D1333101

THE ASSOCIATION FOR
SCOTTISH LITERARY STUDIES
NUMBER THIRTY-NINE

Makeshift
&
Hunger March

TWO NOVELS by DOT ALLAN

THE ASSOCIATION FOR SCOTTISH LITERARY STUDIES

The Association for Scottish Literary Studies aims to promote the study, teaching and writing of Scottish literature, and to further the study of the languages of Scotland.

To these ends, the ASLS publishes works of Scottish literature (of which this volume is an example); literary criticism and in-depth reviews of Scottish books in *Scottish Studies Review*; short articles, features and news in *ScotLit*; and scholarly studies of language in *Scottish Language*. It also publishes *New Writing Scotland*, an annual anthology of new poetry, drama and short fiction, in Scots, English and Gaelic. ASLS has also prepared a range of teaching materials covering Scottish language and literature for use in schools.

All the above publications are available as a single 'package', in return for an annual subscription. Enquiries should be sent to:

ASLS, Department of Scottish Literature, 7 University Gardens, University of Glasgow, Glasgow G12 8QH. Telephone/fax +44 (0)141 330 5309 or visit our website at **www.asls.org.uk**

A list of Annual Volumes published by ASLS can be found at the end of this book.

THE ASSOCIATION FOR
SCOTTISH LITERARY STUDIES

DOT ALLAN

Makeshift & Hunger March

Edited by
MOIRA BURGESS

GLASGOW 2010

Published in Great Britain, 2010
by The Association for Scottish Literary Studies
Department of Scottish Literature
University of Glasgow
7 University Gardens
Glasgow G12 8QH

www.asls.org.uk

Hardback
ISBN: 978-0-948877-96-4

Paperback
ISBN: 978-0-948877-97-1

A catalogue record for this book
is available from the British Library.

The Association for Scottish Literary Studies acknowledges support from the Scottish Arts Council towards the publication of this book.

Typeset by Ellipsis Books Ltd, Glasgow
Printed by Cromwell Press Group, Wiltshire

CONTENTS

ACKNOWLEDGEMENTS

I am very grateful for the help given by librarians in The Mitchell Library, Glasgow, and the Scottish Theatre Archive at Glasgow University Library. Thanks are also due to Duncan Jones for tracing Dot Allan's will, Mary Seenan for information (and comments) about the PEN bazaar, and Yuko Matsui for illuminating discussion about Dot Allan and other women writers.

INTRODUCTION

1. Biography

Eliza MacNaughton Luke Allan, always known as Dot, was born at Headswood House, Denny, Stirlingshire, on 13 May 1886, the only child of a prosperous iron merchant, Alexander Allan. Her mother Jean was the daughter of John Luke, founder of the Vale paper works in Denny. (Dot Allan's 1948 novel *John Mathew, Papermaker* draws on that segment of her family history.) Nothing is known of her childhood; if diaries or memoirs exist, they have not so far been traced. It would seem probable that 'Dot' is a pet name from a little girl's earliest years, and it is tempting to see a passage in her 1929 novel *The Deans* as a reflection or a memory of family life, perhaps of a gentle father-daughter relationship.

> It was . . . one of the nights when the hum of every passing car held a rhythm of its own, when the harsher sounds of the traffic mounting raucously at cross-roads and busy arteries projected through the quiet parts a long-drawn-out note like a minor chord repeated over and over again. Nell adored these singing nights . . . 'Trade,' [her father] would say when the racket grew well-nigh intolerable, 'a' that means grist to some man's mill. Toys and sweeties for some wee lass.'[1]

Most of what is known about Dot Allan's girlhood comes from a single source, a rare interview which she gave in 1931 to the novelist Elisabeth Kyle. The voice of a middle-aged West End lady, reminiscing pleasantly to her interviewer, can almost be heard:

> Although Miss Allan attended classes at Glasgow University for a time, her education was somewhat spasmodic, owing to winter migrations to the South of France, where she had lessons from a very interesting and original Frenchwoman, a protégée of the Empress Eugenie, and one who had had the privilege of teaching Queen Ena of Spain. Later she went to school at Leamington Spa in Warwickshire, a school where M.P. Willcocks, the Devonshire novelist, was at that time English mistress.[2]

By the time of the interview Dot Allan was living at 5 Hamilton Drive in the West End of Glasgow; she and her mother appear on the voters' roll from about 1920. She never married, and this pleasant address, convenient, as estate agents say, to Great Western Road, Byres Road and the Botanic Gardens, was her home for the rest of her life. She sounds like the archetypal daughter at home, and the few references to her in the writing of contemporaries – again, we have no memoirs or letters of her own to fill out the picture – would seem at first glance to bear this out. Elisabeth Kyle certainly makes much of the ladylike setting of the interview:

> I found Miss Allan in a room . . . full of charming things, flowers, shaded lamps, and comfortable cushions. There was nothing in this room to suggest that Bohemian, half masculine creature, the 'lady novelist' in fiction. Nor did its occupant look the part; small and dainty, with grey eyes looking at one from under black, arched brows, she seemed to protest against being debarred, in the public imagination at least, from the feminine delights of life.[3]

The journalist Alison Downie, in a posthumous appreciation of Dot Allan in 1964, indicates that the ambience had scarcely altered in thirty years:

> An invitation to tea in her comfortable home meant an hour or so of talk about people and events in the news; but it also meant tea elegantly served in fragile china cups, and a tempting array of eatables at which the hostess might just nibble but the guests were encouraged to enjoy.[4]

As both Kyle and Downie know, of course, Dot Allan is in fact not only a West End lady but a successful novelist and freelance journalist, a career still unusual enough in 1931 for a woman of her class, place and time. The poet Helen Cruickshank knows it too and expands on the position in her forthright way:

> I used to meet Dot Allan and her frail little mother when they spent short holidays in a quiet Edinburgh hotel. Dot was a fine artist with a most retiring disposition and, because she always shunned the limelight, her work never gained the attention it deserved.[5]

From a twenty-first century viewpoint it seems possible that the dual roles of writer and dutiful daughter, or of writer and West End lady, could make for an uncomfortable mismatch in Dot Allan's life. Some slippage between roles was fairly usual, if not indeed expected, among Scottish women writers of the early to mid-twentieth century. Allan was among the Scottish PEN members advertised as going to be in charge of stalls at a 'writers' fair and bazaar' in Glasgow in March 1950 to raise funds for the forthcoming International PEN Congress in Edinburgh. Other stallholders announced were Marion Lochhead, Nancy Brysson Morrison, Ena Lamont Stewart and Elisabeth Kyle. In the interests of Scottish literature one would rather have seen these considerable writers getting on with their writing, as, it appears, all the men were doing.[6]

Did Allan herself hold any views on this? In the absence of a memoir, should we attempt the dangerous game of inferring biography from fiction? There are certainly some passages in both *Makeshift* and *Hunger March* which would have rattled the teacups if expressed by the gracious Miss Allan. The two personae will be kept in mind in considering her writing career.

At times Dot Allan's writer persona appears to have gone into retreat. During both world wars she abandoned writing in favour of nursing. In World War II and after she was active in the cause of cancer relief and other charities, as Alison Downie recalled:

> Small, soft-voiced, Dot might give a new acquaintance an impression almost of helplessness, yet in fact she accomplished an astonishing amount of work while never appearing to be flustered or out of countenance. There must be scores of people who today remember Dot Allan with gratitude and affection. To some her name may be linked with the recollection of sensible, practical help in time of need. To others it may bring a warm memory of a gift of flowers when they were ill, an invitation to the theatre, a letter or even a telephone conversation . . .[7]

Dot Allan's obituaries, when she herself died after a struggle with breast cancer on 3 December 1964, made much of her charity work, specifying that she was honorary secretary of the Glasgow committee of the National Society for Cancer Relief (an ancestor of today's Macmillan Cancer Support), and mentioning that she had been appointed a Commander of the Order of St John; such an honour is given only in recognition of a considerable period of voluntary service with the Order, a charity of international importance. But the obituaries also acknowledged her writing career, and indeed she was still writing towards the end of her life: her last novel, *Charity Begins at Home*, was published in 1958. Notably, she was keeping an eye on the state of Scottish literature and helping it along where she could. The *Stirling Observer* in its obituary, as local newspapers will, made things a little clearer than this retiring lady might have wished (though the source of the 'fortune' is not revealed. It may have been family money inherited on her mother's death).

> When affluence came suddenly to Miss Allan in the shape of an independent fortune, she was always ready to give material help to literary aspirants through the Scottish branch of PEN.[8]

It is Helen Cruickshank again who gives chapter and verse:

> Since Dot Allan is now dead, it is possible to reveal that she was the generous donor who enabled Maurice Lindsay to edit a selected edition of Marion Angus's poems in 1950 [when no publisher would

take it on without subsidy]. At the time Dot Allan insisted characteristically on anonymity.[9]

Dot Allan's will included a bequest of £2000, no small sum in 1964, to the playwright Ena Lamont Stewart, who had different obstacles to overcome, and similarly was unable to write as much as she might have done.[10] She inscribed a copy of *Charity Begins at Home* to the same writer: 'Ena, with love and admiration from Dot, April 1958'.[11] Dot Allan comes across as a generous woman in both the financial and the emotional sense, and (since Ena Lamont Stewart's best-known play *Men Should Weep* is now acknowledged as a Scottish classic, several times revived[12]), a good judge of writing too.

2. Context

Dot Allan is a Glasgow woman novelist. Until the welcome appearance, around the turn of the millennium, of such writers as Janice Galloway, A.L. Kennedy and Louise Welsh, Glasgow women novelists were few and far between (as, predictably enough, were female central characters in Glasgow fiction).[13] But, considered under the separate headings of Glasgow novelist and woman novelist, she was writing in something of a golden age.

Apart from *John Mathew, Papermaker*, Dot Allan's Glasgow novels all appeared in the 1920s and 1930s, an epic period in Glasgow fiction. These are the decades of George Blake's prentice work *Mince Collop Close* (1923) and his much more successful *The Shipbuilders* (1935); of James Barke's Modernist *Major Operation* (1936) and his masterpiece *The Land of the Leal* (1939), which culminates in Depression Glasgow; of (impossible to omit) McArthur and Long's *No Mean City* (1935); and, almost more pertinently, of a whole host of Glasgow novels by lesser-known writers such as Mary Cleland, John Carruthers, John Cockburn, Frederick Niven, and George Woden. Of varying merit as these works are, Glasgow was the place to write about in those years.[14]

During these prolific decades, much criticism is to be found on the theme that Scottish fiction lacked realistic novels about 'ordinary people'. The critics recognised that Glasgow offered a rich field for the novelist:

> The crowding of our Highland and Lowland populations into busy commercial centres, with the introduction of an Irish element, has created conditions which should lend themselves to dramatic treatment . . .[15]

Where was the Scottish Dostoevsky, Zola, Balzac, Dickens? George Blake's and James Barke's early work is in part a response to this question, as are such long-forgotten novels as John Carruthers' *The Virgin Wife* (1925) and John Cockburn's *Tenement* (1925).

Dot Allan was counted in with this 'Glasgow school' by no less an authority than C.M. Grieve (Hugh MacDiarmid). In his seminal *Contemporary Scottish Studies* of 1926 he pays her a slightly backhanded compliment:

> As belonging to the new Glasgow school may be mentioned Miss Dot Allan with *The Syrens* (some of her more recent work in the form of short sketches has reached a much higher level) . . .[16]

If a writer's individual qualities are perhaps not always to be discerned in her first novel, it became more evident with each subsequent work that, as a Glasgow novelist, Dot Allan was on a track of her own.

Allan's career as a woman novelist overlaps with those of some notable names. Catherine Carswell's two novels are *Open the Door!* (1920) and *The Camomile* (1922); they are in fact partly or wholly set in Glasgow, as are the two novels of the less-known Mary Cleland (the pseudonym of Margot Wells), *The Two Windows* (1922) and *The Sure Traveller* (1923). In quite different corners are the highly popular O. Douglas (Anna Buchan), who produced a string of gentle romances over some twenty-five years from *Olivia in India* (1913) to *Jane's Parlour* (1937), and the far more striking Lorna Moon (Nora Low), whose passionate short stories, *Doorways in Drumorty*, first appeared in Britain in 1926, followed by her one novel, *Dark Star*, in 1929. Nowadays regarded as Scottish classics are the novels of Willa Muir, Nancy Brysson Morrison, Naomi Mitchison and Nan Shepherd; all produced notable work in Allan's first productive period during the 1920s and 1930s, and Morrison and Mitchison in particular were still writing outstanding novels during Allan's second flowering after World War II.[17]

Dot Allan is not often numbered in this roll-call of eminent Scottish women writers, and on balance that is possibly fair. She is probably to be considered a lesser writer than, for example, Carswell, Muir or Mitchison. Hers is a gentle voice; in the majority of her novels her style is not innovative; her views – though they are strong ones – have usually to be sought out. But there are two novels, *Makeshift* (1928) and *Hunger March* (1934), which stand out among other works of their time – because of originality of theme in the case of *Makeshift*, and originality of style in *Hunger March* – and in which her views are presented, in fictional terms certainly, but with vigour and clarity. There is a case for saying that these novels have been unjustifiably overlooked, and they are the Dot Allan works chosen to be reprinted in the present volume.

3. Writing

The *Stirling Observer* obituary already quoted remarks with enthusiasm: 'For many years [Dot Allan], by her pen, supported herself and her elderly mother'.[18] It seems possible from the family background that Allan did not write entirely out of financial necessity (though like so much in her life that remains conjectural), but simply, like most writers, because she wanted to. In any case she did write, and was published, throughout her life. She published ten novels, but also wrote at least two plays, and kept up a constant production of short stories and journalism, except during her apparently voluntary breaks for nursing and charity work in the two world wars.

Plays

Dot Allan's entry in *Scottish Biographies 1938* includes the note 'Recreation: play-going.'[19] Stage-struck and interested in theatre production, as she explains in the Kyle interview, she began her writing career with the plays *Snowdrifts* and *Yellow Fever.* The second, as she points out to her interviewer with perceptible pride,

> . . . was produced by Lewis Casson, the husband of Sybil Thorndike, who was at that time the producer for the old Repertory Theatre in Glasgow.[20]

The Glasgow Repertory Company had a short but significant existence, staging 'plays national in character, written by Scottish men and women of letters' (as well as other work), from 1909 until 1914. The non-Scottish playwrights are notable enough, among them Shaw, Ibsen, Galsworthy and Bennett. The Scottish literati include Neil Munro (of Para Handy fame) and J.J. Bell (similarly then well known for *Wee Macgreegor*) and in the list of Scottish plays is one classic of its kind, J.A. Ferguson's *Campbell of Kilmohr*, a Jacobite drama which remained a staple of community drama festivals for many years.[21] But in general the Scottish plays presented have hardly survived. Dot Allan's plays (which, it seems from the scanty information available, may have appeared under her occasional pseudonym Constance Roy, or possibly Ray) have not so far been traced. They were, however, broadcast on BBC radio in 1928.[22]

Even before she began to write plays, according to the Kyle interview, Dot Allan was

> . . . desperately anxious to meet Sarah Bernhardt, who, old and frail, was paying a visit to Glasgow. The only way I could think of doing so was just to ask for an interview, which she granted. She was kindness itself, listened to my halting French, and answered me with sympathy and courtesy. But I had an awful job selling that article afterwards! The newspapers all said they had had enough of Sarah Bernhardt at the moment; but the *Evening Times* published it in the end.[23]

It seems that in her twenties Allan was already trying her luck at freelance journalism, and displaying the persistence and resilience which that uncertain trade demands.

Journalism

From the early 1920s onwards Allan's articles and short stories were being published regularly in a wide range of newspapers and periodicals. C.M. Grieve's praise of her 'short sketches' has been noted earlier. He does not specify which sketches particularly impressed him, and if we scan a few of Allan's contributions to the *Glasgow Herald* weekend pages during the early 1920s, we may be moved to wonder. 'Chanticleer in Hyndland' in 1924, for instance, is as slight and whimsical as you might suppose, and 'McClintock's New Year Cold' in 1923 somehow doesn't bode well. (For dates of these, and of Allan's other journalism so far as it has been traced, see Appendix I.)

But, as in the matter of biography, the picture of Allan's journalistic work is far from complete as yet. We do know that she contributed regularly to the *Glasgow Herald* during the 1920s and 1930s, and then again in the 1950s. Here is the wartime hiatus in writing previously remarked on, which will show up again in the chronology of her novels. Much of her work has a solid factual base. In 1933, for instance, there is a series on 'Great Hours in Glasgow History', retelling in a graphic, colourful style such episodes as Zachary Boyd's fulminating sermon for Oliver Cromwell in the Barony Church in 1650.[24] 'Personal recollections' of figures like her favourite Sarah Bernhardt (1923), the composer John Philip Sousa (1932) and the pianist Vladimir de Pachmann (1933) go far to balance such flights of fancy as 'Santa's Dream'.

She also contributed short stories to the *Glasgow Herald* among her non-fiction pieces; to *Scotland's SMT* Magazine intermittently (see Appendix I); and to the monthly journal *Review of Reviews* during the 1920s. Some of these stories are workmanlike rather then inspired, but there is hidden treasure too.

'Invisible Mending', from 1935, reprinted here as Appendix II, stands out because of its relation to themes in her novels. It is now a period piece and perhaps a word of explanation is required. Pure silk stockings, the hosiery of choice for wealthy and fashionable ladies in a pre-nylon age, were expensive and laddered easily.

Rather than discard them, a lady, showing the instinct for economy which probably made her wealthy in the first place, would send them to be 'invisibly mended', the laddered threads skilfully caught up and restored. As the story indicates, it was painstaking, tiring work in – literally – sweatshop conditions, a twentieth-century *Song of a Shirt*, and the situation is clearly set out: it is not just that the poor are working for the benefit of the rich, but, specifically, poor women for rich women. If we suspect Allan of presenting a slightly rose-tinted version of the young women's solidarity, and if Carrie settles back into grateful acceptance of her lowly occupation, still the story handles a class issue in feminist terms: there is an echo, as will be discussed later, both of Jacqueline's dressmaker mother in *Makeshift* and of an observant waitress in *Hunger March*.

Novels

Makeshift (1928) and *Hunger March* (1934), reprinted in the present volume for the first time and probably Dot Allan's finest novels, have been given individual Introductions here. Her eight other novels, however, have their own interest, falling as they do into two distinct groups: Glasgow novels (like *Hunger March*, the last and most ambitious in this vein) and novels with a feminist slant (like *Makeshift*, though it is considerably earlier than the others in this group).

Allan's Glasgow novels are *The Syrens* (1921), *The Deans* (1929), *Deepening River* (1932) and *Hunger March* (1934), with *John Mathew, Papermaker* (1948) as an outrider; it is set in industrial central Scotland but is based very directly on her own family history, nevertheless shedding light on social history and conditions in a wider scene.

The Syrens (1921) is the story of a Glasgow merchant; this was the background and the kind of person that Dot Allan knew. It appears from an early press release that *The Syrens* was first announced under the pseudonym Luke Allan[25] (the secret was evidently out by the time it was noticed by C.M. Grieve); merchants' daughters, we surmise, didn't readily admit to writing novels. Her young hero, son of the brief marriage of a naïve girl and a romantic, roving sailor (similar parentage appears later in *Makeshift*) is named Goritholus, after his father's ship: a device perhaps intended to mark him out as innately exotic and unsuited to everyday life in Glasgow, but something of a distraction for the reader. He works his way up in the grocery trade – as his mother and Glasgow expect him to do – but Glasgow the merchant city is a gateway to the world, and he eventually succumbs to his inherited wanderlust. 'One ought to take the world for one's field if one wants to,' Allan observes in the Kyle interview,[26] referring primarily to her own writing, but also perhaps to the outlook of this and other characters in her work.

The Deans (1929) is less successful. It is recognisably Dot Allan's tenement novel, her attempt, in answer to the contemporary critics noted earlier, to write about 'ordinary people'. Unfortunately she has never lived in a tenement. Like Blake in his early Glasgow fiction, she is writing about a world which she does not really know and has not satisfactorily imagined. The pretty daughter and ambitious son of her working-class family are confronting the prospect, and associated problems, of marrying into a higher social class (that grave problems are involved is unquestioned by either the characters or their author). The son Guy is, as the reviewer in the *Times Literary Supplement* remarks, 'financially assisted in an unexpected manner by his mother'.[27] This is a temperate way of describing the mother's stratagem of renting the spare room to prostitutes (in the afternoon, before the younger children come home from school). Allan shows elsewhere in her writing a weakness for melodrama, and this plot twist never approaches plausibility.

The same reviewer kindly enough admits that the novel at times 'shows signs of developing into something more moving than the ordinary tale of conventional sentiment'; these moments are perhaps found in the passages dealing with the mother's arrest and its effect on the family, where a certain sensitivity and empathy goes some way towards redeeming *The Deans*.

Deepening River (1932) is perhaps the Glasgow novel that only Dot Allan could write. Long interested in Glasgow history and sympathetic to the merchant class, she follows the development of the Clyde and of commercial Glasgow through the story of one mercantile family from the eighteenth century on. An early review rightly calls this 'a wonderful and so far a practically untouched subject', though finding the novel (as the reader may) a shade too slow-moving.[28] Whether or not she read this review, Allan's next novel was to be *Hunger March*, which in its compressed, vivid 24-hour structure could hardly be more different from the leisurely saga of *Deepening River.*

But after *Hunger March* Allan's fiction leaves Glasgow. Perhaps it is best to regard *Virgin Fire* (1935) as a practice run for her next preoccupation, the concern for women's lives which had earlier appeared in *Makeshift* (1928). *Virgin Fire* is the story of Marion Bradfute, the (possibly fictional) lover of William Wallace, executed for helping him avoid capture; from this (the story continues, all the way to the film *Braveheart*) sprang his abiding hatred of the English. The choice of such a romantic subject would suggest that Dot Allan was looking for a new direction in her writing, perhaps even contemplating the sort of popular historical fiction which began to be produced a few years later by such novelists as Jean Plaidy and Margaret Irwin.

But this was not in fact how Allan's fiction developed. World War II began, and, like World War I, seems to have caused a hiatus in her writing career. Taking it up again after the war, she published two most interesting novels not widely known now. *Mother of Millions* (1953) and *The Passionate Sisters* (1955) step into worlds not much explored at the time. Respectively, they focus on Margaret Carnegie Fletcher of Saltoun, sister-in-law of Andrew Fletcher, and on the seven Wesley sisters, siblings of Samuel, John and Charles. These are women who accomplished much in their own lives: Margaret Carnegie Fletcher introduced barley mills and weaving mills to Scotland, and if anything is commonly known about the Wesley family, it is that their energetic mother had the daughters, as well as the sons, taught Latin and Greek. But when Allan wrote these women had been lost in the shadow of their male relatives, and to some extent they are still overlooked today.[29]

These novels, together with *Makeshift*, would justify the description of Dot Allan as a feminist writer, but a startling coda to this strand of her work is to be found in her last novel, *Charity Begins at Home* (1958). Paradoxically, it is startling because it is such a measured and quiet examination of character, such a thoughtful portrait of a young woman, such a relentless dissection of an old one. Gone is the melodrama to which Allan has too often been tempted (see the introduction to *Makeshift* later in this volume), and gone are the strained depictions of stereotypes whom she does not fully understand (see the introduction to *Hunger March*). Catherine Shaw is happy in her London childhood with slightly unconventional parents whose love for her is never in doubt, until she has to relocate to West End Glasgow and be brought up by her grandmother. Old Mrs Shaw is one of Dot Allan's most successful and most terrifying portraits: wealthy, miserly, hidebound by convention and unshakably convinced of her own rectitude. Willa Muir had long ago dissected this sort of character in her pitilessly humorous *Mrs Grundy in Scotland* (1936), which Dot Allan may well have known, though it can hardly be doubted that she had also observed such ladies in real life.[30] It is Grandmother's regime, economically favoured but humanly barren, which is held to account for Catherine's perfectly plausible slide into white-collar crime. Allan's condemnation of the well-off middle-class woman has never been more trenchant than in *Charity Begins at Home*.

4. Conclusion

Still Dot Allan, brought up in reasonable affluence – Headswood House in its extensive grounds, and those winters on the Riviera – and, if lines are to be drawn, of the managerial class, seems an unlikely author for the novel most often associated with her name, *Hunger March*.

Edwin Muir, describing Glasgow in the 1930s, detected something which he thought peculiar to the middle and upper classes of that city:

> There may be many intelligent and humane men and women in these classes, but somewhere or other they are blunted or dead;

> they have blind spots as big as a door: the door of their office or their house. They cannot help that; it is not their fault, but the fault of a sensibility which forces them to gather money out of the dirt. But the self-protective need to ignore this involves a deliberate blunting of one whole area of their sensibility.[31]

Dot Allan, a middle-class woman, seems from her work to have been intelligent and humane, but not blunted or dead. Quiet and charming in her drawing room as her interviewer found her, she was all the time unobtrusively observing that blind spot in her mother's and her own generation. She was both aware of and critical of the outlook held by the class and gender to which she herself belonged. We do not know that she was a political or social activist. Perhaps, as a West End lady and a dutiful daughter, she was shackled by the inhibiting influence of the very conventions she depicts, and felt she could not go so far. But as a writer she expressed her disapproval of man's inhumanity to man, and particularly woman's to woman, in novels and short stories throughout her life.

Notes

1 Dot Allan, *The Deans* (Jarrolds, [1929]), pp. 17–18.
2 Elisabeth Kyle, 'Modern Women Authors 3: Dot Allan', *Scots Observer*, 25 June 1931, p. 4. Many thanks to Yuko Matsui for originally drawing my attention to this.
3 ibid.
4 'A.D.' [i.e. Alison Downie], 'Dot Allan: an appreciation', *Glasgow Herald*, 4 December 1964, p. 11.
5 Helen B. Cruickshank, *Octobiography* (Montrose: Standard Press, 1976), pp. 133–4.
6 *Glasgow Herald*, 3 March 1950. The Scottish branch of the writers' organisation International PEN was founded in 1927.
7 Downie (1964).
8 *Stirling Observer*, 10 December 1964.
9 Cruickshank, p. 135.
10 Thanks to Duncan Jones for this information.

11 Copy in author's collection.
12 Colin Donald, 'Familiar echoes' [on Ena Lamont Stewart], *Scotsman*, 3 September 1996.
13 See Moira Burgess, *Imagine a City: Glasgow in fiction* (Glendaruel: Argyll Publishing, 1998), particularly chapter 19.
14 Burgess (1998), particularly chapters 6, 7 and 8.
15 Agnes Stewart, 'Some Scottish Novelists', *The Northern Review*, vol. 1, no. 1, May 1924, pp.35–41.
16 C.M. Grieve, *Contemporary Scottish Studies: first series* (Leonard Parsons, 1926), p. 311.
17 See for instance Willa Muir, *Mrs Ritchie* (1933) and *Imagined Corners* (1935); Nancy Brysson Morrison, *The Gowk Storm* (1933) and *The Winnowing Years* (1949); Naomi Mitchison, *The Corn King and the Spring Queen* (1931) and *The Bull Calves* (1947); Nan Shepherd, *The Quarry Wood* (1928) and *The Weatherhouse* (1930). Several of these titles have been republished in the Canongate Classics series.
18 *Stirling Observer*, 10 December 1964.
19 *Scottish Biographies 1938.*
20 Kyle (1931).
21 David Hutchison, '1900 to 1950', in *A History of Scottish Theatre*, ed. Bill Findlay (Edinburgh: Polygon, 1998), pp. 207–52 (208–14).
22 See *The Times*, 17 April 1928 [*Snowdrifts*] and *The Times*, 29 September 1928 [*Yellow Fever*].
23 Kyle (1931).
24 *Glasgow Herald*, 8 April 1933.
25 See *Glasgow Herald*, 26 February 1921.
26 Kyle (1931).
27 *Times Literary Supplement*, 24 October 1929.
28 *SMT Magazine*, vol. 9 no 4, October 1932, pp. 61–2.
29 There is now a biography of the Wesley women, Samuel J. Rogal: *The Epworth Women: Susannah Wesley and her daughters.* See www.wesley/nnu.edu/wesleyantheology
30 Republished, with other works by Willa Muir, under the title *Imagined Selves* (Canongate, 1996).
31 Edwin Muir, *Scottish Journey* (Heinemann, 1935), p. 108.

INTRODUCTION TO *MAKESHIFT*

Following her debut in 1921 with the Glasgow novel *The Syrens*, Dot Allan attempted something very different in *Makeshift*. It appeared in 1928 from the publisher Andrew Melrose, who had published Catherine Carswell's *Open the Door!* in 1920. While Carswell's novels were (however belatedly) rediscovered and reissued in the 1980s, *Makeshift* has never until now been republished. Like *Open the Door!*, Allan's novel is a *bildungsroman* with a young woman as its central character. Thematically, however, it bears a stronger resemblance to Carswell's second novel, *The Camomile* (1922). Jacqueline in *Makeshift*, like Ellen in *The Camomile*, knows herself to have a gift for writing, and finds that the idea of a young woman writer is all but unacceptable in the middle-class Scottish society of her day.

It is not known whether Carswell's novels influenced Dot Allan; lacking a memoir or papers, her inspiration will perhaps never now be traced. But *Makeshift* is a thoughtful novel in its own right. It makes a clear statement that a young woman does not have to marry, whether out of convention or for security, and that she certainly should not be *used* – the word recurs – emotionally, practically or sexually. In 1920s Scotland, highly conventional as regards the role of women, this was a brave thing to write, with particular resonance since it is written by a woman. It places Allan in the company of such writers as Catherine Carswell and Willa Muir.

Makeshift is not without flaws. Its structure is unusual: Part I (pp. 9–135), the story of Jacqueline's girlhood and growing up, is nearly three times as long as Part II (pp. 139–184), in which the actual theme of the novel comes to the fore. Part I is amazingly leisurely, winding its way through Jacqueline's adolescent feelings, impressions of Glasgow, and first romantic encounters, and only in Part II does the question of writing versus a conventional woman's life really come into focus; earlier, Jacqueline has in fact had some encouragement (admittedly from a writer, himself unconventional). Neither do Jacqueline's various sexual adventures in Part I quite lead on to the writing-versus-marriage theme of Part II. Yet Part I cannot be dismissed: as discussed later, Jacqueline's feelings are here described with remarkable freedom and openness, as startling a feature, in a novel of the 1920s, as the passages concerning Joanna's emotions in *Open the Door!*

The *Times Literary Supplement*, reviewing *Makeshift* on publication, points out a further defect which has to be admitted.

> The principal characters in the story are partly obscured by sentiment and melodrama . . . Jacqueline, the heroine, is a real person in the ordinary occasions of her life . . . But when she is exalted by love or grief she is hidden from us by Miss Allan's overstatements, by a series of violent and useless metaphors.[1]

Melodrama is a failing of Dot Allan's, at least in her early work. It is linked to implausibility, as in the mother's decision to make money by accommodating prostitutes in *The Deans*. Elsewhere Allan may slip into melodrama because she is not comfortable with action scenes; even in the much more balanced *Hunger March*, the scene where Joe knocks down the clerk and believes himself a murderer fails to carry conviction. In the case of *Makeshift* the reviewer is possibly referring to the demise of Jacqueline's lover Owen. While it could be objected that a motiveless murder like his can very well happen in real life, the novelist has to make it, and reactions to it, plausible in the terms of the book, and this (in what is after all only her second novel) Allan does not quite manage to do. The *TLS* reviewer hopes for a future novel in which the main characters are 'as clearly and quietly drawn' as the minor characters here, and to a large extent Allan fulfilled that hope in her later work.

Yet the reviewer appears to overlook – or primly ignore? – the very elements in *Makeshift* which a reader today finds both interesting and important. One is the strong depiction of sexual feelings in both Jacqueline and her lovers. She is brought up in a small town by an unsympathetic aunt and henpecked uncle and begins to write poetry; so far, readers may think, so *Anne of Green Gables*. But, rising seventeen, she experiences the first stirrings of 'sex consciousness' – Allan's phrase. At commercial college, she realises that the tutor fancies her. Should she encourage him? (It might be her last chance, she thinks – Allan rather credibly recalling days of teenage angst.) She is 'conscious only of an imperative urge in [her tutor's] eyes and for a fraction of a second the classroom swung about her' (p. 37).

But she is afraid to keep the proposed date, and when, later, the writer Torrance takes her for a run in his car, she doesn't realise what he's hinting at. (When light dawns, Allan allows her to wonder whether, if she had understood, she would have succumbed.) She sleepwalks into a nasty situation with Mr Shaw from the office; by now the modern reader may be wondering whether she ever will understand, but Mr Shaw makes his intentions fairly clear, and she is no longer quite so naïve when Owen appears. She is ready to meet him halfway, if not more. By the time dull William the bailie's son tries to cuddle her, the passion of her response positively alarms him. Perhaps some of this contributes to the 'sentiment and melodrama' deplored by the *TLS* reviewer, but still it is strong enough stuff for a West End lady to be writing in 1928.

In counterpoint to these adventures runs Allan's presentation of Jacqueline's office colleague Miss Price, elderly, alcoholic, with a 'faint, rather foul smell' (p. 100). She is delicately touched into the story, yet she is all-important, for she is the 'surplus woman' typical of these years after the slaughter of a generation of young men in World War I, and Jacqueline dreads sharing her fate. The sight of Miss Price's squalid room moves Owen to a masterful declaration that he and none other will look after Jacqueline. If that slightly strains credulity, it is much more plausible that Jacqueline herself, terrified of ending up like Miss Price, allows herself after Owen's death to be courted by William.

And how can the *TLS* reviewer have overlooked the Prologue to *Makeshift*? It is, in part, a strong and bitter condemnation of the attitude of middle-class ladies towards the working class, a motif in Allan's fiction which recurs in *Hunger March* and in the short story 'Invisible Mending'. Jacqueline as a child observes their treatment of her widowed mother, who scrapes a living by dress-making.

> Not another stitch would [Mrs Thayer] put in until she was paid for the last order, and the one before that as well. The beautiful lady had opened her eyes in pained surprise. 'My good woman, I haven't got it. If I had, I assure you – '
>
> 'I don't want assurances,' Mrs Thayer had retorted. 'I want a cheque to amount of account rendered. I have bills of my own to meet.'
>
> The beautiful lady had sighed deeply as one who deplores the habits of the lower orders. Then from a ludicrously small gold-mesh purse she had produced two half-crowns.
>
> 'Your milkman's bill,' she had said with deliberate insolence; 'this might serve to meet it.' (p. 11)

But Mrs Thayer's bitterness has its roots in her brief marriage, when from the first – in an echo of *The Syrens* – she saw that her sailor husband was more in love with his ship than with her. As she clutches the green satin destined to make a second-best frock for a minister's wife, this is what fuels her impassioned declaration: 'Second best! . . . That's what my life has been made up of, Jacqueline; makeshift all the time.' (p. 10) She slashes the satin into small pieces, goes into her room and gasses herself. Jacqueline, then and until much later only half understanding her mother's words, nevertheless grows up with the determination that her own life will not be second best or makeshift; this is the overarching theme of the book, fully entitling Dot Allan to be regarded as a feminist writer.

The particular case of Jacqueline as a woman writer, perhaps slightly eclipsed earlier by her romantic experiences, is fore-grounded in part II of *Makeshift*, meshing here in a satisfactory way with the more general theme of women being 'used'. William proposes to Jacqueline. In fact he is using her, with his father's connivance, in order to get out of an unsuitable entanglement in London. Unaware of this, and afraid of becoming a 'surplus woman' like Miss Price, Jacqueline accepts:

> She nodded. All right – would it be all right? At the back of her mind she knew that it wouldn't. (p. 170).

Shortly before the wedding Torrance, the encouraging author, visits Jacqueline and asks how her writing is going. William is annoyed.

> What the blazes did the man mean jawing away about Jacqueline's poetry, puffing up the poor kid she could write? Write! Hell! Didn't he realise she was going to be married – married? (p. 174)

Jacqueline's eyes are opened, and she also discovers how she has been 'used'. It's fortunate, if more of a coincidence than Allan might have employed later in her career, that just then she receives a legacy from a friend of her father's which assures her independence. Remembering her mother's 'second best' speech, she packs her poems and her clothes and takes the train to London.

But there is still a little more to be seen in *Makeshift*. Thinking back over the story, the reader realises – and we may suppose that Jacqueline does too – that none of the men in her life would have allowed her to be a writer, to be herself. We have seen how William regards the idea of a writing wife. Torrance, though he has encouraged her writing, is clearly shown to have unreconstructed views.

> He was violently opposed to all forms of women's rights . . . The mind of woman was not that of a normal human being, he was wont to declare, but of one warped by reason of her sex. (p. 59)

He has found Jacqueline a refreshing change from his colourless wife, 'for while he despised women, he acknowledged that . . .

they had their uses.' (p. 60) So Torrance would not have been a good choice for Jacqueline.

Even the adored Owen is problematic. He does begin to suspect that Jacqueline has 'a spirituality of outlook he had hitherto deemed the prerogative of man' (p. 96), but it is not much of an advance on his previous views, unsparingly delineated by Allan. Jacqueline has said that she wants to be independent.

> Where had the child learned the ugly word? Why didn't some man carry her off and teach her to wipe it out of her vocabulary? She was attractive in her own way, very sweet and quite brainless probably. One, doubtless, of the vast army of women who, God pity them, would never be worth more to any employer than two pounds ten a week. (p. 54–5)

No, Owen wouldn't have done. Any 'sentiment and melodrama' in the novel takes its place as a minor flaw against the cool realism of Allan's denouement. Just as decisively as Ellen Carstairs in *The Camomile*, Jacqueline catches the midnight express for Euston and an independent life.

Notes

1 *Times Literary Supplement*, 1 November 1928, p. 802.

MAKESHIFT

PROLOGUE

Mrs Pullman smoothed out the material with pink beringed fingers.

'Quite nice stuff,' she said; 'quite nice stuff. It should make up into a really serviceable second best.'

Mrs Thayer regarded the lank breadth of green satin dubiously. It was not her way to pander to her customers' propensities for providing their own materials. A percentage, after all, was a percentage. There was precious little to be got out of making and furnishings alone. Her mouth devolved into a resentful pout; a dozen little lines and furrows ploughed her cheeks. Some ministers' wives were awful. Mean wasn't the word. For a moment her feelings wrought havoc on her face. The hiss of her own breathing rose stormily in her ears. What did some folk think she lived on, she and her child – air, the fine, fresh air of Lowerbank Street?

She gave a little apologetic cough. The angry colour faded from her cheeks. Mechanically she measured out the satin breadth.

'Seven and an eighth. Now, Mrs Pullman, how would you like it made up?'

From her niche on the window seat Jacqueline watched the two – the minister's wife, black-clad, studiously affable, with the soft, slithering sort of voice that makes you think of cheap ice cream, sweet-tasted on top, tainted underneath; the dressmaker, tight-lipped, sharp-featured, agreeing in a singularly flat voice to every suggestion.

A cross-over bodice – yes, conceals the bust nicely. A plain – yes, a perfectly plain skirt; easier to do up again with a covering of some sort. Sleeves, too – a touch of lace. Just imitation, of course. And cut low at the neck. Not too low. Just enough to show the skin.

Like a gentle current the burble of talk flowed on, and the daylight waned and the troubled dusk began to steal into the big, untidy room. Jacqueline laid down her picture book and gazed out across the street. The coloured glass windows of the quack dentist opposite were all bloodstained; the big brass plate, smeared likewise with the radiance of sunset, was a molten pool wherein the black letters of his name sprawled like tiny fishes. On the doorstep a woman stood awaiting admission – a stout, overdressed female with feathers flying. Impelled by nervous apprehension, she tweaked the bell a second and then a third time in rapid succession, starting in surprise when the door swung open before her fingers had released their hold. Grimacing agitatedly, she stepped inside. A second, and the big door slammed.

Sighing in sympathy, Jacqueline turned her attention to home affairs. Mrs Pullman was collecting her belongings preparatory to departure.

'Next Tuesday, then, Mrs Thayer. I'll be here at three sharp. I'll trust you not to keep me waiting. My time, you know, is so filled up. If I lose five minutes in the morning I feel as if I were chasing it for the rest of the day. At three, then? As you say, it will make quite a serviceable second best.'

She departed on the last word, and Jacqueline slid down from her perch. There were matches on the mantelpiece; behind her father's photograph – the photograph of the slim, boyish-looking sea captain – the box always lay. She was standing on tiptoe fumbling for it when her mother returned.

'Matches,' said Jacqueline; 'I can't reach the box.' Mrs Thayer made no response. She flopped heavily into a chair and clung to its arms. The muscles of her face and neck were quivering; the meagre folds of flesh that escaped the busts of her corsets were heaving. She gathered up the material in her arms.

'Second best!' she raved. 'That's what my life has been made up of, Jacqueline; makeshift all the time. At home in Kirkton with your Aunt Ruth . . . With your father I thought it would be different. He swore it would be, but it wasn't. It was his ship first, always first. And so it goes on . . . I've missed it somehow; but there's more in life than that.'

Jacqueline regarded her mother with wondering eyes. Only once before did she remember seeing her so deeply moved. That was a year ago, when a very beautiful lady had called to ask her to make another dress. Mrs Thayer had clasped the back of a chair tightly and shaken her head. Not another stitch would she put in until she was paid for the last order, and the one before that as well. The beautiful lady had opened her eyes in pained surprise. 'My good woman, I haven't got it. If I had, I assure you—' 'I don't want assurances,' Mrs Thayer had retorted. 'I want a cheque to amount of account rendered. I have bills of my own to meet.'

The beautiful lady had sighed deeply as one who deplores the habits of the lower orders. Then from a ludicrously small gold-mesh purse she had produced two half-crowns.

'Your milkman's bill,' she had said with delicate insolence; 'this might serve to meet it.'

Mrs Thayer had taken the proffered coins and laid them on a table by her side. 'Yes, five shillings will more than cover what I owe my milkman,' she said, 'for I pay my accounts regularly. I have always kept myself honest and respectable.'

The beautiful lady tilted back her chin and laughed. 'I, for my part, am neither honest nor respectable; but, unlike you, I've got the *nous* not to brag about it.'

It was then that Jacqueline's mother had lost her temper. In her wrath she had thrust over the chair she had been clutching. She had waved her arms and ordered the beautiful lady out of the house. And the beautiful lady had gone, smiling. That had made Jacqueline's mother wilder than ever . . .

The sound of scissors at work recalled Jacqueline to the present. An unusual thing was happening. Instead of describing with her shears the wonderful curves and billows that make a dress, Mrs Thayer was cutting steadily into little pieces the material for Mrs Pullman's second best. Like a tortuous pattern of mosaic the little green patches were falling on the folds of her dress, on the bare table in front of her, on the floor at her feet – minute squares and triangles and roundels of hacked green satin. A last click, and the scissors closed on air; they fell from their owner's hand with a clatter on to the bare table.

For a moment Mrs Thayer sat idle, staring in front of her. Ruins, these tattered squares and roundels; ruins, old and mouldering, of all her womanhood's dreams.

As she surveyed them an echo came to her from out the past; an echo of low, vibrant music that thrilled her veins. She had danced to the music of the Pied Piper once; had up and followed when he called. And all the quick, poignant ecstasy of those days recurred to her now. Into every corner of the little low-ceilinged house to which she had gone as a bride her vision plunged: through the narrow hall with the dark perpendicular stair which led to the bedrooms, queer oblong apartments smelling of the crisp new muslin that draped like voluminous petticoats the spindled legs of the old-fashioned toilet tables; round the sitting room with its creaking, red-plush-covered chairs, its carved model of a merchant ship on the mantelpiece. She had hated that model from the first. Often, noting the expression in her husband's eyes as he looked at its exquisite trellis-work, she was fain to break it into atoms with her fingers. It was the face of her rival, that sleek, well-proportioned craft, the face of the mistress who claimed him for many months in the year, who lured him, siren-like, from safety into danger, and, hardest of all to bear, to whose arms he ever hastened, exultant as a lover ripe for passionate adventure.

Sitting there in the decorous semi-silence of Lowerbank Street, with only the distant hum of the tram-racked thoroughfare drifting rhythmically through the twilight, she could hear the whoop of the wind as it bowled inland from the Channel. She could taste on her lips the salt chill of the blast. Sweet, bitter sweet, those nights and days; sweet, bitter sweet, those alternating periods of bliss and anguish! She could feel the warmth of protective arms, the sense of God-given security with which the nearness of their owner always filled her. And she could feel the raw sweat of terror break out anew on her neck and limbs as across the unfathomable distance of the years there came to her the yearning voices of foghorns cutting the clouds that veiled the bay. At such moments her sanctity had acted as a scourge. Like a cancerous sore within her the knowledge that while she lay safe and warm at home he was out there in the black void of swirling waters.

With thin, nervous fingers she twitched the green fragments on the table; ruins all. Slowly realization came to her.

'This finishes it,' she said, and rushed from the room.

Alone in the darkness, Jacqueline busied herself collecting in a heap the cut-up scraps that littered the floor. Dozens and dozens there were – too tiny to make up even into a doll's hat. Not that Deen ever wore hats. She sat in haughty isolation on the mantelpiece, an unseemly wax nude awaiting the day when Mrs Thayer should be slack and inclined to set about the task of clothing her. Jacqueline, for her part, did not worry about the nakedness of her child; the business was infinitely more amusing than playing with dolls.

The ladies who came and went, shedding their coats and dresses and revealing glimpses of soiled underwear for which they made the unvarying apology: 'The fog; you'd hardly believe they were on clean this morning,' were better fun than dolls. They were the pantomime ladies, and she, curled unnoticed behind the curtain on the window seat, comprised the audience. They acted their parts amazingly well, these unconscious performers. There was one pink-cheeked, curly-headed damsel who, disdaining petticoats, looked exactly like Sinbad when shorn of her frock. Only her tights were dark blue instead of golden yellow, and no flashing sword clanked above her left hip.

There was Widow Twankey, too – a shrivelled old dame with a monstrous nose like a turnip lantern. She came but seldom; but when she did Jacqueline with difficulty forbore to clap her hands. For this person played her part to perfection. She wheezed when she spoke; she scolded at everything. Oh, she made you laugh just to look at her, with her funny old bonnet all awry and the smell of peppermint breathing from her person. And once – once, exactly like Mrs Twankey in the pantomime, she had had the neck of a big black bottle sticking out of her string message bag.

Some days, of course, were duller than others. Days when her mother stitched and stitched and no one came; days when ordinary people with whom it was impossible to play pantomime were the only callers. Red Indians then filled in the time. A curiously exciting game, Red Indians. It consisted of sneaking stealthily down from the window seat while the redskin was being fitted, and in stealing unobserved during this process round the back of the victim and out of the door. If you were seen, you were undone; but you seldom were seen. For when these dull people got dressed up in the holland linings of her mother's contrivances they never seemed to see anything but their stupid selves. The sight of their coarse red arms emerging from a panoply of frills appeared to delight them beyond measure. Like peacocks, they preened and cooed to their own reflections in the glass.

To her last days the conviction then acquired subconsciously remained with Jacqueline that women reveal themselves as they are only when they are divested of some of their outer garments; that to know a woman for what she is you must know her in her camisole, for stripped of the armour in which she habitually confronts the world and unhampered by the cunning devices of the dressmaker, she is wholly and unreservedly natural.

Into the sewing-machine drawer Jacqueline squeezed the bits and pieces. It was dark, else she night have tried drawing them together to make a patchwork robe for Deen. Funny, there was always a something when it came to dressing Deen. Her mother was too busy, or it was dark and she couldn't reach the matches. Poor Deen! She did look silly sitting up there with nothing on; almost as silly as the fashion ladies who lined the walls. And they were funnies, every one!

Beyond the lace curtains the yellow cone of a street lamp gleamed with the misty radiance of a winter star. Within the room the ochreous gas-fire glowed like a mimic furnace. Jacqueline crouched down beside it. It wasn't cold, but she wanted company. It was getting aw'fly dark . . . Why didn't her mother come back and light the gas? Perhaps, as upon that other occasion when she had driven the beautiful lady from the house, she had gone to her room to cry. Jacqueline had followed her then and attempted to rain kisses upon her moist cheeks, only to be bidden to run away and play with Deen. Stupid, unresponsive Deen! Jacqueline looked at the doll now and dragged it down from its perch. But there was no comfort to be wrung from contact with the smooth kid body, and she let it dangle, head downwards, from her lap. Even the funnies were apt to prove better company than Deen.

She searched the wall with her eyes for the grotesque outlines of the fashion plates. Finding her favourites, she let slip a sigh, for the colour had all waned from their features. In the darkness they looked pale and ghostly, frightsome almost as the dummy figure, white-sheeted for the night, that glowered at her from the farthermost corner. At sight of its muffled, indeterminate outline the little bird that lay caged beneath her left breast beat frantic wings against her ribs. Holding her breath, she sat motionless. If she moved about, the little bird was apt to get cross and to flutter the harder. It went to sleep only if she stayed still, very, very still. After all, the frightsome white object was only dummy in his nightshirt. She knew that if the little bird didn't. Silly to be frightened, silly little bird . . . All right, I won't move; I'll stay still, quite still . . .

Jacqueline's head drooped. Over her cheek her hair fell like a silken mesh, veiling her face from the prick of the fireglow. An elfin child lost in a world of shadows she looked as she lay there wrapped in slumber; a gnome king's daughter, dark of hair, slender of body, with shy, sensitive features felicitously coloured.

The room grew blacker; only the crimson bulbs of the little gas furnace burned steadfastly bright. Street sounds grew fainter, more intermittent. Over Lowerbank Street crept the stillness of night.

Jacqueline awoke shivering. It was dark, quite dark. She rose in a panic, groped blindly for the door. As she rushed along the passage the scutter of her frightened feet sounded clamantly in her ears. She tried the handle of the bedroom door. It yielded not at all. In a blaze of fear she wrestled with it until in response to her frantic jerking a paper shaving fell from the keyhole, through which, very faintly, there filtered the smell of gas.

For a moment the child stood trembling, arrested by the strange suffocating odour. Then an overwhelming sense of disaster smote her. She belaboured the door with her fists. But never an answer came back.

Alone in the darkness, Jacqueline screamed and screamed.

PART I

CHAPTER I

Jacqueline strolled leisurely up the street, the ruddy tan of her school-bag a bright smear on her dark clothes.

Rain was falling, a transparent, smoky drizzle, and in all the expanse of villadom that lay clustered beneath the castle crags she was the one living, breathing object.

Today the castle crags, the crenellated walls, were all a mass of wet blackness. A thin spiral of smoke emitted by one of the chimneys gleamed strangely white against the blue-black dome of the sky. An old-time giant the fortress looked, towering above the pigmy rows of red brick houses – an impregnable place set high on a rock, mocking with its invincibility the passage of time.

The rain drops trickled on to Jacqueline's hat. Smilingly, she raised her face to meet them. A soft, kindly moisture in spring, Kirkton rain; not raw and biting like the rain on the East coast of Scotland, but tempered by a gentle wind redolent of clover and wet grass. Jacqueline sniffed the air contentedly. She was very near home now, and her footsteps lagged. The quiet, misty streets held for her a fascination that did not exist in any corner of Lilac Villa.

To the child there was something arid in the atmosphere of Lilac Villa. She had been sharply conscious of it the moment she arrived, tearful and tremulous, in charge of her aunt fully a year ago and had been bidden wipe her feet well on the mat labelled 'Welcome' that lay on the step outside the front door. Wherein lay the difference between her old home in Lowerbank Street and this she was not wise enough to define. Only she realized vaguely that the gods of her mother were not those of her Aunt Ruth. The business must never be referred to here. Bazaar work – yes. Dress-making – never.

Aunt Ruth was a big bony woman, born to rule. On those rare occasions when she had visited Jacqueline's mother she had contrived to dominate the household. 'No eggs preserved?' she would say acidly. 'Now, how do you expect to live in December when they go up to half a crown a dozen?'

Customers, too, she would interview and intimidate. Even the postman's delivery was not immune from her scrutiny. And all attempts to circumvent her were apt to prove useless, for no sound escaped her ears. 'There's the postman's ring. I'll answer it,' she would say. And before Jacqueline, in response to her mother's mute signal, could reach the doorway, it was blocked by Mrs Forsyth's large, purposeful figure. She would return instantly, her gaze ostentatiously averted from the envelopes in her hand; but later it would transpire that she had made good use of her eyes in the passage between the door and the workroom.

'I wonder at you dealing with Thoms – dearest shop in the town,' she would say, apropos of nothing. Or, 'Fancy people still keeping their savings in Consols – such poor return for their money.' Or, more casually still, 'George Buchanan – do you ever hear of him nowadays?' This last enquiry proving beyond a doubt that Aunt Ruth had noted the foreign envelope and the indigo blue stamp.

George Buchanan, incidentally, was a sore subject. The mention of his name never failed to create a battleground whereon the sisters met to spar. Aunt Ruth, blustering like a stump orator, advanced her dislike of him with the delicacy of a battering ram. In his defence, Jacqueline's mother, quietly sarcastic, drew blood with every sally.

Uncle Archie was the exact opposite of his wife; a meagre, bald-headed little man, he went through life apologizing perpetually for his existence. He would, if he had dared, have apologized more abjectly still for that of his wife; but he lacked the quality of courage, both moral and physical. In point of fact, he resembled a dog rather than a man – one of those cringing but not unkindly mongrels, canine outcasts of their clan, who thread the disreputable streets of a city hard on their master's heels conscious that neither they nor their owners have any recognized place in the general scheme of things.

Jacqueline turned the corner into the wide oblong, called by courtesy square, at the far end of which Lilac Villa was situated; a demure, secretive-looking little house by reason of the fact that it had been built by some freak of architecture slightly in the rear of its immediate neighbours. Sometimes, entering the square from the town and spying never a sight of its yellow-curtained windows, Jacqueline would become obsessed by the fear that Lilac Villa had been spirited away in her absence. And she would run on with beating heart, fearful lest something – Something Awful – had happened again. Other days, the spirit of adventure quick within her, she would loiter happily at the crossroads and conjure up visions of what she would do if one day Lilac Villa were really and truly swallowed up by the castle's predatory crags. In those imaginings George Buchanan played a noble part, a George Buchanan whose princely mien accorded ill with the snapshot she possessed of him, arm-in-arm with her father, an absurd straw hat tilted on the back of his head.

Today the flurry of rain that veiled the square concealed its architectural crudities and emphasized the grim lines of the castle, now blackening into shadow. Like dolls' houses, tawdry and ill-constructed, the villas dotted round the square – painted cock-shies seen against this sublimity of rock, this pile of splendid masonry that held vested in its stone something of the quality of eternity.

Jessie, the maid of all work, opened the door. Flushed and self-important, she jerked a finger at the parlour door.

'Comp'ny. A Mistress Thingummy from Glesca'. I'm after takin' them in their tea.'

Jacqueline tiptoed upstairs. Company. She knew what that meant. A scurrying and a flustering and a fussing; the best spoons to get out; the tea-cloth to iron over; the bread to cut, perilously thin; cakes to run for to Ralstons; and flowers, a sixpenny bunch, to be spread out to look as many as possible in the salad bowl, which you must never call a salad but a flower bowl such times as it occupies the place of honour in the centre of the table.

She threw off her hat, toppled her books on to the bed. Arithmetic – she'd done her sums for tomorrow at prep. English – there was still that essay unconsidered. Hamlet; were his difficulties objective or subjective?

Seated on the edge of the bed, her long legs dangling, she ran her pencil through her hair and debated the question. No use asking Aunt Ruth; she wouldn't know; but catch her admitting it! Only the other night Jacqueline had heard her laying off to somebody all about Mary Queen of Scots' visit to Kirkton Castle, and mixing up her subsequent history with that of her English namesake.

'Jacqueline! Jac-quel-ine!'

From the ultra-refined timbre of Mrs Forsyth's voice Jacqueline knew that company still reigned in the front parlour.

Her aunt's agitated gaze shot over her person.

'Are you tidy? Come away in, then. It's Mrs Pullman. She was in the neighbourhood and came to call for me. She wants specially to see you.'

Mrs Pullman held out her hand. 'Dear child, er – Jacqueline, did they say your name was?'

At sound of the soft, slithering voice something snapped in Jacqueline's head. That night – that awful night! Next morning – that awful morning when the dentist from across the way had taken her to his house and given her his horrible, cold instruments to play with! Looking out through the stained-glass windows she had seen the blinds in her own house all drawn. That was because her mother was dead. She had died in the night, so he had told her – that strange, soft-voiced old man dressed like a butcher in a soiled white linen jacket, adding 'Sh-sh!' when his housekeeper had opened her lips to enlighten her further.

Everyone, it seemed to Jacqueline just then, made a practice of saying 'Sh-sh!' when she drew nigh. It was as if her mother, having died, wasn't her mother any longer, but someone else's – the dentist's or her Aunt Ruth's or one of the strange men who came and went with grave, sullen faces.

Did she like Kirkton? Yes, she heard her own voice saying

quietly. Yes, she liked Kirkton. Yes, she liked going to school. Yes, she liked the other little girls.

The wheeze of the front gate broke the senseless refrain of her repetition. Uncle Archie! At a nod from her aunt she ran to meet him. Panting, she hurled herself into his arms.

'Hullo, hullo!' he stammered in pained surprise.

'I hate Kirkton; I hate school; I – I hate everything!' she sobbed as through her head twinged the raw nerve of a dreadful recollection.

CHAPTER II

Jacqueline was entering upon her sixteenth year when she made a discovery that jolted her thoughts out of their even groove.

Prior to this she had found existence rather a drab affair shot with few bright strands. School – the cheap private school at the far end of the town which she attended – was uninspiring. Thrown into it in the middle of a term, when everyone else had chosen her classmate, Jacqueline found herself singularly alone. One girl only had she found ready and eager to meet her advances, a child with long lanky hair and a greasy skin whom no one seemed to have annexed. Her personality did not attract Jacqueline. But someone to walk with, to smuggle notes to at prayers, with whom to exchange foreign stamps and gay little threads of coloured silk was a necessary factor in school life, and Rosie Farrell served well enough as a partner in these youthful social amenities.

Out of school hours Jacqueline missed the stir of her mother's business, the half-reluctant affection her mother had yielded her. Because of the very niggardliness of that affection, the child had not suffered so acutely as she would otherwise have done from its withdrawal. She pined less in actuality for maternal caresses than for the constant bustle that had given zest to her childhood's days. On occasion her thoughts reverted to the fashion-plate ladies in their daring grandeur. She remembered them now not as 'funnies' but as elegant artistic creations a thousand times worthier of wall space than the family groups that gloomed down on you from the walls of Lilac Villa. As opposites to the litter of calling cards on her aunt's hall table, she likened the coloured discs of her mother's pattern books – books seen through the romantic haze of distance which now assumed a superlative degree of loveliness in her eyes.

There was nothing romantic, nothing beautiful about the calling cards. Yellow with age, some of them were, grubby and thumbmarked. But Aunt Ruth took great pride in the litter and refused to allow it to be cast out. Since Mrs Pullman's visit her card had graced the top of the pile. Not because she was the wife of one of the most highly paid ministers in Glasgow, but because she herself – this much Jacqueline had gleaned from her aunt's conversation – was one of the Jacks of Paisley – *the* Jacks, you know . . .

Yes, folks were queer, very queer. Jacqueline had attained the age when she embraced this conclusion as a new thought, unconscious of the fact that a few years hence she would arrive at the further conclusion that it is this very quality of queerness that forms the one uniting factor which binds the members of the human race together and makes them kin. Naturally enough, among the queerest of queer folks, she ranked those persons with whom she was most familiar, her Aunt Ruth and her Uncle Archie. Towards her aunt her feelings were fixed, irrevocably fixed. Her affection for her uncle, on the other hand, was subject to many changes.

One Saturday, when Aunt Ruth had gone to Glasgow for the day, he had taken her to a violent kinemacolour of life and sudden death interspersed with bouts of crude humour. In his seat at the back beneath the gallery, Uncle Archie had rocked with laughter at the comic interludes. The sound of his gleeful chortlings had warmed the heart of his niece. She pressed his arm delightedly when the amusing rustic with the grin like a split melon flickered into view. By way of response he stroked her hand where it lay on the arm of his chair. At the action, so unexpected, so friendly, Jacqueline's heart glowed. Uncle Archie was a dear. They were chums – he and she – real chums.

The rustic was funny, but not half so funny as Uncle Archie's chucklings. She had no idea he could laugh like that. For the moment she adored him as she might an elder brother who has revealed to his admiring sister some new and altogether engaging trait of character.

On the way home her enthusiasm received a severe check. As

they reached the crossroads and came within the confining space of the square Uncle Archie's jollity seemed to slip from him like a cloak. He cleared his throat. 'Er – your aunt,' he murmured, as if she were no wife of his but some eccentric relative of Jacqueline's whose wishes it were wise she should observe, 'your aunt, very properly, no doubt, doesn't approve of picture houses. We won't say anything to her about our little jaunt tonight.'

Poor spiritless little worm! How her vigorous young mind despised him!

It was upon a wet night in October that Jacqueline stumbled upon secret treasure. Mr and Mrs Forsyth had gone to a soirée in the church hall and Jacqueline was left to her own devices. Her lessons done, she looked about her for amusement. Books. She had devoured all the books the house contained, saving, perhaps, the Bible. Solitaire. She had played the game so often that she had come to loathe the sight of the indented board. Cards. There wasn't, so far as she knew, a decent game you could play alone. Restive as a young colt, she prowled the room. Then, wearying of it, she marched to the window, began drumming fretful fingers on the pane.

The square had a funny look tonight, a fly-away, harum-scarum look with the leaves flying and the trees swaying madly to and fro. At sight of them Jacqueline's discontent vanished. She was back in her old role again – that of entranced onlooker, and the square was a stage set for action. Very soon the players began to appear in sight, staid folk clad in oilskins and galoshes. Watching their efforts to dodge the blast, Jacqueline giggled delightedly. Like pantomime ladies of old, they played their parts most wonderfully. They bowed their heads, ran a step or two, then stopped breathlessly beneath the big tree for shelter. They put up umbrellas only to put them down again. They fought their way like tipsy folk uncertain of their goals. Even the teetotal bailie who lived opposite lurched drunkenly across the street when he emerged to pop a letter into the pillar-box. Jacqueline knew him for a teetotaller because he possessed an extremely red nose upon which it was the unkind custom of small boys to comment on in public and for grown-ups to commiserate in private. A sad affliction, a nose like that, to a prohibitionist.

The old square itself seemed inebriated tonight. Plunged in the wild October gale it had shed all its nice airs of decorum, of dapper self-respect. Between the villas the rain blew in gusty streaks, setting the garden shrubs quivering and the street lamps dipping in and out. Like a phosphorescent fish in a glazed bowl the big light at the crossroads swam furtively, now flashing a bright tail upwards, now delving deeper into the rain-dimmed chalice until only a pinpoint of radiance remained. Above the dissolute square the castle seemed to swell vaster and vaster in its immobility, the one changeless object on a night of windy fantasy.

The wonder of it all filled Jacqueline with a kind of awe. The beauty of the old castle hanging over the rainswept town like a doom; the brooding shadows of the green dusk; the tossing trees making of the douce square a termagant, wanton and wild-eyed. And with this sense of wonder which welled up in her in a deep surge of emotion there came memories of her mother, her dead father, of that lordly buccaneer, George Buchanan. In a trice the whole world was changed. The hour was charged with magic. The night air glowed. In that moment Jacqueline savoured happiness as she had not savoured it since the days when her mother had taken her to the pantomime and she had sat, taut with expectancy, during that deliciously thrilling moment when the lights are lowered and the band is playing softly as a prelude to the curtain's rising. Looking out, there came to Jacqueline the impulse that has fired the artist from time immemorial to stay the passage of the hours, to wrest this moment of joy from tonight and to hold it for always. No use trying to stop the clock. Time races on though the ticking ceases.

An idea struck her. She seized pencil and paper. Dusk-castle-wind. Meaningless little words in themselves, but as she set them down a rhyme uniting them floated like a stave of music through her mind. She repeated it eagerly, thrilling at sound of each syllable.

Outside, the wind scampered like a mischievous prank-player between the villas, shrieking and tapping at the window-panes as it passed. Over the table, Jacqueline sat brooding with cheeks on fire. Words – words – words. They waved like flags before her eyes, will-o'-the-wisps beckoning she knew not whither. Up the cobbled steeps of the causeway and back again; over the castle ramparts and down to the foul black dungeon where the great Montrose once lay in chains; along the Drip Road that drives its way through forest and moorland to the North; through the broken arches of the mean, malodorous streets that slope to the river.

Once there, her vision halted, held by what looked like a strange splendid ship dimming the blazing streamers of the sunset. A famous bridge she knew it for, but seen at nightfall from the marshy bank of the river it swam out of distance, a molten galleon with burnished sails faintly fretted by the wind, a Gargantuan vessel upon which the gods might journey.

Breathless with joy, she sat plying her pencil, creating for herself a new heaven and a new earth.

In a night she had entered into her kingdom, a kingdom whose key none could wrest from her.

CHAPTER III

Every Christmas George Buchanan sent her presents, exciting, unusual presents. An enormous feather fan with curling tips into which merely to dip your fingers made you shiver with delight. A gorgeous jewelled chain for the waist with blue stones like forget-me-nots framed in dew, and smouldering green gems like cats' eyes after dark. A shapeless kimono garment from Japan embroidered in fine silk, soft as a baby's hair, and powdered all over with chrysanthemums and frail pagodas.

Then one day out of a storm of snow and rain the donor of all these elegancies arrived, his big bronzed face moist with rain, his burly figure dripping wet.

He greeted Jacqueline boisterously, so boisterously that she never for a moment guessed that he was struggling to overcome the sense of diffidence that always afflicted him in the company of very young females. And Jacqueline was different, quite different from what he had expected. No trace of her mother in her, of those shrewish features, that acidulated voice. A typical old maid spoiled by matrimony he had always accounted Mrs Thayer, all unconscious of the fact that it had been matrimony itself that had added the last spice of vinegar to Mrs Thayer's temper.

Jacqueline bore little resemblance to her father either. A throwback, perhaps, inheriting the grace of her Huguenot ancestor, the first Jacqueline Thayer from whom it had been her father's pride to trace his descent. In her blue dress, her dark hair confined by a wisp of ribbon, she looked to George Buchanan's thinking like an alpine flower. The pale oval of her face recalled to him a miniature he had once seen in a shipmate's cabin of a beautiful young

Frenchwoman painted upon the eve of her entering a convent. Jacqueline's expression held the same exquisite virginity, the same sense of divine content. Her innocence disturbed him strangely. It was so transparent that the thought came to him how attractive she would appear to some lawless marauder who plundered for the sheer love of plundering.

Holding her hand in his, he felt abashed before the sweet scrutiny of her eyes. She made him feel uncouth, ridiculously overgrown. He laughed and talked the louder lest this feeling of inferiority overcome him altogether and set him to flight. A celebration. A jollification. After all these years. Why, she'd been in her cradle – he blushed to recall he had even seen her in her bath – when last he'd been over. Assuredly they must do something to celebrate this merry meeting. A theatre? No, of course not. There weren't any theatres in Kirkton. A dinner out then? Surely that could be managed. There was the County Restaurant newly open and calling out for custom. He would take her there. What time? Righto. Six by the town clock.

The County Restaurant! Jacqueline's eyes grew round; for the County was a new and very ostentatiously grand place that had just been opened in the main street. Jacqueline's knowledge of it was confined to its swing door – a glass affair miraculously fashioned of many compartments which shot its patrons in and out like so many peas in a pod. She knew, too, by sight its magnificent commissionaire – a portly gentleman in a chocolate-coloured uniform whose chief occupation in life appeared to be that of sweeping gaping urchins from the doorstep with a wave of his hands, much as a disdainful housemaid sweeps away refuse with a broom. Until the advent of the County Restaurant, Kirkton had fed frugally in a draper's. On their way to a paradise made up of tea-cakes and tiny tables, blushing young men in company with their women friends had to pass through a purgatory known as the lingerie saloon, where corsets, bust bodices, shamelessly displayed, intruded upon innocent minds. In comparison with these indelicate garments, the artificial palms which lined the entrance to the County Restaurant were sedate indeed.

Jacqueline thought their rigid branches very ugly after those of her flighty friends in the square.

Aloud, she wondered if trees grew like that in foreign parts, if the heat of the Eastern sun caused them to become transfixed. All the way down George Buchanan had snapped thankfully at the crumbs of conversation she had thrown him. This, he thanked God, was more than a crumb; it was a chunk. He chewed it tenaciously until they were well through the fish.

Jacqueline, for her part, was unconscious of the difficulty her escort was experiencing in providing conversation suitable to her tender years. She was savouring too keenly the tremendous business of dining out. It was all so exciting – the big room, the little tables set on an expanse of floor slippery as ice. She wished fervently their table had been in a corner, or at least up against the wall. After the privacy of Lilac Villa, she felt marooned in this sea of feasting folk, of scurrying waiters, of steaming food and popping corks. It made her dizzy to eat amid so much noise and bustle.

Gradually the sense of strangeness departed, leaving her mind clear and receptive to impressions. Extraordinary that so wee a table should hold so much . . . Funny dress that girl in the corner was wearing, fur on it like a winter coat. She wished George Buchanan wouldn't talk so loudly. His voice was the only one you heard upraised, adjuring the waiter to get a move on. She wished he were more like the escorts of other girls, those quiet-mannered young men who ate and drank so matter-of-factly at the other tables. Then she chid herself spiritedly. But for George Buchanan she would not be here; but for him she would never have penetrated these sumptuous regions.

'Drinks,' said George Buchanan. 'What's yours, Jacqueline?'

What was hers? Stone ginger. But it was awfully dear. Wasteful, too. So little in those thick grey bottles. Aunt Ruth was always telling Uncle Archie so.

'Water,' she said, 'or – if you don't mind, stone ginger.'

George Buchanan laughed. 'Stone ginger be —— This is a celebration. We must drink to our next merry meeting.' He summoned a waiter by the delightfully simple device of rattling his knife against the rim of his plate. A moment later two tall green glasses containing a sparkling crimson liquid were placed on the table.

'Here's how!' said George Buchanan, looking across at her.

Jacqueline tasted the wine doubtfully. It wasn't half so good as Uncle Archie's stone ginger. It was sour and not at all nippy, and dried on the tongue. But it was lovely to look upon; just like the juice of a bruised plum crushed on an acid green leaf. Tentatively she took another sip, and then another.

Through her veins ran a thousand tiny beads of fire. Excitement like a fluid seemed to possess her. In the smoke-laden atmosphere she expanded like a sun-warmed flower, and George Buchanan's heart rejoiced at the sound of her gay young laughter.

They walked home through streets silvered over with moonshine, and then, after the fashion of lovers loath to part, they strolled a second time round the square. And George Buchanan told her of the bridges he had helped to build, and Jacqueline told him of the gossamer bridges of fancy which she, in her turn, essayed to build. His enthusiasm brought tears of joy to her eyes.

'Po'try,' he said. 'There's nothing like it, but it's mighty hard to do. We engineers deal in bricks and steel girders. You po'try writers have no material to hand . . . Wonder now what made you think of trying to write po'try? Not much in your mother's line, was it?'

Jacqueline looked up at him. 'There's something,' she said, 'something I'd like to tell you; something I've never told anyone before.'

He laid a kindly hand on her shoulder. 'Fire away, kiddie. George Buchanan's safe as – as houses; he won't give you away.'

'It's something mother said that – that night.'

He nodded. That night. He could guess what that night in Lowerbank Street had meant to this sensitive child. He had heard details from Ruth Forsyth that had made him shudder.

'It was the last thing she ever said: "Second best. Makeshift all the time. I've missed it somehow, but there's more in life than that."'

He uttered a sharp sigh of relief. He had expected to hear some half-crazy saying incapable of interpretation; but this – this seemed sensible enough, uncommon sensible to have emanated from the lips of a hysterical woman on the eve of taking her own life.

'Your mother said that, did she? That was a fine thing to have said. Remember it, Jacqueline.'

The girl's lips compressed. As if she could ever forget! 'But what,' she urged, 'did she mean?'

George Buchanan puffed at his pipe in silent perplexity. He was a simple soul, unused to probing the psychology of any man or woman.

'There's no saying with women, ever,' he observed. Then, noting the look of disappointment on the child's face, he set himself to unravel the puzzle and to outline for her his own simple philosophy.

'I'll tell you, though, how I'd figure it out. It's like this. See that castle up there, with the moon sitting like a top hat on the highest turret? Well, the fella that cast the design for that castle was no second bester. No dodging the timekeeper for him, and bolting on the first stroke of the hour. That fella was an all-timer who worked with his coat off from dawn till dusk. He aimed at being a top-notcher, and he was a top-notcher. And if his fella-workers didn't allow it, we do, and honour 'im for it. See what I'm getting at?'

She looked up at him and, involuntarily, he halted, abashed before the light that shone in her eyes. With her hands tightly clasped, her face upturned in the soft white moonlight, she made him think of a novice to whom the full beauty of her faith has been revealed in a great blinding flash.

'You mean,' she said, groping after words; 'you mean—'

'Just that,' he said hastily; 'just that.'

All unwittingly, it seemed, he had provided her with the articles of a new faith, and he prayed she would forbear to question him further regarding them; for he felt guilty as a man might feel who, having slain a priest, masquerades in the sacred robes of office and officiates at the confessional. True, Jacqueline had told him nothing, and yet she had told him everything. She had revealed herself as a little child reveals itself, touchingly, trustingly, certain of succour. From the darkness of her doubt she had stretched out a hand for guidance, and he had given her – gosh, what had he given her? A snatch of magazine-page philosophy that meant little or nothing; a jumble of slang phrases he hadn't the brains to sort out properly.

He cursed himself for a fool; a fool and a fifth-rate Holy Joe. Why, any ranter running round and scaring folk off from a street meeting with a collection plate could have handed out on the spur of the moment a better working creed than that!

'Best be getting home,' he said, gripping her arm resolutely.

'Yes,' she said, still deep in the trance into which his words had cast her. 'It was a wonderful thing for her to have said; I'll remember it always.'

CHAPTER IV

Jacqueline was almost seventeen before she awoke to a sense of sex consciousness. And then it was not the turgid mutterings of Rosie Farrell that aroused her, but the gradual unfolding of a romance – a real romance – within the precincts of Lilac Villa itself. Jessie was walking out. So, at least, Aunt Ruth put it. Jacqueline, seeing the maid lingering at the gate with a sheepish-looking youth whose hands hung like hams by his sides, or blushing violently when he shuffled up the road while she was cleaning the door brasses, thought there wasn't much walking about it. You couldn't walk far in those shiny tight shoes with the toy heels into which Jessie forced her poor, swollen feet every Wednesday and Sunday evening.

'Where do you walk to?' she asked one day in her guileless way.

Jessie smiled and coloured. 'The old cemetery most times,' she answered after a moment's silent confusion. 'There's some great flat tombs – martyrs' tombs, they call them – where you can sit and talk. It's a great place for walkers out, the old cemetery.'

Her curiosity thus stimulated, Jacqueline went there one Sunday. Sure enough, there were couples strolling aimlessly up and down the slanting gravel paths and giggling shamelessly behind the abutting marble slabs of the ancient tombs. On the way home she met Rosie Farrell.

'I've been to the old cemetery,' she said.

Rosie's boiled gooseberry eyes watered with envy. 'Who with?' she asked. Then she glanced coyly down the street. 'I went there last night with Bob Finlay. We hadn't gone farther'n the first cross before he tried to kiss me.'

Jacqueline snorted. There wouldn't be much trying with Rosie. It was sickening to think of her and that fat-faced Finlay boy despoiling the peace of the old graveyard. Jessie was different. The dead, however wakeful they might be, would never resent her gentle presence. To this mysterious business of lovemaking Jessie brought something sacred, something indescribably lovely, that made you think of the dim light that poured through the blue stained glass in church on sunny Sunday mornings, of the low grumblings of the organ that preceded the triumphant peal the first note of which released you from your seat.

Jacqueline knew all this because she had surprised the maid saying good night to her sweetheart at the gate. As she had slipped from his arms her upraised face had been radiant. In the tarnished darkness her happiness had shone out like a jewel in a dull black casket. From her person warmth seemed to radiate, warmth and an intensive femininity, as though below her finger-tips lay the very protoplasm of life.

Here was a different Jessie from the sturdy young woman who slaved to keep the dust down in Lilac Villa, who scoured the doorstep under Aunt Ruth's direction with a vigour that suggested she was wreaking upon the hapless stone the vengeance she durst not wreak upon her employer.

If love could thus transform Jessie, there must, Jacqueline argued, be something in it. She itched to question the maid, but delicacy forbade. There were so many things – silly little things – she wanted so desperately to understand. And Jessie, tricked out of a Sunday in silk stockings and splashed with *eau de Cologne*, seemed so eminently a person who knew. Privately, Jacqueline believed that Jessie spent too much money on the wrong end of her person. Who noticed your feet if your head was all right?

Jacqueline had left school and was attending commercial classes in the town hall when the opportunity came to her to emulate the examples of Jessie and Rosie. A youthful instructor, breathing heavily in her ears while he made a pretence of glancing over her shorthand notes, uttered a word or two that caused her face to flame. She eyed his retreating figure in stupefied amaze while a tiny quiver of excitement shot up her spine. What a lark! She could walk out in company on Sunday, too. She could; but would she?

With a new spurt of interest she studied the instructor as he patrolled the room beaming, with an absurd assumption of the paternal manner of his chief, upon the class. He was like a weed in a garden, a swarthy, black object with his beetling brows, his oily hair, his wee bristling moustache. Dirt under his finger nails, too, she could bet. She bent over her copy-book with an affectation of interest, but her mind was snared in the meshes of a highly debatable problem. Would she? It was a chance not to be missed. Most likely her one and only. It would be terrible to grow up, to wilt into spinsterhood, to die without ever having made a pilgrimage in the company of a male to the martyrs' tombs. It would be terrible not to be able, when she was old, to regale her descendants with stories of the love affairs of her youth.

She lifted her head to regard again, albeit a shade reluctantly, the person of her last chance. As it happened, he was looking in her direction, and their eyes locked. In that moment Jacqueline forgot the black-rimmed nails, the swarthy brows. She was conscious only of an imperative urge in his eyes, and for the fraction of a second the classroom swung about her.

Next Sunday afternoon a spruced-up youth forged a long chain of cigarettes at the crossroads near Lilac Villa. When dusk fell, he strolled away, whistling ill-humouredly through his teeth. And Jacqueline retired to bed early, fuming at thought of a lost opportunity. She had dressed with the full intention of keeping her appointment. She had even gone so far as to borrow from Jessie a few drops of her *eau de Cologne*. Then, on the clap of the hour, she had peeped down from the best point of vantage, which chanced to be the bathroom window, to see if he were really there. He was. That settled it. At sight of him smoking aggressively beneath the lime trees, his little finger curled affectedly as he raised the cigarette to his lips, she subsided on the ledge of the wash-hand basin in a crumpled heap. She couldn't – no, she simply couldn't!

A minute later she was lathering her handkerchief with yellow soap to eradicate the tell-tale smell of Jessie's *eau de Cologne*.

Jacqueline was eighteen when, having become the owner of

sundry slips of cardboard attesting to her ability to type legibly and to inscribe shorthand creditably, she left the commercial school in Forth Street. At the end of the summer holiday Mrs Forsyth had begun to throw out feelers to her husband regarding her niece's future. Indirect tactics having failed, she was driven ultimately into advancing a frontal attack.

'When are you going to see about a post for Jacqueline?' she demanded one evening.

Uncle Archie twisted round in his chair, depositing his newspaper with a crinkle of annoyance across his knee.

'No hurry, is there?' he remarked, mildly apologetic for the militant crinkle.

Aunt Ruth sniffed. Some men, she hinted derisively, would be hollering there's no hurry and would be leaving their womenfolk to do all the hustling when the last trump sounded. Some men . . .

'Well, well,' interrupted Uncle Archie, 'what do you want me to do? So far as I know, there's not a soul in Kirkton wanting a typist or any other kind of ist.'

'Maybe not,' said his wife; 'but if you had studied the advertisement columns in the newspapers you'd have seen that people in other places do.'

A faint flush stole up the back of his neck. So she wanted the girl out of the place, did she, wanted the house to herself again? He, for his part, would miss her sorely. She was like a tropical bird in Lilac Villa, a brave, flashing creature with her happy laughter, her habit of living intensely.

Mrs Forsyth, guessing at the trend of his thoughts, reached out for a weapon, applied it brutally.

'The fact is, you can't afford to keep her here much longer in idleness. You know as well as I do, Archibald, that your salary hasn't gone up although prices have. Now, if you'd taken my advice and started on your own after the Armistice . . .'

She was off, airing once more a grievance that never withered or grew mouldy, for upon every occasion of controversy it was dragged forth and sunned afresh in the light of day. The sight of it sprouting hale as ever never failed to make Uncle Archie feel a singular hollowness inside, as if he had eaten nothing for weeks but porridge and plum duff.

Writhing in a spasm of sick humiliation – for the woman, confound her, was right, and, what was worse, they both of them knew it – he turned up the advertisement page of the paper.

'Here you are, Ruth; there are one or two likelies here.'

Aunt Ruth choked in the middle of a sentence, scrutinized the place indicated, then, with the triumphant air of a small boy who has succeeded in spearing a minnow with a pen-knife, she stuck a pin in a line of print.

'There!' she said. 'Now, that might do; MacCluskys', the big firm in Rent Street; I'll get Jacqueline to write them tonight.'

CHAPTER V

When it was first mooted that Jacqueline should go to Glasgow a fascinating picture of freedom formed in her mind. Such recollections as she retained of the city were exotic in the extreme – a beatific jumble of pantomime fairies gorgeously apparelled, their sequined raiment shooting sparks of splendour across the dim pit of the orchestra; of dangerously swaying tramcars cleaving their way through the heady surf of the traffic; of shop windows in whose deeps a thousand wonders shimmered; of pavements swarming with all sorts of interesting people. Earning money of her own, she would be at liberty to squander it as she pleased, in picture houses, in hat shops, at book barrows in the street. It was all very exciting. She welcomed Aunt Ruth's suggestion eagerly, squashing Uncle Archie's feebly voiced objections with a flood of eloquent enthusiasm.

It was not until she was jogging out of Buchanan Street Station in a stuffy old horse-cab that the hot rush of expectancy froze in her veins. She leaned back against the dusty blue cushions feeling as she had been wont to feel at times in sight of Kirkton Castle, very small and insignificant. It was as irksome, this feeling of inferiority, as the prick of new wool on the spine. It tended to wear down your resistance until you were ready to wish yourself dead.

Resolutely bright, she took her thoughts in hand, sent them charging down another channel. Weir Street – she wondered if Weir Street was very far away. She had a violent desire to rap on the window with the cockatoo handle of her new umbrella and enquire its whereabouts of the cabbie. But his back, looming like a massive figure of fate before her, looked unapproachable. Not the kind of back you would dare to prod for the purpose of asking even the most important question. And this was important, terribly important. For she knew somebody in Weir Street. At least, she didn't, but she would very soon – an old friend of Aunt Ruth's to whom Mrs Forsyth had written a letter of introduction. In the midst of all the squalor and noise, the thought of that somebody was the sheet anchor to which she clung for comfort until the cab emerged from the dreary curve of the Cowcaddens.

And then she cast it from her with a thud. For there was a theatre, decrepit a trifle, but still a theatre; and there a picture house – *The Woman Tempted Me* – and there, straying off the main thoroughfare, which seemed to go on for ever and ever, were little narrow streets caught at the far ends in a tangle of trees. Jacqueline's eyes lightened at sight of a familiar landmark. The park. Nice and near the park, Aunt Ruth had said, as if her niece's business in life were to be concerned henceforth with the perambulation of sequestered paths. And it wasn't. It certainly wasn't. For subtract eight hours from the twelve that comprise a day, and you have precious few left. And she was due at MacCluskys' in Rent Street next morning and every succeeding morning at ten prompt.

She had visions of herself on the morrow, her heart thumping with terror, shyly opening a side door and tremblingly obeying the mandates of the merest message boy. Then she had visions of herself on some other morning not too far distant haughtily informing the head of the firm, an imposing old gentleman with a massive watch chain girdling his massive person, a gentleman rather similar in appearance to the teetotal bailie in Lilac Square, that she was shaking off her feet the dust of MacCluskys' for ever.

And the imposing gentleman would sigh and shake his head. 'Aye, aye,' he would say in the lugubrious accents befitting the occasion, 'genius cannot be caged.' Whereat she would shake her head depreciatingly, for genius – yes, genius was really going a bit too far. And maybe if he were very nice about it and genuinely perturbed at her leaving, to cheer him up she'd present him with a gilt-edged volume of her newly published poems. 'To Mr MacClusky. In remembrance from J. T.' And she would give the office boy half a crown. 'D'you remember, Tommy, the first day I came here?' 'Deed an' I do, miss! I'll never forget your bonnie blue eyes.' Ah, what a pity it was they were a dirty grey!

Next day Jacqueline discovered that there was no side door. There was no office boy. There wasn't even a Mr MacClusky, only a sandy-haired gentleman of the name of Shaw, who relegated her with a complete absence of interest to a long narrow room at the back which overlooked a lane and ran the whole length of the building. She received a confused impression of clicking typewriters, of curious eyes and shingled heads; then out of the blur one person emerged.

'Miss Carruthers will show you.' Gracefully the sandy-haired one drifted away, leaving the aroma of highly scented tobacco smoke behind him.

Miss Carruthers smiled, displaying a row of tiny uneven teeth, and instantly Jacqueline conceived a liking for her funny, stubby features, her short, squat figure.

'S'quite easy, re'ly,' she said. 'Copying only. You don't need brains for this job. You'll be used to the single keyboard?'

A little later Jacqueline was contributing her mite to the mechanical orchestra pounding out a major refrain; she was a cog in the wheel of commerce that whirs unceasingly from the granite steeps of Maryhill to the many-storied buildings that cluster round the Clyde.

Next night on the way home she remembered Weir Street. Was it very far away? The conductor to whom she addressed her enquiry brushed it aside contemptuously. 'Och, it's on the South Side,' he muttered as though it was inconceivable that any self-respecting young woman who travelled on a westward-bound car should so demean herself as to dream of crossing the river. For a second Jacqueline was daunted. Then, recalling the dismal bedroom called by courtesy 'bed-sitting-room', in which she had spent the previous evening, she persisted. Red car from Jamaica Street, change at the cross, then blue car to Rosadhu Drive. It sounded complicated, but it was worth trying. Much intrigued, with her hands elegantly encased in a new pair of wash-leather gloves, she set out after tea in quest of the sheet anchor – the one person in the whole of this great roaring city who might reasonably be expected to take some slight interest in the person of Jacqueline Thayer.

Darkness was falling when she reached Weir Street, a demure tree-lined avenue which reminded her pleasantly of Lilac Square, and she could scarce see to read the numbers on the doors. A belated errand boy racing down the street paused in answer to her query.

'Fufteen?' he repeated. 'It'll be the auld wife wi' the cats you're meanin'? See yon door a' scarted? Yon's hit.'

Jacqueline's heart sank as she pulled the stiff-resisting bell, a bell whose sorrowful twang seemed to say: 'Let me be. I'm getting old – old – old.' She looked behind her down the street all smirred with shadows, and loneliness, like a high wall, rose about her. Oh, for the sight of somebody she knew! Determinedly she laid fingers again on the rust-ridden pull.

As the last echo died the door creaked open. A maid stared at her in unconcealed surprise. Visitors, apparently, were not as common as cats at 15, Weir Street. Within a few minutes she understood the reason why. Miss Prentice, enthroned in a high armchair, listened without comment to her guest's apology for having come – an apology which something in the older woman's attitude, not to mention the stiff-tailed demeanour of the cats, had made seem absolutely necessary.

In a faraway voice she asked: 'Did you say you were through from Kirkton for the day? Wednesday's the cheap fare, I suppose?'

'Aunt Ruth,' called out Jacqueline. 'Didn't Aunt Ruth write?'

'The cats bite! What an idea! And are the shops looking nice?'

Jacqueline muttered assent. She didn't know whether they were or not, but she realized in a spurt of exasperation that it was useless to try to disclaim anything. How like Aunt Ruth to enlarge upon Miss Prentice's philanthropic deeds and never to let on she was deaf as a post!

And yet, sitting opposite the old lady, Jacqueline was forced to admit that she looked kind in a queer, frizzled-up, mummified sort of way. She handled the Persians as though she loved them, and they responded like faithful dogs to her call. She fed them lavishly on cake brought in presumably for Jacqueline; and once, with a strange little cry, she snatched up the larger animal in her arms, cuddled it close, gazing the while into its eyes as though she hoped to find therein the response which her infirmity denied to her. If only she could have devised some way of establishing contact Jacqueline felt Miss Prentice might have been persuaded to befriend her. As it was, talking to the old soul was like playing a mad game of misunderstandings.

When she rose to go, Miss Prentice accepted her hand with alacrity. Visitors distressed the cats. Fluss was beginning to retch already behind the sofa, and Dearie was rolling uneasily on the hearthrug. A little regretfully Jacqueline looked round the room. It was essentially a home room, very different in character from her hired apartment with its jagged wallpaper, its air of cold discomfort.

'May I come to see you again?' she said a trifle wistfully.

This time, strangely enough, Miss Prentice caught her meaning. She reared her head like an old tired trace-horse determined for all its seeming spiritlessness to resist for once the tug of the rein.

'I'll write fixing a night,' she said.

At the words, scalding tears of humiliation pricked Jacqueline's eyeballs, for she knew as surely as if Miss Prentice had said it that that meant she never would.

CHAPTER VI

Jacqueline had been almost a year at MacCluskys' when there occurred one of those trivial happenings which, while naught in themselves, are sometimes destined to change the whole trend of one's life. She was cleaning her machine preparatory to starting work when Mr Shaw came into the room. He spoke to Miss Carruthers, and Jacqueline was conscious they both glanced in her direction. Viciously she squirted a tiny jet of oil into the shift key. Extra work – that, doubtless, would be the outcome; and today, of all days, she felt particularly disinclined to tackle it.

The previous night she had returned from a holiday at Kirkton. Holidays there were nerve-racking interludes during which she had to wear a guard on her tongue and to make a diligent effort to gloss with glamour her life in town. She told lies because she knew her aunt expected it of her, and her uncle would be humiliated if she didn't. So day in and day out the dialogue ran something like this:

Yes, she liked Glasgow immensely. Yes, she had got to know some very nice people. (Nessie Carruthers, certainly, was a dear.) Yes, she had been to one or two parties. (One, to be accurate. The staff dance.) Yes, the park was nice and near her rooms. And the shops, too. She refrained from telling how often she passed them with eyes averted lest the demon of covetousness awake in her, weakening her resolution as it had done that day of the staff dance when she had succumbed to a black *crêpe de Chine*, a dream of shimmering loveliness smooth in texture as the petals of an ebon flower.

Mr Shaw came towards her with his sidling catlike movement.

'Er, Miss Thayer,' he murmured. 'There's a special piece of work I'd like you to take on this morning, nothing to do with business. It's for a friend of mine. His typist is down with flu and he wants to catch the American mail.'

As he laid a pile of MS by her side, a well-known name leapt up at her. She uttered an exclamation of surprise. 'R. F. Torrance – does he live in Glasgow?' Like many country-bred Scots, she had been brought up in the belief that no one lived in the Second City who could possibly live out of it.

He nodded. 'He's living here just now. In Althea Terrace. A short story, I believe this is. Do your best with it anyhow.'

She unfolded the closely written sheets with an expression akin to awe on her grave young face. 'Thanks for trusting me with it,' she said; whereat he looked at her curiously out of his soft brown eyes, detaching her mentally from the other girls in the room. She was different from them without a doubt. There was something distinctive about her, a certain aloofness, a kind of gracious spirituality. Beautiful hands she had, too; perfectly shaped. He couldn't recall having noticed her before, not even at the staff dance. If he had he would have asked her to waltz with him, although he doubted if she'd dance well – her body for all its slimness would be too unyielding.

'Let me know when you finish this,' he said brusquely, conscious that his scrutiny had led her to believe that he had some further instructions to give. He sidled away, fondling his upper lip and wondering if the April sunshine had gone to his head. For, just for the fraction of a second before he turned away, he had had the impulse to sink his fingers in the sombre pool of the girl's soft hair.

Nessie Carruthers ran over to her. 'What fun! I love Torrance's things. Is it a love story?'

It was. And Jacqueline wept with joy as she clicked out the last few sentences. Then very carefully she read the typescript on the outlook for errors. There was one only, a trifling misplacement of letters, and she thrilled with pride as she pinned the pages together.

Mr Shaw looked up when she entered the private office. 'Finished? Good! Let me see.'

He laid the MS on his desk, looked not at it but at her, and involuntarily his official manner fell from him and the words slipped out: 'You've been crying.'

She clapped her hands to her cheeks. Her eyes, doubtless, were red as raspberries. Why couldn't she cry genteelly like the girls in books?

'I believe I did sniff a little,' she admitted. 'It's an awfully lovely story.'

'Hm,' he said, ruffling the pages. 'A love story, I suppose.'

'Of course,' she said, rubbing her eyes in the fashion of a child who is fain to obliterate by violent means the traces of a shameful emotion.

He smiled at her, and some probing quality in his smile made her retreat within herself.

'Why of course?' he queried in his soft voice. 'Why of course?'

She squared her shoulders and again the thought came to him how unyieldingly she would carry herself in a waltz.

'Because most of R. F. Torrance's things are love stories,' she retorted. Then a shade of anxiety forked her brows. 'It's after three now. What time does the mail go?'

Mr Shaw fiddled with the ruler on his desk. He was uncertain whether she was inspired by genuine anxiety, or whether by thus turning the conversation she was snubbing him, pushing him gently albeit decisively back into his proper place. Ah, well, if she preferred the employer, she should have him. The reflection that he was in a position to dictate to her for the better part of each day afforded him a certain lively satisfaction.

'You'd better put your things on and take it along to him yourself,' he suggested. Then, as she left the room, he cursed the universe at large, for he had intended, in his turn, putting her in her place by using her as a common messenger, and she had flushed up and thanked him as if he had conferred on her yet another mark of signal favour.

Half an hour later Jacqueline sat awaiting Mr Torrance in one of the most beautiful rooms she had ever seen – a room full of rarely bound books and gleaming mahogany, the darkest corners of which were lit by flares of yellow lilies in blue lustre jars. There was a sense of space induced by the seascapes on the walls that sent her fancy roving. She built up a mental picture of the author which was a cross between Lord Byron and Robert Burns. She pictured him as an ascetic with luminous eyes and sweet reluctant smile. She imagined him entering the room slowly with pensive mien and languid gait.

Instead, he burst open the door like a rowdy schoolboy and proceeded to rustle over the typescript she handed him for all the world like a jovial grocer checking the price-list of a rival.

'Did you type it, Miss – er—?'

'Thayer,' said Jacqueline. 'Yes. I hope the spacing is right.'

'Capital, capital!' he said, as though the subject under discussion were a prime cheese. 'I'm tremendously indebted. Thanks very much.'

The interview so far as he was concerned was ended. What the deuce, he wondered, was she waiting for? Money? No, he couldn't offer a girl with her air of breeding a tip. In a day or two, perhaps, he might send her some flowers or chocolates to MacCluskys'. Meanwhile she was standing trailing the tips of her shabby gloves along the tip of a tall chair as though her life depended upon the tracing thereon of some invisible pattern.

'You'll convey my thanks to Shaw?' he said, merely for the sake of saying something.

She did not answer. The pattern, it seemed, was engrossing every particle of her attention. Then, suddenly, she lifted her head. The colour was gone from her cheeks, causing them to appear pinched and thin. She looked like a woman on the verge of making a desperate confession. A second and she had blurted it out.

'Poetry; I write poetry. Is it very hard to get it published?'

He regarded her with a becoming solemnity. 'It depends on the poetry.'

The colour trickled back to her cheeks. She loosened the collar of her coat. How hot it was, intolerable! The white-domed ceiling, the orange-coloured lamp seemed about to descend on her head. 'Mine – mine isn't much. Only little things.' (What on earth had come over her? Why couldn't she express herself properly?)

'What sorts of little things?'

His voice seemed to come to her from a distance – the voice

of an inquisitor dragging the truth from out of her. Kindly its tones were and free from patronage, but in replying to its questionings Jacqueline felt as if she were being divested of her clothing in George Square.

'Got any of your poems on you?' he asked at last, as casually as if he were asking for the loan of a lead pencil.

She shook her head, exhausted by her efforts at explanation. 'They're all in a wee notebook in my trunk.'

He mused for a moment in silence. He was busy, infernally busy. There was that article to finish for the *Tribune*, notes for the lecture he'd promised to deliver on the 23rd. Still, youth had a right to be listened to. One of the tenets of his creed was that the successful artist in common with the capitalist owes something, not only to the unsuccessful, but to the tyro, and that he who deliberately withholds that something is no better morally than a miser who gloats secretly by night over his treasure and stares by day with unseeing eyes at the misery around him.

'Like me to have a look at your poems?' he volunteered, and was rewarded by the rapture in her eyes. Then, to cut short her embarrassed expressions of gratitude, he waved an arm at the bookshelves behind.

'I've got most of the moderns, you see. I believe in youth, in the new men.' A thought struck him. With characteristic abruptness he voiced it. 'Do you get enough to read?'

The question, put thus starkly, was almost equivalent to – do you get enough to eat? And for a moment Jacqueline was on the point of protesting that she did; oh, yes, thank you; more than she could read. Then something in Mr Torrance's simplicity provoked her own.

'Only shilling shockers I buy or borrow from the other girls,' she said.

He glanced at his shelves. 'Take what you like,' he said. Then, hawk-eyed, he watched to see what manner of book would be her choice.

She was conscious of his gaze, conscious that the kindliness which had inspired his offer was now swamped in curiosity. She was the raw specimen by whose taste in literature that of the herd might be gauged. As she hovered unhappily before the well-lined shelves she felt herself squirming on the pinpoint of a psychologist's investigations.

She drew out a volume of travel. 'May I have this?'

He shook the fine film of dust from its covers. 'You'd like to see the world – go abroad?'

She assented. Her father had been a sailor. He had been all over the world. From the eyrie of her sensitive mind she watched Torrance add this scrap of information to the mental sketch of her he was compounding. Typist. Would-be poetess. Sailor father. Romantic – quite. Not for worlds just then would she have revealed the fact that her mother had been a dressmaker in Lowerbank Street . . .

She sat up late that night reviewing in a frenzy of excitement the contents of her little black book. Every now and then she would thrust out her chin, assume a critical attitude and set out to read calmly, dispassionately, as she could conceive of Mr Torrance doing. Then a wave of recollection would rout her critical sense. That – that was the night when the green slits of sky showing between the turrets of Kirkton Castle had looked like islands floating through the mire of black cloud; that – that was the day she'd gone with Uncle Archie to the Trossachs and spied Loch Katrine in the distance, a bar of bright blue enamel clasped across the tumbled breasts of the hills.

Midnight struck on the University clock. She banged down the book, every fibre of her critical faculty starting into life. The awfulest rubbish – that was what it was. Not fit to show a cat. Ah, but she'd deluded herself sadly when she had thought that stuff worth talking about. Mr Torrance would never go beyond the first page . . . And she'd go on hammering the keys of a Smith Premier all the days of her life, and she'd get old and grubby-looking like that poor pathetic Miss Price who sat at the far end of the room at MacCluskys' and tried to pretend she wasn't deaf at all, although she couldn't even hear the stopping bell. And maybe, she, too, would forget in time like old Miss Price to take the wee black men out of the corners of her eyes when she washed in the mornings, and would breed a whole colony of warts on her neck and chin.

Certainly Mr Shaw would never shake his head and say sadly: 'Aye, aye, genius cannot be caged.'

She bowed her head over her book, pressed its shiny boards to her hot cheeks. It was a part of herself, that wee book. Oh, the pity of it that that part should be such awful rubbish! She decided to burn it straightway. But the fire had dwindled low. There was no coal in the box, only a thick powder of dross. In desperation she seized a Liberty calendar, with a picture of Anne Hathaway's cottage on it, that Nessie had given her at New Year time, and tore it up for firewood. It flamed up briskly and she bore down upon it with the black book. Its varnished boards shrivelled, refused to ignite. With a sharp cry of alarm she picked it from the spluttering embers. Awful rubbish though it was, she couldn't stand by and see it burn.

Next morning she wrapped it up neatly in brown paper and addressed the parcel to R. F. Torrance, Esquire.

CHAPTER VII

During the next week Jacqueline's anxiety was almost unbearable. A hundred times she told herself that Mr Torrance was a busy man, that she must be patient – patient! And forthright she put her machine out of action by belabouring its keys in a fierce attempt to work off the superfluous energy that was pent up in her desire to hear from him.

It was at the conclusion of one of these days, a day during which her mind had striven painfully to combat the blankness of waiting by reviving some of the old childish fantasies, that her landlady announced the arrival of a gentleman to see her.

Her pulses fluttered. George Buchanan! Some instinct told her it was he. All day he had been the companion of her thoughts. He had entered the Grind House with her. She had talked to him in the tram coming home, and at tea she had recalled the sumptuous dinner she had once enjoyed in his company in Kirkton.

'Bring him up,' she cried, her mind bright with plans. If he were to invite her to dine with him now she would be able to do him credit. There was the new *crêpe de Chine* and her little rose hat and she'd buy that scarf she'd seen at Fortune's . . .

The nimble shuttle of her thoughts fell to the ground at sight of a stranger. 'Oh,' she gasped. 'It's not—'

The stranger felt her outstretched hand grow limp in his grasp. 'I'm sorry,' he said; and felt it. 'You were expecting someone—'

In her moment of dismay she struck her visitor as oddly pathetic and just a trifle ridiculous. With her big wistful eyes, her mouth awry with disappointment, she looked like a child whose cake has been snatched from it. The litter of the disordered tea-tray caught his eye. How did some people live? She must be poor, pitifully poor to live in such a place. He wondered if George Buchanan knew . . . He had, of course, he realized now, made a mistake in calling unannounced. And yet he had carefully chosen the hour – neither tea nor dinner. But for all that here was this girl finishing some nondescript meal already. He lifted his eyes from the table to her face. It was warmly coloured now, as if during the interval his eyes had been averted some invisible being had dabbed the tops of her cheeks with rouge.

Hastily he proffered explanation. 'Did George Buchanan forget to tell you he'd given me your address, asked me to call? We were together in New York for a fortnight before I sailed.'

When he had gone Jacqueline locked the door and looked fondly at the *crêpe de Chine*. It was to dine out after all, only its escort was to be this quiet 'Englishy' young man in place of George Buchanan – this man whom in evening dress she could envisage looking like those other immaculate young men she had observed dining at the County Restaurant many years before.

Lights! Lights! Lights! How dazzling they were, how merciless! They revealed every blemish. They proclaimed every flaw. In such a place the *crêpe de Chine* looked cheap. Its doubtful lines showed wantonly. The grey-haired woman who took her cloak handled it as if it were mere shoddy beneath contempt. Jacqueline wondered if by chance she had seen it ticketed with its fellows in the shop window at the corner of Broomielaw Street.

Mr Southwold was waiting for her in the corridor. Earlier in the day she had ruminated happily upon what he would think of the *crêpe de Chine*. Now, she hoped rather miserably that he wouldn't notice it at all . . .

She was relieved their table was up against a wall. She was relieved her escort didn't address the elegant young foreign waiter who looked like a duke in disguise as 'young f'la me lad'. She was relieved he didn't clink his spoon on the rim of his plate when he craved attention. Instead, he talked to her in a low conversational voice, listened to her utterances with a delightful air of deference, smiled at her jokes. Nevertheless, for all his well-bred show of interest, she surmised he was just the wee-est bit bored. For George Buchanan's sake he was entertaining her, but he was finding no entertainment in the business himself.

She rallied herself to prick his interest, to hold it. She thought of some of the actresses she had read about who by sheer force of personality could hold an audience with the flicker of an eyelid. She forced herself to become vitalized, to throw out. But it was almost as though she and Mr Southwold spoke different languages. His world was not hers. Hers – resentfully she acknowledged it – was narrow, hatefully confined. For tonight she had stepped out of it. She was playing with a gallant assumption of the *beau geste* the role of a woman of the world. But tomorrow she would go back, back to the Grind House, to the throbbing machines, as though these fleet-footed waiters had never ministered to her, as though this shaded, scented world had never been . . .

He leaned across the table, a gleam of interest diminishing the dark pockets beneath his eyes. The slightly artificial smile which had trembled on his companion's lips all the evening, had disappeared. She recalled to him momentarily the girl he had blundered in upon last night, the girl who had risen eagerly from the disordered tea-tray and then had grown rigid at sight of him, like a peevish babe.

'A penny,' he said; 'or must I bid higher? Are they very precious?'

She smiled at him; without artifice this time, and again she struck him as oddly pathetic.

'My thoughts? They're cheap, they're sordid. I'm thinking of tomorrow morning. Going out at nine-thirty to the Grind House. That's what we call MacCluskys' – the office where I work.'

'Must you?' he asked.

She nodded. Then she blushed at the shamelessness of her own avowal. Even to this stranger the amiable fiction must be upheld. 'My people didn't want me to,' she murmured. 'But I like to be independent. It isn't as if – I have only my uncle and aunt, you see.'

He had heard of them from George Buchanan – 'two damned old wives, one male and one female'.

'It's much better,' he agreed gravely. Independence! Where had the child learned the ugly word? Why didn't some man carry her off and teach her to wipe it out of her vocabulary? She was attractive in her own way, very sweet and quite brainless probably. One, doubtless, of the vast army of women who, God pity them, would never be worth more to any employer than two pounds ten a week.

It rested his eyes and his soul to look at her as she sat there in the soft light – her hair purplish-black beneath the reflection of the blue shade, her wistful eyes drenched in shadow, and the soft round ball of her chin thrust forward like that of a defiant babe who by reason of its very innocence is immune from fear. He liked her clothes, too. Cheap, obviously, but quiet. Blatancy in a woman was to Owen Southwold the scarlet sin . . . Often at night, when he was far from port and had not heard the rustle of a woman's skirts for months, he would pace the deck and out of the fine white spume and his curling smoke wreaths would arise the figure of the Immortal She – an ice maiden austere as the scene about him, cold as death to all men save her conqueror. Then he would shiver and look out across the white wild, and remind himself that she was not for such as he.

A fluffy miss all softness and swift to mirth; a buxom beauty with feelings flaccid as her fat; a sinuous siren all poses and extravagant gestures, would be fitting mate for a wayfarer, a 'gangrel body' as the Scots mate had it, on God's good earth. Any one of these would wave him a tearful goodbye from the quayside and then go off and console herself innocently an it be the first, wantonly an it be the last, with some other man. But the ice maid would beat her breast in agony. She would be like tragedy's twin sister in those days when he was gone from her into the white wild.

They drank coffee in the lounge seated opposite each other at a tiny table. There was no band, only the roar of traffic. Beyond the window, the glass vaults of the station rose like the curves of an enormous tent in the arena of which vast numbers of people scurried. Jacqueline was absorbed watching them, when a slight movement at her side arrested her. She turned to her companion.

'Like a circus, isn't it?' she said.

He bent forward, scanned the crowd.

'Jove! There's the clown.'

She followed the direction of his eyes, laughed at sight of a white-faced, red-nosed man shambling beneath a load of family luggage. Then she let slip an ecstatic sigh. For this – this was the first time in her life she had shared with another this secret source of entertainment. And she felt responsible as a child who, in an agony of apprehension lest its companion miss any of the exciting features of the show, keeps on pressing his hand and calling his attention to this and that as if he himself were possessed of neither eyes nor ears.

The ladies' cloakroom was empty when she went for her things. Even the superior attendant was not visible. Only a tray with a solitary coin remained to reproach her. She forgot it as she went down the broad staircase. How spacious it was! How – to use the old word – sumptuous!

They drove in a taxi to Hentzau Street. On the way she studied her companion's side-face. Seen in profile it was extraordinarily vital. This was due, she decided, not to the tanned complexion alone but to some latent force, untamed and untameable, that lurked beneath the surface. She had seen such a look in picture-books on the faces of the Crusaders. She had seen it on the faces of soldiers on leave during the Great War . . . Vaguely, it occurred to her that she didn't know what Mr Southwold's occupation was. That he had one she never doubted, but she couldn't conceive of him sitting at an office desk from ten till five, or even devising word pictures after the manner of R. F. Torrance.

Simply, she asked: 'What do you do?'

He smiled at the *naiveté* of the question. 'Nothing very definite, I'm afraid. I potter about a good deal from place to place, you know.'

'I see,' she said comprehendingly. But she didn't. Nor did she until the arrival of a long-delayed letter from George Buchanan enlightened her. Then, because she felt she would have burst with excitement if she hadn't confided in somebody, she danced into the Grind House calling for Nessie.

'D'you know,' she said, and paused impressively; 'do you know, Mr Southwold – the man I told you about – is Owen Southwold, the explorer?'

CHAPTER VIII

Through the windless air soared the long-drawn-out notes of the University chimes. It was funny, Jacqueline reflected, how their refrain seemed to vary with her moods. Last night, and the day before that, and the day before that again – ever since Owen Southwold had gone away – they had dinged heavy as lead. At night they had rung in her ears like a death-knell. In the morning, when she had thrust down the bedclothes and stepped, shivering, on to the waxclothed floor, they had reverberated like the crackling laughter of an evil spirit fain to wreck his spleen upon all within earshot. This morning they had rung out on a different note – come to tea, come to tea. And she had reread for the twentieth time R. F. Torrance's letter, and marvelled at once at his kindness and at the oddness of his beginning:

'Dear Jacqueline Thayer.' No Miss about it!

Half-past! She threw a backward glance at the spangled fans of sunlight and hastened along the terrace. Number three looked different from the other houses, distinguished in some queer inexplicable way. Was that because a genie lived within? Did the very stones recognize their owner's greatness and assume accordingly a superior air? Or did the explanation lie in the more prosaic fact that R. F. Torrance had a wife or a sister with a pretty taste in window curtains?

A wife, Jacqueline recognized, as a slim, exquisite woman rose to greet her with a murmured, 'My husband will be here directly,' a wife as different from other men's wives as the house from its neighbours. R. F. Torrance was quite obviously a connoisseur, if this delicately featured woman, these mellow-toned landscapes that lined the walls, were evidences of his taste.

A moment later he came into the room, dispelling its tranquillity as a German band chases peace from a quiet back street. He started right away to speak to Jacqueline of her poems, oblivious of her discomfiture. She slunk back into the deeps of her chair as he discussed them with frank impetuosity, uttering a word of commendation that sent her hopes soaring, a flicking phrase that whistled like a whiplash in her ears. And then, just when she felt as if the hot ball that had risen in her throat would cause her to die of suffocation, Mrs Torrance interposed in her toneless voice: 'China tea, Miss Thayer. I hope you like it?'

Before she left Jacqueline summoned up courage to hark back to the subject of her poems. 'I suppose I'd better burn them,' she said.

Mr Torrance stared at her in horror. 'Good God, no.'

'But if they're so – so feeble,' she stuttered.

'Who said they were feeble? They are full of faults, but not irremediable faults.' He drew the book from his pocket and, opening it at random, proceeded to explain his meaning, the while his wife sat with hands locked staring dreamy-eyed into the fire.

During the summer that followed Jacqueline's visits to Althea Terrace stood out bright splashes in the ordered monotony of her life. They were cram-full of excitement, these visits, of mental stimulus. R. F. Torrance she came to regard as a modern Quixote who tilted in the sanctity of his study at half the windmills of civilization. Mrs Torrance was always kind and cordial; but to Jacqueline in those days she seemed little more than a shadow in the house whose presence would not be missed if it were suddenly withdrawn. She addressed few remarks to anyone, and fewest of all to her husband, but when she did she called him by endearing names and her voice cooed and her lips pouted adorably as though she was cajoling with all the charm of which she was capable, a fractious but much-beloved child.

Torrance himself was to Jacqueline a fount of wisdom in whose depths she found constant inspiration. He bubbled with crystal clarity one day; the next she found him long-winded, obscure as an old-fashioned metaphysician, and she was forced to content herself with her own interpretation of his meaning. He was violently opposed to all forms of women's rights. The mind of woman was not that of a normal human being, he was wont to declare, but of one warped by reason of her sex.

'Take the average woman,' he propounded one day. 'See how she makes of the things she loves either dolls or heroes. That is why childless marriages so often founder. The husband, formerly the hero, is relegated by his wife to the ignominious position of doll to appease her lust for littlings. And he resents it – loathes like sin the gentle pawing that takes the place of the once passionate embrace.' He puffed fiercely at his empty pipe. 'From the time she's toddling till she's closed her eyes for the last time, every child-woman must have her doll.'

Jacqueline digested the idea and found it wanting. 'I haven't got a doll. I haven't got a hero either.'

He laid down his pipe, dug his thumb in the bowl and grinned across at her. So like a woman to argue the abstract from the personal! 'Then we'd better advertise. But think again before you waste the money.'

She obeyed him with the little birdlike droop of the head characteristic of her in moments of reflection, and then she turned away her face, for in it she felt the colour mounting. White wastes of snow. A solitary figure pacing a ship's deck . . . Yes, she had a hero in the person of the debonair young man who had answered her artless query so nonchalantly: 'I potter about from place to place, you know.'

Communal life was at that time another of R. F. Torrance's crazes. The one house, one family idea he deplored as retrogressive to progress. Seclusion, he contended, was a sort of mental incest in which the vices of the family multiplied and the virtues decreased. Take the case of two persons living together. One inevitably drained the vitality of the other. With persons as with voices there must always be a sound and an echo. In the midst of this diatribe Mrs Torrance glided into the room as though to give pictorial illustration of the truth of her husband's theory. Once she had been an operatic star. Now she was just an echo – a wraithlike creature with a long swan neck and soft colourless eyes that smouldered with a lustreless fire beneath a mop of ashen-gold hair. Looking at her seated in a low chair, Jacqueline wondered she did not die of sheer inanition. And yet for all her languor she was hauntingly beautiful. There emanated from her person a flame-like quality that made Jacqueline link her with the world's wonder women. Like Helen and Beatrice and Lady Hamilton, she seemed to realize that in her person was vested a power sufficient to enthral a legion and that, unlike her less gifted sisters, she had no need to expend one ounce of her vitality in order to attract any man.

Beside this strange still woman with the brooding eyes that seemed to see so much and to care so little, Jacqueline felt herself crude, undeveloped. When Mr Torrance was talking she was trying so hard to follow him, to be worthy the overflow of his wit that she could scarce sit still. His most revolutionary theories drew from her little soft cries and ejaculations she was powerless to suppress. In how far these acted as the huzzas that inspire the showman she had no conception. Certain it was, however, that in Jacqueline he found for a time the audience his artist soul required. For while he despised women, he acknowledged that, like all the objects on this earth, they had their uses. Every gladiator is the stouter hearted for catching a glimpse as he enters the arena of the bright eyes of his lady behind the grille.

At the Torrances' Jacqueline met all sorts of interesting people, people among whom she felt like a lame duck, for she alone lacked a label. One day, bracing herself to meet unflinchingly a storm of ridicule, she approached Mr Torrance. 'Do you think I might try one of my things at the *Tribune*?' she asked.

He regarded her in such a way that she felt a flare light in her cheeks. 'My dear child,' he said, 'haven't you tried your stuff all over the shop already?' As she shook her head, his bushy brows met in an amused grimace. 'Surprising woman! Type out the "Grind House" and post it to the editor tonight. It will come back most likely, but there are a dozen other possible places.'

It failed to come back, but in due course there came instead a postal order. And instantly Mrs Torrance affixed to Jacqueline her tag. 'Writes poetry for the *Tribune*,' she murmured in her toneless voice, introducing Jacqueline one Sunday to, of all persons, Mr Shaw. He held her hand in his for a long second. How tremendously alive she looked, not aloof and distrait as she had seemed when he had first noticed her at MacCluskys'! Wrote poetry, too, by Jove! That, he supposed, was how she came to be accepted in this *galère*. Funny thing for a typist to do in her off-time. Movie shows he understood to be the usual recreation of the key-thumping tribe.

'Funny – didn't know you had a side line,' he said. 'What do you write about, by the way?'

Dare she tell him? A spirit of mischief set her eyes dancing. From beneath their decent black veils two grey imps looked out at him.

'Shall I tell you?' she said. And at the provocative note in her voice his pulses stirred. She was fascinating all right. What had made him think her stand-offish? Yet she had frozen him that day he had spoken of a love story, and now he could swear she was going to mention the tender passion herself.

'The Grind House,' she said. 'That is what we – Miss Carruthers and I – call MacCluskys'.'

He was staggered and showed it. His hand flew to his upper lip. But Jacqueline's eyes knew no mercy. There was malice in them more than a trace. For she didn't like him. She did not know why.

Some weeks later, on a Saturday afternoon, Mr Torrance arrived unexpectedly at Hentzau Street.

'I've got my new bus outside,' he announced. 'Will you come for a run? There's a wind rising that will blow us to Kingdom Come and back before dark.'

It roared in their ears all the way through the suburbs of the South Side. It shrilled above the clatter of the traffic in Port Glasgow's narrow twisting streets, and it reverberated like a paean above the ripple of the tide on Langbank's dank, weed-ridden shores. R. F. Torrance drove quickly, erratically, with the same fierce intentness that marked all his actions, and he whistled the while, now the catch of an old Border air, now a bar of Italian opera, and occasionally the refrain of a foxtrot. Once, as he swerved perilously near an elderly Airedale who surveyed the approaching wheels with soft incredulous eyes, Jacqueline clutched with a little screech at his arm. He put on the brakes, admonished her solemnly. That way accidents occurred. Lack of self-control didn't spell cowardice alone. It spelled something worse – febrility of purpose, a febrility which led in time to the development of suicidal tendencies.

At the words her muscles grew rigid. The gentle beauty of the glancing river, of the brown and yellow blur of trees on the rocky hillside gave place to the narrow confines of a city street. She saw again from a darkened room the bloodstained windows of the quack dentist opposite.

'What's wrong?' asked Torrance sharply.

She regarded him with sombre eyes. 'My mother killed herself. Gas. When I was a child.'

He lifted his hand from the wheel and laid it on hers. She clasped his fingers convulsively, finding comfort in their warm pressure, balm for a wound that all neglected had festered for long in the darkness of her being. It was the first time since she had gleaned the truth about her mother's death that she had spoken of it voluntarily, and now she felt as if some of the bitterness of grief were being wiped clean from her soul. For this silence of Torrance's was a healing thing. It soothed and it salved by virtue of its very sincerity. For a full moment they stayed motionless, heedless of a big touring car that shot by them noiselessly. It was only when sprinting ahead a few minutes later they overtook it that Torrance noted its occupants and uttered an exclamation.

'Charlie Shaw,' he said. 'Damnation!'

'Why?' said Jacqueline. 'Why?'

'If you must have it, Miss Baby Innocent,' he said, 'because my wife is jealous, terribly jealous.'

'How – how queer!' Unconscious of their implied meaning, the words escaped her. It was queer, truly; for Mr Torrance was old, quite old. His hair was greying at the top, even his eyebrows were whitening. Of course, he was clever, terrifically clever. Still—

His youthful laugh interrupted her thoughts. 'I'm not Methuselah, you know. Besides, has it never struck you that the finest mental tonic in the world may be a love affair?'

She crinkled her brows. Tonic in such a connection was a funny word.

'Don't you realize that in certain circumstances a kiss may be as good a pick-me-up as a cocktail?'

He glanced down at her as he spoke, and as he did so something turned to ice within him. Only a moment ago he had bragged that he wasn't Methuselah. Now he was none so sure. For in this girl's eyes his glance had kindled no answering spark. He was the most brilliant man on her orbit. But he was old. He had held her hand. She had clung to his. But that meant nothing to her because he was old. He might, he dared swear, take her in his arms an he willed, and she would stay passive in his embrace as she would in that of a parent . . . God, was he so old as all that?

Proof indeed was here that he required a dose of his own prescription.

'We'll turn,' he said. 'It's growing colder.'

And he drove slowly, carefully, back to town in the manner of a man who, seeing the days of his life draw in, determines to take no needless risks.

That night Jacqueline lay awake thinking over his words. Her own ignorance, she reflected, upon certain subjects was colossal. She was still meditating drowsily upon the similarity between cocktails and kisses when the University clock struck twelve.

CHAPTER IX

A few nights later, Jacqueline was leaving the Grind House when Mr Shaw overtook her.

He made a remark regarding the fineness of the weather, then he focussed his soft brown eyes full on her face. Instinctively her back stiffened. He was about to fire some unpleasant shot and she braced herself accordingly.

Casually enough, however, his words slipped out. 'You've heard R. F. Torrance is off again?'

'Off?' she repeated uncomprehendingly.

He nodded. 'Gone abroad. So they say.' There was the suggestion of a sneer in his words, almost of a snigger that set her nerves tingling. He was observing her closely, she knew, testing her feelings as an amateur cook may sometimes test the condition of a roast by digging a skewer into its various parts. At a loss for words she bit her lips, and for a moment they stood together in silence, the hunter and the quarry, isolated in a little glade of darkness that seemed all the blacker by reason of the fact that it lay just without the beam of light emanating from MacCluskys'.

A new and altogether unaccountable emotion stirred in Jacqueline. Flight – she ached to take refuge in flight. So strong was this impulse that she could scarce control her heels although her sense of decorum forbade any unseemly display of haste. She must remember she wasn't a child any longer. She must remember that she was grown up, earning her own living. Shut up, she admonished her quivering nerves.

Touché, her companion crowed inwardly, elated at his success. So there was something in that after all! Strange the attraction

Torrance had for women. Men of the artist tribe – actors, authors, and the like who didn't know what work was – always seemed to play the deuce with women, while a business man, a steady, decent chap like himself, didn't have a look in.

The clang of a bell drifted up the street. 'My car,' cried Jacqueline, and ran for it. Once inside, she sat bolt upright, afire with an indignation she could not reasonably explain. What, after all, had Mr Shaw said? Only that R. F. Torrance had gone away. Well, and if he had, what about it? His going was no business of hers. No, it wasn't that that had excited her. It was something – something queer in Mr Shaw's manner, something at once insolent and prying and judicial. In that moment they had stood together in the darkness he had dragged her into the dock. He had tried her for some unnamed crime; and she had resented the unspoken charge, had resented it fiercely. For one moment she had irked to hit her judge between the eyes. That was before the impulse to flee had assailed her.

She had not been in the habit of calling at the Torrances' uninvited, but tonight she determined to do so to probe the mystery for herself. That there was something amiss she felt convinced, when in place of the trim parlourmaid an elderly woman opened the door and bade her go upstairs unescorted. Clearly, for the moment, the household was disorganized. Outside the drawing-room door she paused, doubtful if her intimacy with Mrs Torrance were such as to justify this intrusion. Then, with a little clear of her throat for announcement, she turned the handle.

From the low seat by the fire Mrs Torrance rose, stared up at the incomer, her face hardening with surprise.

'You!' she said. 'You!' Then all at once she crumpled up in her chair and began to cry.

Had gouts of blood appeared in the eyeballs of one of the sculptured goddesses in Kelvingrove, Jacqueline could not have been more amazed. She stared for a second at the stricken woman, then, 'Oh, don't,' she implored, a catch in her voice. 'Please don't!'

Mrs Torrance pressed her handkerchief to her eyes. The storm of emotion which had shaken her momentarily was spent. She clasped Jacqueline's hand and drew her closer.

In low vibrant tones she began to talk, and Jacqueline, harkening to the rise and fall of her voice in the still room, was obsessed by the feeling that a relentless tide was bearing her swiftly away to an unfamiliar shore. Veiled as that shore was in mystery, peopled by foes and friends so strangely masked that it was well-nigh impossible to tell the one from the other, Jacqueline shrank from landing on its mist-ridden slopes. She cleaved as never before she had cleaved to the simple land of childish things, the familiar friendly land from which this relentless tide was steadily dividing her.

Sitting thus quietly with Mrs Torrance in the twilight Jacqueline recalled those times when as a child she had stolen into the little back parlour where her Aunt Ruth and one of her women friends had been closeted, their heads wagging, and she had been bidden sharply to run away and play. At such times, she had gone lingeringly, athirst with curiosity to know what they were talking about so softly, so secretly. Now – ah, now, she knew. And she wished she didn't. Knowledge brought with it a sense of shame, of cruel unease. Knowledge – but what knowledge, after all, had she?

She longed to hide her face, to conceal its youthful contour lest Mrs Torrance should awake to the discovery that her listener was no mature woman accustomed to the confidences of her fellows, but a mere fledgling whom on an instant she would bid sharply run away and play. But with no thought of the administration of any such rebuke the vibrant voice continued its unhappy tale. Only the previous morning he had told her he was going. As excuse he had adduced the all-sufficient reason that he was fed up, couldn't stand it any longer.

'It?' she had queried dully. 'Everything,' he had answered irritably. 'Houses – streets. Smug, hypocritical Scots people.'

Mrs Torrance paused at that, her head bowed on her breast, her brooding eyes bent on the trail of smoke that rose from the waning fire to scuttle miserably up the chimney.

Jacqueline nodded in mute comprehension. Himself a Canadian by birth, R. F. Torrance had no liking, she knew well, for Scots people. The women, he voted superior – sturdy, sincere creatures, worthy descendants of their Highland ancestry. The men, on the other hand, he had been wont to declare possessed all the vices of a polyglot people. While their women stayed at home, they had been forced to fare forth from their native glens in quest of gain; and being receptive, after the manner of most untutored persons to outside impressions, they had acquired the worst traits of the traders with whom they had come in contact. Thus in the composition of the average Scot you could trace the cruel greed of the Spaniard, the class-consciousness of the Teuton, the arrogance of the American, the brainless conceit of the Cockney. The Scot, in short, being the last man in Northern Europe to come within the confines of civilization, appeared to be the tree upon which all the vices of the nations had been grafted. That was why he was so damnably objectionable . . .

Mrs Torrance was speaking again, this time in quick tortured accents. '"You're going alone?" I asked him. "No," he answered. That was all.'

A screw tightened round the muscles of Jacqueline's throat. 'Oh,' she cried. 'Oh! And you thought that I – I—' She stopped, smothered in the hot blanket of her emotions.

Mrs Torrance caught her by the wrist. 'Don't be self-righteous. You'd have gone if he had asked you. You know you would. Any woman would. He despises us. He tells us so to our faces, and yet if he crooks a finger we follow. I did thirteen years ago. And I don't regret it today. I haven't regretted it any of the other times.'

'Other times?' breathed Jacqueline.

Mrs Torrance looked with indifference at her face of horror. 'Oh, yes,' she said. 'There have been other times.'

Jacqueline drew a quick jigging breath. Here was a phase of love new to her, a phase stronger, more deeply satisfying than anything she had ever dreamt. A man, it seemed, might commit adultery, murder, perjury – all the crimes in the calendar – and still be beloved by his mate. Of such unwieldy tenacity was this insoluble bond.

As she lay awake that night Jacqueline knew that she had left the land of childish things behind, and that she stood alone on an unfamiliar shore. Groping amid its shadows she thought of many things; of the instructor at the commercial class who had looked at her with such an imperative glint in his eyes, of the moment outside MacCluskys' when Mr Shaw had haled her into the dock, of the day at Langbank when the author had boasted: 'I'm not Methuselah,' and compared cocktails with kisses. She grew crimson at the recollection of their conversation. Had he – had he meant anything then? And if he had and she had understood, would she – ah, how could she tell?

He had realized, at any rate, what his wife hadn't – that she was still only a little girl. Thank God, he had realized that! Thank God, he had left her alone.

CHAPTER X

Nessie Carruthers hovered in the doorway, uttering little ecstatic squeals. 'Isn't it lovely? Aren't the lights dinky?'

Jacqueline made a murmur of assent, but her nostrils dilated. Scent – cheap scent – it came towards them in waves. It impregnated the place like a drug that drains vitality, produces coma.

At the head of the hall the conductor presided over his band. With volcanic energy he paced the narrow rim of space allotted to him, bursting every now and then into a bar of song. He was like a windmill, Jacqueline thought, in a dun-coloured stretch of country, a dynamic force pitting himself against a torpid world.

Nessie's fiancé made a forward movement. 'This way, ladies.'

They entrenched themselves at a white-clothed table overlooking the shining oval of the floor – Nessie and her fiancé, Jacqueline and Nessie's young brother, Bill.

'First time you've been here, isn't it?' said Bill, jogging his elbows on the table to the refrain of the band. 'Used to be a church, y'know. There's still the pews in the gallery and the band's in the place where the choir used to sit.'

Jacqueline looked at the alcove where the perspiring fiddlers were penned, and then at the pews overhead. The scuffle of the dancers' feet, the racket of the music, aroused in her a sense of recoil as piece by piece she traced the outline of the old church. Almost she could hear R. F. Torrance's voice saying in her ears: 'There's Scotland for you. Who but a Scot who at one and the same time prides himself upon keeping what he calls a teetotal house and invests all his savings in whisky, who but a sanctimonious Scot could have conceived the notion of converting a hallowed building into a dancing hall?'

The dark wooden flanks of the pews rose in a steep incline from the front of the gallery to the wall at the back. To all appearances that section of the building had been left untouched. The seats remained just as they had been in the days when Sunday after Sunday whole families of worshippers had filled them. In her mind's eye Jacqueline could see these families – steps and stairs of chattering boys and girls awed into silence as they shuffled along the pews; whiskered gentlemen, florid of face, breathing hard as they bowed their stiff necks in prayer; fragile dewy-eyed women who dreamed the hours of service away wrapped in romantic reveries in which the Lord had no part. Did the spirits of these gentle souls ever steal into their accustomed seats at eventide, to be jolted out of their dreams by rattle of drums, rasping of fiddle-strings? Or did the stench of perfume, catching at their throats, cause them to swoon and to see things through a mist hazily, so that the alcove where the players were penned became the altar again in front of which the pulpit rose, and the giggling couples at the white-clothed tables reverent partakers of the Holy Sacrament?

Bill's voice checked the sentimental current of her thoughts. 'Like a turn?' he said.

For the fraction of a second Jacqueline hesitated; then the lilt of the music banished the faces of the unseen watchers from her mind.

It was almost eleven when she disengaged herself finally from his arms and declared her intention of going home. 'Don't bother seeing me off; I'll be all right,' she said casually.

Bill looked at his feet and then at her. He didn't want to go so soon, and yet go he must if he were to be true to his reading of the role of perfect cavalier. But if he once went he didn't suppose that old buffer at the door would let him in again, and he'd not been in the place above two and a half hours. You got into the 'pictures' for a bob and if you looked slippy and changed your seat when the lights were down you could stop the whole evening if you chose; whereas, to get into this place you had to plank down two-and-six. Crivens! What it costs to be a gentleman! For the first time in his life Bill was brought face to face with the fact that true gentility is made up partially of generosity, partially of a deeper regard for the feelings of others than for your own.

The band, arrested in a tedious process of tuning, swerved into a waltz tune, a flood of romantic melody that enveloped the hall in a mist of gold and silver sound. Bill sank in it like a drowning man.

'Sure you'll be all right?' he said. 'Well, so long. Cheerio!'

Jacqueline's feet dragged as she went upstairs. The exhilaration which the exercise had induced had gone, leaving her a victim of foul air and fatigue. She stood for a moment outside the cloak-room door, drawing her wrap about her. A chink of light at the end of the passage disclosed the gallery with its stark walls, its regular ridge of pew-backs. She peeped down at them. There was no one in any of the seats. On tiptoe she descended the stone steps and sank into a maroon-coloured cushion. As she did so there arose a faint dry smell of dust, of incipient damp. And she recalled those Sundays at Kirkton when she had been obliged to sit stiffly upright beside her Aunt Ruth for two and a half hours night and morning, hearkening to the 'greetin'' voice of old Mr Gray, who was a cousin of Mrs Pullman's and of the Jacks of Paisley, *the* Jacks, you know . . .

Below her, on the glassy floor, the dancers, like fate-driven figures, circled round and round. Looking down on them, Jacqueline felt as if she were gazing into a box from which God had lifted the lid. With its livid lights, its raddle-cheeked women in their tawdry dresses, the revelation suggested hell, not Heaven, and there came to Jacqueline the phantasmagoric thought that below every Scottish kirk there perchance smoulders this seething crater of underground movement, these rags and ribbons of rapacity and desire.

The advent of a party of newcomers caused a stir near the door. The women were better dressed than the majority of those present, the men moved with an easier grace. Even when they separated into couples and mingled with the foxtrotting crowd they were distinguishable from the rest. As one of the couples swung closer Jacqueline recognized the man's features. Conscious, perhaps, of her gaze, he shot a glance in her direction and on that instant she determined upon flight. Mr Shaw. And she hadn't seen him save in the distance since that night he had haled her into the dock. On that occasion she had not realized the nature of her supposed offence. She had not realized it fully until she had been swept by the relentless current of Mrs Torrance's voice into a thicket of dimly apprehended shapes and forms where she had been left like a castaway thrown at darkling upon the slopes of an unfamiliar shore.

Descending the narrow stairway she ran tilt into him. He made a gesture of apology. 'May I have a dance?' he said.

She shook her head. 'I'm just going home.'

An idea took root in his mind. 'Let me get a taxi and take you there.'

She demurred for a moment. He brushed aside her objections. It was only as she was stepping into the car that conscience smote her. What was she doing this for? To save herself the trouble of taking a definite stand and adhering to it despite opposition? No, it wasn't that. Rather it was the desire to familiarize herself with those things she only dimly apprehended, to test her feelings on these strange slopes . . .

Mr Shaw, she realized, was speaking, making a surprising announcement in his soft rounded voice.

'I told the man to take us a little run first. Anniesland. The Stockiemuir. I hope you don't mind? It's a ripping night.'

Anniesland. The Stockiemuir. Why not? It was, as he said, a ripping night. She loved the swift lunging movement of the car, the leaping gnomes of shadow. Idly she watched them straddle the tramlines, start back in grotesque fear of the competent glitter of the headlights.

'How's the poetry getting on? Any sequels to "The Grind House"?'

So he hadn't forgotten that! Her hands relaxed. Conversation wasn't going to be so difficult after all. So long as he didn't mention R. F. Torrance . . .

'Oh, heaps of sequels,' she retorted. 'Some day there will be a whole volume immortalizing MacCluskys'.'

'Can't think where you get all the ideas,' he murmured.

'No, you wouldn't,' she agreed inwardly.

They talked gaily while the car sped over the switchback road to the suburbs and thence up the hill to the moor. There silence fell upon them.

On either side straggled miles and miles of bare country, broken here and there by the cold gleaming of a stream. Jacqueline strained her eyes for a twinkle of light, a sign of human habitation. But, locked in the fastness of the moors, they seemed to be gliding on and on through a wilderness of shadow, of grey stone that rolled back in shapeless waves until it was drawn into the black ridges of the hills.

The solitude seemed to Jacqueline as heavy as sleep, a sort of dark stuperose stillness masking the face of death. Shaw's voice when he spoke unexpectedly surprised her with its note of conscious refinement.

'You'd think we were a hundred miles from the Palais. Look! There are the lights of Drymen.'

He indicated a pale luminosity that leapt like the puny splutter of a match in the deserted void ahead.

'Just a few yards farther on – stop a minute, driver – there's a road to the left that leads to a summer bungalow of ours. What d'you say to going up and getting them to give us a bite of supper before we trek back to town?'

She glanced at him in surprise. 'But your people – won't they think it queer?'

He shook his head. 'They're still in town. There's only the caretaker and her son. She was an old maid of ours – decent old soul. She'll cook us something in the twinkling of an eye.'

For a second Jacqueline did not answer. Back there on the moor she had felt lost, stranded as a child on a long journey who has lost count of time and cannot visualize where it is going. And now, lights, the walls of a house, food – all these comforting adjuncts of civilization proferred to her magically in this drear wilderness of a world seemed to her things not lightly to be set aside.

'What do you say?' he urged.

She smiled up at him. 'Supper,' she said. 'I'd love it. Wouldn't you?'

CHAPTER XI

In the dim light the bungalow, with its verandas, looked an odd sort of place, a castle of cards that you felt might collapse at any moment. Shaw put his finger on the bell and then without waiting an answer thrust his latch-key in the lock.

'Sophia's gone to bed, most likely. Come into the lounge and I'll go and prospect.'

He left Jacqueline there and she heard him run upstairs and knock loudly at a door overhead. Almost immediately he returned.

'Here's a nice go. Birds flown. I wonder if they've left any fodder? Shall we raid the back premises and see?'

He opened a door for her. 'Through the lobby, this way. That's the kitchen ahead . . . Fire's still in. Jove, we're in luck. They've left their own supper set.'

There was a large piece of boiled gammon on the table. There were scones and a loaf and a pat of fresh butter. Shaw's eyes went from the edibles to Jacqueline's face.

'First come, first served, don't you think? Shall we cart the stuff through to the lounge or squat down here?'

'Here,' she voted. 'It's cosier.'

As they sat supping together Jacqueline was oppressed by the curious intimacy of it all. It was almost as though Mr Shaw at the head of the table were the jocose young husband and she the shy, rather shrinking young wife. He pressed food upon her, then drink. But she refused the latter determinedly.

'I wish you'd take some,' he said, helping himself liberally. 'Keeps the cold out. And we've a long ride home.'

'Then isn't it time we started?' she said bluntly.

He lifted his glass to his lips, pushed back his chair. 'Wait a jiffy. I'll give the driver a drop.'

He was absent fully ten minutes. When he returned his cheekbones were flushed, his speech was a little less consciously refined.

'Awfully sorry,' he murmured. 'That damn fool of a driver must have misunderstood me. He's gone.'

'Gone!' she repeated blankly. 'But – but his fare. He'd never go without—'

'Oh, he wouldn't worry about that. We've an account, you see, with Wilburs'. That same chap has driven me out often when we've been staying here.'

She sprang to her feet in swift alarm. 'What on earth shall we do?'

He prodded the fire with a poker, addressed himself to the embers.

'It's pretty obvious. Stop where we are and not squeal about it.'

He did not seem appalled at the prospect. Almost, judging by the covert smile that traversed his lips, he appeared to relish it. His indifference stung Jacqueline to a frenzy. She hurled at him one suggestion after another. The telephone. Why not phone for another car? Wasn't there a bus they could take back to town? The village – Drymen – couldn't they walk there? Or the high road – wouldn't some passing vehicle give them a lift?

He looked at her pityingly. 'My dear Jacqueline, you're not in Rent Street. There's no one passing, no bus at this hour. As for a telephone – the nearest is in the village and that's a good five miles away.'

She subsided at that rather abjectly into a chair. From the dryness of his tones she gathered that he considered she was making an unnecessary fuss – almost a scene. She supposed she was; she knew, indeed, that she was. But she felt more like screaming than sitting here quietly. For it was hateful – hateful being stranded with Mr Shaw.

'If it's a chaperone you want the Kers will be back any moment. Sophia, you may depend, didn't leave that spread for the mice.'

She shook her head. But he noted the rush of colour to her cheeks, her evident embarrassment, and instantly he laid fingers on the sensitive spot.

'You're afraid of being here alone with me, I suppose. Do you dislike me so much?'

She threw back her head defiantly. 'Sometimes I dislike you intensely. Other times you're different – nicer. I don't understand you.'

Her display of spirit warmed him. He had no use for direct methods himself, but he appreciated the daring of those who trafficked in them.

'Do you understand any man?' he queried. 'Do you understand our friend Torrance?'

She hesitated, weighing her words. 'I think I do. But he isn't like ordinary people.'

Shaw uttered a kind of a laugh. 'He's more promiscuous. It's not a dancer this time. It's a waitress from Crabs', I hear. At one time I thought it was to be you.'

She averted her eyes, fearful lest the commotion his plain speaking had set up in her brain should cause them suddenly to overflow. There was no use, she reflected fleetingly, trying to pretend she didn't know what he was talking about, no good trying to work up a righteous show of indignation. For if it came to strict truth, she didn't know – she could never tell, whether if R. F. Torrance had asked her to go with him, she would have said 'yes' or 'no'.

He drew his chair closer, laid a hand on hers. 'Getting sleepy, dreamy-eyes? Like to stay and talk a bit or go right off to bed?'

Talk or go to bed? No, she couldn't accept the situation so matter-of-factly as all that. There must surely be some alternative. Desperately she cast about for one. Drymen – Drymen, he had said, was only five miles away.

She voiced her thoughts precipitately. 'Five miles is nothing really. I'm sure I could walk it. I think I'll try.'

He cut the ground from under her feet with a word or two of raillery. If she really liked walking in the rain . . . And once again she felt as though she were behaving like a fool, creating a scene which appeared to him as a sane fellow merely silly.

'Honestly,' he said, 'you're better by the fire than out in that. If it's as wet as it was when I was talking to the driver, the road will be flooded by now.'

Yes, she supposed she was better where she was. But sitting here with him had its disadvantages. His hand, for instance. She hardly liked to draw his attention to the fact that it still rested upon hers, heavy as a lump of wet putty she was fain to fling off.

'Baby fingers,' he murmured, comparing her thumb with his own. 'Baby fingers.'

Did he think she was an imbecile or an infant?

She jerked away her hand. 'If there's no help for it, if I've got to stay here till morning, I may as well go to bed. Will you ask the woman, Mrs—'

'Ker,' said Shaw. 'Sophia Ker.'

Ker – Sophia Ker. Funny, Aunt Ruth used to have a washer-woman named Sophia Ker. Nice if it should turn out to be the same.

On the way upstairs Mr Shaw stumbled. 'Damn!' he said violently. 'Damn!'

She affected not to have heard and went on ahead.

'Door to the right,' he directed. 'My sisters sleep there as a rule. 'S'll right, isn't it?'

'Quite,' she said. 'And you'll be sure to ask Sophia to call me in the morning?'

'Won't forget,' he repeated, backing out. 'Good night, sweet-heart.'

Had he really said that, or had she only fancied it? Her pulses were thumping so loudly that she could scarce hear above their din. For on the way through the hall, before the stumble on the stair, she had divined a possible reason for Mr Shaw's 'different-ness' – an empty decanter which, when she had first set eyes upon it, had been almost full.

She slipped off her hat, ruffled her hair with her fingers. In the cheval glass she looked very cool, very composed. Only the pupils of her eyes were dilated and a little nerve in her right lid twitched incessantly. She pressed a finger on it, forcing it into temporary submission. Sleep was out of the question. It was not merely that her brain was too excited, but she could not rid herself of the thought of that empty decanter . . . Not, she told herself, that Mr Shaw was actually the worse of drink. He was only queer, uncon-trolled, jumpy. But no, she wouldn't try to sleep just yet. She would listen for the caretaker coming in. She did hope it would turn out to be old Sophia who used to come to help Jessie every second Monday.

She wandered over to the long French window. Outside, the darkness seemed to have thickened. There was a sound as of heavy rain falling on flagstones. She unfastened the window latch, peered out. From the narrow veranda a row of steep stone steps disappeared in a maze of wildly writhing shadows – trees, tall trees waving their tortured branches to and fro in the storm.

Shivering a little, she closed the window.

No use listening for Sophia now. She could hear nothing for the drumming of the rain. She snuggled down in her chair, tucked one foot beneath her. Sleep – no, she wouldn't sleep. She would just shut her eyes and pretend to herself she was home in her bed at Kirkton, and that Jessie had waked her, and that it was high time she was up if she were to be in time for school. But that she wanted five minutes more – just five minutes . . .

Nightmare. Yes – of course, it wasn't real. It was nightmare. And yet it was all so clear – so terrifyingly clear. The turning of the key in the lock. The fumbling footsteps. The sight of Mr Shaw groping his way across the room. And then his face like the close-up in a film, all eyes and gaping mouth. She would die if those great coarse lips closed on hers. She would die of horror and disgust.

She forced herself to speak quietly, dispassionately.

'What is it?' she said. 'What do you want?'

And then panic seized her. For at sound of her own voice – her own pitifully strained voice – she had realized that this was no nightmare at all.

He regarded her from under drooping lids, checked by her affectation of composure.

'What are you playing at?' he said, a tang of ill humour scraping the velvety quality from his voice. 'You know well enough what I want. You're not a pal of Torrance's for nothing.'

Her face, she realized, was breaking into hot little quivers. Her muscles were dissolving in a palsy of trembling. She dreaded lest she should lose consciousness, lose control, and he would have his way with her. His way! God! What would that way be?

She played for time. 'You startled me. I was half asleep. Hasn't Sophia come back?'

He smiled slyly. 'Not yet. But it won't matter. Her quarters are at the back. She couldn't possibly hear us. As for the taxi – I dismissed it if you'd like to know the truth, sent it back to town.'

She clenched the arms of her chair. 'Then the man hadn't gone when you went out? That was all a trumped-up lie! Oh, you – you—'

The sharpness of her exclamation sobered him momentarily. His features grew sullen.

'Don't take it that way. Honestly, Jacqueline, you needn't be frightened. I'm not such a bad sort really. 'Course, I don't come up to the governor's standards. But I've more moral sense than our friend R. F. *I* don't keep a couple or more households going.'

He drew nearer, imprisoned her hands in his.

'Look here, Jacqueline, be sensible. Don't try to fight me. You can't, y'know, with those baby fingers.' Then suddenly his voice thickened. 'Don't glare at me like that or I'll kiss the life out of you.'

His forehead, like that of some fabled monster, loomed above her own. His mouth descended on hers with a fierce searching pressure. Blindly she struck out, savage in her instinct of self-defence.

The thud of her fist upon his throat winded him, set him gasping for breath. In that moment she sprang from him, unfastened the window and fled down the veranda steps.

On the gravelled walk she met a couple hurrying towards the house. As they passed her, she heard Shaw's voice on the veranda cursing and calling her name aloud. And on that instant she bent her head and ran right out of the gate and along the rainswept road.

CHAPTER XII

Rain. Slanting sheets of rain with the coldness of ice in it.

Crouched beside the wall that girt the high road, Jacqueline felt the conflagration in her blood burn slowly out. Her brain which only a short time ago had been afire was no longer flexible and alive, but a numb useless member atrophied by shock and an acute sense of chill.

What to do she could not bring herself to decide. Her hat, her bag containing her purse, were in the bungalow. She dared not go back for them, and yet, dishevelled and without money, she could not beg shelter in the village. In any case, she doubted if she could walk that distance. For quite suddenly while still she had been running her limbs had given way and she had been obliged to stagger to the side of the road for support. There she had stayed huddled against the stone, letting the rain sweep over her.

To think that only a few hours ago she had been safe in the Palais, surrounded by lights, by people! If only she had never – but how was she to know that this nameless horror lurked on the horizon?

Aunt Ruth – Nessie – no one had warned her. Mrs Torrance alone of her friends had hinted . . . And she in her ignorance had listened, open-eyed, but had only half understood.

She wrenched herself upright. There was someone – two people coming along the road. A man's voice, taut with anxiety, cut the stillness.

'I tell you, Sophia, I must find her. By God, if anything's happened—'

It was Shaw looking for her, Shaw with the blazing eyes, the outstretched arms! The rigidity that prisoned her limbs dissolved. There was a steep hill ahead, but she breasted it without stopping to take breath. And once again there came to her the feeling that this was nightmare. Impossible that it should be aught else. In real life things like this didn't happen. The world wasn't a trough of darkness wherein rain drummed incessantly. In the world there were people, music, lights . . .

Lights! But there – there in the darkness was a light; there were two lights.

As she neared them she realized they were the rear lamps of a stationary vehicle, of a taxicab, the very cab she recognized when its yellow panels became discernible in which she had driven with Shaw from town.

The driver was not in sight. The car had no visible owner or occupant. She opened the door and went inside. There was a bundle on the seat which proved on investigation to be a coarse red rug. She gathered it round her shoulders, nestled down in a corner. Here was sanctuary, shelter from the rain. She shivered as she watched it drifting past in slanting sheets, driving before it the scatter of snow that lined the roadside.

A loud clearing of throat, the guttural hiss of violent expectoration warned her of the driver's proximity. She slunk back on the cushions, but he gave never a glance behind. Slowly, reluctantly, he cranked up the engine, cursing it as though the mechanism were a dour, unwilling horse. Then he mounted his seat and the car slid forward.

She drew a deep breath. It were better so. To be obliged at this juncture to explain would be hopeless. She would let him drive her right back to town before she apprised him of her presence.

Grr! Grr! How the engine throbbed and rattled, just as if there really were something amiss! She was so tired, so tired . . . If only it were quieter she might sleep. But no, she mustn't sleep. She would dream, of a certainty, of Mr Shaw precipitating himself upon her, and she would scream and scream!

She stared out through the darkness. The moors had been

lapped up by the rain mist that stretched, a drear waveless sea, on either side. The world seemed drained of colour – a lonely, light-forsaken planet through which the car meandered without purpose like a needle-less thread.

Grr! Grr! Almost it seemed as though the engine were talking to itself, deploring the fate that impelled it to nose its way through these inhospitable regions on such a night. At the top of a long hill it wheezed and choked in the manner of an elderly asthmatic. Then all at once, as though the paroxysm had cleared its tubes, it spurted ahead with a singing rhythm. In the distance a vast fan of dusky light smouldered. Jacqueline's heart leapt as she recognized the city cupped in the Renfrewshire hills. It was not until the white curves of the canal bridge at Temple hove in sight that she rattled her fingers on the glass window.

The driver slowed up. With a dazed air he dismounted, opened the door.

'Well, I'm – I'm—' he stuttered.

'I want you to drive me to 23 Hentzau Street as quickly as possible,' she directed.

His cheeks were crimson. Possibly he, too, had been drinking. Jacqueline could not tell. She only prayed he would waste no time. It was even colder here than it had been on the moor.

'But – but when – where did I pick you up?' he persisted stupidly.

While she hesitated, Jacqueline followed with her eyes the lazy sweep of the canal. Above the stagnant water there swayed a square of yellow light, a ship's lamp gleaming dulcetly above the rain-sodden banks.

'Near Drymen,' she said. 'And now, please hurry – 23 Hentzau Street.'

The following afternoon Shaw was in his private office when a knock fell on the door.

'Come in,' he called without looking up.

'It's about Miss Thayer,' said a voice at his side. He wheeled round violently. But in Nessie Carruthers' eyes there was no sign of rancour.

'What about her?' he queried.

'She's ill – very ill – I'm afraid. I ran round at dinner-time to see why she hadn't come. I found her in bed, delirious.'

The ruler he was fiddling with slid from his hand.

'Delirious! Did she – I suppose she talked a lot of nonsense then?'

'She doesn't know what she's saying, of course,' said Nessie apologetically. 'She talked about you and the Grind House and about someone called Sophia, and she cried and cried.'

Cried, had she? Cried! If she had done that last night instead of struggling – no, that wouldn't have availed her any. If she had laughed, shouted at him instead of letting the silent horror she felt creep over her like a disease and transform her so pitifully before his eyes – yes, if she had laughed loud enough and long enough the lusting devil in him would have known defeat. As it was, her fluttering terror had flogged his desire. If she hadn't winded him with that biff on the throat—

He averted his eyes lest they should quail before Nessie's straightforward gaze.

'There's not much doing just now. D'you think you and Miss Price could manage—'

'Oh, we'll manage,' she promised gaily. 'No fears about that.'

When she had gone he sat fiddling with his ruler, reflecting upon the extreme awkwardness of the situation. If the girl were really ill it was up to him to do something. There was no denying the fact that it was he who had driven her into the roadway at two o'clock in the morning. 'Course, her being so thick with Torrance had misled him. He'd been all wrong about that. Things had been strictly on the level there. If he had consumed less of Sophia's cheap whisky he'd have tumbled to that and not have made a ruddy fool of himself. No wonder the child was scared. Her first affair, and him in that sottish state!

He rose, pushed open the window. The shop opposite was having a sale. There was a big placard in the window: 'REMNANTS SLIGHTLY SOILED. 6/11¾.'

Slightly soiled – damnably soiled – not worth 6/11¾. That was how he felt. Yet what could he do? Go and ask for her – send her things? He didn't dare. He had too many relatives skulking around, spying upon his actions. If they got hold of this – a typist – Charlie's latest! Lord, how they'd yap about it! He had seen his sisters on the warpath before.

There was, too, Sophia to be reckoned with. He had paid her well to keep her mouth shut, but there was always the chance that she might blab. She had been honey-sweet until about half an hour before his departure, when she had come to him with tightly buttoned lips, a small black reticule from which an envelope bulged in her hand.

'I've seen that writing, let me tell you, many's a time,' she said vindictively. 'It's Mrs Forsyth of Kirkton's writing, and that bag belongs if I'm not mistaken to her niece that lived with her.'

Irritated beyond endurance he had taken the bag from the woman without a word. It lay in his pocket now. He took it out and examined the contents: the letter, a tiny purse, a crumpled handkerchief which he recalled having watched Jacqueline twist between her fingers in the kitchen.

From the black silk a faint fragrance emanated. Deliberately he savoured it, then he thrust the bag back in his pocket. Whew! Surely it must be getting on for tea-time . . . He reached for his hat, opened the door. As he passed the window his eyes fell on the flaunting placard: 'SLIGHTLY SOILED. 6/11¾.'

CHAPTER XIII

To Jacqueline the days that followed were a blur. Vaguely she remembered tumbling into bed and waking with the intention of dressing and going out to the Grind House. But when she stretched for her stockings they eluded her. She looked at them where they hung over the bedpost and just then she noted a strange thing. The bedposts were little men leering at her. She could not possibly rise with their eyes upon her. She huddled down beneath the blankets. Funny how the little men had got there. She never remembered seeing them before. No, nor all those other people who filled the room. She didn't care who they were or how long they stayed so long as they didn't ask Mr Shaw to their party. She'd never dance with him again, never. But had she danced with him or was it with Bill? Funny, going to the 'Pally' with Bill and Sophia! Funny place all dripping with rain! Why didn't the dancers take umbrellas with them? But it was time she got up.

She tugged on her stockings. They felt cold and clammy on her skin. So, too, did her petticoat. The shoulder-straps were like strips of solid ice. Her teeth chattered. She couldn't stop them. She hoped to goodness she wasn't going to be ill . . .

That was her last recollection before the whole world reeled. When she recovered from the stupor which succeeded that convolution, her landlady was by her side and a strange man.

'You'd better telegraph her people,' he was saying. 'No, there can be no question of moving her, not with that— What? Oh, a day or two will tell.'

Her next recollection was of Aunt Ruth, a strangely gentle Aunt Ruth holding a glass containing orange juice for her to drink. It was the most wonderful stuff in the world, that orange juice. Sometimes when Aunt Ruth was out and she was alone in the room, she would lie and look at the fluted glass, the plate of yellow fruit, and yearn for the kindly liquid to cool her parched throat.

One morning she heard the University chimes. What time is it, she was on the point of asking, when another more vital question occurred to her.

'What day is it?' she asked.

'Tuesday,' said Aunt Ruth. 'You've been in your bed a week.'

A week – only a week since that awful night. Aunt Ruth came nearer.

'It must have been that nasty hot dancing hall. I don't hold with these places myself – never did. All the bad breaths!'

Jacqueline plucked at the bedclothes. No one knew then – thank God, no one knew!

'The doctor says it must have been a chill at the start – threatening of rheumatic fever, that's what he says. All the same,' Aunt Ruth consoled herself, 'things might have been worse – MacCluskys' have been very pleasant. There's a friendly letter from a C. Shaw saying you must on no account hurry back until you are quite well again. They're paying your salary, too, just as usual.'

Jacqueline writhed. 'I won't take it,' she cried.

'Don't be so soft,' admonished her aunt. 'Every good house does that. You don't need to feel beholden to them.'

Jacqueline gathered all her breath for an emphatic utterance.

'Aunt Ruth,' she said, 'I'll never go back to MacCluskys' – never.'

Mrs Forsyth's eyes widened. Was the girl raving again? She took up the clinical thermometer.

'Now then, keep it flat under your tongue . . . Ssh! Not another word!'

In a week's time Jacqueline was able to go out. On the day following Mrs Forsyth took her to Kirkton. For a full fortnight she basked in the soft familiar air, in the affectionate enquiries of Uncle Archie, in the kindly attentions of Aunt Ruth. Then one day the atmosphere changed.

Jacqueline, who still remained in bed for breakfast, was dressing when her aunt returned somewhat earlier than usual from her morning shopping. Something in the harsh metallic click of Mrs Forsyth's heels on the stair set the girl's heart thumping with a quick sense of alarm.

Mrs Forsyth's cheekbones were livid when she entered the room. There was a sort of naked fury in her expression before which Jacqueline recoiled.

'I met Sophia Ker in the town,' she said.

Jacqueline's heart missed a beat. Sophia Ker. She had forgotten about her! She, doubtless, was the woman she had passed in the garden, the woman to whom she had heard Shaw say: 'By God, if anything's happened.'

The weakness of her illness came over her again. She crumpled up like a child caught out in a fault. For a moment she stayed motionless, then a sob escaped her lips, a harsh tearing sound that turned away Mrs Forsyth's wrath.

She moved towards her niece with a little fluttering movement of her arms, a gesture wholly alien to one of her creed and temperament. But before she reached the girl's side her eyes lit on a garment lying on the bed.

Crêpe de Chine – pink *crêpe de Chine*! It was a stigma of iniquity in Mrs Forsyth's eyes, a piece of damning evidence. For the woman who was fool enough to go about in January with a thing like that on her back was fool enough for anything. In a flash she recalled Jacqueline's extravagant admiration of George Buchanan; her way of caressing Uncle Archie's cheek with her fingers; her habit of lighting up when he came home at night although she had seemed tired and listless during the day. And then, casting her thoughts farther back still, she recalled how Jacqueline's mother had gone off and married a man they knew nothing at all about, after the scantiest of courtships. She remembered when she had reproached her sister for making herself so cheap to a man and a sailor with a girl in every port at that, she had rounded upon her and said things – bitter, impassioned things that had violated her sense of decency, married woman herself though she was. These things came back to her now, stiffening her resolution. For like mother, like daughter.

'Tell me,' she demanded, the corners of her lips twitching, 'what were you doing at a house near Drymen alone with a man? You, brought up so carefully!'

In the face of her aunt's implacable anger Jacqueline's weakness fell from her. A spice of her mother's shrewish temper awoke in her.

'I won't be talked to in that way,' she cried. 'I'd rather get up and leave the house right away.'

For a second Aunt Ruth's upper lip twitched so terribly that Jacqueline thought it could never again return to its rightful place. Then it reverted into a tight line.

'You *will* leave this house, that's certain,' she said firmly. 'I won't harbour a wanton – no, not for a single hour!'

CHAPTER XIV

When Aunt Ruth had retired in a fury from the room, Jacqueline had dressed hurriedly, cast her few belongings into her suitcase. This done, she stared for a moment out of the window at the familiar contours of the square. Her favourite tree at the corner looked grey and stale this morning, rather like a draggled old woman.

Jacqueline shuddered. Goodbye, Kirkton. Best go at once and get it over . . . Uncle Archie? No, she wouldn't wait to speak to him. She could not bear to see the glint of kindliness in his eyes give way to an expression of incredulous contempt.

She went slowly downstairs. Aunt Ruth was in the hall.

'I'm going,' she said, a ray of hope buoying her that Aunt Ruth's set features would on a sudden quiver and grow human.

Whether they did or not, Jacqueline never knew. For Mrs Forsyth turned smartly on her heel and the kitchen door slammed behind her.

On the way to the station Jacqueline kept thinking: 'I don't care. I don't care. I can get on without her.'

Lying awake at nights in Hentzau Street she chanted the same defiant refrain. But in the mornings a sort of cold sweat broke over her, converting her defiance into fear. If she should fall ill again! If some morning the room should reel again around her!

After a week of broken sleep and anxious days Nessie Carruthers exclaimed at sight of her:

'My dear, you look awful! Whatever's up? I know there's something.'

Jacqueline felt the colour flood her face. For a moment she could not bring herself to speak without emotion.

'It's lack of work,' she said at last. 'These last few days I've answered – oh, scores of advertisements. I've climbed hundreds of office stairs. It's no good. Nobody seems to want me.'

'But – but your job's waiting you at the Grind House. Why, in the name of goodness, go looking for another?'

Jacqueline's lips whitened. 'I won't go back there. They know that. I wrote to Mr Shaw from Kirkton.'

She did not tell Nessie that in reply she had had a letter refusing to accept her resignation and enclosing a cheque for a fortnight's salary.

Nessie looked thoughtful. 'It was last Monday – no, it was Tuesday I mentioned something about you coming back and Mr Shaw never said a word about you having written. Honestly, Jacqueline, you're making a mistake. I've no brief for the Grind House, but as Bill says, "there's a dam' sight worse".'

'I know. It's not that. It's—' She groped for a credible lie. 'It's monotonous. I'd like a change.'

Nessie's good-humoured face puckered. 'You're lucky if you can chuck a certainty like that. I didn't know you'd inherited a fortune.'

A fortune! After Nessie had gone Jacqueline counted her money, the money that stood between her and want. Exactly one pound, thirteen shillings and fivepence! At sight of the neat little piles of coins ranged on her toilet table she laughed and laughed until the tears rolled down her cheeks and she was obliged to go to bed because her head ached so badly that she could not hold it upright. From her pillow she lay contemplating the future. Of these little piles of coins only the small silver one would remain after Mrs MacAndrew's bill for board and lodging was paid on Saturday. There was, too, the pound she had in the purse she had left at the bungalow. Mr Shaw had written saying he was keeping her bag safely for her. After that pound was exhausted – but she would have found work by then. She must find work. Any sort of work. Charring, scrubbing, sewing. Wasn't there supposed to be a shortage of domestic servants?

She reversed the pillow beneath her head. 'I don't care. I don't care. I don't – ah, but I do, I do!'

The following afternoon she answered an advertisement for a between-maid. The lady of the house regarded her in surprise.

'I'm afraid you're not just the type of girl I want,' she was murmuring when a tall good-looking youth lounged into the room.

At sight of a stranger he halted. 'Won't you introduce me, mater?' he said.

The lady rose in a flurry. With a word or two of regret she shepherded Jacqueline to the door.

On her way home Jacqueline passed the Torrances' house. It was shuttered and locked. There was not even a card with an address for letters in the window. Another fragment of anchorage torn up! Jacqueline walked quickly away from it down the hill to Hentzau Street.

She found Mr Shaw on the doorstep.

'It's you!' he said. 'I've been waiting. Look here, I must speak to you—' He broke off as she made to brush past him. 'I've got your bag here, your purse. You can't send me away without a word. I want to apologize. For God's sake, Jacqueline—'

He had raised his voice and she cast an anxious glance at Mrs MacAndrew's door. If she should hear— With a violent effort of will she conquered the sense of repulsion the sight of him had aroused in her and controlled her voice.

'If you must speak to me, come upstairs . . . Now, what is it you have to say?'

'This – this cheque,' he stammered. 'You sent it back. Why, in the name of thunder, why?'

'Because I've severed my connection with MacCluskys'. You had my letter.'

'I know. I know. But don't you see, I can't let you make a martyr of yourself because of my folly – my dam' folly. Fact is, I lost my head. That filthy whisky – thank God, nobody knows but the two of us.'

'Someone else knows. Sophia Ker.'

'I've sealed her mouth,' he said confidently. 'She won't blab.'

'She's blabbed already. She told my aunt at Kirkton – exactly what, I don't know.'

He leapt to his feet with a savage exclamation. 'I wonder –

look here, get your aunt to repeat word for word what she said.'

Jacqueline smiled wryly. 'I can't do that. We – we quarrelled. My aunt turned me out.'

He stared at her aghast. 'You mean because of this? Oh, my Lord! Look here, if there's anything I can do—'

'You're the last person in the world I'd ask.'

His lips flapped. 'I deserve that, I suppose. But – dash it all, Jacqueline, in a way you led me on. You rode straight for the high jump and then you shied when you got up to it. Mind you, I'm thankful you did. I'd have felt a pretty cur today if—'

He stopped short and, half turning, stared out of the window. From the sultry thundercloud that all day had threatened the city a few tepid drops had begun to fall. In the wan light Hentzau Street resembled a tunnel in whose clotted darkness people and vehicles seemed to have lost their distinctive personalities. Jacqueline alone appeared to have remained immune. She looked jolly even now, he reflected, although her cheeks still showed traces of her illness and her wrists were painfully thin. He remembered how he had felt after that last go of flu . . .

'Look here,' he said, 'you're not fit to trail about cadging for jobs. Won't you come back? Can't you bear even an occasional sight of me? I give you my Bible oath I won't look the road you're on.

'Don't you see the awful position you're forcing me into,' he persisted, heedless of her emphatic head-shake; 'employer tampering with innocent girl's virtue sort of thing? Don't you see that – dash it all, if you're thrown out of work through this, it is I who've chucked you out. If anyone's got to suffer through this business it should be me, not you.'

He was in deadly earnest, nevertheless he could not help feeling a faint glow of appreciation at his own generosity. For the moment the mantle of his father had fallen upon him, the mantle of old 'Preaching' Shaw, so called because at one time it had been his habit to preside at mission meetings in the East End and in immaculate evening clothes to clasp the hands of unwashed sinners.

'I won't suffer,' Jacqueline retorted. 'There are other firms. It's no use arguing about it. I wish you'd go.'

He rose reluctantly. She ignored his hand, busying herself with the contents of the bag he had returned her.

At the door he halted to voice a final plea. She wasn't listening though, he feared. Or was she? He could hardly tell, for her eyes were bent on that confounded bag . . . She looked up. By the Lord Harry, she seemed moved at last!

'Say you'll let bygones be bygones,' he reiterated; 'say you'll come back.'

He was taken utterly by surprise when quite suddenly she gave way.

'Very well,' she said woodenly. 'I'll come.'

He went away consciously elated that his oratory had got him out of an awkward hole, a hole his conscience had rendered thoroughly untenable.

As it happened, however, his oratory had had nothing to do with it. What had weighed the scales with Jacqueline was the discovery that the pound note she had had in her purse when she had left it at the bungalow was no longer there.

'To take my pound and then to go and tell Aunt Ruth,' she thought to herself as Shaw went down the street. 'Oh, Sophia, how could you?'

CHAPTER XV

To one of Jacqueline's temperament, creative work is well-nigh impossible during a period of mental or emotional strain. For weeks the Grind House exhausted all her energies, then gradually the impulse to express herself in other terms than those dictated by Messrs MacClusky & Co. reasserted itself. She set to work upon a narrative poem which she called ambitiously her white saga, a drama in verse of modern pioneering, a picture as she conceived it of the desperate battle waged by man in the remoteness of the wild. In spirit she lived with her characters through the long soundless nights, through the days like years that stretched into a seeming eternity, through the deathless struggles when the grey spectre of the ice-floe bared fearful fangs.

The Grind House held her by day, but it was by night when the blinds were drawn and the theatre cabs began to rattle home that her real life began . . . Often she would listen to them as they throbbed, hooting, round the corner. Sometimes she envied their inmates, warm and palpitating still in the spun-gold wrap of illusion woven out of the actors' gallant gestures. Other times she gave them no more than a passing thought. Despite their worldly possessions they were worth, as the saying went, less than she. For their riches lay exposed on their persons and in their homes for any thief to make off with, while hers lay locked securely in her breast.

The day she concluded her poem she had a letter from Owen Southwold announcing his return and inviting her to tea with him in town. She beamed with delight. The very person she wanted to see. He would be able to inform her on all the points that had baffled her. To her chagrin, however, he turned the conversation. He fenced with her so adroitly that it was only after they had parted that she realized how determinedly he had avoided speaking about his voyages. At the end of their next meeting, in a fit of pique at his persistent avoidance of the subject which she guessed lay nearest his heart, she thrust a typewritten MS on him. That would show him she wasn't just a child!

He took it courteously. 'One of your poems? Yes, I'd like to read it very much.'

But he was quite sure he wouldn't. She was a delightful kid, sincere as they make 'em. He was awfully sorry for her, liked taking her about. She had the most attractive way of lighting up when she was happy, of letting go the past and seizing hold of the present. He liked to watch the slow dawn of laughter in her eyes, gradual at first, then spilling over in a spasm of uncontrolled mirth. He liked to watch the birdlike droop of her head when she was immersed in thought, the eager poise of her shoulders when you made her a present of a new idea. It was easy to do this last, surprisingly easy. And it excited her, you could see, almost as much as a present of a box of sweets.

The degree of enthusiasm, however, provoked by the sweets depended, he had discovered, not so much upon the sweets themselves but upon their ribbon garniture. To her, ribbon, coloured ribbon, was quite obviously a rubble of delight. He had known her to slide rapturous fingers over a fanfare of pink silk, to utter an exclamation of sheer horror when he had proposed to slit it with a knife. To obviate this wicked procedure he had seen her go through a tremendous performance of knot-wrestling, and tugging and ironing out with her hand the wrinkles and creases after which the object of her care had been folded into her bag to disappear for ever from his ken. Once he had fancied he had caught sight of it in the form of a shoulder strap slipped down on her arm, and pushed hurriedly out of sight. This instance in mind, he punctiliously selected sweets for their exterior furnishings. For while he couldn't very well, he argued, give her a bale of ribbon to play with, he could give her scraps wherewith to tie things on. And she was a delightful child. He liked talking to her. But – no, he didn't want to read her stuff. It would be jejune and of a certainty it would bore him.

As he put the MS in his pocket Jacqueline divined his thoughts and her lips quivered. She went to bed feeling as humiliated as though she had proffered someone she was fond of a kiss, and been put off with a pat on the back of the hand.

Next morning on her breakfast tray lay an envelope in his handwriting. She tore it open fearfully, then as she read its contents a wild joy filled her.

When next they met Jacqueline realized instinctively that their relationship had undergone a change. No longer was it a remote impersonal one blurred over with vague ceremonials, but a naissant flower of fine-blown intimacy. It was as though across the pages of the written word their eyes had exchanged a long confidential look, their souls had pressed together in sympathy with the result that the barriers on both sides were down. Of their overthrow Owen's first words showed consciousness.

'Why did you never tell me you felt things like that? Why have you always hidden your real self away?'

'Have I?' she asked breathlessly. It was a little startling, this sudden stride into friendship.

The innocent grey of her eyes, the deepening bloom of her cheeks lured him to greater candour. This child whom he had hoped to please with coloured ribbons was no child after all, but a woman of infinite reserves with a spirituality of outlook he had hitherto deemed the prerogative of man. He had the impelling desire to sound the depths of those reserves, to explore their farthermost reaches. Yet all the while he knew and exulted in the knowledge that the reaches of the human soul are unexplorable.

'Your poem was a revelation to me,' he said. 'I never guessed you felt things like that.'

'You imagined I was content with just – just this?' Her eyes swept the drab little room.

'D'you suppose women never get bitten with the desire for freedom?'

'I thought instinct bade the average woman walk softly, eschew danger. There's danger in breaking loose, you know.'

She pondered his words in silence. Yes, the caged bird was safe, secure. But, oh, the fun it missed not being free to flap its wings, to fend for itself. She rose, shook herself clear of the clouds of reflection that threatened to engulf her.

'Is it not about time we started?' she hinted.

'It is,' he admitted, but he was vexed with her for reminding him of the fact. He hated to break off their conversation just as it had got going satisfactorily. Still, she was right. There was no help for it. A week ago he had engaged a box for the first night of a musical comedy and had invited two friends of his to join them. They had followed up his theatre invitation by bidding him to supper at their house after the performance, and upon his refusing on the score of having a guest of his own Jacqueline had been included in the party.

To Jacqueline a theatre box was a new experience. To begin with, she was not at all sure if she were going to like it. Delightfully private, of course, but you had to crane your neck to see your side of the stage. And in the strong light you felt oddly conspicuous, cocked up there as if you were one of the players whose every movement was being observed by the crowd below. She was thankful she had put on her *crêpe de Chine*. Early in the evening she had looked tentatively at her best jumper, her coat and skirt. Then she had recalled a mention of the word box, and a box, she had decided, with supper to follow at a strange house, had to be lived up to. Of course, if this Mrs Wray turned up in tweeds she'd feel awful, vulgarly overdressed.

The curtain rose. There was a movement behind her. Owen's friends were arriving. Even in the darkness Jacqueline was conscious of the perfumed elegance of the newcomer's attire. And to think she had actually hesitated between what she had on and a coat and skirt! She would have died of shame, she told herself, if she had been daft enough to come out in her best jumper.

Introductions were effected in the interval. From beneath drooping lids Jacqueline studied Mrs Wray. She was dark, befurred, mysterious. There was the shimmer of diamonds at her throat, her wrists, and her eyes were two black pools of changing light. From the crown of her head to the tips of her toes she was elegant, one of those perfect beings whose figures seem part of their frocks, whose every movement is fraught with fascination. A cosmopolitan, Jacqueline decided. And instinctively she slid a little deeper into her shell. So this – this was the type of woman who was Owen's friend. How crude in comparison he must find her, how lacking in charm and assurance.

Like a shadow Mrs Wray's husband loomed at the back of the box, a tall distinguished figure of a man, dark-eyed and very dignified. While he stood beside her chair Jacqueline felt she should converse with him and leave Mrs Wray and Owen to their *tête-à-tête* uninterrupted. But she was tongue-tied. There seemed nothing to say. She could only envy the ball of badinage that leapt so lightly between Owen and Mrs Wray. She could only reproach herself for the jealous tug of envy that shook her when every now and then the tinkle of Mrs Wray's laughter trickled out afresh. Later, during a vibrant song of love and passion, a song that made Jacqueline want to drop her face in her hands and sob, she observed Mrs Wray steal a long glance at Owen. If he were conscious of it he gave no sign. No reflection of an answering smile broke through his mask.

At supper Jacqueline's suspicions acquired a sharper edge. With a show of good generalship Mrs Wray kept her in the conversation, but always she seemed to be trying to turn her inside out, to disclose the ill-furnished condition of her mind, her dreadful inexperience. Mrs Wray's smile was very sweet. She deferred to Jacqueline's opinion very charmingly, but all the while the girl knew instinctively that her hostess was fain to throw her to the dogs because she was a friend of Owen's.

When she rose to go her blackest doubts were confirmed. Mrs Wray held up her cloak with an exclamation.

'My dear, you'll catch cold. This is so thin. Have you no fur?'

In her hands the wrap looked like a beggar's garment picked up by a pitiful queen. 'Cad!' said Jacqueline below her breath; 'cad!'

A moment later, bowling down the hill with Owen, the incident went from her mind. Why did the car go so fast? The lamp posts slipped by like pendulous beads strung together by a feverish hand.

Never before did she remember seeing the city so still. Over the trees the mist had spun a gossamer net. The night air blew soft and humid. In that moment Jacqueline felt as if this – this was what she had been waiting for all the days of her life, this swift flight through the darkened streets along with Owen.

Did he savour it all as keenly as she did? She could not tell. Only he held her hand at parting as though it were a precious thing he was loath to relinquish, and he looked into her eyes as a man might look who is seeking a light that if once descried will illumine his path through life for ever.

She did not sleep very soundly that night. At early morning she awoke and lay wrapped round in a mystic robe of new-found happiness. Something had happened overnight. Something that even in the raw cold of dawn set every nerve in her body singing, every vein tingling to a muted melody. She made no effort to analyse her feelings. It was enough that this inrush of rapture enfolded her. From now on her world was changed.

Life, she mused, was wonderful. A dark cocoon from which all unexpectedly there emerges a gleam. She let her soul bathe in it as a child bathes its limbs in a tiny pool of sunlight on the pavement, smiling all the while to itself. Then, for fear of satiety, she stepped for a minute outside. How awful to die before life has given all it has to offer! She thought pitifully of the hundreds who never attain adolescence, of the girls who die before they understand the meaning of life . . . And then the shimmering pool lured her once more. She lay basking in it, beating with her fingers a tattoo on the bedclothes to the tune of the actress's song: 'Love! Love! Follow the gleam of it!'

Gleam, yes, that was it – a gleam of radiance piercing the grey.

CHAPTER XVI

That same week there came another invitation from Owen. It was to dinner this time at his hotel. Jacqueline read the note propped up against the china salt pillar on her breakfast tray, and its perusal lent a fine flavour to her straw-tasted scrambled egg. She received few letters of any kind, only an occasional abruptly worded epistle from George Buchanan; and twice she had had a hastily written line from Uncle Archie enclosing a postal order which he begged her upon no account to acknowledge as he was sending it to her with his love 'on the sly'.

The meal over, she folded up Owen's letter and placed it in her bag. When she was filing references at the Grind House she liked to remember that the letter was there. It filled her with an absurd sense of superiority when she said no, thank you, to Nessie's invitation to supper. It fortified her when old Miss Price, ambling in at lunch time, stopped to peer into her face and to mutter: 'Eh, but I had bright cheeks, too, at your age.' Thereon the old woman had sighed prodigiously. For what, after all, had the brightness of her cheeks availed her? What had they won for her in her old age? A stool near the fire in a city office, a top-floor bedroom at the end of a toilsome climb which nightly seemed to grow steeper and steeper. She laid a claw-nailed finger on Jacqueline's arm.

'Make the most of your time. It's not long in the passing.'

Jacqueline quailed. There were times when Miss Price resembled a malevolent old witch with her predatory features, her rheumy eyes, her faint, rather foul smell. At such times the words that fell from her lips were like toads from which you shrank in terror lest they entrap you in a loathsome circle you could not escape. The circle they connoted began at the Grind House and ended at Hentzau Street. Without that circle Lilac Villa stood, a pleasaunce of delight impossible of attainment. The outer world ringed the circle round so that ever and anon stray glimpses of it were granted the prisoners, kindling in them wild aspirations, wilder desires, torturing them with the pangs of frustration. Hentzau Street to the Grind House. The Grind House back to Hentzau Street. For one dread moment Jacqueline stood bound in the horrific chain of the old woman's spell. Then she shook off Miss Price's detaining hand. In her bag was her talisman. At that instant the thought of Owen's letter was like balm across her heart.

As she left the Grind House an unpleasing possibility occurred to her. She might not be the only guest at Owen's hotel. Mrs Wray might be there. Mrs Wray got up to kill in all sorts of marvellous clothes. A wave of rebellion coursed up in her, a wanton wave spiked with envy, with hate. She hated Mrs Wray for what she had. She hated herself still more for what she hadn't. She recalled the women who had posed and pirouetted before her mother's pier glass in Lowerbank Street. No wonder they had behaved as though they had been above themselves. That glass, she realized, had been to them a magic mirror wherein they had seen themselves not as they were but as they wanted to be – stately princesses in shimmering cloth of gold, cherry-lipped coquettes twisting the hearts of men as they might the yielding stems of a rose.

She turned up the main street, and instantly the glare of the shops added fuel to the fire of her torment. On a fine night the hilly street was a great white avenue swept by searchlight, a switchback arcade with set scenes on either side.

These set scenes with their simpering wax ladies, their dangling furbelows and glistening baubles, drew Jacqueline like magnets. She was a fool to pause, she told herself, but tonight of all nights she couldn't help it. Before a pink-and-white figure tricked out in Pompadour silk she stood transfixed, her heart hot with the fever of desire. Oh, the grace of it, the fragrance and the charm! It was a dress such as Marie Antoinette herself might have worn. Jacqueline could picture her own arms emerging from those tiny wisps of sleeves, she could feel the curve of the bodice clinging to her shoulder blades. Almost she could inhale the faint indescribable perfume of new silk that pervaded it. Then all at once she recoiled. So had the blood-lusting hags of the Terror seen themselves in the laces of their Empress.

Doggedly she walked on, breasting with never a pause the crest of the hill. But with every swing of her body her desires grew sharper-edged. Woman was built for conquest. Clothes were her rightful weapon. Why should some women be condemned to walk through life unarmed while others went caparisoned at every point? It wasn't fair – no, it wasn't fair!

She uttered the words aloud, but they were lost in the hubbub of the street. At that point there was a little crowd round a corner window. 'Eh, isn't that bonny?' Above the clatter rose the shrill notes of a woman's voice. In spite of her resolution to walk straight home and to look neither to right nor to left, Jacqueline swerved to one side. She pressed forward towards the gleaming plate glass and then she caught her breath. To think that there was such loveliness in the world! She caressed in fancy the glowing satin robe, the fur, still instinct with savagery, that flanked it. She flirted the great fan of tawny feathers to and fro in a ballroom where Owen bowed over her hand. She smiled to think of her feet encased in those little loves of slippers, slid them across the mirrored surface of a parquet floor above which swaying baskets of red roses swam voluptuously. She laughed as she made play with the gossamer lace that fashioned a handkerchief . . . And then she slunk away. No wonder some women stole! She felt all at once cowed by the noise of the crowd, beaten by the stupendous glare of the arc lamps. She must get home quickly or she would scream aloud.

A woman in an open car swept by. Mrs Wray smiling enigmatically at the world at large from out a luxurious nest of sable furs. Jacqueline ground her nails in her palms. How dared she smile? How dared she look so sleek, so self-satisfied while hundreds of her sister women starved for the lovely things of life? It wasn't clothes alone. No, it wasn't merely hats and dresses and shoes. There were other things – dozens of other things. Face creams and perfumes in glistening bottles with gargoyle stoppers. Powder in great glass bowls delicately scented, bath salts like coloured sweets in lovely transparent jars, stuff in tiny enamel boxes to make your nails pink and shiny, brighteners for your hair.

Oh, it was like a craving for drink, this thirst of hers for finery. It informed her whole being, ravaging her until she felt faint, indescribably weary. It was all so hopeless. For she wanted so much, so much! Not one meagre garment to make shift with on all occasions, not a something that 'might do', but all the adorable fripperies, the toilet toys that are the playthings of modern women.

In a stupor of despair she made her way up Hentzau Street. How could she ever hope to look aught but shabby in Owen's eyes? Shabby and second-rate. She wished she had never gone to Mrs Wray's, never known the women who were his associates. She would rather, she told herself in a burst of embittered extravagance, he had introduced a street woman to her as his friend than this glittering, scintillating creature, this exotic bird of a modistic paradise.

Mrs MacAndrew opened the door to her.

'You're late,' she said sourly. 'Your fish'll nut be worth the eatin'.'

Jacqueline forced her lips to the semblance of a smile.

'It doesn't matter,' she said. 'I'm not hungry.'

She went upstairs followed by her landlady, tray in hand. The sight of that tray with its egg-smeared cloth – it was nearing the end of the week – its huddle of coarse dishes and plate of blackened haddock made Jacqueline shudder.

She went to bed. She wept. She watched the darkness ebb and the morning shadows dawn. Then she dropped off to sleep, a smile on her face. She was going to dine with him tonight. What did anything else matter? He, thank Heaven, had never said: 'My dear, your cloak is so thin!'

CHAPTER XVII

There was a red weal in the sky above George Square, a long lurid slit cleaving the irregular ridge of the house-tops from the ebon shell of the sky. Above the statues and grass plots twilight clung like a transparent drapery, frayed every now and then by a fan of light projected by a passing tram. In the waning light the tunnelled entrance of the station with its belching smoke clouds, its sporadic trickle of vehicular traffic, assumed a monstrous aspect. Like an entrance to the regions of darkness its cavernous slopes all wet with a steamy moisture and stained with posters. Like a reflection of hell fire the sparks starting above the grey smoke clouds, the spluttering of engines getting up steam.

In the narrow recess of an oriel window Jacqueline and Owen sat together, apart a little from the lounge behind. They had lingered over dinner till the clatter of cups had aroused them to the fact that breakfast was being laid at the adjoining tables and that the morning menus were replacing those of dinner.

'Boiled or fried?' said Jacqueline foolishly as they rose.

'Jove,' he chuckled, 'that's an idea. Won't you come tomorrow to breakfast and see the last of me?'

But she had refused. She wasn't certain for one thing if he were in earnest or not. In any case, all sorts of people might be turning up to see him off – the Wrays, the men at Dumbarton with whom he had been negotiating about ship fitments. She would hate, she reflected, to be one of a crowd. Besides it wasn't as if he were going for good. The date for the next expedition wasn't even fixed.

'Let's get clear of the mob,' he had said, and piloted her to the window alcove. Once there silence had fallen upon them, one of those portentous pauses which punctuate the advancing stages of intimacy between two persons of the opposite sex.

Jacqueline leaned back, looking out at the sky. Here, with the chatter and glare behind them, the blur of George Square in front, they were isolated as on a cloud-bar and infinitely more comfortable. She looked across at Owen. Their eyes met and she flushed. For thoughts, she knew now, were transparent things. It was terrible the way he read hers at times. He had guessed, for instance, at her dislike of Mrs Wray, had commended the correctness of her intuition, but had hinted gently at the inadvisability of becoming over-censorious. The Scots as a nation, she had defended herself, are hypercritical. 'Are they?' he doubted. 'I don't believe you can label a nation with definite characteristics. So much depends, as my old nurse used to put it, on the boiling. I wouldn't vouch for the boiling that evolved Enid Wray, but she's amusing, she's charming. What more can you ask of a casual friend?'

A casual friend. The description had been effectual in restoring Jacqueline's temper. Then all at once the phrase had driven its way inwards. Did he regard her, too, as nothing more than a casual friend? 'Charming – amusing.' Ah, but she wasn't even that! Compared with Mrs Wray she was crude, ignorant, provincial.

A tremor fluttered her lips, her nostrils. He eyed her anxiously. 'Feeling faint?' he had asked, and a word had dropped from his lips that eased the tightening pain at her heart. She gave no sign that she had heard that word, but it dwelled continuously in her mind like the memory of a caress.

As their eyes met now the jewelled word came back to her and she burned to ask him if he had made love to many women and where and when and how. There were so many things about him she wanted so desperately to know, things that even George Buchanan could not tell her. Oddly enough, Owen tapped the stream of her thoughts, diverted its current to his own purpose.

'Do you know there are great gaps in your life I don't know anything about?' he said. 'Some day you must fill them all in for me. You know the sort of thing I mean. Born at Kirkton, whenever it was. Started writing poetry at the age of three. Threw over the Muse and went in for typing at the age of ten. Fell in love at fifteen. Who was he, Jacqueline?'

She shook her head. 'You first,' she said. 'What made you go in for exploring?'

His face darkened. For a second his eyelids drooped heavily on his cheeks as though her question had stirred up a welter of recollections he was fain to merge in the more wholesome happenings of the present. When he looked up she realized that the mask which he habitually wore had fallen from his features. In the grimness of his lips, the glint in his eyes, she recognized the reflection of a conflict that had at one time torn at his soul. And she thrilled inwardly. For this was Owen Southwold, the real man, this was the daring explorer who pitted his strength against the many-fanged spectre of the ice-floe.

'Tell me,' she begged, and in her own ears her voice sounded very small and childlike.

'What made me go in for exploring? A woman, if you must have it.'

Her face kindled. 'You mean a woman inspired you, fired you with the desire to discover virgin country?'

He answered her brutally, eyes averted. 'Inspired me with the desire to put as many leagues between us as possible. My mother, Jacqueline.'

She uttered a little hurt cry of surprise. On that instant she could have wept in sympathy with him, wept at thought of his desolate youth, of the arid years of adolescence uncomforted by mother love. Somehow, she had never thought of him in connection with other people; she had never visualized him surrounded by a bevy of sisters and brothers, the idol of doting parents. Instinctively she had recognized in him one of those who stand apart from their fellows, who carve their own destinies unaided. But to think of him standing alone as a little child – oh, it was wicked, it was heartrending!

'Wasn't she nice to you even when you were wee?' she cried.

Owen's eyes grew sombre. It was the first time for years that he had discussed his mother and his feelings were those of a man who strips a bandage from off an ancient wound which he fears will have gone septic for want of cleanly care.

'Nice!' he derided the word. 'I was an only child and she smothered me in devotion, shut me in on affectation of delicate health, from the world. Schools were hotbeds of infection so I never went to one. Playing fields were death-traps, so I saw them only from the top of a bus. She became ill, hysterical if my father argued with her. The tyranny of weakness – that was what it was.'

He stopped, staring into the square. It was dark now and the trams seemed to trundle by more slowly, their energy spent in the turmoil of the day.

'Things came to a head when my father died. I was twenty then and the net was growing tighter and tighter. I had no friends, no life outside four walls. I used to pace my room at night and make plans. God! What plans!' In the haze of cigarette smoke he reconstructed them, smiled at the phantasmagoric picture they presented. 'Then I got a poisoned finger. The doctor, who was seldom out of the house, lanced it for me. He was old and doddering. I'd never paid much heed to him, nor, so far as I know, had he to me. My mother was his friend. She was lying down that night – the sight of my finger had sickened her – and we were alone, he and I, in the library. He scraped the thing clean; then, as the pain went shooting up my shoulder, he laid a heavy hand on it. "Get out, my lad," he said. "Take the bit between your teeth and go." I stared at him in stupefaction. "But my mother?" I stuttered. "Isn't she ill?" "Ill!" he scoffed. "She's no more ill than you or I. I'll tell you, Owen, what I told your father a score of times – if your mother had been a working man's wife with half a dozen children clinging to her skirts there would have been none of this. She's sound, organically sound. Her only disease is selfishness, heart selfishness. And it's no life for you here if you're to remain whole. You've got to get out."'

He stopped short, ringed round by the book-lined shelves of the old, musty-smelling library, conscious once more of the little runnels of moonlight which had eddied through the shutters of the Venetian blinds. Then he became aware of the girl by his side, aware of her flushed, expectant attitude, of the fact that like the writer of a cheap serial he had stopped in the middle of his narrative at the most vital point. With an effort he resumed it.

'We argued the question until all hours. "If I went and anything happened to her I'd feel like a murderer," I told him. "If you stop on you'll merely be shifting the guilt on to other shoulders – she'll be the murderer then," he retorted. I'll never forget that night – the hot needles of pain raging up and down my arm and the prospect of freedom sending me raving mad. I was on fire in every fibre. Next day I booked a passage for the Cape. Frisson, the Danish explorer, as it happened, was one of my fellow passengers. That was the beginning of it all for me.'

'And your mother?' cried Jacqueline, her sympathy reverting to the woman upon whom only a minute ago she had been ready to cry shame.

A whimsical smile lit his eyes. 'Her health improved with my departure. She's in Paris now, interesting herself in a home for orphans.'

Jacqueline's eyes grew moist with pity. A pack of friendless boys and girls as substitutes for a son, and such a son! How awful, how perfectly awful.

She said accusingly: 'And do you write to her, go often and see her?'

The veiled antagonism of her tones amused him.

'Of course,' he assured her gravely. 'We are the best of friends. I admire the work she is doing, refining the orphan riff-raff. And she's been awfully decent about mine, although she doesn't approve of it. She holds that if the Almighty had intended man to discover the Pole, he would have laid down a nice cushy track for him in the beginning. As there is nothing of the sort she considers it downright sacrilegious of us to attempt the going. In her eyes we are on a level with the girl in Bluebeard who persisted in prying into the forbidden chamber.'

Jacqueline laughed, then her thoughts harked back to the days when with no thought of fulfilment he had built his castle of plans.

'All that might have made you a woman-hater,' she pronounced solemnly.

He flirted for a moment with the idea. No, he thought not. For, following the example of his father, he had never regarded his mother as a woman grown. As a child rather, a mental weakling whose whims must for peace's sake be indulged.

'A mob of sisters might have done that, but not one mother,' he disputed. 'As it is, I've been too busy all my life to get to know any woman really well.'

Two imps of mischief entered Jacqueline's eyes.

'Only Mrs Wray,' she said.

'And Miss Jacqueline Thayer.'

'But you don't know me, the real me,' she countered.

He dropped his tone of badinage, looked her in the eyes.

'I'd like to,' he said.

Something in his gaze sent her heart thudding. She grabbed up her gloves, cast an agitated glance at the clock.

'D'you see the time?' she cried. 'It's getting terribly late.'

He called himself a fool as he followed her through the lounge.

CHAPTER XVIII

They lingered for a moment in the entrance while Jacqueline fumbled with the buttons of her gloves. Now, when it was too late, she regretted her precipitancy. For this, she reflected dully, was his last night. She might not see him again for months. And a vision of the circle came to her again, of that monotonous pathway she trod day after day.

She peered out into the darkness. With its gaunt statues, its stealthy paths intersecting the grassy patches, the square looked like a deserted graveyard, dismal as the pit dug by her thoughts. On the edge of it the great blue globules of electricity burned steadfastly, streaking with their pallid searchlights the cobblestone tram track, creating on the grassy stretch beyond a maze of shadows.

Out of it ambled a familiar figure at sight of which Jacqueline's heart constricted. For it was Miss Price who all unconsciously had suggested to her mind the horrific circle, and here like a grotesque ghost haunting the arid ground of her own creation was the old woman herself. Beneath the hard bright lights she staggered uncertainly, stopping every now and then to stare vaguely about her, to exchange a sentence with an invisible companion who walked apparently on her right hand.

As she watched the crazed old figure potter along the kerbstone Jacqueline was conscious of a clutch at her heart. She felt she could feign indifference no longer. She touched Owen's arm.

'That's old Miss Price,' she cried. 'D'you remember I told you about her? She's always rather queer, but tonight she's worse than ever. Let's go after—'

She clapped her hand to her lips in horror, for just then, as though felled by a treacherous blow, Miss Price lurched sideways, slipped, and fell softly on the pavement's edge. A loafer went forward. He was still leering at her with bloodshot eyes when Jacqueline and Owen drew near.

'She's no' deid,' he said sadly, regretful of his inability to provide them with a proper sensation. 'Mebbe she's fou'.'

He slunk back in the shadow, his interest gone. Drunks were a common enough spectacle to him and there was nothing distinctive about this one.

For the fraction of a second Jacqueline hesitated, a feeling akin to affront making her heart dissolve. She had wanted Owen to hold her sex sacred, to regard woman as a white unblemished being, and she felt ashamed, humiliated to the very roots of her being that he should see a member of it in this state. She had the impulse to interpose her body between his and the huddled form on the pavement, to implore him to go away before he could remark the dust-raddled cheeks, the thin, yellow trickle of saliva between the gaping lips, the faint, rather sickening smell that floated towards them. Then shame stung her. What a snob she was. The poor old soul!

Owen laid his fingers on the old woman's pulse, then he looked up at Jacqueline reassuringly.

'She's all right. We'll get her off before a crowd gathers. Do you know whereabouts she lives?'

Fortunately Jacqueline remembered, and in a few minutes with the aid of the loafer who procured from the station an appropriately shabby cab, they were hurtling round the corner out of the square. All her life Jacqueline remembered the details of that ride – the stuffy cab that groaned like a tortured animal as it struggled up the sharp incline; the old woman lying in a huddled heap on the cushions opposite; the small tip-up seats upon which she and Owen were perched and which threatened to dislodge them forcibly at every moment. Once she was thrown almost into his arms. As he released her smilingly, she wondered if he felt as she did, that Miss Price was watching them, prying mockingly out at them from her bleary eyes.

The final jolt of the taxi as it stopped acted like an alarum clock going off at the old woman's ears. She stirred fretfully, opened her eyes.

'S'you,' she said affably to Jacqueline. Then she stared out at the closed door of her abode.

'Home,' she said. 'There's no place like home.' But she showed no inclination to enter its portals. She wept and protested, she called in turn upon the Lord and Jacqueline to protect her when Owen lifted her bodily over the threshold.

In the background a deformed girl stood, watching the little scene. On enquiry she gave voice to the disquieting information: 'They're oot. I'm ma lane.'

Owen glanced at the stair and then at the stupefied old woman. Beyond her drooping head, against the dull red wallpaper, Jacqueline's face was focussed. The sight of its distressed expression decided him. He turned to the gaping child.

'You go ahead,' he commanded, 'and show me the way.' Then, very carefully as though she were an awkward parcel, he gathered Miss Price in his arms. This time she made no demur. Her head lapsed sleepily on his shoulder, strands of her hair sagged out, brushing his face. Following them up the twisted stairway Jacqueline wondered if at the back of her muddled brain the old woman were conscious of a sense of security, if her deep sighs were indicative of content.

On the threshold of Miss Price's bedroom the feeling of shame that had overcome Jacqueline momentarily in the square rushed in on her again. The attic smelled bedroomy. A litter of soiled clothes, of stale rubbish formed a sort of unlovely façade round the walls. There was dirty water in the basin. A torn nightgown lay on the bed. Owen deposited the old woman on it and turned to Jacqueline.

'That's that,' he said. 'She'll sleep it off all right. We may as well go.'

But with an inaudible murmur she shrank back from him out of the light. She could not bear at that moment that he should look her in the face. For shame and pity were contorting her features, making them weak and tremulous. She masked her quivering mouth with her hand, then realized with a twinge of disgust that her fingers, too, were shaking.

She made a pretence of glancing round the room.

'I'll wait and tidy up a bit,' she stammered. And, indeed, there was much need. What a state the place was in! And to think she had brought Owen here . . . What would Mrs Wray say if she knew? The recollection of Mrs Wray as she had seen her last nestling in her frame of sables drove the softness from her heart. The unfairness of things braced her like a douche of cold water. It was the parasitical Mrs Wrays of this world, she told herself, who are responsible for the Miss Prices. She had a momentary impulse to shake an accusing finger in Mrs Wray's face, to tear the silks and laces from off her back, to tell her that it was thievish magpies such as she who, by snatching more than their rightful share of the world's spoil, make derelicts and drunkards of their weaker sisters.

There came a low groan from the bed. With a pang Jacqueline went towards it.

'Are you sure she's all right?'

He nodded. 'Absolutely. She is as light as a feather, poor old thing. Probably she hadn't eaten much all day and a very little went to her head.' He looked round the room. There were no signs of drink about the place, only of poverty, unmitigated poverty. 'God!' he said. 'What a hole! The typical home of the surplus woman.'

A sob broke from Jacqueline's lips. She turned her back on him, her shoulders heaving.

'I'll wait for you,' he said and shot from the room. He dared not, he felt, have trusted himself to stay. And that old woman for all her stupefaction might spy out at them any minute from her half-shut lids.

He encountered the deformed child on the landing.

'May I wait here for my friend?' he asked, pushing open a door that stood ajar.

She assented sourly and stole away. He was a toff. That was clear enough. Mebbe he'd walk off with the candlesticks, mistaking them for genuine. That was the sort of thing, she brooded darkly, toffs did. Well, it wasn't her that was to blame anyway. It was them for it, them that left her by her lane.

In the frowsy back room Owen smiled grimly. What a night! What a house! Its dirt-seamed paper, its bulging walls stank of rot and decay. To his way of thinking a dwelling such as this, semi-detached and still hanging on to the shreds of gentility, was infinitely more tragical than the one-roomed hovels of the destitute. A house of this sort was like a woman whose pride and dignity have been worn down by age and ill-usage, and whose one-time loveliness is blotched by the marks of some hideous disease. This, he reflected, was the kind of place in which 'Reds' are born, the kind of place in which lawless and perverted instincts spring as naturally as daisies in grass. No wonder the old woman upstairs drank. Considering the home she lived in her vice was a remarkably robust and honest one.

He drew a chair to the fireside oblivious of the fact that a heap of dirty yellow and saffron shavings was all the cheer the grate contained. He pulled from his pocket a packet of letters wherewith to beguile the time. But even as he did so, a vision of the ice-maiden rose from out the empty fireplace as she had done a hundred times from out the sea spume to bear him company. He caught his breath as he recognized the patch of purple-black hair that swept her forehead, the passionate perturbation of her eyes.

'Jacqueline,' he said aloud, 'Jacqueline.'

In a neglected heap his letters slid from his hand.

CHAPTER XIX

When Jacqueline came into the room he was staring fixedly at the ornate canopy of the fireplace as though he were photographing upon his mind with infinite pains the copper scrolls that intertwined until they formed an aureole for the podgy copper head.

During the time he had waited there alone his thoughts had doubled on their tracks. Memories, like deep borders of stinging nettles, rose about him, filling him with a vague unease. Scene by scene these memories were linked together in one long irregular chain, starting with that night in the library when the moonlight had silted in through the chinks of the blinds and the doctor had lanced his finger and made him at one and the same time a present of his freedom. Thereafter, like the penny panorama booklets of boxing matches he had bought as a boy, and rejoiced in on the sly, the struggles, the forced surrenders, the lightning conquests he had known flipped his mind's eye.

That night on board the *Afric* . . . Hot as hell it had been in the low-ceilinged saloon, and the ship's whisky had burned the back of his throat like salt on a wound. Despite the jeers of his companions, he had risen determinedly from the card-table, and had flung himself out of the door. Thither the jibes of his opponents – for he was losing – had followed him, cleverly worded taunts calculated to rouse the tiger in him. He had wheeled round on the threshold burning with rage, when a voice outside had uttered a word of warning that had cleared his brain, sent his anger coursing in another direction. These chaps might be sharpers right enough. But what business had this foreign johnny to interfere?

When he wanted a nurse attendant, by the Lord Harry he'd have a Britisher and no blasted foreigner.

On deck a little later he had lurched into his rescuer who had conducted him with due courtesy to a deck chair where, the fires of his wrath allayed by the night air, he had discoursed upon this subject and that until bedtime. Next morning he awaked with the conviction that he had made a fool of himself. As he dressed, and refused breakfast, he tried to eject this conviction from his mind, but in vain. It stayed with him until his friend of the previous night hove in sight, hailed him with a smile. The warmth of it melted Owen's reserve, dispelled his sense of inferiority. He plunged into confession. 'I was losing heavily last night. That vile concoction they call whisky on board . . . I've you to thank for putting me right about those fellows.' Frisson nodded, the smile wiped from his face. 'It is a long time, a very long time since I made my first voyage, but I have not forgot.' He stopped, shrugged his shoulders, let fall an English slang word that rippled oddly from his tongue. 'Strewth! I have not forgot.'

Of South Africa Owen remembered little or nothing. The menacing outline of Table Mountain, the white streets with their surprising aspect of super-civilization had served merely as a background for the personality of the Danish explorer. Incidentally they were the starting point of his own ambition. From that period of his life, the colt period, only one other picture survived – that of a room, blue-painted, heavily curtained, clouded with tobacco smoke; of a bevy of women lightly clad who paraded in and out its maze of little tables, teasing the men who sat drinking at them, tousling on occasion their hair. Curiosity had driven him thither. Nausea drove him thence, a fastidiousness implanted all unwittingly by the chalk-white hand of a painted harridan, springing in his breast.

Later there had been other women. Foreigners for the most part who had angled openly for his favours. And a young English high-school mistress who in a paroxysm of hero-worship had flung discretion and modesty to the winds as a woman on a doomed vessel may in a panic fling her garments. The convulsiveness of her sobs had angered him beyond measure. For he had asked nothing more from her than the common currency of social intercourse and she had wilfully misinterpreted his meaning, falsified his every utterance. Then in a quivering nerve-storm she had grovelled before him, let loose a torrent of impassioned words before which he had grown colder and colder, nauseated as he had been years before by a different form of indecency in the blue-painted parlour in the Cape.

After that experience he had gone out of his way to avoid women, having been awakened to the fact that the pioneer, in common with the pugilist, is a species unknown to the opposite sex and one therefore of a consuming and romantic interest. He had maintained this aloof attitude until after a long voyage he had encountered a Spanish dancer whose stabbing glances had penetrated his defences. After days and nights in the company of a rough-spoken, bearded crew, her lustrous eyes seemed to him rarely beautiful. But always, even in moments of passionate emotion, he had held himself in check, conscious of a curb upon his impulses. As a child he had been woman-ridden. As a man he would be free. And he treasured this freedom of his as a woman treasures her virginity. It was to him the very flower of existence, a sacred bloom he would allow no momentary flick of passion to despoil.

Later there had been Mrs Wray. But while she amused him with her shrewd, daring impertinencies, he recognized her for what she was – a social parasite who in another age might have been a king's mistress. For she belonged to the feline tribe, the cat-women who care not by whose hand they are fed so long as the cream be of a sufficient thickness. For the sake of a sable set or a bauble for her hair, Mrs Wray, he knew well, would dance to any man's piping. She had tried to play upon his sympathy, had hinted plaintively at marital unhappiness. But all the while he had suspected that she and her distinguished-looking rake of a husband were in league to extract all they could out of himself and their other acquaintances no matter at what expense of truth and honour.

Glasgow, certainly, was dull for a woman of Mrs Wray's calibre. The society of the worthy, solid people in which she now found herself bored her intolerably. She welcomed Owen's visits, she told him frankly, as she welcomed bursts of sunshine.

He, for his part, likened her to the gamins who stride alongside you at holiday resorts, turning somersaults for your edification every other moment. And she meant to him neither more nor less than those amateur gymnasts whose antics you reward with smiles and sixpences and straightway forget.

Jacqueline, on the contrary, was unforgettable. He had tried to put her from him, and failed. For matrimony he had long ago decided was not for such as he. Any time he might come home broken in mind and body. There was old Scrabbles . . . Once it had a place in your mind it was not easy to be rid of the picture of old Scrabbles. It was one of those persistent nightmares daylight cannot dispel. Old Scrabbles on one of the worst voyages had been his right-hand man. Then quite suddenly he had gone to pieces. He had wept like a woman at sight of home waters. He had sobbed hysterically when he had boarded the Bristol train. A week later Owen had received a heartbroken letter from his girl wife beseeching him to come at once. He had gone, to be greeted by his former shipmate with a silly smile. 'He went away a man,' the girl had upbraided Owen; 'he has come back a child.' Then she had fallen to weeping. 'It's not fair,' she had cried through her tears. 'Men like you and him have no right to marry.'

And it was truth, Gospel truth. As such Owen acknowledged it. Yet given time, a quiet life, there was every chance, he pointed out, that Scrabbles might recover . . . He grew, however, steadily worse and his wife ran off with another man. Fortunately, her departure meant nothing to her husband. He continued to smile just the same.

No, marriage was not for men such as he. He told himself so again as he stared at the dusty canopy. Then, as Jacqueline appeared at his elbow, a pale ghost of herself, a personification in the flesh of the ice-maiden, all his resolutions scattered before the pain in her eyes. He caught her hands in his, comforting them.

She whimpered like a hurt child. 'The poor old thing! All that makes me frightened of the future.'

Frightened! His little love! He slipped an arm about her

tenderly, mindful that she was no practised experimenter in passionate emotion, no brainless primitive to be taken by storm.

'Won't you let me look after the future?' he said. 'Won't you? Won't you?'

He was pressing her for an answer, forcing the pace. And he hadn't meant to do that. God knew he hadn't meant to rush her. But in another minute his lips must touch hers, his man's strength must measure itself against her soft fragility. That was the worst, he reflected fleetingly, of repression. When you let go . . .

'Won't you?' he said again, and this time in burning agony the words spilled from his lips. Then all at once a perfervid amaze filled him, the dim apprehension of the happening of a miracle. For against his face fell the caress of her hand.

CHAPTER XX

When Jacqueline entered the Grind House next morning her eyes went to the place usually occupied by Miss Price. It was vacant, but almost immediately the door opened to admit the old woman. She ambled towards her accustomed seat, bestowed no look to right nor left. With growing surprise Jacqueline watched her remove the cover from her machine, adjust her copy paper. Her hands to all appearances were no more tremulous than usual, her sight no more defective. Only once in the course of the morning's work did she stop to stare in front of her, her lips moving, her head twitching as though she were being worsted in a lusty bout of argument. Observing her, Jacqueline wondered if she were addressing the invisible companion with whom she had traversed George Square the night before, the treacherous friend who had felled her and fled, leaving her at the mercy of a street loafer.

Her carbon sheet slipped from Jacqueline's hand. She gazed out above the carriage of her machine, lost as Miss Price had been lost a moment before, in her own thoughts. Once again, as though the mere recollection of Owen had a vitalizing effect that stung her senses, she reacted to the memory of his caresses. For the first time in her life she had discovered the sanctuary of a man's shoulder and she had tasted the sense of completion that follows spiritual surrender. For almost an hour they had stayed together in the back room of the lodging house, mute for the most part, merged in the glow of a happiness that had reflected warmly upon the dull apartment, transforming it into a place softly bloomed with shadows, starred with flowers. Above the empty grate the yellow gas-jet had spluttered and fizzled in feeble protest against the cold that threatened to freeze the pipes. Through the door an unsavoury smell of cooking had drifted.

But romance, hardiest of all homogenous plants, thrives even in the sterile haunts of the semi-genteel. And its magic dust lay thick upon their eyes, blinding them to the things about them, translating them into terms of beauty.

Owen, for his part, was conscious that for the first time in his life he had let go the curb that had kept him hitherto from assuming the full responsibilities of a lover, that had restrained him from attaining the full meed of rapture that comes to a man when he regards the future no longer as a lone trail but as a path which it behoves him to make smooth for the feet of his beloved. And he felt an exaltation of spirit so strong as to be almost lifegiving in its intensity. As he held Jacqueline's hand in his, he asked himself – was it contact with her woman's weakness that had inspired in him this fine flush of strength, this illusion of godlike omnipotence? Or was it the mute worship proffered him by her eyes? Whatever its source, this new-found virility of his, he vowed, should be harnessed in her service. It should never do her bodily harm.

Even as he laid this votive offering on the altar of his love, the loose features, the vacant mouth of old Scrabbles rose before him. Doggedly he set about the task of laying his old shipmate's ghost by relating the story of his misfortune.

To Owen's surprise when he had finished Jacqueline sat silent, a smile on her lips the nature of which he could not divine. And again there came to him the impelling desire to explore the cavities of her mind, to drag into light the feminine traits he could not understand. Then he cursed himself for his savagery for, on a sudden, the droop of her head had given him clue to her thoughts. The eternal mother in her had awaked. Just for one moment she was wrapped in contemplation of herself comforting him in her arms as she might a little child.

He choked at sight of her rapt eyes. He wasn't worthy of all she was prepared to give him. In a blaze of panic he writhed inwardly lest she should find this out and fling him back into darkness. Then, bracing himself, he advanced to the confessional.

'I'm not good enough,' he muttered, a dull flush on his cheeks.

She opened her arms with a little crooning murmur. 'Good enough! Oh, my dear . . .'

Later, when they had gone into the quiet street, Jacqueline had recognized that for her henceforth the world was transformed. Burnished with starlight, the little street, darting downwards in an ever narrowing slope, was like the swift clean lunge of a sword plunged lightly into the city's heart.

As she walked Jacqueline held her head higher, conscious that there had come to her a definite purpose in life. To become as perfect a being as he believed her . . . Ah, but it wouldn't be easy. For he didn't look on women as mere appurtenances to men as R. F. Torrance did. To his thinking women were torchbearers. The reflection of their radiance shed light on dark places. They stood at the summit of man's ambition, bidding him advance although danger threatened. And when he had attained the farthermost peak, then – and then only – did they give him rest within the fastness of their arms.

She sighed. She slipped with her forefinger the paper in her machine. He would be speeding towards Carlisle now. 'Fair fa's the sun on Carlisle's walls.' . . . She wondered what kind of people would be in the compartment with him. She hoped his fellow travellers were men, not women. The type of woman who travels first-class on a long journey is always so terribly immaculate. Soft eyes looking out of a misty veil, swan-neck ankles sheathed in silk . . . As like as not, she'd be too fragile with her way of it to hoist down her own attaché case from the rack, she'd appeal to him with a little helpless gesture. And he'd recognize as she stood erect, swaying with every movement of the train like a dancer waiting her turn to pirouette to the centre of the stage, the lissome grace of her, the perfumed elegance . . .

With a little grunt of disgust Jacqueline jammed the brake on her imagination. What a fool she was, jealous of a woman who in all probability didn't exist!

When she opened the door of her room that night an unaccustomed sweetness smote her on the threshold. As she lit the gas she gave a little gurgle of delight, for upon her table lay a great bunch of perfumed blossoms – pheasant-eyed lilies with velvety hearts of burnished amber, parma violets conjuring up for their beholders little painted images of southern skies and blue waters, pale yellow daffodils wet with dew, their drooping bells harbouring the crystal beads of a morning frost, frail sprays of milk-white lilac, tokens these last of the evanescent spirit of spring as it manifests itself in the north to set against the riper blues and purples of the south.

Most precious of all was the message attached to the flowers. This she fondled with her fingertips, slipped into the folds of her dress. When she stooped it emitted a faint rustle that filled her with a secret rapture. In the long ago she remembered the rustle of a paper poke similarly concealed had been wont to thrill her with the knowledge that she had still one chocolate left . . . She smiled when she recalled her solemn greed in the matter of sweets, the gambler's instinct that had caused her to hoard on occasion her pennies and to expend them all at once on a 'surprise packet' in the hope of finding within something more delectable than she had ever dreamed.

Life was pretty much like a surprise packet. A collection of ordinary things like trekking out on wet days and taking off your shoes to dry when you came in, and 'tea-ing' in town for a treat. Her meeting with Owen was the delectable you rarely found, the delectable after which she had hankered all her life. Her mother, she reflected sorrowfully, had been cheated out of that something. Her surprise packets had contained only makeshifts, second bests.

Later that evening she walked through the park along Sauchiehall Street to Lowerbank Street. The rain had stopped but the streets still glimmered pitch black in the brittle light. It was one of Glasgow's rarely beautiful nights, a night peculiar to the Second City when the steamy humidity of the day seems to have sweated all the excrescence out of the haggard concaves of its commercial buildings. Above the inky pools of blackness they rose – dim, mysterious as the palaces of the Doge with here and there the staring eyes of a lamp, rapacious as a forest beast, swung out in front of the retiring portals, violating the remote dignity, the ecclesiastical austerity of the old grey stones. Intersecting these grave exteriors tenement fronts showed like flippant curtains pricked by a dozen varying lights, each unshuttered window exposing a coloured slide and a cameo of home life – a man in shirt sleeves lathering his chin with foamy soap, a woman red with rage screaming at someone unseen, a stack of greasy dishes over which the head of a pale child bent laboriously.

Above the tenements the night clouds were parted as though slit in twain by a rusty blade and a copper glow smouldered in the hollow, fusing it with the high chimneys and the cauldron of the lighted thoroughfare below. Along it, like ships in full sail, the splendidly lit trams swayed and curveted, their trolleys clinging delicately to the twin wires suspended overhead. Far into the distance these silvering wires stretched – twinkly-white as a twin necklace of platinum to which the raindrops adhered like baroque pearls.

Enchanted country the undulating street with its balloons of white light swung high over the cobblestones, enchanted country with the shuffle of feet, the smothered clanging of bells, the frenzied note of the traffic swelling upwards in a perfervid carousal of sound. To the tune of it, the tune of the city's pipes, Jacqueline betook herself through the lighted maze of Charing Cross down the hill that led to Lowerbank Street. She had left it a frightened child stalked by a mystery she did not understand. She was returning to it a woman grown, flushed with the consciousness of a woman's power.

The blinds of her old home were drawn, but behind the shrunken holland was a sea of light. There was a brass plate on the door. As she went up the steps to read it the thin jet of a fiddle trickled out, audible corroboration of the fact that the Misses French were 'Teachers of Dancing' as the black lettering proclaimed.

Jacqueline listened in a kind of dream to the shuffling movements of the dancers, the insistent beat of the pianoforte. Above it all she could hear her mother's voice shrill with pain: 'Second best, Jacqueline. That's what my life has been made up of.'

That, seemingly, was what most women's lives were made up of. Only the other day Nessie had confided to her that Bert was none too steady . . . Poor Nessie! Funny how persistently the world of women revolved round that of men. Funny – she said the word aloud, misusing it in the familiar Scots fashion which causes folk to use it with no thought of jocularity.

Funny! The word prolonged itself on her lips to accord with the fitful breeze of the dance music which dipped and then soared again, a gust of melody in her ears.

Dear God, how happy she was! She danced down the steps she had once trodden so sorrowfully.

CHAPTER XXI

The perfume of Owen's flowers lulled Jacqueline to sleep that night to dream of the meadowsweet that starred Kirkton's fields, of the bright buttons of blooms that flowered miraculously in vivid patches upon the stony slopes of the castle crags. In a slumberous drowse she spun the web of her future, a web of shot-silk dazzlingly irradiated.

Once only in her dreams of the future did the demon of melancholy lay heavy fingers on her eyelids. The expedition was due to depart. The ship had weighed anchor and the waters beyond the bay were rolling queasily, yellow and greenish red as though they had been sprayed with blood and boiling oil. Owen had strained her tightly in his arms and then he had turned abruptly on his heel and left her to go ashore alone.

As she climbed the perpendicular hillock of the gangway a man brushed past her. She had stopped dead, looking back at him and as though conscious of her regard he, in his turn, stopped and looked back at her. Then he smiled and by his smile she knew him – old Scrabbles whose soft silly smile had driven his girl wife to seek shelter in another man's arms. And she had uttered a wild cry that sent a white gull wheeling in distress above the basin of the bay, that caused a group of dock labourers to lift their heads and to stare at her. But old Scrabbles never stirred. He stood motionless, smiling, smiling.

When she awoke she extended her fingers to caress the daffodils that browsed closest to her bed. Then as her eyes, roving the room, realized its fresh loveliness she tore at herself for selfishness. The idea of her having so many and never thinking to share them!

She took an armful of flowers with her to the Grind House. Half she pressed on Nessie, the remainder on Miss Price. In the dim light of the passage the old woman eyed her strangely.

'I had nightmare the night afore last,' she mumbled. 'You were in it, you and a strange young man. He carried me up a stair, a long dark stair, but he was giving never a thought to me. It was you all the time was in his mind.'

She stepped closer to Jacqueline and emitted a malevolent chuckle.

'You'd best look out,' she said. 'I worked it out on my cards this morning. The Black Jack was uppermost every time.'

'The Black Jack?' repeated Jacqueline, mystified.

The old woman nodded, proud of her ability to curdle young blood.

'That means death or misfortune. You had better beware the dark young man.'

Mr Shaw, who was passing, overheard the words. What impelled him to pause he did not know, possibly the consciousness that the atmosphere was weighed by something unpleasant, possibly the look in Jacqueline's eyes.

'Like me to fire the junior clerk?' he exclaimed. 'He's a swarthy beggar and no mistake.'

The lightness of his words broke the spell. Jacqueline laughed and escaped. For once in her life as she unlocked her machine she said 'Thank you' to God for Mr Shaw.

The sense of disquietude awakened by the old woman's words stayed with her until she reached home and descried on the mantelpiece an envelope in Owen's handwriting. Tucking one foot beneath her on a chair she settled down to the delicious business of devouring its contents. As she did so her excited imagination staged each scene of his journey, each happening, touched upon however lightly by the writer.

His arrival at Bristol, his meeting with So-and-so, his call upon the business magnate who had professed himself eager to share in the financial responsibilities of the next voyage. Incidentally, the magnate had rather an amusing device in his study, a dog's kennel containing an animal who at a shout of 'Towser' bounded forth from his painted doorway . . . For a moment Jacqueline played with the idea of the dog Towser, of the grey-bearded company promoter who was not above having a toy in his study. Then her eyes lit and lingered on a line in the next page. He was going the next day to see old Scrabbles. The poor old chap was worse. The doctor wanted to certify him insane.

Old Scrabbles. She hadn't liked his smile when, in her dream, he had stared back at her. She sat very still, the pulse at her heart she used to call a little bird beating hotly against her ribs. Owen was going to see old Scrabbles tomorrow, he had written. That was today, this morning. By now he would be back in the Bristol hotel. The thought of that hotel comforted her. There was such an atmosphere of ordered harmony about these big hotels, a superb normality that warred against the intrusion of an old Scrabbles. She could imagine the lounge with its rows of little tables, its scatter of newspapers, and at the far end the homely click-click of a tape machine trickling out the latest quotations from the Stock Exchange. Impossible that anything untoward should happen in such surroundings. Impossible, impossible!

She glanced at the clock. Ten minutes past seven. The lounge would be emptying now, spilling its contents into the glittering *salle à manger*. In the bottlenecked doorway the head waiter would be directing the traffic of diners, controlling the vortex of incomers and outgoers with regal gesture. And the air would be glutted with the smell of rich warm food and tinctured by the slightly sour flavour of sparkling wine. And somewhere, perhaps, a band would be playing . . . She rocked her shoulders to its melody, resisted the impulse that bade her bury her head in her hands and cry. For his letter was lovely, but she was lonely. Bristol was – how many miles away?

She opened a drawer in search of a handkerchief. Alongside her case lay a notebook containing her last poems. She drew it out, ruffled at random its pages. Immediately her critical faculties awoke. Unreal, up in the clouds, mazy-Annie sort of stuff her verses seemed to her now. Lacking in what R. F. Torrance had been wont to call the red corpuscles. She crouched beside the fire poring over the written words. They were colourful enough, but she realized they held more of sound than sense.

She closed the book with a sigh. So much for her rotten poetry! She had essayed writing before she had known the first thing about life. Who was it who opined that nobody should write a novel before he was fifty? That was as may be. Certainly no woman should attempt to write poetry until she had emerged from the chrysalis stage, until she had experienced the glow of contentment that comes of giving up the keys of self into another's keeping. That, strangely enough, instead of barring the door upon self-development was the surest way of opening it wider. For through the eyes of another, life reveals itself in a thousand different aspects, little gemmed facets, bright as fire.

Falling in love with Owen she realized had meant for her a quickening of the senses, an increased urgency in the habitual demand she made upon life. It meant a sudden efflorescence of spirit that gave off a dazzling aroma like that of the soft yellow balls of mimosa crushed hard in the hand. In the intensity of its sweetness she revelled fiercely, full of an exultation that riddled her being, set aside all thought of self.

She laid down her book. So much for that! Writing was all very well. But she had Owen. To become as perfect as he believed her was going to be an all-time job. In the meantime she must read more, get hold of some decent books. Newspapers, too. The leaders in the *Herald* were said to be awfully educative. Music. He was keen on music. She, for her part, didn't know Debussy from Irving Berlin . . . Would an occasional manicure be ruinous? Amateurs, she had heard Mrs Wray declare, never quite got the look.

She employed the next half-hour polishing her fingernails. Then, as a newsboy ran screeching up the street she went to the window, rapped upon it briskly with her chamois pad. He delivered a paper to her on the doorstep, and because she was happy and it was still raining outside, and his feet were bare and bleeding, she pressed a sixpence upon him in place of the right coin.

She went upstairs humming to herself the refrain she had heard that night in the theatre with Owen and the Wrays. 'Love, Love, follow the gleam of it . . .' Ah, she'd be bold and start straight off with the leader, the longest and stuffiest she could see. But before she had found it a line in the stop-press had ripped her mind, leaving it a gaping wound of agony and despair.

CHAPTER XXII

With fingers that wobbled and refused to stay quiet Jacqueline flung on her hat, fumbled at her coat buttons. The holes were too small. Funny, she'd never noticed that before! Gloves – wherever had she left her gloves? Oh, but what did gloves matter so long as this wound at her heart might be staunched?

She gulped at something that stuck like a bite of raw apple in her throat. Then turning, she caught sight of herself in the glass. Strange how you can come through hell and yet look the same as you did before its jaws have savaged you. Nessie or Miss Price meeting her would know no difference . . . Owen might. Owen . . . The sound of his name steadied her. She slipped back again into the comforting illusion that had insinuated itself in a wheedling murmur through the tumult raging about her head. 'It couldn't be true – it couldn't be true.' . . . She had his letter here, delivered only a few hours before . . . Newspapers exaggerated everything. There might have been a fuss, a fracas of sorts, for old Scrabbles was mad, mad as a hatter. She had known that when he had looked back at her and smiled . . .

Up the street there reverberated the swinging sound of a half-empty tramcar. She ran after it, boarded it breathlessly. Funny to sit still and calm, looking out of the window opposite as if nothing had happened. Ah, but nothing has, she told herself, gulping on the sour apple in her throat. It can't be true, it can't . . .

A penny fare, or was it three halfpennies? She didn't know. It didn't matter anyhow. Good-humouredly, another passenger argued the point with her. 'A ha'penny's better in our ain pockets nor in the Corporation's. The Corporation takes plenty aff us as it is.'

'Does it?' said Jacqueline, bound by her own reflections.

The woman looked at her and snapped: 'I'm thinkin' you're nut a ratepayer.'

Ratepayer! The word penetrated the mist clouding Jacqueline's mind. It was a nice normal word to pit against that abnormal monstrosity, murder. It was reminiscent, that word ratepayer, of portly, bald-headed men, of discreetly décolleté women, their noses shining purplish-blue through a hasty smudge of face powder. It was of a piece with the lounge of the Bristol hotel with its litter of tables, its carefully folded newspapers. In such an atmosphere, death would seem a sheer indecency. And yet somewhere, sometime, somebody must die in a hotel. She sat for a time contemplating the fact, then miserably her thoughts scuttled down another glooming alley. Life was so short, so pitifully uncertain – how did anyone dare to make plans for the future, to say as she had said: 'We'll write and tell Uncle Archie when you come back, we'll beg him to come to town to meet us for the day.' Old Scotswomen, she knew, had a way of adding 'If we're spared.' Ah, they were wise, those old women! They had eaten of the husks of experience.

The guard touched her arm. 'Hyndland Cross, you said, didn't you?'

She tumbled out of the car. Her limbs were shaken, her feet stone cold. It was a mercy she hadn't far to go. Mrs Wray's house was the first in the terrace. She recognized the curious Siamese lantern outside. She rang the bell, essayed a frantic boggling with fate as she stood waiting in the hall. If something must have happened, let him be maimed, hurt, blinded, only let him live, let him live . . .

Mrs Wray came running downstairs.

'Miss Thayer, how d'you do? Come into the library. It's Miss Thayer, Harold. You remember – Owen's friend?'

The good-looking rake she had tried to talk to in the theatre rose from the fireside, made a gesture of welcome. She sat down, and a wave of terror overcame her, choking her utterance. For these people knew something as she had surmised they would. They knew – but what she dared not ask. On that instant she prayed that they would tell her nothing, that they would let her keep the last shred of hope she had garnered so painstakingly about her. She clung to that hope as to a garment the abandonment of which would expose her to a mortal blow.

It was coming. She nerved herself to meet it, to hide from their watching eyes the awfulness of her hurt. Only let him live, she implored, until I see him again . . .

'Tragic business this about our friend Southwold,' Mr Wray was saying.

She clung to the rail of the armchair. Draggingly the words came out:

'That was why I came. I thought you – you would probably know the truth – what truth there is in the newspaper rumour.' Rumour. She was pleased with herself for remembering the word. Rumour. Yes, that was the way to dispose of that outrageous line in the stop-press.

Mr Wray hesitated. 'I was on the phone with Mr Durton of Dumbarton a minute ago. They had rung through to Bristol, got details.' He flicked the ash off his cigarette with excessive deliberation. 'Seems he'd gone out to see an old shipmate, Scrabble or some such name. They'd been walking round the garden together when the fellow went right off his head, seized a gardener's knife, struck Owen in the back. A man passing saw him fall. Instantaneous, the doctor said.'

So it was true. No good that voice in her brain keeping on shrieking it can't be true, it can't be true. No good huddling over the fire hoping for warmth. There was no warmth to be found anywhere any longer.

She rose, swayed towards the door. Mrs Wray caught her arm.

'Don't go like that. You're upset, and no wonder. It's ghastly, horrible!'

She dabbed her eyes with her handkerchief, dallying with an emotion that was obviously surface, while Jacqueline stared at her with unseeing eyes. If only she had turned back and thrown herself upon old Scrabbles! But that, she told herself, was a dream. Perhaps this, too, was another nocturnal horror and she would awake from it sweating with terror but safe – safe with Owen's letter next her heart.

She shook herself free of Mrs Wray's burble of talk; accepted, because he forced it upon her, Mr Wray's company to the tram terminus, heard as he said good night, his encouraging 'Steady on. Things won't look so black in the morning.' From force of habit she tendered her fare to the conductor, followed some ten minutes later in the wake of her fellows who descended *en masse* at George's Cross. The sky sign wasn't working yet. The horizon was black. Very slowly she went up Hentzau Street.

Alone in the darkness she sat contemplating the future. On and on it stretched – an arid road with never a rift of light. And always this gnawing ache, this memory of the might-have-been, pricking like a goad in her side. That morning – that last morning. If only she had clung to him, implored him to stay! If only she had wound her arms round his neck, told him how much she cared . . . Looking back upon it now she realized that their parting had held in it all the elements of finality. He had gazed at her eyes, her hair, her lips in the wan light in the hall as though he were trying to engrave on his mind every line of her features. He had repeated her name softly as a man in the throes of death may repeat the name of the Virgin Mary. He had said it without passion, without emotion or ardour, only with such a world of reverence in his voice as to make her livid with shame that she was not worthier to wear this crown of worship which he had bestowed upon her.

Round and round in an anguished circle her thoughts fluttered, torn at every point by regret for the things she had left undone, the little loving words she had never uttered. In a passionate effort to lessen the darkness that enfolded her spirit she chid herself for that coldness. Sheer *Scotchness* – that was what it had been. The fear of letting herself go that impels an emotional person to simulate indifference when all the while a thousand feelings are crying out for utterance . . . They kept belabouring her, like little hammers, these feelings, raining down curses upon her sluggish blood, creating in the dim room a harsh unseemly din. Dawn was piercing the black coffined slit of her window when it subsided. In the queer unnatural silence that followed she grew sick with fear. Without Owen her world was empty . . . Oh, God, that she should be left in this wilderness alone!

PART II

CHAPTER XXIII

Death, thought Jacqueline as she lit the gas, comes in a sort of epidemic.

With the taper still alight in her hand she leaned against the table listening to the sound of movement overhead. Poor old Uncle Archie! He had professed himself tired, had promised to go to bed, and there he was pacing to and fro, to and fro . . . She longed to go to him, to throw her arms around his neck, to soothe him out of the fullness of her strength. But as her mind followed him back and forward on his aimless journeys she realized with a momentary feeling of strangulation at her throat that it wasn't her touch he hungered for, that no token of affection could give him comfort.

She blew out the taper, snuffed it with irresolute fingers. The room looked forlorn tonight as though like a faithful animal it were fretting for its mistress. The sweet sickly smell of hothouse flowers blown in from the hall still clung to the plush curtains, to the heavy folds of the overmantel. A minute trickle of tea-bread crumbs encircled that end of the table where the minister had sat, munching steadily the while old Bailie Macfarlane had striven with a heavy hand to uplift the dispirited banner of the conversation. In the end, wiping the butter off his long moustache with the back of his hand, he had owned himself vanquished. 'Aye, aye,' he had said, rising abruptly, 'things must aye be someway.' And he had made for the door, overcome by emotion or the desire – Jacqueline wasn't sure which – for a stronger brew than the now tepid tea of his neighbour. Thereafter, one by one, the others had dwindled away, leaving only the disordered table as reminder of their presence.

Jacqueline had had the unhappy conviction as she gathered the plates together – what a mess of jam Mr Macfarlane had left on his! – that the meal had been a mistake. It had only prolonged the agony. For no one had known what to talk about, least of all Uncle Archie. He had pressed food upon his guests indiscriminately; he had passed cups of tea with hands that trembled. And then on a sudden he had uttered a loud shuddering sigh that had robbed the table of its air of decent decorum and imposed upon the vision of his friends the primitive spectacle of a raw sore.

After a second's palpitating silence the minister had cast a veil over it by fluttering aloft the threads of a fresh topic of conversation. The new glebe. He didn't think much of it. Marsh ground one half. The others had backed him by setting up a noisy chorus: 'D'you tell me so? Is that a fac'?' Only among his fellows, Uncle Archie sat apart, prisoned in the stocks of grief, a sorry sight with affrighted eyes and blue-tinged cheeks from which in pity his guests turned their gaze. Yes, the meal had been a mistake. But Aunt Ruth, said Uncle Archie, would have liked it. So for Aunt Ruth's sake it had been provided – a memorial in the form of a meat tea served on the snow-white plains of her best tablecloth.

To and fro, to and fro . . . Uncle Archie was still pacing the room trying to secure rest for his mind in the exhaustion of his body. The sound of his dragging footsteps made Jacqueline's heart ache. So had she, too, tried to cheat herself into the belief that her limbs were weary, so had she tried to lull the cry that would not be stilled.

She pressed her cheek against the worn flap of the armchair. How quiet the square was after Hentzau Street! It was only a fortnight since she had left her lodgings, but so intensively had she lived during these last few days that time seemed to have exacted from her a treble toll.

Only a fortnight ago she had risen from bed, her head light with lack of sleep, and had said: 'A year ago today since Owen – since it happened. It's getting easier to bear.' Then a tearless sob had torn her throat. For it wasn't getting easier – to her tongue her heart gave back the lie. It was just as bad. And in a tempest of mutinous sobs she had cried: 'I can't bear it – I can't!'

Just then a knock had fallen on her door. And a spark of hope had flickered up in her to burn out as swiftly as it had arisen in a fierce little twist of pain. For miracles, she told herself bitterly, don't happen nowadays.

Mechanically she had risen from her crouched position by the bed to open the door. In Mrs MacAndrew's hand there had been a yellow envelope. Jacqueline tore it open, then a deep flush had overspread her brow. For she whom she had thought in her hours of desolation nobody wanted was wanted now. Uncle Archie wanted her – wanted her so badly that he had telegraphed without counting the number of words. 'Your Aunt Ruth taken ill. Very serious. Come immediately at once.' For a second Jacqueline had stood on the threshold, tearing the form into tiny pieces. Aunt Ruth, with her upper lip twitching well-nigh up to her nostrils, her face featureless with rage – Aunt Ruth ill! There was something grotesque in the thought.

It was not until a few days after her arrival at Kirkton that Jacqueline had become acutely conscious of an alien presence in the little house – Death, waiting, watching, manifesting his nearness in sundry little intimate ways – in the smell of toilet vinegar pervading the landing, in the low eerie peal of the muffled doorbell.

Like a distraught ghost Uncle Archie haunted the sickroom.

'She's a bittie better the day,' he would nod cheerfully to the indeterminate figure hunched below the bedclothes. And Aunt Ruth would stare back at him out of eyes grown strangely clouded as though to say, 'Hark at him, poor fool! Why does nobody tell him I'll never be better – never?'

One day when Jacqueline was tending her she stretched out her hand and caught at her niece's. The look in the tired eyes caused the girl's heart to move queerly. Through her mind sped the thought: 'She wants to say she's sorry, sorry for having suspected me of—'

Acting upon impulse she dropped on her knees beside the bed, kissed the toilworn hand.

'You're thinking of that – that night near Drymen, of what Sophia told you, aren't you? I was there with a man. But it was all right. I mean, there wasn't anything, really. But I don't wonder you doubted me. I'm sorry—' Her voice broke as the tired eyes brimmed over with tears of thankfulness and the fingers that lay in hers moved in a mute caress.

She rose softly, fearful of the effects of overexcitement on the invalid. But her pulses were thudding. To think that Aunt Ruth had really minded as much as all that! Oh, what a fool, a silly blind fool she had been to fling out of the house that morning, letting her silence convict her, instead of refuting Sophia's insinuations right away!

Seeing her aunt after this long absence, Jacqueline thought she had the appearance of one for whom the struggle to live has become too harsh, and who has embraced quiescently the decision to give it up without further effort. Uncle Archie was the sole link that bound her to the things of this world. Gradually it seemed as though this link weakened, grew less. One night she ignored him when he nodded at her as usual. Within an hour she was dead. And on that instant the terrible tension that had racked the household snapped. Time all at once was of no account. Jacqueline was conscious of an overwhelming desire for sleep. Uncle Archie alone seemed unable to stay quiet.

He was moving about upstairs still. His footfalls were like blows directed upon her breasts . . . Nine, ten, eleven, twelve months since Owen – oh, Uncle Archie, take comfort, it will be – it *is* easier in twelve months' time.

CHAPTER XXIV

To be a cog in a wheel is fifty times easier than to be the mistress of a little house. Very quickly Jacqueline arrived at this conclusion. The inefficiency of the daily maid who had succeeded Jessie filled her with amaze. For the first time in her life she came into contact with the cruel snobbery of the servant class. And the continual pinpricks frayed her temper, imbued her with irritation at the octopus claims made upon her by this five-room and kitchen house.

At times, abetted by the 'daily' whose unspoken motto appeared to be, 'What's the use of doin' much? The place doesn't look onything anyway when a's done,' Jacqueline would lapse into indifference. Rising late, she would move about the house listlessly. When night came she would lie awake, reliving the hours she had spent with Owen. Sometimes she would drop off to sleep at early morning, to dream that the long voyage was well-nigh over, and that tidings had reached her that he was hastening to her side. Upon wakening, her agony was acute. In the effort to check her sobs, to escape the feeling of hopeless longing that weighted her, she would rise early, rush about the cold grey rooms. But at such times her energy seemed without purpose. She would essay one task, leave it unfinished, fly to another which, in its turn, she would suddenly abandon.

Then, jogging her elbow, would arise the spectre of Aunt Ruth, the perfect housewife, spurring her to action. The drawing-room – she could see Aunt Ruth's brows meet in sorrowful condemnation of its unkempt state. The meat-safe – she could hear Aunt Ruth's audible sniff of disgust as she descried the untidy heap of scraps left to waste on a dusty plate. The tradespeople spoke of

Mrs Forsyth with awe and respect. 'Your aunt would never have been ta'en with the like of that,' the butcher opined lugubriously when Jacqueline, after scant deliberation, had selected a joint. 'Your aunt kenned a prime cut when she saw one.'

Yes, she was a disappointing understudy upon all counts, Jacqueline recognized. Even Uncle Archie accepted her services disparagingly. 'Yon tax papers?' he would cry suddenly. 'Are they paid yet?' And upon her confessing that they were not because she wasn't sure whether the full amount was due on the first or the second date, he would shake his head as though deploring the feebleness of her intellect while frankly admitting ignorance of the matter in question himself. 'Your aunt looked after all that. She had the business head of the family.'

Thereon his face would pucker up and grow scarlet like that of a small child who, mindful of the admonitions of its elders, is fighting a natural inclination to cry. At such times Jacqueline always ached to coax him with endearing phrases until the pinpoints of moisture melted from his eyes. But her affectionate gestures, she was quick to note, embarrassed him. Aunt Ruth had been undemonstrative and such tokens of endearment as Jacqueline proferred took the old man by surprise, causing him to eye her with suspicion and to doubt whether she weren't too fond to be sensible. Ruth, he recalled, had all her days been sensible. Even before they were married she had upbraided him for his habit of buying Forfar rock – a famous sweetmeat – on Saturdays. It would, she hinted, be far more sensible for him to be saving up for a bit furniture . . .

Their first joint purchase had been a rocking-chair, an uncouth object, but possessed, as the youthful salesman who had disposed of it to them had pointed out, of 'a rare swing'. For years that swing had intrigued them and always when Aunt Ruth was indulging in it he would nod at her and say: 'Better nor Forfar rock, eh, wumman?' Aye, Ruth all her days had been sensible, real sensible. It was only in her last hours that her face had lost its shrewd expression, that her eyes had grown bemused. That, maybe, was because even then she was peering into the Unseen . . . He wondered how she was getting on with the lot of them up there.

She had a way of sorting folk that might not be looked upon with favour by the Lord. No, he couldn't picture her in celestial regions at all with a harp and wings. Ruth who all her days had despised trollopy fal-lals. Jacqueline now, would look quite the thing in them. There was a kind of Frenchifiedness about her that made her different from other folk. Of late he had thought she was getting to resemble her mother. There was the same look about the eyes, a driven look . . .

He glanced over at his niece where she sat, the white disc of her face rimmed by the shadow of the fireglow. Maybe her black dress was to blame for that look. Maybe it was just his fancy. Nobody and nothing seemed to him to be looking over-blithe these days. Certainly Jacqueline wasn't so bonny as her aunt, with her ripe plum complexion, had been at her age. Still there was some, no doubt, who might fancy her.

Abruptly he broke silence. 'The bailie was telling me his son William's coming home the night from London. D'you mind on him, Jacqueline?'

She shook her head. The only male in Kirkton who had impressed himself upon her mind was the teacher assistant at the commercial class, who had waited for her in vain that Sunday in the square.

'The bailie used to blow a lot about William. He was a harum-scarum rascal as a laddie. Your Aunt Ruth couldn't abide him.' He sighed, and the skin of his gnarled old face wrinkled into a pitiful fretwork. Jacqueline regarded him compassionately. This was a very different Uncle Archie from the jovial little soul who had taken her to a picture house on the sly and had chortled with mirth at the oncarry of a dusky comedian. An idea occurred to her.

'Uncle Archie,' she said, deliberately plaintive, 'Kirkton's awfully quiet after Glasgow. I wish you'd take me to a cinema one night.'

He stared at her in surprise, doubtful of the decorum of the request.

'Is it not ower soon?' he said. Then he pulled himself up. The lassie was feeling Kirkton dull. That accounted for the driven look. 'Hoots,' he cried, 'that doesn't matter if we've the mind for it. What about going the night? We'll slip in at the back and nobody'll notice us. And if we meet anyone that knows us on the way home we'll just let on we've been out for a bit saunter.'

They met no one on the way home, only from the gates of the big house opposite glimmered the lights of a cab. Out of it a young man alighted, calling a greeting to someone who was advancing down the steps to meet him. From the open door light gushed in a warm stream, transforming the tree-shadowed path into a shining corridor.

As the young man swung up it Jacqueline stared. So like to Owen's was the easy gait, the slight sturdy figure, that for one moment of madness she believed the miracle had come to pass. Her lips cleaved to her teeth else she would have called aloud to him, but so strong in her was the sense of his nearness that she felt there was no need for speech. He would divine the thoughts she could not utter. In an inarticulate murmur his name broke from her lips.

Uncle Archie edged nearer. 'What's that you're saying?'

On that instant her heart froze. She tucked her hand into his arm while he lingered, innocently curious, beside the cab.

'It's too cold to loiter,' she urged; but in vain. The bailie's son was back, directing the cabman about this and that. Just for a moment he turned in their direction, killing her reminiscence, for, facially, he bore no resemblance to Owen. His skin was sallow, his eyebrows bushy and his features expressionless, as though he wiped every vestige of feeling off them each morning when he shaved. His eyes alone betrayed his youth. They were round and enquiring like a child's. Unexpectedly he swept off his hat.

'Hullo, Mr Forsyth,' he sang out cheerfully. 'I've just got home.'

'So I see, man, so I see,' stammered Uncle Archie, startled by the unceremonious greeting and at being caught out in the act of spying upon his neighbour's cab. 'Ah, well, you'll be over one of these days with your father most likely?'

The young man looked at Jacqueline as he responded, and for the second time that day she was reminded of the youth who had signalled a message to her with his eyes above the bowed heads of the pupils of the commercial class.

Uncle Archie inserted the key in the door lock.

'If William comes over the morn with the bailie, we don't need to say where we were.' Then, lighting the gas in the hall, he opined: 'A wise-like lad, William. But I wonder what's brought him to Kirkton the now?'

The following evening Jacqueline was ironing in the kitchen when the bell rang. The bailie, doubtless, and William . . . She opened the door and a gushing young woman bore down on her.

'Jacqueline dear! The same as ever, I do declare!'

The light of welcome waned in Jacqueline's eyes. There was no change in Rosie Farrell either – she could see that at a glance. With an effort she infused some degree of cordiality into the tepid tones of her voice.

'Uncle Archie, you remember Rosie Farrell? We were at school together at Miss Cree's.'

Uncle Archie rose, extended an awkward greeting; then he wavered towards a chair at the far end of the room. Rosie's grandeur was overpowering. It got on his nerves. He never remembered seeing a woman with as many jingling bangles in his life!

Looking at the visitor's extravagant attire Jacqueline recalled the quiet elegance of Mrs Wray. She was still recalling it when above the shrill uproar of Rosie's chatter there echoed the emphatic ping of the bell. It was William this time, and Jacqueline, ushering him in, observed with a sort of secret shame the colour mount to Rosie's cheeks, the crudity of the wiles wherewith she sought to attract him.

A queer game of cat and mouse it was – Rosie, her eyes humid with excitement, advancing and retreating, riveting William's attention with some bait of saccharine flattery, forfeiting it again by a gesture of over-friendliness from which he fled in evident distaste. Once or twice he rounded upon her, threw back such sallies as to silence even her babbling tongue, but for the most part he was content to play the game, to retreat when she tended to go too far, to wriggle a little and to lure her on when she showed signs of tiring, to lie prone at her mercy when her audacity was checked by a timely interjection from Uncle Archie.

Jacqueline looked on fascinated. She had never before seen a woman exploit all her stock in trade in a barefaced attempt to subjugate a man. Almost it was as if Rosie were a determined saleswoman who was forever delving into this drawer and that, producing silks and satins to flutter before the beholder's eyes – bright glances, contagious sighs, sudden unexpectedly flamboyant smiles. Jacqueline wondered if William were aware that this glowing merchandise was all displayed for his benefit, whether or not he approved any of it. There was, she surmised, something of the mountebank in his composition. He was quite capable, she knew instinctively, of simulating an enjoyment he was far from feeling. And yet, she reflected, he must be enjoying himself or he would rise and go.

Rosie made the first move.

'Dear me,' she said, with a sidelong look at the blinded windows. 'It's dark already. I hate the streets at nights. So rough with all these soldiers about. D'you go my way, Mr Macfarlane?'

The game, so far as William was concerned, was ended. Bluntly he asserted himself. But, although his cavalier disclaimer made Jacqueline squirm, Rosie, apparently, did not notice it, for she lingered, praising him, in the hall.

He stayed until after eleven. By the time he left Jacqueline had accorded him a free pardon – he was so wonderful with Uncle Archie. With no apparent effort he had moved the old man to mirth as uproarious as the dusky comedian of the screen. With a gesture or two he etched for them a series of lifelike portraits, mimicking deliciously the Cockney whine of this person, the wheezing solecisms of the next until they moved before one – grotesque figures of fun jogging hereaway, thereaway, with every hitch of his shoulders, every jerk of his tongue.

When the door closed upon him Uncle Archie wiped his eyes. He hadn't laughed so much since— Man, that was a rare one about the old woman and the champagne bottle! He let slip a chuckle, cleared his throat in a shamefaced attempt to cover it.

'Hm – hm! A fine gift of the gab has William.' He turned the key in the door, affixed the safety chain beneath the lock. Then once again he ruminated aloud: 'I wonder what's brought him to Kirkton the now?'

CHAPTER XXV

A fortnight later Jacqueline could have enlightened him. For William himself proved communicative. Perhaps, as she suspected, he was a trifle proud of having been recalled home for wrong-doing. It isn't every Scots bailie's son who in the course of a few years' sojourn in the Metropolis becomes liable to citation as a co-respondent in the forthcoming divorce case of a popular musical comedy actress.

He confided her name to Jacqueline. 'Maimie Fouldern. She's married to a stockbroker called Ferguson, Ronnie Ferguson. Easy-going sort we all thought him until this . . . Maimie Fouldern – you'll have heard of her? Her photograph is all over the place. Miss Maimie Fouldern in her Morris Oxford. Miss Maimie Fouldern in one of our model velours.'

Jacqueline nodded. Yes, she had heard of Maimie Fouldern, knew by sight her teethy smile, her wide-open baby eyes. Obviously William expected her to be impressed. And she wasn't – she just wasn't!

The fact that she wasn't, and in her transparent way showed it, caused her to bound upwards in William's esteem. He leaned forward with the ingratiating air of a small boy, laid a hand on hers. Later, she was to learn that this small boy attitude of his, alternating as it did with an assumption of gay masterfulness, was one of his engaging mannerisms. They were alone in the parlour, Uncle Archie having shuffled off to bed fully an hour earlier with no word of apology. They'll ne'er miss me, he would have made excuse had he deemed excuse necessary. But he didn't. For already he had ceased to look on William as a visitor. Almost – and he smiled slyly to himself – the bailie's son was one of the family, so often and so casually did he drift in and out of Lilac Villa.

William's hand tightened on hers. 'If it weren't for Maimie,' he said, 'if it weren't for Maimie – look here, Jacqueline, if she turns me down after the proceedings, will you have me?'

His meaning was clear despite his incoherency. Above his eyes his brows were jigging. Like those of a stage demon they forked upwards in funny little furze bushes when he was excited. He was excited now, Jacqueline realized. But she could not wholly rid her mind of amused resentment at the boyish insolence of the proposal. If Maimie won't, will you? Second bid. Going – going – gone!

Misled by the glancing smile on her lips, he took her in his arms. For a second she resisted, then as the rough of his coat sleeve brushed her cheek her defences went down. In the crook of his shoulder she might recapture a whiff of the ecstasy she had believed lost to her for ever, she might lose herself momentarily in the current-whorled stream of passion he had released. Almost, she could lull herself to rest in the belief that this was no stranger who held her next his heart, but the lover who had bestowed upon her the bright jewel of his adoration.

A mist rose before her eyes. She wept softly, and William, feeling her stir in his arms, stroked her hair. Dear little dark horse, he had had no idea she was so keen on him! Damn Maimie! Damn Ferguson! Damn everybody! What a blasted fool he had been! A tear falling on his hand moved him still farther. He made to hold her closer, but to his stupefaction she shirked the contact of his lips, struggled free. For a second she stood glaring at him, her eyes black with anger, then with a little sob her head drooped again.

Mechanically he fondled her wrist while his brain worked furiously. He was blowed if he understood her! She had clung to him with an ardour that had surprised him. She had lured him on with her tears, her sighs, and then she had turned on him like a tiger; she was a dark horse sure enough. With Maimie now, a man knew where he was . . . All the same, give him the modest violet every time. Not that you'd call Jacqueline that exactly. She was a hybrid really, a cross between a wildflower and an exotic. For all her clinging ways she would not be easily culled.

He tugged at his tie. 'I've been straight with you, Jacqueline. I've told you exactly how matters stand between Maimie and me. I'm dashed sorry. For you do care, don't you?'

She looked at him with eyes that reminded him strangely of those of a snared animal. With a flicker of her long lashes she emerged from her unhappy preoccupation.

'Care?' she said dully. 'Care for you? No.'

'Then why the deuce did you—' he blurted, then stopped. However exasperated a fellow may be there are some questions, he told himself, he cannot very well put to a lady.

'I don't know,' she said, pushing the problem back and forward in her mind as though trying to focus upon it a clear light that should result in its elucidation. 'I've been pretty miserable lately. Have you never felt when you've been lonely, down on your luck, that you'd give the world just to feel someone's arms round you – someone's – oh, if you're miserable enough – anyone's.'

He nodded. The girl was a rover and didn't know it. Ye gods, who'd have guessed it to look at her?

'Rath-er!' he agreed. 'That was how I got in tow with Maimie.'

Maimie. She shuddered. Only that morning in Milne's, the stationers in High Street, she had seen a magazine frontispiece of Maimie, incredibly blonde and baby-eyed. William noted her gesture of distaste and retracted his unspoken accusation.

'I'm not comparing my feelings with yours,' he said hastily. 'A man's different. I suppose now there's been some fellow with you and something happened to prevent it coming off?'

His perspicacity astounded her. 'How did you guess?'

Could he tell her without giving offence? Diffidently he splashed out of the shallows.

'Because, to be frank, you take to that sort of thing as a duck to water.'

She blushed crimson as his meaning broke upon her.

'Do I?' she murmured.

Without intending it, he reflected, she was provocative, infernally provocative. That was the worst of innocent women. They led you on and on and then left you standing.

'You know,' he admonished her, 'you're far too attractive to be cooped up like this. You should make up your mind to forget the other man and give someone else a chance. You're the sort who ought to get married.'

'What exactly do you mean by the sort who ought to get married?' she demanded, frankly curious.

He quailed before her unruffled gaze. He was floundering in deep seas again and this time he durst not own it. You couldn't with any decency tell a girl that with an emotional nature such as hers marriage was the safest course.

'I mean,' he said, 'I mean—' Hell! What did he mean? 'It isn't as if you had a special *flair* for anything. You don't act or dance, do you?'

'No–o,' she admitted. 'I don't act or dance.'

And then she remembered her little black book. She had buried it in a drawer on her arrival at Kirkton and in the stress of continuous trivial happenings and the anguish of her recurrent fits of depression, she had let it lie there all these months untouched. Once or twice on odd scraps of paper she had scribbled a few lines of verse, but on rereading them she had destroyed them hurriedly, deeming the self-pity that had inspired them an ill to be hid from sight, not paraded in public like the sores of an Eastern mendicant.

'You're quite right,' she said thoughtfully, 'I'm making an awful hash of life. I should try to do something.'

He flashed upon her his engaging small-boy smile.

'Marriage,' he said. 'I'd recommend marriage if it weren't for Maimie.'

CHAPTER XXVI

In the days that followed the blank wall of existence seemed to Jacqueline to be ringed round with portraits of William. William, haggard and hunted-looking, at such times as he had received disquieting letters from London. William, gay and masterful, when one day's silence had succeeded another. William peevish, inclined to sulk when she rejected his lovemaking. This, however, was seldom, for with the astuteness of his type he had tumbled to the one way he could procure her favour.

A hangdog air, a sigh symptomatic of deep depression never failed to awake in her a tremulous kindness that took the sting out of her earlier protestations of indifference. The fact that Maimie was always in the foreground of his thoughts seemed to make such lovemaking as she suffered him to indulge in, safe. For Maimie, she argued, had claims upon him which no man could in honour disregard; no matter how much he might wish to become engaged to herself the obstacle of Maimie bulked in the way. So far as she was concerned Maimie stood for safety as surely as the thin rail round the uppermost rampart of Kirkton Castle. But for that rail a light-headed person leaning forward might lose balance and be hurled to the rocks below.

Sometimes, when William persisted in threading the seam of their relationship with a romantic twist, she wondered with a wry sense of doubt whether she weren't depending overmuch upon a frail support. Supposing anything happened to Maimie! But untoward accidents, she told herself, never do overtake the Maimies of this world. The worst that befalls them is the loss of their jewels at the start of a none too promising autumn season.

One evening, after a visit to the picture house, Uncle Archie opened the subject of William. Upon Mr Forsyth enjoyment had the same effect as alcohol has on a younger man. After these excursions to the cinema his tongue invariably wagged as though oiled. His natural vigilance relaxed and he appeared to lose that fear of contempt which had beset him ever since association with Ruth had convinced him of his own miserable inferiority. Like a mountain-climber who has drunk just enough to feel the chill pains of fatigue ooze in a goodly sweat from his thighs, he was conscious of the need for companionship, and because of this consciousness he was lavish in the expenditure of such confidence as would gain him the right of entry into another person's world.

'The bailie and I went down the road together this morning,' he said. 'I think like me he's wondering if you and William are going to make a match of it.'

So Uncle Archie didn't know about Maimie. The bailie had kept his thumb upon that.

'I'm not in love with William,' she protested.

Uncle Archie regarded her intently, an expression of mingled relief and regret on his face. He wasn't so sure that to be in love as the lassie put it was an altogether desirable state. It meant the suppression of a thousand doubtful impulses, a desperate sensation of dangling head downwards in mid-air. He had experienced it before marriage, not after. Marriage, he mused, with no thought of disparaging his partner in the adventure, was the best cure going for that desperate dangling sensation . . .

With a nervous movement alien to him, he thrummed his fingers on the arms of his chair.

'There's something,' he said, 'I've been minded to say for awhile back. It's this, Jacqueline. There'll not be much left when I'm gone. If I'd taken your aunt's advice and started business for myself after the Armistice . . .'

With a gesture of bravado she attempted to stem the doleful tide of his thoughts.

'But I can keep myself. I could go back to MacCluskys'.'

'I'm none so sure. There's a pressure now there wasn't a couple of years back. Anyway, supposing you could, what's to it when all's said? A mere pittance you could scarce scran a penny off to put by for your old age. And there's that to think on, lassie, there's that—'

He fumbled for his handkerchief, rubbed with it on the misty ovals of his glasses. Now he had dragged it out into the open he couldn't say he liked the look of it – this problem of Jacqueline's future.

'Mind you, I'm not advising you to marry for money. But' – his left eyebrow contracted in the semblance of a wink – 'there's no harm in marrying where money is. And the bailie could buy and sell the half of Kirkton.'

Jacqueline threw back her head. 'He can't buy me,' she was on the point of crying out. But at sight of Uncle Archie puffing unsteadily at his half-empty pipe she bit back the words. He was too old to comprehend the crackling flame of her defiance. He would only think she was trying to pick a quarrel. Then another aspect of the case occurred to her. She let her darning slip on to her knee.

'Do you – do you—' she began, then stopped.

At home for once in the world of another person Uncle Archie had followed the track of her thoughts. Genuinely affected, he laid down his pipe.

'No, you're not to be thinking I want rid of you, lassie. It's only that I've a mind to see you settled. There's too many women wanting homes of their own these days. I'd miss you. You know that brawly. But I could do fine wanting you if I saw you happily settled with William.'

'And do you think,' she said, spearing with the wrong end of her needle the heel of the sock she was working at, 'd'you think I would be happily settled with William?'

'And what for no?' demanded Uncle Archie truculently. 'He comes from a well-feathered nest, I warrant you.'

That fact, doubtless, had weighed with Maimie. But it carried no weight with her, Jacqueline reflected. In the jargon of the storybooks she'd sooner work her fingers to the bone than be beholden to William . . . The needle she had driven in, head downwards, retaliated upon her at this juncture by inflicting a savage prick. As she squeezed the tiny squirt of blood from the base of her nail she told herself she was an idiot to worry. It didn't matter a hoot what Uncle Archie or the bailie thought. There was Maimie – thrice-blessed Maimie.

Her figure was one around which Jacqueline's fancy played continuously. It amused her to lift Maimie bodily from the scented hothouse of her Mayfair flat and to set her down against a background of snow-scarred hills and sloping country. It amused her to hearken to the jingle of Maimie's bracelets, the clopper-clopper of her Louis heels on the crazy-path terraces of Kirkton.

One day she found herself searching for words to imprison on paper her conception of Maimie in Lilac Square. She sent the miniature comedy in verse that resulted with a note to R. F. Torrance at his London club, the one address he had once told her that never failed to find him. By return she received an exuberant reply.

'There is no longer a future for sentiment,' he wrote, 'but there is for satire. It takes a soft heart and a hard head to smite with a blow that will strike home without maiming its victim and so exposing him as an object for compassion. The combination, as you've discovered, of a sneer and a smile does the trick. Bravo, Jacqueline!'

His approval warmed her, spurred her to further effort. She couldn't act or dance, but she could – yes, she really could write a little. Owen had believed in her ability. So did R. F. Torrance. Unfortunately her talent was not one out of which she could hope to earn her livelihood. Long ago R. F. Torrance had told her with great cheerfulness that there was no money in it. There wasn't. But there was something else – a quickening of interest in the things of life, an outlet for such feelings and emotions as she could not damp down with the black dross of common sense.

With the recession from her spirit of the dreary weight of grief, her vitality had increased, and along with it her need for some mode of self-expression. Since Owen's death she had fallen into the habit of looking backward. Now the future started looming up again in front of her. This time upon its slopes no gallant figure awaited her, no promise of passionate companionship, only a maze of words out of whose manipulation she must glean happiness. Some nights when the wind went stravaiging through the streets and the whispering couples at the crossroads clung to each other for support, the old longing would convulse her, drive her thoughts down forbidden alleys. And she would let them drift on until the glint of old Scrabbles' knife arose to rend them anew.

All unwittingly one such night she gave William a welcome that sent him home in a jubilant frame of mind. He encountered his father in the doorway, foisted upon him the glad burden of his belief.

'If I were free, I believe Jacqueline Thayer would have me.'

The bailie did not answer. He was reflecting deeply, searching for the instrument most likely to aid in the solution of a problem that had sorely perplexed him.

'I've an idea mama should have a hand in this,' he said at last.

William emitted a low whistle of surprise.

'What the hell—' he stuttered.

'Ssh-ssh!' reproved the bailie. 'There's things weemen can handle far better nor men. Have you not learned that yet, laddie? What now about a bit feeling letter from mama to Mistress Maimie Ferguson? The girl you were engaged to before you ever clapped an eye on her is fretting herself into a decline – sentiment, ye ken, laid on with a trowel. Mama's a grand hand at that.'

'But she knows – we all know I never set eyes on Jacqueline to my knowledge until a month ago.'

'Toots! What does that matter? Your mama'll believe anything if it's put to her peetiful enough. She's like a roll of cheap wadding that'll absorb anything.'

'But Jacqueline—?'

The bailie snorted, stalked indoors. A poor-hearted, doubting Thomas, this son of his!

'Ach, is it no' worth a trial?' he shouted, banging the big front door.

CHAPTER XXVII

May, and with its opening days there came a heat wave that dispelled the cool grey serenity of the little town, that saturated in a crimson glamour the cobbled terraces, the lunging ramparts. About the fields the wind-coloured river twisted – an endless tide of stagnant water indistinguishable in its steadfast impassivity from the slopes of the encroaching shores.

In the distance the galleon sails of the famous bridge quivered like a mirage – a dream-ship dimly blue against the livid blood-orange of the sky. Poised for flight like a sculptured bird of the ocean, it defied this miasma that had stolen in during a night of tempest upon the little northern town, impregnating its pent-in alleys, its douce squares with strange scents, strange languors transported by some freak of alchemy from a torrid courtyard of the East.

Looking down upon the town from the heights of the castle was like peering into a bowl of boiling broth. The grey-lozenged slates of the house-tops, the mincing gardens resembled a clutter of cut vegetables lying sodden below vast clouds of choking steam.

On the night before the heat wave began, a night of thick air and clammy cold, Uncle Archie and Jacqueline had been invited to supper at the Macfarlanes'. When she entered the big old-fashioned drawing-room Jacqueline felt as though she had stepped into a mesh. Mrs Macfarlane, nodding and blinking at her out of small beads of eyes half lost in loose bunches of flesh, enveloped her in an atmosphere of sentiment that made her feel like an insect crawling miserably up the oily surface of a flypaper which grows stickier and stickier as you near the top.

Alone in the drawing-room with Jacqueline after supper, the old lady wiped her eyes and rambled on about William. William in his wee sailor suits. William in a bonny blue jersey with white stripes toddling to school. She minded the night he was born. She minded the bailie – ah, but he wasn't the bailie then – tiptoeing into her room and looking down at the pair of them. 'Hoots, wumman, is that a' the size of him? Never heed, we'll be gey and proud of him yet.' And she was, she always had been until this . . . Not that she blamed William . . . It was that London – London. She rent the word in two.

London was no place for a man to live alone. The temptations – oh, the temptations! You couldn't walk the length of Regent Street without being accosted. She knew that for a fac'. The very last time she'd been there she'd been spoken to by a strange man. Such a fright she'd got – she'd run so that you couldn't see her heels for stour!

And, as it had turned out, it had all been a mistake. For next day from Fullers' window she had seen the selfsame youth stopping dozens of people, trying to sell scraps of white heather he kept hidden in his pocket because he was ower young, she supposed, to possess a hawker's licence. Oh, a queer place, yon London!

'Overrun by Scots,' said Jacqueline, in a reminiscence of R. F. Torrance.

Mrs Macfarlane bridled. 'If it was it'd be a decenter place to bide in.' Then she smoothed her face with an effort. Dear, dear, she was surely never going to lose her temper with William's intended and this her first visit! It was false policy, too, on her part to miscall the town he would be taking her to, if . . . With a self-conscious smirk she made a brave effort at recovery. 'Fine and lively though, London. The the-aters now, you could go to a different one every night in the week. Not like Glasgow.' She stopped, groping after dimly remembered facts. Glasgow – wasn't this girl a native of Glasgow? If so, she was putting her foot in it again. Och, it didn't matter anyhow. Glasgow was the kind of place nobody had a good word for and yet that everybody went back to . . .

'And the shops,' she went on, harking once more to London with the laudable intention of underlining its attractions with the heavy pencil of her approval. 'You never saw such shops! A'thing in the windows. That's typical English, the bailie says. All show that will show. But they're grand to look at. Silk every time, never a stitch of decent hard-wearing winsey.'

Listening to her harsh uncultivated voice, Jacqueline marvelled how William, born and brought up within sound of it, had escaped contamination. He had no trace even of the pseudo gentility affected very often by those members of the second generation who are fain to mark emphatically the difference between themselves and the first. That was one of the things she admired about William. He must recognize even more acutely than she did the utter commonplaceness of his parents and yet he clung to them. Never by word or look did he disparage either of them.

On the way home that night Uncle Archie paused outside his own gate.

'I'd have liked a bit turn,' he said wistfully. 'But I doubt it wouldn't do. If they were keeking out their windows and saw us it would look as though we hadn't enjoyed ourselves comin' away before we needed to. But I've no mind yet for my bed.'

He sighed as he drew his chair close to the parlour fire. Pipe in hand, he looked sideways at Jacqueline.

'You're gey and fond of William,' he opined. 'But I doubt your aunt wasn't far wrong about him. He's been a thought wild, it seems.'

Jacqueline started in surprise. While Mrs Macfarlane had been talking to her about William upstairs the bailie, apparently, had been talking about him to Uncle Archie downstairs. In the dull light the old man's face struck her as rather pathetic. It had the ill-washed look that worry imparts to the cheeks of the elderly.

'Have they been telling you about Maimie?' she asked.

'Maimie?' he repeated, 'Maimie?'

Uncle Archie wasn't a good actor. There was no use his trying to deceive her. She knew without his saying another word that he had heard all about Maimie. Silly of him to try to play the innocent!

Then her irritation evaporated as she reflected – Uncle Archie was getting old. In his young days women like Maimie were never mentioned. That was what was wrong. He couldn't bring himself to speak freely about a lady whose conduct he must naturally deplore. To her astonishment – for William, after all, was in the same boat – Uncle Archie began to praise him sky-high.

'There's no telling,' he wound up with a little smack of his lips, 'there's no telling to what heights William may not rise. He may have a handle yet to his name.'

Imperceptibly with the lengthening of the days the mesh, it seemed to Jacqueline, grew thicker. The consciousness of it chafed her continuously. She tried to escape it by absorbing herself in creative work. But always there were interruptions. William wanted her. And, oh, it was lovely to be wanted in that way again!

They went to the County Restaurant and ate ices to the strain of the newly imported jazz band. They went on a day of sweltering heat up to the centre to look down upon the steaming ravine that was Kirkton below. You felt like God, Jacqueline thought, poised on a day like this on the topmost rampart. But surely God did not look down upon the world with such listless eyes. Or was humanity's travail accounted for by the fact that the pigmies below meant as little to Him as they did to her viewed from this giddy height? Then through her mind drifted the words, 'Male and female created He them.' And a blessed little pulse of relief bounded in her side. For, if mortals love so jealously those things that they create, how much stronger must not the love of God be for the world, and the things of the world that owe their being to His divine breath?

She stepped back from the rail, her eyes shining. William, the watchdog, pressed closer to her side.

'You're beautiful,' he muttered. 'By God, in this light—'

She turned on him reproachful eyes. 'Don't,' she said. 'We're too near Him here to take His name in vain.'

In various little ways Jacqueline found herself testing her affection for William. He was a great dear. A dozen times a week he proved his devotion to her in unexpected acts of kindness. Nevertheless she arrived always at the same conclusion – if he were to go out of her life tomorrow she wouldn't lose more than a few nights' sleep repining his absence. She would miss him badly, of course, but not agonizingly. For in their relationship there was not that element of camaraderie that atones quite tolerably for lack of love.

'D'you know,' she taxed him one day, 'you and I have really nothing in common? We don't talk – we can only play at this sort of thing.' She indicated their interlaced fingers.

He smiled down at her. 'What can one talk about in this fœtid hole? Wait till we go to London.'

'We?' she took him up sharply.

He nodded, his eyebrows forking. 'For pity sake don't take it like that, Jacqueline. If it weren't for this blasted business . . . I'm crazy about you. I can't get along without you. You do care – you must care for me a little, don't you?'

Weakly she threw him a crumb of comfort. 'A little, perhaps. I don't know.'

After all, why withhold it? There was always Maimie, thrice-blessed Maimie.

CHAPTER XXVIII

It came over Jacqueline one morning like a wave – the longing to look upon the close-pressed house-tops of the Second City, to sniff the acrid mixture of smoke and chemicals that pricks the nostrils at St Rollox, where a cumbersome fabric of chimney stacks, of squat black houses debouching on the railway line gives the stranger warning of the great cauldron of cobblestoned streets, of rain-bleached buildings that lie beyond.

She itched to let her gaze wander unchained through the large light caves of the shop windows, to hearken to the frenzied orgy of sound beaten out by the hammering traffic round the Broomielaw and swelling in a low hoarse road to mingle with the puerile blast of motor horns at Charing Cross. She itched to walk up Renfield Street again – slowly, lingeringly, letting her eyes switch from left to right.

For of all streets in the town Renfield Street had always seemed to her the most sharply characteristic. It sprang at the bottom from a thick black clustration of buildings. It ended at darkling in a smoky blur that merged with the base of the sky, a blue-black sky shot with the red and yellow twinkling of the city lights, a lustrous couch for that loveliness that broods sweetly over mean streets and dark thickets of old, old mansions rotting in decay.

It is, in reality, the dry river of the town, this slanting street – a turbulent river swollen by a dozen eager tributaries, banked alternately by mean houses and splendid opulent windows blazing with colour. Flooded by brightly postered vans, by panting lorries, and twin chains of ascending and descending tramcars, this cobbled thoroughfare with its incessant drums of sound is a richly coloured film reflecting no less truthfully and romantically than the river traffic on the Clyde the manifold activities of the Second City.

'Would you mind,' said Jacqueline, looking up from the maze of tiny figures in the timetable, 'if I went to Glasgow tomorrow for the day?'

Uncle Archie stared as though she had said Timbuctoo. William emitted a low whistle.

'Great idea!' he said. 'I'll come, too, and we'll make a day of it.'

But she demurred emphatically. William had no part in her memories of the town. She had no mind to go with him to any of the places she had gone with Owen. There were some shining hours she was fain to keep untarnished.

She arrived at Buchanan Street shortly after eleven. By two o'clock she was wondering a shade disconsolately why she had come. For it was lonely wandering about without an object and rain was falling in sheets. At midday the city was like a stifling arcade roofed not by a single dome but by a ragged awning of demented umbrellas. She lunched at a tea-room where the thin flaky wedges of marzipan underlying the pink-and-white icing on the cakes made up for the thickness of the cups; then she went by tram to Nessie's.

The warmth of her welcome thawed the ice that was crusting about Jacqueline's heart. Nessie plied her with questions, interspersed by protestations of sisterly affection. Here was no element of criticism, only of kindness. As she basked in the sunshine of Nessie's approval Jacqueline felt as though she were enjoying a brief respite from the harassing business of living.

'And when is *it* to be?' she asked, diverting Nessie off the trail she was pursuing of interested enquiries.

Nessie's face altered subtly. So did her voice.

'Quite soon now. Bert's job's improved – just last month they gave him another rise. We've got our house taken now – a lovely wee villa out Burnside way. Hot and cold in the scullery and the windows look on to the Braes. It's beautiful when the sun shines. Only it shows every speck. I'll have my work cut out to keep things spotless out yonder.'

Was it imagination or was she talking with greater enthusiasm about her house than about her future husband? Tentatively, Jacqueline voiced her thoughts.

'And Bert, Nessie, is he—? Are things all right now? D'you remember you hinted once—?' She paused, fearful of fraying by a word the gay composure of her companion.

Nessie lifted soft doe's eyes to her face.

'Yes, I remember. Oh, sometimes, I think it'll be OK. Other times, I wonder—'

With fingers that laced and unlaced themselves on her lap she strove to combat her doubts. Failing to down them completely, she set them back from her, bared others that for years had pressed more closely upon her.

'You know how it is, Jacqueline. You can't go on at the Grind House for ever. And Bert's bucked up of late. It's not so often now and I'm more used to it. He's an awful dear, re'ely. Generous isn't the word. And, as mother says, there must aye be a something.'

A something – drink or a Maimie. But it wasn't that in every case. With Owen . . . ah, but there had been old Scrabbles. She shut her eyes upon the picture of his tortured face.

'And the others?' she asked. 'Old Miss Price?'

Nessie's eyes narrowed. 'Did *you* know about her?'

Jacqueline nodded. Did she know? Who better?

'None of us did until the other day when she suddenly toppled down on the floor. We thought it was a kind of fit, flew for a doctor. He said she was drunk, dead drunk. I could scarcely credit it. She's not been back since, so last Monday I went to ask for her. Oh, Jacqueline, it was awful. She'd had nothing decent to eat for days. I didn't know what on earth to do. In the end I went to Mr Shaw. He was frightfully decent – gave me a fiver to get things for her. What I'll do when that's exhausted I don't know. For she's not fit to work. Oh, the filth of that place, the smell!'

She wrinkled up her stubby nose and Jacqueline had a vision of the two houses side by side – the one whose scullery was fitted with hot and cold; the other with its façade of dirty underlinen, its evil odour. No wonder Nessie voted for the villa at Burnside despite Bert's failing . . . Through her mind sped Uncle Archie's words: 'What's to it after all? A pittance you can't scran anything off against your old age.'

She smiled up in William's face when he met her at Kirkton station. William, like Bert, stood for security. Yes, she'd had a tophole day in town. That was to say it poured all the time. Miss him? We-ell, she'd hardly got as far as that! But she was glad – oh, yes, jolly glad to be back again.

CHAPTER XXIX

That same evening it happened.

Looking back upon it, Jacqueline recognized that her own mental and physical lethargy were in part to blame. But above and beyond that there was Miss Price – Miss Price as she would always remember her, with her dusty cheeks pressed close to the pillows, her long spindly legs like crutches thrust out above the bedclothes. A surplus woman, Owen had said. And his words were the lettering below the picture, the clue to this tragic caricature of debased womanhood.

Old age, Jacqueline was young enough to think, should be a blessed state, an ebbing fire framed in yellowing laces, in amethyst silks decorously smooth. With it should be associated books, leisure, flowers and friends. Cut off from these mellow attributes of age the surplus woman flees its approach. In a futile attempt at self-deception she plasters paint on her haggard cheeks, hangs beads on her wizened chest – beads which she makes believe are pearls her lover has given her.

Uncle Archie's voice raped the tremulous motif of Jacqueline's thoughts.

'And did you have a grand day in the town?'

She nodded, striving to lessen the load on her mind by a lightness of speech.

'It rained all the time.'

At that moment William burst into the room. His eyes were rapt, his hair rumpled as though in a moment of unbridled excitement he had combed it wildly with his fingers.

'It's all right, Jacqueline,' he cried. 'It's come off all right, Mr

Forsyth. Everything's going to be all right. A wire from Maimie. She's done with me.'

Jacqueline stared at him in a sort of baffled stupor. Impossible that this bulwark should have failed – impossible, oh, impossible!

William went on babbling to Uncle Archie. 'It's jolly well all right, isn't it? We've got your blessing, haven't we?'

Through a mist Jacqueline saw the old man flush, formulate a stammering sentence or two. Then her hand fluttered to her throat. Her heart felt bleached. She could hardly breathe . . .

She fled the room, sought her own. Opposite the window the big hawthorn tree at the foot of the bailie's garden bowed its head in the attitude of a reluctant bride. Its pearly blossoms were tinging rapidly with yellow, a dirty yellow like tartar on a tooth. That was old age. A decay that cannot be arrested unless you have someone to look into your eyes and to avow you dear . . . And William loved her. Always it came back to that. Like a horse exercising on the eve of a big race her thoughts galloped round and round in a circle, spurred by a frenzy of the blood that was a kind of fear. Uncle Archie would miss her. No, this was an obstacle she cleared at a bound, Uncle Archie's own words recurring to refute her. She didn't care that for William! But didn't she? She'd been mighty glad to see him a few hours earlier emerging from the crowd round the book-stall at the station. Braced by the unrestrained gusto of his greeting she had veered away from the disturbing reflections that had companioned her in the train. Poor Miss Price! As William's wife she would be in a position to help the Miss Prices in the world. She would rather do that than busy herself eternally with bazaars like Mrs Macfarlane. *She*, incidentally, would be pleased . . .

They would all be pleased, all except herself. And she might be too. You never knew. It would be nice to travel first-class, to litter the seats with the latest magazines, to wear silk next the skin. But she wouldn't waste much money on clothes. Why should she when there was no one for whom she cared to beautify herself? William. She supposed he'd like to see her looking smart. A discredit to a fellow, a dowdy wife, he'd say. And tell me what a married woman wears and I'll tell you what her husband is. That was the kind of glib utterance William was fond of perpetrating. In years to come she could see him, top-hatted, magnificent in frock coat and massive watch-chain as befitted a business magnate, mouthing stale *mots* spiced with vulgarity the while his juniors squirmed and adjusted their lips in the semblance of a smile. For Mr William Macfarlane was a personage. His puns were given publicity in the press. Poor William! His mother would be terribly proud of him!

Outside her door Uncle Archie's voice sounded. 'William's for off, Jacqueline.'

'Let him go,' she cried, with the superb recklessness of a raggle-taggle urchin who spans his nose at authority. She, at any rate, would never suffer the recital of his lordship's questionable jests.

But Uncle Archie did not hear her and called out louder.

'William's for off. Are you not coming down? Will I tell him you're tired?'

The tender solicitude in his voice touched her. She opened the door, clutched at his coat sleeve.

'Oh, Uncle Archie,' she sighed. 'Be good to me. I'm so lonely.'

He patted her clumsily between the shoulders as he might a child in whose throat a prune stone has stuck.

'Tuts, tuts, lassie, there's no need for you to be that, with William down the stair there wanting you.'

'And you don't?' she said softly, without spirit.

Uncle Archie fumbled with his handkerchief.

'I wouldn't say that; no, I wouldn't say that. But I'm an old, done man, Jacqueline. And you're young. You've a lot of years before you that I haven't.'

She saw those years – a grey chain of days uninspiring as tags on a tear-off calendar and ending, perhaps, as those of Miss Price were ending. She brushed past Uncle Archie, stooped over the banisters, and called out a gay 'hallo' to William who stood waiting, bareheaded, in the hall.

He ran upstairs three steps at a time, and Uncle Archie faded away into the bathroom, the door of which he slammed to let them know he was safely out of the way and that they could take their freedom.

William's attitude was chastened. He was none too sure of his ground. With the Maimie type a man knew where he was. With Jacqueline – that, he reflected fleetingly, was why she was so dashed attractive.

'I'm sorry, blurting it out all of a heap. The mater thought I should come right over. We only had the wire a minute ago from London.'

He did not offer to show her the telegram. A few weeks later Jacqueline remembered the omission.

He came a step nearer, touched her wrist. The unshaded gas cone below which he stood revealed him to her as a forlorn small boy, uncertain of his fate.

'It's all right, Jacqueline, isn't it?' he said humbly. 'You'll have me, won't you?'

She nodded. All right – would it be all right? At the back of her mind she knew that it wouldn't.

CHAPTER XXX

Being engaged, Jacqueline thought, would be pleasant enough, but being engaged, she discovered with a little shock of surprise, was only a prelude to getting married. And there was a conspiracy to rush matters. William had an important business appointment. He sulked at the prospect of returning to London alone. Mrs Macfarlane shook her head over it. Even Uncle Archie went out of his way to emphasize to Jacqueline that he could do fine wanting her.

'Maggie,' he opined, 'is grand at redding up.'

She wasn't, but Uncle Archie was not observant. Unlike his niece, he was not haunted by the memory of Aunt Ruth, the perfect housewife. He recalled her only as the perfect woman forgetful of the many occasions when he had chafed at her habit of domination.

Jacqueline felt a little helpless among them all. Even William seemed to have ranged himself against her. She wished she had someone to whom she could look for guidance, someone whose word she could accept unquestionably as a child accepts the word of an elder. She thought of Mrs Torrance. But Mrs Torrance, she realized, with her infinite capacity for selfless love would have naught but scorn for those others of her sex who traded ungenerously in counterfeits. And counterfeit, Jacqueline knew well, was the measure of all she could offer William.

From Mrs Torrance her thoughts went to George Buchanan. He was an understanding soul whose frequent silences had invited confidences. But George Buchanan was too far away. In any case, since Owen's death she had not heard from him. Her last two letters had gone unanswered. She thought of Nessie. But – no, Nessie was no use. Nessie's own line of conduct was proof of her philosophy. Poor Nessie! Hot and cold and a fine outlook on to the Braes. She smiled wryly as she reflected – a year hence she might be sighing 'Poor Jacqueline,' oblivious of her own hot and cold. A year hence – possibly sooner. From the very start her material comforts might smack unpleasantly of makeshift, second best – 'And there's more in life than that.' She thanked God that whatever might befall her in the future she had discovered the high meaning that underlay her mother's words.

One day when the discussion of dates was at fever heat, William reproached her directly: 'One would almost think you didn't care for me.'

She glanced at him sharply. 'I've never pretended anything. I like you, but I'm not in love with you.'

'Still thinking of that other man?'

'No,' she answered him truthfully. 'I don't very often. It wouldn't be fair to you.'

'Meaning I don't come up to standard?'

'No one ever will.'

He glared across at her where she sat, framed in the alcove of the bow window, a fork of sunlight raking the sweep of her dark hair.

'The fact of the matter is,' he said slowly, 'it's a good thing for you you didn't marry him. For you couldn't have stood disillusionment and no man born could have been all you thought him. He's come to be a sort of legend with you, a living Arthur.'

A pained flush pricked her skin. It hurt her to hear William refer thus lightly to Owen. It was like the slow mauling of something infinitely precious. And yet she recognized that in what he was saying there lurked a certain element of truth. William was no fool. Often, quite unexpectedly, he compelled her admiration of his astuteness. He had a way of piecing out the scrappiest bits of evidence and of presenting them as a credible whole that amazed her. His knowledge of human nature was surprising in one whose imaginative faculties were to all appearances nil. It was only where a certain type of woman was concerned that he appeared devoid of even the rudiments of common sense. This weakness was a soft streak in a nature otherwise glacially cold and brittle. William belonged to that select body of Scots whose governing motto is 'Deil tak' the hin'most', a body that once started on the upward path never looks back lest the sentimentality that is a national weakness should work upon it to halt, help some laggard on the way.

Sometimes Jacqueline wondered if when they were married she would be able to hold him. Her pride alone would suffer if she failed. And then she took herself to task for her callousness. William, after all, was kindness itself. She liked him, on the whole, better than she had done before they had become engaged. His manner was less strained, easier. He had begun to treat her more as a normal human being and less as a wilful child. And she had rather he talked to her than touched her.

The bailie, too, had been overwhelmingly kind. He had pressed a handsome cheque upon her and bidden her away to Linton's, the biggest shop in the place, and buy a trousseau. Then, while still she laboured beneath a sense of gratitude, he had struck a blow for the cause.

'William's due in London on the tenth. What about making the fifth the great day?'

'That's awfully soon,' she murmured, the impulse hot upon her to throw down the cheque, to cry: 'No, no, if these are your terms!'

He put a hand on her shoulder, a watery gleam in his eyes.

'It's like this, Jacqueline. No matter when it is, it'll seem awful soon to you. Girls, I've heard tell, are like that. You'd best bite on the bit and be done with it.'

Gravely she pondered his words, forgetful for the moment of the fact that he was one of the chief figures in the conspiracy.

'Ask mama,' he went on. 'She'll tell you the same thing. And she wasn't sensitive like you either. Mind, I'm not saying your attitude isn't the right one. Keep a man guessing and he'll stick to you. If you'd fallen to William like an overripe grosset, he'd have been off down the road long ago.'

Bewilderment and panic filled her. This business of marriage as these people saw it bristled with mystery, with intrigue. Was she wise to rush, all blindly, into it? Men, it appeared, were just children and their wives their nurses whose duty it was to keep their charges in good humour by a display of their talents. One pretty charm after another they must, perforce, have ready to dangle before the fractious infant lest, hey presto, his eyes should go a'roving; and that for infants was against the law.

And then, realizing that his last speech had been taken amiss, the bailie said something that had transformed her from a granite statue into a gentle protective creature with dewy eyes. He said it of set purpose because he was a shrewd man and recognized as none of the others did that the fires of Jacqueline's affection for his son wanted vigorous fanning if they were to become ignited at all.

'You'll be good to Will'um, Jacqueline? We set great store on him, mama and me.'

Brimming over with exalted resolutions she hugged his hand, blind to the histrionic quality of his gesture.

'I'll try,' she promised. 'I'll try to set great store on him too.'

A few days before that fixed for the wedding Jacqueline had a telegram from the Torrances. They were motoring in Scotland and expected to pass through Kirkton on their way north. They would call on chance that afternoon between four and five.

Jacqueline murmured an inarticulate 'hurrah' as she crumpled the flimsy paper between her fingers. Between four and five – splendid! Uncle Archie was never home before six. She would have them all to herself. Then with a sudden cooling of the blood she remembered William. He would be sure to come over and spoil it all.

He came, and stung by self-consciousness she introduced him as her fiancé. He accepted congratulations charmingly. But he didn't like Torrance. The author, with his habit of rapid articulation, his jeering laughter, irritated him. What the blazes did the man mean jawing away about Jacqueline's poetry, puffing up the poor kid she could write? Write! Hell! Didn't he realize she was going to be married – married? Wasn't that a sight more worth talking about than this 'modern movement', this 'rhythmic feeling', and all the rest?

William ground his teeth as he reflected that Torrance was the type that, left to himself to judge, he would never let off with the option of a fine. No. Six months hard for him every time! In a different way Mrs Torrance likewise was an irritant. Try as he would, he could not compel her attention. She was all eyes and ears for this hulking brute of a husband of hers who monopolized the conversation so unblushingly. Once, like a spoiled child who is huffed at not being taken notice of, William started deliberately to talk to Jacqueline about some trivial arrangement for their wedding.

At the door she found herself saying nervously: 'I hope you didn't think William rude just now? He's a dear really.'

'He must be if you're going to marry him,' said Mrs Torrance sweetly. R. F. Torrance frowned and said nothing, and Jacqueline knew he was curbing his tongue with difficulty.

As their car disappeared Jacqueline lingered, looking across the parched vista of the square. She wasn't married to William yet; only engaged. But already she had begun apologizing for him to her friends.

The thought troubled her as she went indoors.

CHAPTER XXXI

Jacqueline eyed the long narrow envelope dubiously. There was an official look about it that roused her misgivings. A second later she let its contents fall from her fingers.

'George Buchanan,' she exclaimed. 'Uncle Archie, George Buchanan is dead.'

Uncle Archie scraped clean the bottom of his porridge plate.

'George Buchanan,' he mused, drawing in his breath. 'I mind him fine. Your Aunt Ruth couldn't abide him.'

That finished George Buchanan so far as he was concerned. For, having slept fitfully, he was in a sentimental mood. Waking early, his thoughts had plunged forward, then back – forward to the morrow which was to be Jacqueline's wedding day, back to that afternoon when in old Mrs Grierson's hotel parlour he and Ruth had been united man and wife 'till death do you part'. They had neither of them given much heed to that sentence then. There had been too much laughing and chaffing and popping of corks. One glass half full of wine, he remembered having been warned, was all old Mrs Grierson had allowed in her modest estimate of the catering, but it had sufficed to create an atmosphere of jollity that had lingered pleasantly in the minds of those who shared it.

Jacqueline picked up the typed sheets, proceeded with a deepening sense of emotion to digest their meaning. Then with a little catch at her throat she handed them to Uncle Archie.

'Read that,' she said.

The old man thrust back his plate, reached for his glasses. As he proceeded to polish them with his coat sleeve Jacqueline felt she could have screamed out at him for the slowness of his movements.

'Hm . . . hm . . .' he grunted, turning over a page. Then surprise sharpened his voice. 'To you five thousand pounds'; he dropped the letter, tapped the table with his fingertips. 'That'll bring you in roughly – roughly, mind you – about three hundred and thirty pounds a year . . . three thirty per annum. A nice round sum, eh? Not, maybe, to a man like the bailie – but to you and me—'

He stopped, for his niece, he saw, was not listening. She was thinking of George Buchanan, the big bluff friend who had enriched her childhood with his gorgeous unsuitable gifts, who had evolved for her out of the shreds of her mother's last utterance a brave philosophy of life.

She sighed. Uncle Archie looked across at her.

'It's no sighing matter,' he said heavily. 'It's a matter for – for congratulation. William, you'll see'll be bonny and made up with it. Every man likes his wife to have a pickle pin money and he's all the better pleased if he's not called upon to provide her with it.'

Jacqueline assented listlessly. She wished Uncle Archie would go. It was high time he was off, but he stood flipping the letter against the toast-rack, 'hm-hming' over it, deploring the fact that the bank rate wasn't what it was – 'No, not even what it was in your Aunt Ruth's time' – that explosives were still falling, that oils weren't what they were, that there was never a sign of trade taking up.

When he was gone she stood drumming her fingers on the window pane. So that was why George Buchanan had never answered her letters. He had been lying all those months in hospital. It hurt her to think of his great strong limbs pinioned in the cramped space of a ward bed.

Later, out of a curdle of personal belongings, she raked the snapshot she had of him arm in arm with her father. It wasn't a flattering likeness, but it was the best she had. The absurdly small straw hat tipped on the back of the head made the brawny figure look ludicrous. She hoped William wouldn't laugh at it; but, no, she reflected with a little tightening of her lips, there was no fear that William would laugh. For this was a photograph of the man who had left her money. And money was the one thing for which William and the bailie had a profound respect. They held it sacred as Owen had once held her . . .

She spent the morning packing, tossing this and that into the big trunk that had belonged to her mother. She did not expect to see William at all that day, but in the evening he arrived. It had been arranged that he was to dine at the County Restaurant with three of his friends who were coming from London to be present at the ceremony next day, and she was surprised when his familiar rattle fell upon the door.

'Got fed up, came off early,' he said airily. 'I didn't want to wake tomorrow of all days with a thick head. Won't you come out for a bit? It's stifling indoors.'

The square had a queer unreal look, she thought, as they traversed it. The trees weighted with foliage looked smudged and glazy like piecrust decorations plastered unevenly on the gargantuan pudding basin of the sky. The castle soared above them, a star-pointed ethereal structure builded not of stone but of that substance of which dreams are made. The heat of the day still held and the haze that accompanied it imbued the square with a strangeness wholly foreign. Almost you expected to hear the thrumming of Chinese gongs among the trees, the guttural chatter of native voices, so completely in the torrid heat did the West seem to have merged itself in the East.

William walked by Jacqueline's side talking volubly. They had had a snorting dinner – Brett, Joe Duncan, Chitty and he. He'd met them at the station. To his surprise a fourth had stepped out behind them. Hanged if it wasn't Vigors. Jolly decent of him to have come. He'd never thought of asking him with railway fares what they were, and the old boy's business none too flourishing. He was a forty-second cousin, by the way, of Ferguson's – Ronnie Ferguson. Funny thing, he'd met Maimie – Vigors had, at the Grafton Galleries one night this week. She'd bidden him give William her love and congrats. She'd called him a clever boy. But no wonder with such a mother! Undoubtedly, the mater's letter had done the trick with Ferguson when all else had failed. Maimie had taken it to him, tremulous voice, tearful eyes sort of stunt.

Maimie, bless you, wasn't a top-liner on the bills for nothing . . .

William's voice was like a succession of dark waves that circled round but never penetrated Jacqueline's consciousness. Round and round, meaningless and insistent – a sort of syncopated frenzy in the hot stillness of the square. Green and orange its gardens were now – muggy little byways sucked dry of beauty by the sun. Even the sloping roofs of the bailie's greenhouses had lost their polished lustre . . . Suddenly – the slumbering spark in Jacqueline awoke. Letter – Maimie – Vigors – what was it all about? She turned from contemplation of the blurred glass to William's face.

'What letter?' she asked. 'Did your mother write to Maimie?'

William guffawed. Excitement and the heat had combined to make him reckless.

'It was the pater's great scheme. But he put it to the mater so that she thought it was all hers. The letter she wrote was her own right enough. It was a masterpiece, the silliest, most artless letter imaginable. Your Uncle Archie saw it. He can tell you.'

Jacqueline's face changed. 'But – what had he to do with it?'

William laughed again. She wished he wouldn't. It was grotesque – that braying beneath these tired trees.

'It was all about you, my child,' he said. 'The mater pitched it strong, I can tell you. Sob stuff with a vengeance. I'd been engaged to the sweetest little girl in Kirkton for years. This scandal was breaking her heart. If it went on Maimie and Ferguson between 'em would be responsible for the slaughter of an innocent. Maimie took the letter direct to Ronnie. Thrilling third act in stockbroker's office. "Read this, Ronnie." Sob. "Oh, my darling, can't you forgive me?" And he did – why, what's up?'

She had stopped short, her eyes fixed on his face in a curious stare . . . So she had been the victim of a conspiracy to free William. The bailie, Mrs Macfarlane, even her own Uncle Archie had not scrupled to use her as an instrument. Her temper mounted dangerously.

'And you pretended to be in love with me – you professed to care—'

He pressed her arm against his side with a force that astounded her.

'Before Christ, I do care. You'll soon realize that.'

He was so close to her that his breath swept her face. And quite suddenly there came to her a recollection of that night in the bungalow when she had struggled with Mr Shaw. She stepped back from William, writhing inwardly, in a sort of sick, fearful repugnance.

He let go her hand. 'I can wait,' he said sullenly, his eyes glinting like a tiger cat's in the dimness.

She recoiled before the implication of his words. Tomorrow there would be no Maimie to save her. There would be no railing between her and the rocks.

CHAPTER XXXII

Jacqueline's heart was pounding as she went upstairs. She lit the gas in her own room and drew down the blind. She didn't want to look out at the bailie's house opposite. She wanted to sit down on her bed and think. Lately she seemed to have gone on and on muddle-headedly without ever having stopped to think. That was stupid, terribly stupid. For life, after all, is very much like a spring-cleaning. No use embarking upon an orgy of effort that leaves you spent unless the result is to be a clean orderliness that will afford you joy and leisure for many a day to come. She had muddled things all along the line. She ought to have stuck to her poetry writing and not thrown it overboard like a piece of unwanted cargo whenever Owen had come along. It would have been something to have held to fast when the storm broke.

Had she possessed that something she would never have drifted into this dangerous intimacy with William. As it was, she had been grateful to him for having helped to fill a vacuum. She had had no thought of marriage.

What had made her rush into that? She fain would have evaded the answer to this question, but it pressed in upon her with the insistence of a nightmare through which there ambled the figure of old Miss Price. Behind that nightmare lay the truth. She would not have promised to marry William if George Buchanan's legacy had been hers a few weeks earlier. That, humiliating as was the admission, was the bare truth. That blessed five thousand would have saved her from the rocks.

Everything, she reflected, comes too late. Those clothes bought with the bailie's cheque – how she would have loved to have peacocked in them before Owen! George Buchanan's money – had it come a month ago, what might it not have saved her from? But it had come too late.

Then, sweet as the savour of forbidden fruit came the thought – is it too late, is it?

She buried her head in the pillow, strove to stifle the thought. Lots and lots of women, she told herself, marry caring no more for their husbands than she cared for William and it seemed to work all right. Ah, but lots of women had never loved as she had done, lots of women had never trodden the heights. They had no splendid legends to carry with them into eternity.

And then the awful realization came to her. In giving herself to William she would be throwing away what Owen had worshipped, she would be defeating herself and him. For if she cared naught for herself, he had held her in reverence. He had counted her body dear.

Too late? Too late? Lured by the distant echo of the Pied Piper's magic, she crouched on her bed, planning rapturously what she would have done had it not been too late. She would have left Kirkton and gone to London. Save at first, Uncle Archie had never really wanted her. A housekeeper would serve him better than ever she had done. She would have lived frugally, for five thousand pounds wasn't a fortune, although it seemed one to her. She would have worked hard at her verse making. The Torrances would have befriended her. Mrs Torrance had held her closely in her arms at parting the other day, as her own mother might have done. R. F., too, was fond of her in his queer unstable way. He would have helped her with her work, given her advice, introductions. She might, of course, be a little lonely. But she had her legend to live on, to colour her days until such time as the future should widen out and yield her, please God, other bounties – books, friends, a home of her own where in sweet tranquillity her dreams should be born.

And then, as though tugged by some inner cord, her mind switched back, back to the old days in Lowerbank Street, when her mother had stitched and stitched. In her ears rose again her mother's tense voice – 'Second best. Makeshift all the time. I've missed it, Jacqueline, but there's more in life than that.'

More in life – she knew there was. Yet tomorrow she was going to marry William, William for whom she didn't care *that!*

She rose, jerked up the blind. The trees had lost their glazed look, the leaves hung limp. Over the way the electric bulb in William's room showed, an immobile fireball through the minute squares of the soft net curtains. Once across the white frame of the window his figure passed in shirtsleeves.

If she failed him, his vanity would suffer. That would be all. He was the type, she realized instinctively, who would console himself quickly. Had he been an Eastern potentate and the chief wife in his harem had flouted him, he would have passed on without a flicker of hesitancy to the chamber of the next. It had been Maimie first and then her. Tomorrow it might be Rosie Farrell.

She turned from the window, made a rapid survey of the room. Her big trunk, bulging with its lid open, occupied almost the whole of one wall. Beyond it, on either side of the fireplace, stood a brand new hatbox, a battered suitcase. Jacqueline's eyes went from the one object to the other. At the moment they stood, these inanimate things, for the old life and the new.

She knelt down beside the trunk, fumbled with her fingers through the folds of silk paper covering a set of glossy black furs. With a slight shock she realized that these pretty things belonged to her no longer. They were part of Mr Macfarlane's present to William's bride.

In a corner of the tray she found what she sought – Owen's letters, the snap of her father and George Buchanan, and the notebook containing her poems. That was about all, she reflected, that she was entitled to take with her – that and the workaday clothes she had worn at the Grind House. For the contents of the big trunk were made up without exception of garments bought at Linton's with the bailie's cheque.

She pressed down the lid of the trunk, turned the key. She placed it conspicuously on the toilet table where it could not fail to be observed. Then she lifted up the suitcase. Precious little room in it, she thought, as it yawned open over a chair. Just as well she had precious little to take!

Her spirits mounted as she stuffed her stockings into the toes of her shoes, rolled an old knitted cardigan round the glass of her hand mirror. Half an hour later she slipped downstairs, slid back the heavy bolts of the door. The stars crusting the rim of the sky above the castle beamed down on her and smiled sweetly back at them. In the valley over the fields glittered the red and green lights of the railway track, the track that leads south. Along it flashed the gleam of a receding train. What was that song she had heard in the theatre with Owen? 'Love, love; follow the gleam of it'?

She stood motionless until there was only a mere pinpoint of light in the darkness, then resolutely she swung round the square.

The midnight express for Euston stopped at Kirkton station. She crooned a little pæan of joy as she stepped aboard.

THE END

INTRODUCTION TO *HUNGER MARCH*

Dot Allan's major novel *Hunger March* (1934) is a treatment of the contemporary Depression and the class struggle in Glasgow. In discussions of Glasgow 'proletarian fiction' of that decade, two other novels on the same topic are much more often cited than *Hunger March*: they are George Blake's *The Shipbuilders* (1935) and James Barke's *Major Operation* (1936). (The alert reader will note that Allan's novel was published before either of these.)

Major Operation is an angry, colourful, polemical novel which brings together, in a hospital ward, a Glasgow businessman and a shipyard workers' leader, with their opposing points of view. Barke, the son of a farm worker, took great pride in his proletarian roots: there is no doubt where he is coming from. Blake, like Allan, was by birth and upbringing middle-class, and an awkward class-consciousness runs through *The Shipbuilders*, as he himself came to recognise:

> He [Blake] pleads guilty to an insufficient knowledge of working-class life and to the adoption of a middle-class attitude to the theme of industrial conflict and despair.[1]

Hunger March, like these novels, contrasts working-class with middle-class as they come into contact, and sometimes conflict, in the diverse city that is Glasgow. But Allan takes a different line: she is continually concerned to observe the attitude of middle-class towards working-class, specifically as displayed by women. She might well, like Blake, have acknowledged 'an insufficient knowledge of working-class life' – that has hampered her before, notably in *The Deans* – and it does show at times in *Hunger March*. But the character who may be considered the central one – the novel begins and ends with him – is a Glasgow merchant, of the class to which Allan herself belonged, and to that extent at least she is at home in her story.

Hunger March as a novel is both ambitious and carefully planned. The action is confined to one foggy day, the day of a hunger march. Hunger marches – massive demonstrations by the unemployed – were not infrequent occurrences in both Britain and the United States in the Depression years of the 1920s and 1930s, and Allan aligns them with other such marches, from biblical times onwards, in a Proem (pp. 195–203) which is perhaps somewhat overwritten and obtrusive, but certainly foregrounds the anger behind *Hunger March*.

Except for a very few passages which briefly follow the characters elsewhere, the novel is also confined to the particular city through which the march is passing on this day, and largely to the Square at its heart. The city is in fact never named, but it can clearly be recognised as Glasgow, not least from the description of the Square with its statues and Council Chambers, which is George Square.

It can therefore be suggested that the hotel from which several of the characters observe the hunger march was, in Dot Allan's mind, the building on the north side of George Square which for many years was the North British Railway Hotel. (A hotel is a good place to bring characters together: Allan may well have known Vicki Baum's bestseller *Grand Hotel* of 1930, later a popular film, and much more recently Ali Smith has used the device in her 2001 novel *Hotel World*.) Arthur Joyce's office, the other main locus of action, seems to be placed on the opposite side of the Square, in the building which until comparatively recently, in real life, housed the General Post Office. It is, of course, not essential to know this – what matters is not where the location is, but what Allan does with it – but the idea that she is envisaging a real place does illuminate one of the notable features of *Hunger March*: the lyrical passages of description of 'the city'.

> Soon after midnight, a blustering wind sprang up which swept the streets like a zealous scavenger determined to leave behind no trace of the day that was spent. It shrilled through the narrow bottle-neck, blew in wild gusts about the Square, and battered loudly against the tall buildings. A late [tram]car, gliding round the corner, met the clamour of the gale with the triumphal lilt peculiar to a lightly weighted vehicle of its kind. On that instant, the Square resolved into a dim harbour for the golden galleon whose bow-wave, spreading to the frost-white grass, shone in the darkness. (p. 428)

If Allan, deciding on the shape of her novel, shows a true writer's instinct in choosing to pare it down to one day in one city, she gives evidence of great ambition in her selection of the people who are to inhabit that place on that day. There are nearly a dozen major characters, who all have their stories, most of them treated at some length. Allan attempts to link all these stories together, and to a large extent succeeds.

Thus Arthur Joyce, the merchant, is the employer of young Celia and Charlie, who will lose their jobs if his business goes down, and of the cleaner Mrs Humphry, mother of the long-term unemployed Joe whose story forms a major strand of the novel. Mrs Humphry also cleans for suburban housewife Mrs McGregor who is in the hotel to lunch with her holiday romance, and Arthur Joyce is the lover of opera singer Adèle Elberstein who entertains him in her suite. (These two ladies may appear rather irrelevant at first, but, unable to leave the hotel once their engagements are over because of the hunger march outside, they serve to illustrate a main theme of Allan's work, as will be found.) Jimmy the journalist, a casual boyfriend of Celia's, is there to interview Adèle, but is swept into the hunger march itself through his admiration of the charismatic radical Nimrod. And this is not to mention the waiter Carlo, terrified to the point of paranoia by experiences in his past – his body, when he hangs himself, is found by Adèle – or Mr Joyce's chauffeur and parlourmaid on their awkward teatime date. Allan's vision is that in her novel, on this one day in Glasgow, she is presenting all the city's life.

Not all the strands of the novel are presented with equal confidence. The story of Jimmy and Nimrod actually gets lost; they are arrested during rioting in the Square on pp. 325–6, and we hear no more until they are found musing in the cells on pp. 419–24. Jimmy is a cub reporter straight from the cinema screen; Hamish Nimrod (an awkward conjunction of names, perhaps intentionally so) is probably meant to recall such charismatic figures as John Maclean and James Maxton, who entered Glasgow legend among the Red Clydesiders of the early twentieth century. Allan is really not comfortable with either of these characters. Yet their reappearance at the end of the novel makes a point, usefully contrasting Nimrod who draws his inspiration from the past and Jimmy who looks to the future. Which attitude, Allan asks, is going to bring about change?

The story of Mrs Humphry and Joe suffers from Allan's customary uncertainty with working-class characters. It wavers between melodrama and sentimentality; with a mother like Mrs Humphry, we are tempted to suggest, no wonder Joe all but brains her with a chair (p. 241). But, again, it is plausible enough that he is reacting to her thoughtless remark: 'I'm never happier than when I'm [working].' He has never worked in his life, and Allan points to that as the cause of both his bad temper and his anarchic dreams.

Adèle Elberstein is another character straight from central casting, but Arthur Joyce, the merchant, is a different matter. Allan is in touch with him, as she is not with either the opera singer or the cleaner. In almost our first sight of him, he is reading a balance sheet which indicates that he should 'get out, and quickly' (p. 210); close down his business and retire. His first thought is that he'll be lost without the business, but a close second is his realisation of the plight of the staff who will be thrown out of work, and that unselfishness is what makes him struggle on.

Hunger March was well received on publication. The anonymous reviewer in the *Glasgow Herald* sees and appreciates what Allan is doing.

> The drama is immeasurably heightened by the concentration of events into the limits of one day, and one of the finest artistic points

> in the book is the inevitable way in which the various people and their stories are presented and made to impinge one upon the other. . . . By thus focusing her action Miss Allan has netted an enormous number and variety of characters from office, club, hotel and slum.[2]

He (if the writer is a 'he') finds Mrs Humphry and Joe 'the most realistically conceived of all the characters and the most humanly lovable' (possibly a predictable verdict from a comfortably placed *Glasgow Herald* reviewer), but he finishes with a perceptive point: 'When [Dot Allan] has strengthened and chiselled her prose, how far beyond this will she go?' He has noticed the lapses into distinctly unchiselled prose, the longeurs and overwriting, which diminish Dot Allan's work even as they are intended to enhance it. But he gives her marks in other areas:

> The theme of *Hunger March* is one which has cried out to be tackled, and Miss Allan is to be congratulated on having the imagination to see its possibilities for the art of fiction and on being the first in the field.

The *Times Literary Supplement* reviewer also approves of the book, but there is something strange in the very first words of his piece.

> Mr Dot Allan has adopted an ingenious and effective technique for his story *Hunger March.*[3]

It isn't a typo, for the review ends in similar appreciative vein, but still mistaken in one particular.

> Mr Allan has written an honest, inspiring book; his impartiality, his realisation that pain and conflict are not the monopoly of the poor, make his sympathy for them and his description of their sufferings all the more convincing.

The misidentification is interesting. Allan was evidently not known to the reviewer (though *Makeshift* had previously been reviewed in the *TLS* with a correct attribution,[4] presumably by somebody else). Thus the assumption has been made purely from reading the book. (The jacket blurb is of no help, saying only 'In this novel Dot Allan breaks fresh ground.')

So is it simply that *Hunger March* does not read as a 'woman's book'? Is it the case that women are not expected, in 1934, to write this kind of book? If any of this is so, perhaps it is, in a way, a compliment to Dot Allan, who in *Hunger March* has written as she (and many another woman writer) *could* write, untrammelled by any sort of 'women's writing' convention.

And yet, in another sense, it is a 'woman's book', as the reviewer should have seen. Allan uses the two women in the hotel, Mrs MacGregor and Adèle Elberstein, deliberately to point up her recurring theme: that if the middle class never notice the working class, middle-class women are most neglectful of all. We have seen a strong statement of that in the Prologue to *Makeshift*. Here in *Hunger March* both Mrs MacGregor (p. 299) and Adèle (p. 315) are carefully made to notice the demonstration – at last – and to react. If their reactions are almost comically inadequate – Adèle dashes off a cheque, thinking mostly of how the press will praise her generosity (p. 321), Mrs MacGregor buys a pennyworth of parsley instead of an expensive cantaloupe (p. 375) – still, Allan is saying, it's a start. And she overtly makes Mrs MacGregor muse (p. 375) on 'women like her who hadn't realised until now how bad things were in the city, and who had never done a hand's turn to help.'

But much more subtle is Allan's treatment of the waitress Fanny, an important character in *Hunger March*, though given only a few lines. She is deftly enough deployed to pull the chauffeur Burns and the maid Flora into the picture, as they tentatively get to know one another in her tearoom (pp. 344–5), but her significant moment is earlier, when she stands by the window watching the hunger march pass below. She hears, as we do, 'the late-lunchers, the tea-drinkers', at first rather frightened by the shuffling mass of humanity outside and then turning indignant, asking one another

> why Somebody didn't do Something About It. . . . Of course the real sufferers [unlike the marchers] didn't advertise their woes. There was such a thing as good Scots pride. . . . Disgraceful to allow a mob to control the streets. . . . (p. 287)

Fanny has her own thoughts. In her sympathy for the marchers and her anger at the women, she madly pictures herself opening the window and throwing cakes and pies out to the hungry men below. Of course, she doesn't.

> 'That everything you require?' [she asks her customer] Then without waiting an answer, for in her opinion they had all and more than they deserved, she drifted over again to the nearest window.
>
> 'It shouldn't be allowed, that sort of thing,' a thin, wheezy voice complained. . . . 'I thought I'd be late for my tea with you. I'm sure and I don't know what the world's coming to!'
>
> 'I'm sure I don't know either,' echoed Fanny, her heart thumping uncomfortably in her side; but in the clatter of cups, the murmur of many voices, no one heard the fat waitress speak. (p. 288–9)

Though Fanny echoes the customer's words, it is with completely different import. She is sensitive, intelligent, working-class, and female. She is ignored by – indeed invisible to – the middle-class women who see her every day. But Dot Allan has seen her. In *Hunger March*, in 'Invisible Mending', and in much of her writing, Dot Allan is trying to give the fat waitress a voice.

Notes

1. George Blake, *Annals of Scotland 1895–1955: an essay on the twentieth-century Scottish novel* (BBC, [1956]), p. 32.
2. *Glasgow Herald*, 3 May 1934.
3. *Times Literary Supplement*, 17 May 1934.
4. *Times Literary Supplement*, 1 November 1928.

HUNGER MARCH

'. . . And the famine was over all the face of the earth.'

PROEM

'. . . And Joseph gave them bread in exchange for horses, and for the flocks, and for the cattle of the herds, and for the asses; and he fed them with bread for all their cattle for that year.'

The first hunger march took place in Egypt. Jacob's sons, the ten brethren of Joseph, come to seek corn when the famine was in their own land, the land of Canaan, were the first hunger marchers. They marched, not as our ex-servicemen, our neo-pagans, our paid incendiaries, our honest men and our Communists do, brandishing crude weapons, shouting defiance, but in the peaceful manner of a pastoral people whose faith in neighbourly charity is undefiled. They came their way unto Egypt slowly, upon the backs of their asses the sacks wherein they hoped to bear back corn to Canaan. And as they entered the presence of Joseph, the Governor of the land, and he who sold corn to all the people of the land, they bowed themselves down before him, with their faces to the earth.

A strange tale, this, of the first hunger march – a tale of filial devotion, of tribal affection, of brotherly love interwoven with many manifestations of that perverse strain inherent in Eastern psychology, the love of masquerade, of stagecraft, of complicated expression as opposed to candid exposition which still distinguishes the Jew of today from that simple fellow the agnostic or the Christian.

You may read in Genesis of how Joseph, knowing his brethren but making himself strange unto them, spake to them roughly, calling them spies come to see the nakedness of the land. And of how they, knowing him not, made answer, they had come but to buy food, adding: 'We are all one man's sons . . . We are the sons of one man in the land of Canaan; and, behold, the youngest is this day with our father.'

And of Joseph's reply: 'If ye be true men, let one of your brethren be bound in the house of your prison; go ye, carry corn for the famine of your houses:

'But bring your youngest brother unto me; so shall your words be verified.'

You may read of the fear that fell upon them when on their homeward journey one of them opened a sack to give his ass provender at an inn, and found in the sack's mouth the money he had rendered unto the Governor's man for corn. You may read of Jacob's reluctance to let his youngest son fare back to this strange land in obedience to the Governor's behest, and of that second march into Egypt when, driven at length by famine, the sons of Jacob took with them their youngest brother, Benjamin, and, to propitiate the Egyptians, presents consisting of the best fruit of the land in vessels – a little balm and a little honey, spices and myrrh, nuts and almonds.

You may read of how at last, his passion for circumlocution sated, Joseph wept and made himself known unto his brethren, saying: 'I am Joseph, your brother, whom ye sold unto Egypt . . . God sent me before you to preserve you a posterity in the earth, and to save your lives by a great deliverance . . . Thou shalt dwell in the land of Goshen, and thou shalt be near unto me, thou, and thy children, and thy children's children, and thy flocks, and thy herds, and all that thou hast:

'And there will I nourish thee; for yet there are five years' famine; lest thou, and thy household, and all that thou hast, come to poverty.'

You may read of all this in Genesis, and as you read you may picture the first hunger marchers – patient, bearded Israelites urging their beasts down to Egypt. With the red sand of the desert on their hair, and their brown robes limp in the heat, they draw near the walls of the city in which is gathered up all the food of those seven plenteous years when the earth brought forth by handfuls. They draw near the city silently, the limpid blue light of approaching nightfall raying upon them as upon the figures of saints. Hunger marchers out of Gilead, on the lips of each one a prayer: 'Give us corn that we may live and not die, both we and thou, and also our little ones. Give us bread!'

Thus in the desert, within sight of the walls of ancient Egypt, this cry was formulated by ten pilgrims, a cry destined to crash through the centuries like the first hoarse mutterings of revolution; a cry destined to evoke emotion in the breasts of stoics, to set those in high office trembling, to kindle a flame that consumeth all that harken unto it or unto its echoings.

Give Us Bread!

The great hunger march of the New Testament took place in the reign of Herod. Five thousand men, beside women and children, took part in it. They took part in it at the bidding of Jesus, whom they had followed on foot out of the cities into a desert place, and who, on hearing of their hunger, said unto His disciples: 'Bring them hither unto Me.'

And He commanded the multitude to sit down on the grass, and took up the five loaves and the two fishes, and looking up to heaven, He blessed and brake, and gave the loaves to His disciples, and the disciples to the multitude.

'And they did all eat and were filled.'

Again and again through the New Testament the hunger march recurs. The return of the Prodigal Son to his father's house from the swine-troughs was a hunger march. So was the march of Christ and His disciples on that second sabbath after the first when He with His disciples went through the cornfields, and His disciples plucked the ears of the corn, and did eat, rubbing them in their hands.

So it may be said of Christ that He was the first of the great hunger marchers. So with equal truth may it be said of the meanest hunger marcher today, perambulating a city square in defiance of authority, that he is following in the Divine footsteps. He is walking in the shadow of God.

It is probable that the first Ice Age, the age that ended that known as the Golden Age, brought about the first hunger march in these isles. The hunters, roaming the hills in quest of wildfowl, or seeking fish in rivers that reflected the white gleam of their naked bodies, were not hunger marchers in the real sense; for so keen was their aim, so buoyant their movements, that they never went long a-hungered.

It was with the coming of the Ice Age, of the bergs with their glacier peaks and grey cold, that the winds of adversity blew shrill over the land. It was then, when beasts perished in the louring blast, when every summit was wreathed in fog, and fish died below the ice freezing the streams, and a sense of fearful chill made heartbeats laboured – it was then, of a certainty, that the first hunger marches in these isles began, marches of desperate men bewildered by this strange white doom come so swiftly down upon them.

One can picture these men, brave hunters of yesterday, running amok in the grey solitude as they sought for trails they had followed from infancy, for the familiar scents that were wont to guide them. One can see their eyes searching for landmarks so strangely travestied by the sinister sky, and the enclosing bergs, as to seem gone for ever. Gone – everything gone in this dank grey darkness! One can imagine them marching on and on, the beat of their blood urging them forward although they knew at the back of their bemused brains they had lost all sense of direction, all hope of salvation. On and on . . . So, centuries later, modern hunger marchers, bearing rude weapons, blaring harsh music, were to encircle our cities' squares, our Government buildings, voicing the prayer of Joseph's brethren:

Give Us Bread!

Through ancient Rome, through Greece, through Tyre, the cry in sundry tongues has echoed. Caesar's legionaries plundering Egypt; Napoleon's soldiers stumbling back from Moscow, Prince Charlie's followers replacing from Carlisle, all have uttered it. It has arisen in every corner of the world: outside Tyburn, beneath the walls of the Kremlin, on the shores of the Caspian Sea, in the kraals of Africa, on the sun-baked Chinese plains.

Paris awoke to the cry one wet October morning in the early days of the French Revolution. It awoke to the beating of a drum in the Quartier Saint-Eustache, where a young woman set out crying upon all mothers and Judiths to descend from their homes to seek food and revenge. Thus began the greatest hunger march in all history, the march of the maenads on the King's palace at Versailles. Carlyle describes the women, ten thousand strong – women of all classes, all types, robust dames of the Halles, housemaids with early brooms, slim mantua-makers, virgins on their way to mass – hurrying, tumultuous and wild-shrilling, towards the Hôtel-de-Ville. He tells of their attack upon the Armoury, their seizure of guns, of money-bags, and of cannon yoked with seized carthorses.

Past the city barriers, across the ancient bridge of Sèvres crossing the Seine, they roll on their way – this vast regiment of women marching to the rhythm of drums; drums whose tapping notes echo their heartbeats as the press grows closer and the lovely inheritance of royalty comes in sight. Through the splashing rain they advance up the leafy avenue of Versailles with its four rows of elms – the women and their followers, members of the National Guards from every district, and all the ragtag and bobtail of those villages through which they have passed.

'Bread, and speech with the King,' is their demand as they swarm over the Palace esplanade, where the rain beats down upon their bedraggled locks, their rusty pikes, their tree boughs and their billhooks. *'Du pain, et parler avec Roi.'*

Sequel to this hunger march and, stranger still, the march of the maenads back to Paris with the King and the royal provision wagons in their midst. No pleas now for bread, but a loud triumphal singing of ribald songs, a lewd chanting, with a sidelong jerk of a weapon towards the royal carriage: 'We shall not want for bread now; we have brought back with us the Baker and the Bakeress.'

'Processional marches not a few our world has seen', writes Carlyle. 'Roman triumphs and ovations, Cabiric cymbal-beatings, royal progresses, Irish funerals; but this of the French monarchy marching to its bed remains to be seen. Miles long, and of breadth losing itself in vagueness, for all the neighbouring country crowds to see. Slow; stagnating along, like shoreless Lake, yet with a noise like Niagara, like Babel and Bedlam. A splashing and a tramping;

a hurrahing, uproaring, musket-volleying; the truest segment of Chaos seen in these latter Ages!'

And now in a generation made outcast, one half, by the machine, the cry of Joseph's brethren, of the maenads, is dinging into the ears of politicians, of philanthropists, of men in high places, every hour of the day. You can hear it, if you have a mind to listen, above the throbbing of piston rods, the plunging of dynamos, the scream of escaping steam, the fierce shudderings of electric road drills, the thunder of blasting. You can hear it, a thin hoarse cry as of a force imprisoned deep down in some gigantic chasm gashed in the face of the earth, and made stiff by the devilish contrivances of modern excavators and builders.

You will see nothing, however, if you go forward to look into such a chasm, but a scattering of men controlling monster cranes operating great buckets which dip into the ground for the purpose of collecting rubble which they then draw upwards to dispose of in trolleys before seeking the underground again. You will see nothing but a framework, where the rubbish has been cleared; a framework of iron girders set firmly in a great wedge of the soil. Iron, steel, ferro-concrete everywhere. The Machine Age concentrated in this chasm of mechanical industry.

Small wonder the cry of man echoes but faintly here. For here where the machine is all powerful man matters little enough. But can you make man realize this? Not in a hundred years!

With ingrained stubbornness he still prates of the right to live. He still believes, as Joseph's brethren believed, in the necessity of preserving his tribe from extinction, in the need for seeking provender for his house and for all that he has. He has less faith in the charity of his neighbours than had Joseph's brethren. Perhaps this is why when he asks for assistance, as they did of Egypt's Governor, he does not bow down before the potential giver, his face to the earth. Instead, his attitude may be likened to that of the street urchin, who cries, 'Gimme!' and snatches. Indeed, the only person before whom he is inclined to bow down is before him who has snatched so ruthlessly that he has succeeded in amassing riches in a world where riches are few.

Yes, despite execration, despite the fact that again and again it has been proved that a simple machine can do quite neatly and effectively, and without any song about it, the work of a gang of labourers, man still claims his right to live. Within recent years, he has taken to asserting this claim in accents louder than courtesy permits. His brain, addled by confused justice, by the jargon of diverse politicians, and stupefied by the incessant din of clattering machinery, works only in spurts. His opinions, never soberly accumulated, or carefully gestated, are ruled by his passions. And his ruling passion is the desire to live.

Give Us Bread!

You can interpret that cry today into a desire for the decencies of life, into a plea for respite from a struggle that is desperate in the extreme.

The last hunger march to secure headlines in the world's press occurred in June 1933 in Edinburgh,[1] where, at the end of a three days' march, unemployed men and women from all parts of Scotland camped and slept in a street famed for its beauty and historical associations. Dawn saw the red banners, tied to the railings of Princes Street Gardens, fluttering gently in the cool breeze above irregular rows of recumbent figures. Later, on the opposite pavement, Edinburgh shop girls and office workers, on their way to business, lingered to stare at the marchers rousing themselves from slumber and seeking out a nearby fountain in which to bathe their tired faces. The advent of a horse-drawn lorry bearing food for the demonstrators, and pulling up outside the Gardens, caused the black-coated brigade to halt once more. There, the lawyer's clerk, the corset maker, may have thought as they gazed open-eyed at the famished marchers devouring tea on the chilly pavement – there, but for the grace of God, go I! And it is probable that the clerk and the corset maker expressed their gratitude to God by hurrying hotfoot to their respective tasks, and by bringing to those tasks such a spurt of energy as to cause their employers to reflect at the end of the day on the possibility of cutting down staff. They might manage with a man, or a woman, less, if old Thomson, or Miss Jones, kept it up . . . An ironical acknowledgment, this, on

1 This was written before the hunger march in February 1934.

the part of the Deity, of the gratitude of Miss Jones and old Thomson for their comfortable states.

About midday a crowd of some thirty thousand followed the red banners through ancient ways where the gilded cavalcade of Mary, Queen of Scots, once swayed, and where the Leith mob, after the failure of the Darien Expedition, swarmed, crying out for the blood of the English captain whose vessel lay captive in the Forth. Unlike those men of Leith, the followers of the red banners raised no shout for other men's blood. With only a confused murmur rising from their ranks, they rolled on over the stony ways like a gulf current which, without unwise struggle, or show of violence, must sooner or later wear down all that which opposes its passage.

Almost a year before the Edinburgh march, Washington had been the scene of a similar happening, when thousands upon thousands of ex-servicemen from all parts of the United States assembled and camped in Pennsylvania Avenue, just four blocks from the Capitol. The marchers ensconced themselves in hovels, dugouts and dilapidated shelters on a Government property in process of being cleared in a scheme for beautifying the city. From there, they proceeded each day to demonstrate before the Capitol and the White House.

Their demand was for further payment on their War Bonus certificates, a demand refused by Congress under the strong advice of President Hoover. But most of the banners flaunted by the veterans who assembled in all the glory of their old uniforms bore the simple legend: 'We Want Bread.'

The full story of that march has yet to be written. It suffices to record that it forms a chapter unique in the history of the United States. Beginning in the State of Louisiana, where the first seeds of rebellion were sown by fiery spirits, and ending rather ignominiously in a free fight, with bricks flying, in the streets of Washington, amid a populace whose sympathies were sharply divided, it has no real parallel in the story of our times.

One vital fact emerges from the record of all these marches – the fact that in place of being a splendid outpouring of humanity knit together by a common cause, the marchers tend to resolve almost invariably into a shuffling mob trailing half-heartedly at the heels of their leaders; a mob wasting its strength in shouts of imprecation, in paroxysms of passion as objectless as they are pitiful to behold.

Yet still they persist, those marches – bubbles on the stream of a Great Unrest. They persist, and who shall say but that the reflection of their sombre hue does not alter the colour of other lives, that it does not cast its shadow upon the swift flow of current happenings?

On through the centuries, they pass and repass, those marching figures – brethren of Joseph, sansculottes; American ex-servicemen, our own unemployed. They pass and repass, creating today the merest blur, like that of a human breath on the mirror of our consciousness – wiseacres and fools, saints and sinners, rogues and visionaries, honest tradesmen and vagabonds, boys in their teens, doddering old men, mothers with infants in their arms, wild-eyed viragos, waving and shouting. They pass and repass, and so long as we suffer them to do so unaided, the drumming of their feet rises in our ears liked the doom-peal of our civilization.

Bread! We Want Bread!

From the deepest of human needs that demand arises. To reject it is to damn ourselves for ever as unworthy vessels of the Godhead spark which differentiates man from beast.

PART I

MORNING

CHAPTER I

It was one of those days when you felt God had forgotten the city. Hours ago, dawn had swept softly round the world, destroying the thick, tense silence, transmuting darkness into light. Yet here in the city's heart, the burden of outspread wings still lingered. A drab grey sky, indeterminate as down, sloped above a confusion of black stone. The sun, suffused by cloud, resembled a purple globe held by unseen hands against the sky. In the streets, vehicles moved reluctantly; men and women walked dully, as in a dream. It was as though in these pinioned gullies the stored-up vitality of centuries was all spent, as though a sense of doom were hooding the lyrical images evoked by youth, converting ecstasy and exaltation into a stuporous gall that chilled the blood.

Outside the town, the sun had driven clear of the clouds' dark fleece. Its rays cast garlands of changing light on the fields, the hills. At their base, tall young trees stood up like pure white flames springing miraculously from the blackened crust of the earth. So bright likewise with the glitter of hoar frost was the coarse grass fringing the river that the water appeared glowing and silver-edged as it flowed out to sea.

In the keen clear air there was peace and the sense of eternity. But even while he savoured this sense, Arthur Joyce was aware that within himself was a lurking disquiet.

He was conscious of it while he breakfasted and scanned his letters. There was nothing much in them to arrest him. A few bills, a couple of dinner invitations, a begging letter from a man who claimed to have served in the same battery in France as his son. What was the fellow's name? Higgins, Joseph Higgins, 7 Steeple

Street, Littlehampton. The name and address conveyed nothing. Well, that would have to be enquired into . . . 'Captain Joyce'. For the fraction of a second, sitting there at his breakfast table, Arthur Joyce saw a brown-eyed schoolboy talking eagerly – life even at the age of fourteen had seemed a tremendous thing to Jerry – the while he devoured porridge and cream.

Unlike many bereaved fathers, Joyce was fortunate in that he never saw his son as other more imaginative men saw their dead – stunned and blinded, maimed and maddened by the insensate din of gunfire. When he thought of Jerry, it was not the adventurous young man known as Captain Joyce, but the ardent schoolboy, who took shape before his eyes. Perhaps, unconsciously, he had trained his thoughts to avoid those years when reason seemed to have fled the world; or it may have been that, recognizing the futility of keeping on rubbing at a sore, he had deliberately narrowed the sweep of his horizon, ruled out the brief period that elapsed between his son's departure from school and his death in France.

Meticulously, with his paperknife, as was his wont, he slit open another envelope and set the letter it contained against an empty toast rack in front of him. The writing on the thin sheets was that of Constance, his only surviving child, a young woman with a passion for foreign travel. Why Constance wanted always to be rushing off abroad he never quite understood. Words were all Constance garnered in foreign parts; that was all places meant to her. Never, by any chance, did you see through her eyes remote temples with sacred bells at whose awakening nimble brown people prostrated themselves in the dust. Never through her eyes did you see the snake charmers outside the native bazaars making their strange reedy music. No; wherever she went – to South Africa or the Ind – she was always surrounded by the hum of well-bred English voices, by the chaste tinkle of teacups. The absolute spinster, Constance – God help her!

What her father had never realized – or else, of a certainty, he would have tried to help her himself – was that his daughter was a victim of the Great War. Although she had never set foot in the war zone, or heard so much as the bang of an anti-aircraft gun, she had suffered from a vicarious form of shell shock, so that for months, after Jerry's death, when she laid her head on her pillow at nights the thunder of artillery had pounded loudly in her ears.

She never spoke of this. Nor did she talk much of Jerry. Her father's policy was to ignore the dead, as though by dying they had disgraced themselves; to segregate them from the living. She could not recall ever having heard him utter her dead mother's name. And now, suddenly, Jerry had gone through the gap in the hedge. And because you couldn't see him, because all that was left to you of him was the echo of the guns that destroyed him, you must wear a guard on your lips and not say thoughtlessly: 'That was the year Jerry had measles,' or, 'That was the summer Jerry and I went to St Andrews.' It was difficult when every single incident in your life was bound up with Jerry.

Sometimes it occurred to her to wonder what would happen if she violated this unspoken rule, if she invaded her father's private fastness and forced him to speak of her brother. But as a child is shocked and terrified at sight of an elder in tears, so her heart recoiled from the possibility of provoking emotion in her father. She had been on a visit to friends when the telegram had come from the War Office. By the time she reached home, Mr Joyce had regained his self-control, if, indeed, he had ever wholly lost it.

That things should go on just as usual after Jerry's death seemed to his sister revolting, and somehow lacking in respect to his memory. She had an absurd impulse the day she came home to snatch the sweet peas from their slender vases, to blot out the candles that created little pools of radiance on the dinner table. So young was she then, so brimful of vitality, that her instinct had been to turn the spear in her own breast, not to pluck it out and to bury it, as her father, with the wisdom born of age and experience, had done.

In the end, the continued booming in her ears had alarmed her. She determined on flight. 'I'd like to travel,' she said one day. 'D'you know, Daddy, I've never been across the Channel since I was a kid? I want to see places – Vienna, St Moritz, Madrid.'

She had gone off with an elderly widow for companion soon

afterwards. On her return, her father, after a few tête-à-têtes, decided she had got nothing out of the trip. Nor had she. But she had rid her mind of much of the evil wrought in it by self-repression. She had entered new tracts of country which she had never trodden in company with Jerry, and gradually, because she brooded less frequently upon him, and upon the circumstances of his death, the nightmare of the guns left her.

Travel she hastily assumed to be a cure for all ills. Consequently, whenever boredom or some minor ailment attacked her, she ticked off on her fingers such places abroad as she had yet to visit. South America, New Zealand, India.

She was in Madras now. But even had she been at home, Joyce reflected, it would have made no difference. He wouldn't have told her about this. Not until it was all settled.

This – in a flash, it bared itself to view, the source of his disquiet. A balance sheet which even he, with his talent for avoiding the unpleasant, could not delude himself into mistaking for cheerful reading. For the past few months he had hedged, held back from coming to a definite decision. But the course, summarized briefly in the words, 'Get out, and quickly', seemed now to be plainly indicated. He had nothing to worry about, nothing to reproach himself with, so Jacks, his friend and legal adviser, had been quick to point out.

No; he had nothing to worry about. Nevertheless, his mouth twisted wryly as he visualized the announcement: 'Joyce and Son, closing down.'

Well, they wouldn't be the first of the India merchants in the city to put up the shutters. There was Hintons', a far bigger concern than theirs had been; and Fuljacks' – both gone. To this day Fuljacks' offices were standing empty – narrow, winding premises reeking faintly, or so he always imagined, of the mysterious produce of the Orient. He had taken on one of Fuljacks' bright young men, a likeable youth with more than an average share of ability. For a second, it occurred to him to wonder who, if anybody, when Joyce's shutters were closed, would take on Joyce's bright young men.

But in business there is no room for sentiment. That had been one of his father's maxims, and the old boy had lived up to it for all his profession of godliness. Joyce could remember when every newspaper was banished from the rooms on Sundays, when by his father's command a certain cuckoo clock in the lobby was stilled because its frivolous notes profaned the silence of the Lord's Day. Monday saw the cuckoo clock restored to voice, and his father, unburdened of his weekly piety, seated four-square at his desk, controlling the destinies of his firm with a deadly incisiveness that rarely failed to impress his subordinates, and secretly to amuse his son, who could not help contrasting the humility of the sober-miened elder of yesterday with the truculence of the man of affairs today.

Yes, get out, and quickly, Arthur Joyce was pretty sure would have been his father's mind of it. Certainly, he would retire a richer man now than if he hung on for a few more years.

He sat staring at the litter of dishes on the table, trying to think clearly what this business of retiring would mean to him personally. He had never contemplated it until such time as his limbs or his wind should give out. And so the future yawned before him uncharted. Had he been a younger man, or a man of a different temperament, he would have dubbed the prospect 'exciting'. But armoured as he believed himself to be in cynicism, he fancied the stoppage of his activities would affect him little, if at all. He might develop a paunch, he reflected wryly, and become a regular diner-out with a fund of 'good stories'. But the raconteur, like the professional comedian, requires a second – an adoring wife or daughter to murmur: 'Do tell them that other one, the one about the menagerie.' And he possessed neither. Constance, somehow, didn't count.

He wondered what would have been her mother's mind of things. Not that it mattered really. No one had paid much attention to Aggie's opinions when she had been alive. He didn't know what made him think of her now. Perhaps because, although Aggie had been the vaguest creature on earth, and incapable of managing servants, of ever catching the right train, she had on rare occasions the faculty of throwing an extraordinarily clear light on a troublous problem. It was as though her usually muddled thoughts, floating hereaway, thereaway, suddenly threw up a prize in the shape of a deep-water pearl.

Yes, there had been times when Aggie had unexpectedly made him sit up and listen, and when, more surprisingly still, he had taken her advice. But when you went to her for further counsel, it was a thousand to one you found her floundering again, immersed in some deep incomprehensible muddle, astounded and tearful because her dressmaker or some tradesman or other persisted in declaring that two and two made four instead of the five she insisted it should be. Poor Aggie! When he married her, that vagueness had seemed to him the evidence of an abnormally sensitive temperament, of a gentle shyness which he deemed a lovely quality in a woman at a time when shyness among women was going out and hardihood was coming in.

Aggie had been educated at a ladies' school, at one of those polite seminaries where prizes are given to every child no matter what its intellectual shortcomings. Aggie's prizes were all for good conduct. It was characteristic of her that she kept all these little books, that she had even brought one, a maxim on good behaviour, with her on her honeymoon. Her behaviour had been 'correct' enough then in all consciousness! Poor Aggie!

He had a quite vivid recollection of her sitting opposite him in the hotel at Carlisle where they had spent their first night together. Her eyes the colour of jonquils, her slim face faintly flushed, she had looked, he thought, ethereal, as though she might suddenly float away before his arms could enfold her. But a minute later he was smiling at her helpless indecision over the menu. Thick or clear? He had made up his mind for her on that point as he was to make up her mind for her on other, profounder, issues all the days of her life.

Yes, it was a thousand odds to one at this juncture that Aggie could have given him any counsel worth taking. In any case, Aggie had died before the war. She had not survived to experience that stupendous change in the world's outlook. He wondered how it would have affected her. Would she have drifted on, all unaware that the old order was changing, or would she have felt, as others of her generation had felt, as though she were being torn up by the roots and transplanted in some rude and alien soil?

The process, all the same, in his case had been fairly easy. Just a change of values, that was all; and the influx into the office of women of the type he dubbed 'smarty'; casual-minded young creatures rather too well dressed, in place of reverent, middle-aged men. Margarine instead of butter – that summed up the change pretty well in a sentence. Something that tended to grit between your teeth instead of gliding suavely over. Yes, that had been practically all there was to it until Jerry. Then suddenly the smooth ring of existence had been wrenched asunder. Mingled with the violence of his grief was that sense of shocked surprise common to those who have enjoyed a long immunity from Fate's harsh blows. A feeling that his soul had been rudely violated, torn and trampled upon, preceded a wave of self-pity which he recognized as a mawkish sentiment to be instantly damned up. Accordingly he kept his emotions under constraint until he began to feel the pain, which had almost blinded him with its searing pangs, recede farther and farther away. Today, it was no more than a pinpoint set at the centre of his being, a pinpoint never wholly insulated but capable of inflicting torture on nerves that were exposed and quivering.

As he sat there, a tall, muscular figure relaxed in his chair, the strong sunlight beat upon a face subtly altered by the thoughts passing behind it, a face unmasked and so a little pitiful as the face of any grown person is apt to be who is unconscious or asleep. Gone momentarily was the expression of shrewd alertness, of disdainful scepticism. In its place was a strange wistfulness, a bleak hunger that knew no let.

It was the sound of his car, driven round to the front door from the garage, that rescued him from the depths of the pit into which he was slipping. He jerked himself alert with an impatient movement. A blue lookout for the future if, at contemplation of the first lull, he let himself go raking up the past! And yet it was perhaps because he had shut the door so resolutely upon it that the past, when he regarded it squarely, still hurt so damnably. He had known women, half crazed over the loss of a child, brood over their grief until its fangs were withdrawn, and their sorrow had appeared to companion them friendly-wise like the pattering feet of their dead child. Mock sentiment, of course! Soft as muck! Determinedly, he drove his thoughts down other channels.

But, even as he made plans for the occupation of his leisure and rejected them, he was dogged by a sense of loneliness, of something lost. He had gone on and on, passing milestone after milestone without noticing them, and now suddenly he was brought to a stop. Without the interest of business, the glamour its excitement lent, he realized one day would be much like another. Weeks would tend to drag tediously as they had done in his early youth, when as an only child and before he had learned to read, his plaint in a house of elderly grown-ups had been: 'I've nothing to do.'

The thought flashed upon him – second childhood, and the lines on his long, weathered face hardened. Had it come already to that?

He leaned forward, a faintly bitter smile biting into the folds about his mouth. Thank Heaven, he had hobbies to spare and money, not to burn, but to make enough of a blaze to provide fireworks for his own entertainment.

While he sat contemplating the prospect ahead – a fishing on the Spey; a house in Surrey; an occasional cruise; not east: he'd had enough of that, but to the northern capitals and perhaps Florida – the ping of the front-door bell echoed through the kitchen lobby.

Burns, the chauffeur, stood on the step, swinging his arms vigorously. He stopped exercising when the door opened.

'Hullo, Flora! What's up? What's keeping the governor?'

'And how should I be knowing? Hadn't you better be going in and asking him yourself?'

Burns rubbed his chin with his hand. A big stolid fellow, with watchful grey eyes, he had not the type of mind capable of evolving pert repartee. He stood staring at Flora, the Highland tablemaid with her high-coloured cheeks, her big hips bulging the thin cotton of her light blue wrapper, until suddenly her colour grew higher still, and she shut the door smartly in his face.

He lounged back to his car feeling slightly indignant. If she thought – if she thought anything, she was far wrong! He hadn't rung the bell for the sake of speaking to her – the great Highland heifer! – but because the governor was usually so on the nail that he had begun to think something must be up.

He sauntered over to the top of the hill, looked down on the rolling fields below. If they had been going country-ways, he mused, instead of town, it might have been as well to take chains. They'd had heavy snow overnight further north, the papers reported. A right skiddy day, a gruelling day for horses. That was one thing about a car – no fear of it skinning its knees.

He turned and looked at the Rolls – a proud shining object in the sunlight. Set against the grey façade of the many-windowed house, a house whose sloping stone roof and mellow walls bespoke an antiquity which they did not in actuality possess, the modern streamline of the car suggested another sphere. It suggested a speed-bird, wings suspended, blown by some wild black hurricane across the barriers of time into an earlier age, an age of frost-girt stillness and repose. Unconsciously, Burns' nerves sucked up that repose. For a minute he stood breathing deeply, then his eyes, resting on a thin line of smoke drifting skywards from the chimney of his cottage at the top of the hill, came back to the window of the room where Mr Joyce habitually breakfasted. If he were the governor, he'd be blowed if he'd go into town on a day like this! He'd be off with the car to the back of beyond.

What was the use of a mint of money if it mewed you to a city desk? The last few weeks, the Rolls might just as well have been a blinkin' bus. Tuppence each way. Into the office and back again. Ruddy that with a new car that thought nothing of seventy on a clear road! Instead, it was tram-dodging all the time, avoiding old women skittering like hens across the street. There should be a law against it. White lines confining the old birds to a run.

'A fine mornin', Burns.'

Burns nodded assent, and the old gardener, wheeling a barrow full of frost-nipped plants, straightened his back.

'The master's late this mornin'. Are you takin' him into the office, Burns?'

'Suppose so, George. Why?'

'Oh, nothing, nothing. But my grandson – you mind Annie's boy? He's workin' for a saddler in the Low Wynd – he telled me last night there was to be a great demonstration in the Square today. That'll mean a terrible thrangity in the town, I'm thinkin'.'

A confident smile transfigured Burns' rather stupid, good-looking features. He jerked his head backwards towards the waiting car.

'Och, she'll win her way through anything. It wouldn't be a bad job if she did for a wheen of them when she was at it.'

The old man nodded. 'Aye, these politeecians filling the laddies' heads with their trash! When I was young, you voted Tory and you took what came to you and were thankful. But now' – he spat disgustedly, and an infinite scorn sharpened his voice – 'now, what with their National Government as they call it, you don't know which is gentry and which is scum. I'll nutt vote for scum, I telled them when they came canvassing to me. I've risen from scum myself and I know what scum is. I'll vote for my betters, or nutt at all.'

'Hear hear, George!'

Mr Joyce was visualizing, not unhappily, the leisurely days ahead when a clock chimed the hour.

He scraped back his chair, flung into the hall where, summoned by his hasty movements, Flora stood in readiness with his coat and hat.

Briefly he acknowledged his chauffeur's salute.

'We're late, Burns. Drive like blazes.'

As the car swooped confidently down the avenue – a monstrous black raven flying between rows of white frozen trees – an odd little smile rose to his lips.

What was all his hurry? Putting up the shutters wasn't a long job.

CHAPTER II

In the lounge of the hotel directly opposite Joyce and Son's office, a young journalist awaited the arrival of Adèle Elberstein. The lady was travelling by road. It was quite on the cards she might not get here for another hour. In that case, she might be too tired to grant him an interview, too intent upon conserving her energies for her appearance at night.

He yawned, looked about him for distraction. The lounge, despite its blaze of electric lamps, had a chastened air. It was the sort of lounge, he thought, which only the outburst of a spurious gaiety plus the company of a pretty woman, regarded through the mellow haze induced by cocktails and champagne, could redeem from the blight of semi-gentility. A strange setting for Adèle Elberstein!

For a time he lost sight of the glooming room with its high bare walls, its pillared recesses and tedious litter of little tables. He was stalking Europe on Elberstein's trail, seeing her name emblazoned outside the opera houses of Paris, Madrid, Bucharest, Milan. It was at Milan she had made her debut, at Milan she had achieved her first, her most sensational, success. It was there, according to rumour, she had met the Crown Prince. It was there a queen had gone to her as supplicant, desperate to reclaim from the diva's influence her eldest son.

They said Elberstein flaunted some of the Prince's jewels on the stage that night as a gesture of contempt for royalty; and that on the following morning she crammed the priceless rubies, the diamonds, the sapphires, carelessly into an empty chocolate box and sent them back, by letter-post, to his Highness. A month later she was gadding about France with a notorious Bolshevik agent. She was photographed outside a Montmartre cafe in his company. At a meeting of Communists, she was reported to have sung the Internationale and to have roused her hearers to such a fine fever of frenzy that within an hour shooting affrays were occurring in various quarters of the city.

But behind all the fantastic posturings, the foolish, exaggerated gestures, there lay the artiste. As he sat there, Jimmy pictured Adèle Elberstein as a woman gifted by nature with a voice so pure, so exquisite, that its preservation was her chief care. Men pursued her, flattered her – princes, politicians. journalists – and, womanlike, she was swayed by their wiles. But only temporarily, for she was a star set in her course; and those who paid her homage, who flattered her, who contributed to her triumphs, were no more than the uneasy clouds that flit in a planet's wake.

'Coffee, sir? Scotch and soda?'

Jimmy fixed the intruder with a stony gaze. Hang it all, he couldn't go on consuming liquid refreshment. If Madame Elberstein didn't turn up soon . . .

'Neither,' he rejoined curtly. Then it struck him that the waiter, oppressed like himself by the aridness of the atmosphere, was probably eager to establish some kind of human contact in a room which, for all the life it held, might be the interior of a superintendent's office at a cemetery.

'Many people stopping here?' he asked. Not that he cared in the least, but that was one of the remarks you could make to a foreigner without impairing your British prestige.

The man shrugged. His head, which was too big for his body and set too far back on it, wobbled unpleasantly.

'Not many, sir. But in this weather . . .' He shrugged again, set to work to polish the table as though loath to leave the proximity of an affable patron.

'Ah, well, you've a celebrity coming today. Adèle Elberstein.'

'So I have heard it said. The last time I listen to Madame Elberstein – it was in my own country, at the opera in Milan.'

'They think a lot of her there, I dare say.'

With a flourish of pride the little man threw his napkin over his arm. He resembled momentarily a strutting bantam which, seeing no farther than its own farmyard, believes itself cock of the universe.

'A lot?' he jeered. Then a wealth of sincerity strengthened his voice. 'They love her, they—'

He stopped short as the glass doors swung open to admit an incomer. Instinctively he lowered his eyes; his shoulders drooped obsequiously. Only his voice remained free from the taint of servility.

'I know,' he said confidentially. 'I know, because I have a daughter, little Giovanna, in the ballet at Milan. I give her good lessons, I pay a great deal of money, so that one day she may be a coryphée there, little Giovanna.'

But Jimmy wasn't interested in little Giovanna. His attention had strayed to the newcomer. He was trying to recall who he was, and where, if ever, he had seen him before.

'By gum,' he exploded, 'that's Nimrod, Hamish Nimrod! I bet he's here for the demonstration.'

'Demonstration? There is to be—'

'This afternoon. You'll see all the fun from here.'

Jimmy spoke absently. His gaze was on Nimrod, otherwise he would have surprised a look of fear in those bulging eyes. He would have recognized, clever as he was at detecting the real person behind the trappings, that here was a terror-stricken soul whom life had consistently betrayed.

Over at the fireplace, the man called Nimrod stood warming his long limbs. He was younger looking, Jimmy decided, than you would judge from his photographs. His curly black hair showed no trace of thinning, no tinge of grey. His features, lean as a hound's, looked as though they might have been cast in iron. A sportsman, and a member of the ruling class you would have taken him for, had it not been for the deep pallor of his skin. Slum pallor, Jimmy dubbed it, and stared the harder at this man who embodied in his person all that was most vital in the revolutionary movement in Scotland today. Almost you felt that here was the hard core of an aggressiveness which no weight of arms, of argument, would ever wear down. It resembled in its essence the glint of cold steel.

Behind those keen, knife-like eyes, what dreams were evolving, what spectacular processions of strange, startling events? Outbursts of sansculottism, perhaps, or a slow, sure pressure that would regenerate Scotland, and, through Scotland, Europe itself? Burnings and parades and haranguings, futile although alarmist, or some supreme coup whereby the mob would gain mastery? But the mob would not retain that mastery long. How could it, composed as such mobs are of a thousand inflammable elements fused together by a common passion, which, consuming itself, burns swiftly out? No, the mob would not retain its mastery long, but Nimrod – the man who set flame to its fiery particles and then stood aside coolly, calculating where the hottest sparks would fall – Nimrod would retain the sceptre himself. No king on his throne, surrounded by the full panoply of state, would ever dominate his subjects as this advocate of democracy would dominate his followers. God in heaven, cried Jimmy inwardly, didn't the poor fools recognize in their leader a potential dictator, who would arraign to himself, perhaps unconsciously yet none the less determinedly, the powers of life and death?

Nimrod stooped at that moment to cast a match into the fire. As he did so, the glow of the leaping coal flushed his face, and Jimmy was aware of a brooding melancholy, a tenderness, that cancelled the eyes' dark glint. Then Nimrod rose to his full height, and it struck Jimmy, as he stood there smoking aggressively, that there was at once something pitiful and tragic about the solitary figure. Pitiful because although he was of the people, he was no longer one of them. He was isolated from his kind by reason of the visions he saw, and by the fire of his intellect . . .

Tragic? Jimmy hardly knew why he thought that. It was not because Nimrod was solitary. Some men preferred to play a lone hand, and Nimrod, no doubt, was of their company. It was more a feeling than a reasoned conviction that here was something fine doomed to frustration, a rare and courageous spirit born too late. A hundred years ago Hamish Nimrod would have been among those who led brave expeditions to unknown countries overseas. Or, chained to his own land, he would have been among the first, when the madness of battle swept the glens, to go out to meet death singing, the glint of moonlight making a halo about his head.

In these days there was more likelihood of handcuffs than of a halo. Nimrod was accused by his enemies not of being a traitor, which term has a certain dignity, but of being a 'damned twister', of taking money from Russia. His own people repaid him by their trust, but sooner or later they must exhaust him; sooner or later the sight of their sores must lacerate his soul. And in the end the strength that was his would be broken. It would be all spent on a barren strand.

There was a movement behind. The nervous little Italian waiter had let the door swing with a clang. Jimmy looked round. There was no one about. He crossed over to the fireplace.

'Mr Nimrod, isn't it?'

Nimrod nodded, his body tense against the wall. Frowningly, he surveyed his interrogator. Police or press – which did he represent? The latter, most likely. There was just a trace of the Oxford manner.

'Is this demonstration to be on a bigger scale than usual? I'm on the *Wire*. There are rumours.'

Nimrod removed the cigarette from his mouth with a gesture of grave courtesy.

'You go to blazes!' he said.

Jimmy smiled good-humouredly. 'I'd a notion to mingle with your marchers. Maybe it's the same thing.'

Unperturbed by the snub, he seated himself in a chair between the fire and the window, a loosely knit figure with a head so well shaped as to suggest the heroic mould, had it not been for the foreshortening of the nose. A handsome fellow but for that one defect, and far from stupid-looking, Nimrod thought. Odd how journalism keeps on attracting that type and disappointing it. For where intelligent youth expects to find a mouthpiece, he encounters a muzzle. This youngster with the disdainful mouth looked as though he had had a few bouts with authority and been worsted. Nimrod had the impulse to say to him, 'Get out of it,' but he refrained. After all, there were enough lone dogs in the world. Let this one hunt with the pack so long as the pack didn't turn round and rend him. Heaven knew, he might go on hunting with them long enough before they would smell out he was alien to them, a thinking animal, and so of a different breed from themselves.

Unaware of the other's scrutiny, Jimmy leaned forward looking out at the Square. There was little traffic this morning, and the statues, ranged at intervals in the grassy plots and unobscured by the veil of constantly passing vehicles, had an air of formality reminiscent of participators in some ceremony of state. A queer, inarticulate spot, Jimmy thought; the heart of the city and yet at the moment so sedate, showing never a trace of the tremors that shook her, of the misfortunes that had befallen her. Poor but proud. Maybe that was it.

In the half-light the tramcars, gliding by, seemed shriven of their usual clear colour. The faces of the passers-by, the loafers, had a ghostly look. A big saloon car shooting round the corner was the only purposeful object in the square, and even it seemed affected by the prevailing lethargy, for already it was slowing down. It pulled up dead at Joyce's, the India merchant's over the way. Mr Joyce himself got out. There was some talk, Jimmy recalled, that if trade didn't look up his would be the next big firm to find itself in Queer Street. A pity, for there had been a Joyce trading with the Far East since Trafalgar.

Jimmy turned on impulse to Nimrod. 'Tell me,' he said, 'would you have everything go in the holocaust? The old businesses, the old traditions – everything?'

'"If thy right arm offend thee . . ."' quoted Nimrod grimly.

'But does it offend you?'

'The whole system offends me. It stinks because of the corruption it is founded on.'

Jimmy's eyes narrowed. If only he could get Nimrod talking – 'Look here,' he said, 'I don't want to argue – I've not wit enough, Lord knows, to cross swords with you! – but what I'd like to be at is this . . .'

He leaned forward, letting fall his cigarette in his eagerness to marshal the thoughts which leapt like a torrent in his mind, to manacle in words all those impish doubts which at times tormented him. At that moment, Nimrod thought him rather engaging, with his reddish fair hair slightly ruffled, his irritating man-of-the-world air abandoned. Yes, perplexity became the young. When a man used his brains as this journalist fellow was using his now, it was as though a light flowed from his being, as though stone was turning into flesh. Jimmy spoke slowly. 'If humanity will muck about inventing machines that take the place of manpower, and if the Roman Church persists in tabooing birth control.'

The glass doors opened. On the threshold stood a middle-aged woman with a high forehead and a tiny chin, whose tendency to recede contradicted the intelligence expressed by the upper part of her face. She wore a very tight black silk dress. Her hair was set in the stiffest of marcel waves.

'Friend of yours?' said Nimrod.

Jimmy drew rein. Glancing up, he encountered the eyes of Miss Smithers, the hotel receptionist. She gave him a little flurried nod.

'Madame Elberstein has arrived,' she said, then vanished.

Jimmy rose reluctantly. 'Sorry; I'm interviewing her. In any case, I expect I was boring you. I expect you've heard all this a thousand times before.'

'A thousand and one,' amended Nimrod. 'It's comic, all the same, to hear you doubting Thomases. We underdogs are the only folks who have no doubts at all. We are the only ones with faith.'

'Faith? But in what?'

'The future,' said Hamish Nimrod.

Jimmy stood for a second in silence. Over Nimrod's head, breaking the gloom of the high bare wall, was a globule of electricity. It sprang from a bracket embellished by grotesque black leaves whose reflection, on the panel behind, composed the features of a leering gargoyle. The devil jeering at the halo surmounting the head of a revolutionary!

This thought was in Jimmy's mind as he left the lounge.

CHAPTER III

It was very hot in Madame Elberstein's sitting room. The atmosphere, heavy with the scent of flowers and the reek of some Oriental perfume, was redolent of the footlights. Jimmy felt as though he had come down from a high mountain peak into a ravine where the winds of Heaven never blew and the light of the moon never reached – a sterile place of tarnished lights and the exotic glow of tulips out of season.

From the company of a man in whom life burned at white heat, he had come into that of a woman eaten by conceit as a stricken body is eaten by disease; a woman who for so long had dramatized her every action that she was no longer aware of her histrionics. She was one of those people, Jimmy recognized quickly, you couldn't talk to. She was too busy composing the next sentence she intended booming at you to listen. In a trice, his conception of her cherishing her voice, preserving it from harm as an artist might preserve from contamination his love of pure colour, fell to pieces. That voice, like the Madonna face sometimes bestowed by the Almighty on a woman with the soul of a Medusa, was a sheer accident. It was a divine gift disposed in a graceless body. Jimmy fidgeted on his chair. After the rarefied atmosphere created by Nimrod, the egoism of this exuberant creature revolted him.

She was handsome enough, he conceded, in her way. A big strapping woman superbly proportioned, and with tolerable features. Her person exuded an animal magnetism which, in another mood, might have attracted him to her. That, no less than her voice, would attract most men, irrespective of class, of nationality. Well, they were a pretty mixed bunch, her admirers – a crown prince, a French Communist, the nervous little Italian waiter downstairs.

He rose, looked down at her where she sat, clutching her chinchilla cloak and surrounded by her aura of self-complacency – a proverbial queen of song with orchids pinned to her furs, diamonds glittering at her breast, ostrich plumes drooping from the preposterous hat that crowned her thick black hair.

'Thanks very much,' he said. 'You've given me some interesting copy.'

But nothing, he added inwardly, to what you might have given me if only you had shed your confounded egoism. For truth composes the best copy in the world. It is the *vox humana* in life's confused symphony. It is at once scarifying and sublime. Then, abandoning phrase-making, he reflected that to dig the truth out of Elberstein you'd have to strip her of her velvet sleekness, her affectations. This done, as like as not you'd find the soul of a French pension keeper underneath, cold and mean and calculating. Yes, he could imagine those eyes watchful of the helpings on the plates as they circled the dinner table at nights.

She extended her hand to him in farewell. Because he guessed she expected him to bow low over it, he gave the jewelled fingers a hearty grip.

'Please tell the concierge I will see now the other gentlemen of the press who are waiting,' she murmured.

'I do not think there are any others,' he said blandly.

He glanced into the front lounge on his way out. There was a sprinkling of people round the fire, two podgy-faced women laughing loudly, and two stout, overdressed men. The little Italian waiter hurried in with drinks on a salver. What a scared rabbit the fellow looked! For a second Jimmy lingered uncertainly, then he went on into the entrance hall. Miss Smithers, emerging from the manager's office, glided over to him.

'Charming, isn't she?'

'Who? Oh, Elberstein. Would you call her that?'

Miss Smithers' features went flat. Her determined affability faded out before Jimmy's candid gaze.

'Well, she seemed so delighted with everything. Of course, you never can tell,' Miss Smithers sighed. Hotels, as she knew from experience, tended to bring out the worst side in human nature. She wondered frequently if it was because a hotel with its keys, its numbered doors, was so akin in its way to a prison.

'Number thirty-three-ee, please,' a page went past her calling. She stared with hostility at the boy's red neck bulging above the green collar of his jacket. As she did so, she recalled having been at Holloway to see a hall porter in whom she was interested. That was when she had first gone into the hotel business. A Swiss by birth, with no friends in this country, he had been taken up for 'cooking the books' as they called it. For all that, he had been the most efficient hall porter she had ever come across, a fine old chap bearing a strong facial resemblance to the popular pictures of Santa Claus.

She had never quite got over the shock of hearing him referred to as 'Convict Twenty-nine'. She had returned to business that night with a new, but intense, loathing for a system which affixed a number in place of a name to each registered guest. Since then, she had cherished the rooted conviction that it was this system which was in part to blame for the perversity of hotel visitors. Mr Smith, she argued, suffering subconsciously from the fear that he would lose his identity in this place where he was no longer known as John K. Smith, but as a hundred and twenty-seven, instantly sought to assert himself, to preserve John K. Smith from spiritual annihilation, by launching complaint after complaint. That was his defence against submersion in a sea of nonentities, a river of numericals. Bad service, poor food, cold baths, neglected fires. It didn't matter what, so long as John K. Smith could raise his voice sufficiently to dispel from his mind the rising fear that here he was of no significance at all, here he was merely a number, not a man.

'You must get pretty fed up here sometimes, Miss Smithers.'

The colour rose faintly beneath its smothering of pearl powder. 'To the back teeth,' she said. Then it occurred to her that her back teeth were not her own save in the sense that she had bought and paid for them. They were like many other things in the hotel world – artificial, although they didn't look it.

She smiled cautiously, mindful not to show the gold.

'I'll look out for you in the *Wire* tomorrow, Mr Carruthers.'

He nodded absently and went on. She looked after his retreating figure and thought: 'A pleasant young man; but I suppose if he were here he'd be complaining like the rest at the end of a couple of days.' Then, at sight of one of the permanent guests in the hotel bearing down upon her, she hurriedly assumed her normal expression of cheerful affability.

'Miss Smithers, look at this! Toast sent up for my breakfast. I'm taking it to the manager to see. Disgraceful! I shall write about it to the directors.'

Miss Smithers regarded the charred pieces of bread held up for her inspection with an air of gentle interest.

'Really!' she murmured in a shocked voice. 'To send that up to you, Mrs Ferrell!'

'To me, as you say, of all people!' cried Mrs Ferrell, triumphant, or so it seemed to the receptionist's sensitive ears, at having successfully established her identity. 'Well, we'll see what the directors have to say about this.'

Jimmy, passing back to the telephone box, shot a glance at Miss Smithers playing the part of sympathetic friend to a raddled old dame with hennaed hair. Fed up to the back teeth! No wonder! He extracted two pennies from his pocket, unhooked the receiver.

'Hullo!' he said. 'Give me Central, double two, double two. That Joyce and Son? Put me through to Mr Joyce's office, will you? . . . Mr Joyce's secretary speaking? Darling, I've just been interviewing Adèle Elberstein, and I'm done with women. Lunch with me usual place, will you? . . . What? I'm making no mistake. Darling, I love you to distraction. I'd die for— Oh, damn!'

Cut off, he spun a coin. Heads she comes, tails she . . . 'Ah-ha,' he chortled. 'Thank Heaven for that!'

Celia's fair skin was warmly coloured when she replaced the telephone. 'You're making a mistake,' then, 'Wrong number,' she declared, with an energy which deceived her employer, whom the call had interrupted in the midst of dictation. Mr Joyce disliked being kept waiting. Today he disliked it especially, because the task he was engaged upon was an uncongenial one which he wished to be ended with quickly.

He studied the typed sheet on the desk before him. 'Yes, that's all right. You might send a note to Mr Jacks asking him to come down here at five – no, better make it five-thirty, when we can thrash things out. Send it along by hand with these documents enclosed. I want them delivered at once. Now, who is this next?'

Celia's fingers trembled as she lifted the telephone to hush its insistent call. If it were Jimmy again . . . !

'Hullo,' she said, 'hullo. Yes, this is Mr Joyce's private office. No, I'm not sure if he is in or not. If he is, who shall I say? . . . Who? Sorry, I don't quite . . . Yes, I've caught it now. Miss Mitchison's sister. Hold the line, please.'

Celia turned to Mr Joyce. 'A lady, Miss Mitchison's sister, wants to speak to you privately.'

'Where is she speaking from? London?'

'Sounds more like a local hotel call to me, Mr Joyce.'

'Got a newspaper handy?' Mr Joyce ruffled the leaves until he came to the centre page. Sure enough, there was the announcement in letters large enough to arrest. Enormous Attraction! Adèle Elberstein! Famous Operatic Star! And he'd missed it! That showed how preoccupied he'd been.

'Right. Say I'll speak myself, Miss Ker. And that's all I require you for meantime. Send that note to Mr Jacks right away. Oh, and you might order flowers for Madame Elberstein; she's singing at the concert tonight. Roses or something. Never mind the price. Send a lot. That's everything. Hullo, Adèle! Is it really—?'

That was all Celia heard before she left the room.

Mr Joyce's face was flushed when he resumed his seat. At a moment when his peace of mind was threatened by the necessity of his enforced capitulation, and his pride, in consequence, was smarting, it was pleasant to come in contact with a woman for whom reality did not exist. In the company of Adèle Elberstein you were drawn into a warm, rose-coloured sphere in which most of the people, Adèle included, were a little mad, like players in a film. You were part of an atmosphere you knew well enough had no vitals in it, but which lapped you round with content.

Mr Joyce sighed happily as he bent over his desk. Miss Mitchison's sister – that was an old jest. Years ago he had run down from London for the day to visit Constance at her boarding school on the south coast. There was a concert that afternoon. Several artistes were coming from town to perform, a young violinist who was all the rage, and a singer whom no one had ever heard of, but who appeared to have been engaged on the strength of her being Miss Mitchison's sister. Miss Mitchison was the 'head's' right hand, a spectacled young woman with watery eyes which seemed always to be regarding the world in a gentle appeal. When her sister swept on to the platform in a vivid green dress that emphasized the rouge on her cheeks, a little stir had rippled the ranks of the uniformed schoolgirls. At tea, which the artistes had with the staff and any visiting parents who were present, everybody tried to behave as though Miss Mitchison's sister were in no whit different from themselves. But she was, and they knew it. Watching Miss Mitchison hand sandwiches to the 'head', Mr Joyce fancied the gentle appeal in her eyes had deepened to a sudden anxiety.

As it chanced, Mr Joyce travelled back to London in the same compartment as the singer. Almost at once she began to inveigh against the narrow-mindedness common to high-class schools. 'Those old women looked at me as though I were a – a . . .' She stopped short, wavering.

'And aren't you?' he wanted to say, but didn't. 'Aren't you? For, by George, you look it!' And then she proceeded to rage about her sister being cooped in with those old hags. What opportunity had Ella of making good, of getting anywhere? And yet she had had the best education of the family . . . She calmed down presently and told him she was leaving England next day. She had an engagement to sing for a week in the Casino at Ostend.

About a year later, Constance handed him an illustrated paper with a flamboyant wedding group on the second page.

'Look, Daddy, d'you remember that ghastly woman – Miss Mitchison's sister? You were at the school concert when she sang. She's married Elberstein, the conductor. Fancy him looking at her! And he'd taken her to Italy to study. Did you think she'd much of a voice?'

'I don't know. Perhaps she had more personality than voice,' he said unguardedly.

'Personality!' scoffed his daughter. 'Paint, you mean. If you'd heard what the girls said about her . . . !'

He never heard what his daughter's classmates said, but later he heard what the Continental critics were saying. He saw photographs, paragraphs everywhere. And then, as though her voice had failed to focus upon her a sufficient meed of public attention, her private life began to figure prominently in the limelight.

She left Elberstein. Filthy little Jew! No wonder, thought Joyce. Simply walked out and left him. There was a pianist, they said, in the case. But it was with a senator, no less, that she went about during her tour in the States. After that, innumerable exalted names were coupled with hers. There were lots of scandalous stories. Joyce believed them all. She was that sort. Couldn't help it any more than her sister could help being a milksop and a drudge.

It was with a feeling of lively interest that he learned on one occasion when he was on his way home from the West Indies that she was coming on board at Vigo. The passengers prepared to give her a rapturous welcome. Her stateroom was filled with flowers. When she came in to dinner the first night, in a green dress, paint on her cheeks, he recalled the school concert. But in place of antagonism, she was surrounded by admiration, by solicitude. No need now to try to behave as though she were in no whit different from the rest. She was different, and everyone knew it. She was a world-famed diva. Miss Mitchison's sister. Lord, it seemed hardly possible, seeing her at the captain's table that night.

She was leaving the dining saloon when her eyes encountered his gaze. She uttered an exclamation. Both her hands flew out to meet his. From the warmth of her greeting, strangers took them for old friends fortuitously met.

There was a fog in the bay. The *Alcasar* had gone at half-speed. For his part, Joyce wouldn't have cared if she had stopped altogether, so complete was the circle Adèle Elberstein had drawn about him. The ship, the sea beyond, enclosed in a field of iron-grey cloud, represented an empty and vacuous world. The centre of his universe was here, in this stateroom banked in hothouse blooms.

Days passed as in a dream, a vivid, extravagantly coloured dream that was at times oddly disturbing. There was the evening Adèle sang a cabaret ditty in the lounge, and the wife of a Colonial Governor walked out in the middle. Wicked Adèle! But who cared for the Governor's wife, anyway? Certainly not the Governor. He was always hanging around, trying to make up to Madame Elberstein. Not that there was much chance for him, or for anyone else, so the passengers said. Not with Joyce in possession.

'One marvels at a man like Mr Joyce,' the Governor's wife was reported to have said disgustedly.

'Why wonder, my dear?' said the Governor. 'He's a man, isn't he?'

So close was their alliance that Joyce was incensed, on arrival in England, to find her claimed by her press agent, her impresario, her secretary. He chafed because their engaged compartment was invaded by journalists, by photographers, before the express started for town. When they reached it and they went their separate ways, he realized he was behaving like a fool, and that his resentment was in no way justified. Adèle was wiser far than he. She shed personal relationships as she shed her furs, and assumed them as easily. There was real fellowship that way.

Accordingly, when once or twice it happened that the strands of their separate existences crossed, the old intimacy was resumed. Adèle hardened gradually into the role of celebrity. She became less spontaneous, more of the actress. But when, as now, she called him up on the telephone, her voice still had power to divert his thoughts into mellifluous channels, to release his mind as alcohol releases certain minds from anxiety.

Yes, it was providential, he thought, Adèle turning up today. Not for a minute did it occur to him that there was aught of blasphemy in his giving credit to the Almighty for the coming of such as Adèle Elberstein.

CHAPTER IV

The Palatial is one of the largest restaurants in the city. So large it is that you may toil up half a dozen stairs, or shoot luxuriously up in an elevator, and on each landing see people with half-open mouths plying knives and forks amid a maze of white-clothed tables. Within its walls you may partake of all kinds of food: of wholesome table d'hôte luncheons incredibly cheap; of horrid mushes described as *à la Française*, although why France should be called upon to sponsor Scots leftovers, Heaven alone knows.

While he waited for Celia, Jimmy amused himself by watching a group of businessmen topping their three-course lunch – Scotch broth, roast mutton, fig pudding, with tea and buns.

'Funny thing,' said one, a tall, oily-haired man with the unctuous air of a commercial traveller – 'funny thing, the fellow in charge of the Rolls-Royce stand at the Show says they've taken double the orders this year to what they did last. In these times, mind you! Funny, that!'

'Funny!' echoed Jimmy inwardly. 'According to the Englishman, we Scots have no sense of humour, yet to us every blamed thing is funny. Funny Uncle Tom getting run over by a tramcar. Funny Scotland's done! . . . Sorry, I don't want to order anything just yet. I'm waiting for a lady. Funny she's so late. Lord, I'm at it myself now!'

At what? the waitress pondered as she hurried away, but her curiosity was swamped almost immediately in a spate of orders. 'Three fruit salads, miss, and a plate of mixed cakes . . . Two sausage and mash . . . A black coffee and a ham sandwich as quick's directly, please. I've to catch the one-thirty train.'

'It's often the way,' said the elderly bearded man who presided at the head of the commercial travellers' table. 'It's often the way. Big orders one end of the pole, poverty at the other end.'

He sat back with the air of one who has uttered a profundity; then, realizing a shade surprisedly that his hearers were unimpressed, he took refuge hastily behind his napkin with a toothpick. He emerged from covering to enter into a colloquy with a plump waitress whom he addressed affectionately as Fanny, a big, bouncing creature whose ready smiles and luscious gaze served to rehabilitate his self-esteem.

'Old geezer,' she murmured to herself as she went from his table, and hoped that the time she had wasted on him would result in a silver coin instead of coppers being left for her under his plate.

'I'll tell you what it is,' volunteered a square-jawed young man sitting next him. 'It's' – he looked round, suspicious of eavesdroppers, whereat Jimmy, feeling guilty, affected a sudden consuming interest in the bill of fare. Lowering his voice to a whisper, the square-jawed young man thumped the table so emphatically that the teacups shivered and an ice-wafer, perilously poised, slid off the rack. There was a scraping of chairs as his companions drew closer in anticipation of an important pronouncement. Jimmy strained his ears, but only a disconnected phrase fluttered against them. 'Beaverbrook . . . Distribution of wealth in wages . . . Trust the people.'

Well, the people were all right. They always were. But that didn't prevent the Bread Riots. That didn't prevent Europe from being devastated by the Great War. That wouldn't prevent— He looked up, smiling. Celia was threading her way towards him – Celia, looking a little cold and haughty among all these food-flushed people. She halted to allow the plump waitress they called Fanny to pass, and Jimmy, studying her as sometimes one can best study the familiar in an unfamiliar setting, and amid a crowd, saw the milk-white skin, the deep grey eyes, the defiant tilt of a chin, which in contour still resembled that of an untried child.

As she stood there waiting, like youth wavering on the threshold of knowledge, he felt a flicker of wrath rise up in him against a civilization which conscripted virginal young girls into the ranks of wage-earners, against a world that destroyed the lovely solitude which should by rights have been hers. Here was another person born too late. A hundred years ago Celia had blossomed from girlhood into womanhood as naturally as a flower and as exquisitely. While still laughter brimmed her eyes, and her rioting imagination had reached out to garner delight from the sunshine and the storm clouds alike on her horizon, she would have stepped across the threshold all unwittingly. She would have been that delicious person of the eighties, a demure young matron carrying behind her soft doe's eyes all the deep wisdom instinct in the woman who loves and is loved. Instead of which, she was an unwitting victim of mass-production. She was caught fast in the artificial pressure of modernity.

'Hullo!' he said. 'I knew you'd come.'

She drew off her gloves; too short at the wrist they were, and rather shabby.

'The conceit of some men! I very nearly didn't. D'you know what brought me?'

'Hunger, plus your kind heart. You couldn't bear to disappoint me.'

'Disappoint – Jimmy, I could have slain you this morning. Curiosity. That's what brought me. Tell me, what's Adèle Elberstein like? Old or young? Plain or ravishingly beautiful?'

While they fed, he told her; not in the usual grudging way of the average male, which is to leave out everything of interest, such as what the lady in question wore, and what, if the occasion were a meal, they had to eat, but with a lavishness of detail that would have justified the raising of half a dozen libel actions had a fourth of it appeared in print.

'So that's what she's like. I wondered,' said Celia thoughtfully.

'Why this interest?'

A little shade came down over the clear grey eyes. The perfect confidential secretary never gives anything away. Her employer's secrets are safe in her keeping. Celia was new enough at her job to revel in the sense of responsibility it gave her. Not infrequently, indeed, when she was tired and near to tears, the vision of the competent Miss Celia Ker, Mr Joyce's right hand, restored her drooping spirits and revived her confidence. 'The main thing,' the chief of the business college where she had learned typing and shorthand had impressed upon her – 'the main thing is to keep cool and never lose your head.'

When Mr Joyce had selected her out of a score of older and more experienced applicants, it was with this motto ever before her eyes that she started work. Out of it had gradually sprung her conception of the competent – nay, the magnificent Miss Celia Ker, whose calm demeanour is never ruffled, not even when importunate young men ring up in the middle of the morning's work to declare their love.

It was a little difficult, all the same, to reconcile that Miss Ker with the other Celia, who, having been brought up very quietly in the country, hated trams and buses, and being jostled by strangers and eating alone in crowded restaurants. It was this dislike of eating in restaurants alone which had caused her to welcome Jimmy's suggestion that they should lunch together when his work permitted. They came from the same village and had known each other casually when he, as the minister's son, had felt it to be expedient upon him to break speed regulations on his motor-bicycle in order to prove that a manse did not necessarily breed milksops, and she, driving her father's trap – he was the doctor of the district – had dreaded meeting this harum-scarum road hog.

Slight as had been their acquaintanceship in the country, when they met again in town it was with a rush of mutual gladness they greeted each other. Instinctively, Jimmy assumed towards the girl a protective attitude coloured by a mild sentiment. She had turned out confoundedly good-looking. More in her face than ever before. To her father's death and the difficulties she had subsequently experienced, he attributed that sweet gravity which endowed her shyness with dignity, a quality from which shyness as a rule is definitely divorced. To Celia, Jimmy was someone in this noisome city she could hold on to, someone she could trust and talk to freely. She couldn't talk freely to anyone inside the office. The competent Miss Ker must never so far forget herself as to unburden her mind there.

'Why this consuming interest in Adèle Elberstein?' he asked again.

She rose and pulled on her gloves, a little smile playing at the corners of her lips . . . Don't go and tell, Celia. The competent Miss Ker would never forgive you if you did.

'Oh, I don't know. Just because she's famous, I suppose. I've never met anyone who was.'

'It doesn't alter the person really. Fame is only a label affixed to a person by public opinion. The contents inside are unchanged.' He thought suddenly of Nimrod, and realized he was talking nonsense. Public opinion had changed Nimrod. It had converted a visionary into a leader, a ruler of men. That was the worst of this writing game. It tended to atrophy thought, to make one glib and overflowing like a leaking fountain pen.

'I'm talking rot,' he said.

She smiled at him. 'I know. I like it. So few people do.'

Upon the shadowy pavement the glittering façade of the Palatial shed a tongue of light. Beyond, tall buildings dissolved to ghostliness in the deepening gloom. The boundaries of the city seemed narrowed down to this one long street, a street of incessant yet futile movement, for, so far as eye could see, it led nowhere at all. Threatening clouds swallowed it where it swept upwards to the sky, and, slanting down to where the streak of a sky-sign glittered courageously, it was submerged in the clammy dusk that was deepening over the city. In the warm doorway of the restaurant, Celia shivered as she regarded the dark shapes of men and women passing swiftly into the gloom. They, and the coil of traffic caught in this shallow tunnel, seemed all to be a part of something unknown and terrible that threatened her.

She glanced round at Jimmy. Usually he made her feel more certain of herself, secure – as though he could prevent the rushing crowds from breaking in upon the secret places of her soul. But now it was as though he too were armoured against her, sheathed in some brittle substance she could not pierce. Although upon his lips there still lingered the half-quizzical smile her questions invariably evoked, she knew instinctively he was far away. He was not actively resisting her. He was simply oblivious of her. And because she cared for him only as a child cares for its protector or for its playmate, and not as a woman cares for a man, she did not feel wildly resentful, only a little bewildered and fearful at being left to face the world alone.

'Goodbye, Jimmy,' she said on impulse, and pushed off along the street.

The Square was crowded when she reached it. There were little knots of policemen at the corners. Another hunger march probably, another gathering of desperate and despairing men. She tried to imagine what it would feel like to be unemployed, to go on from day to day weighted by a sense of failure. How the competent Miss Ker would comport herself in these circumstances, Celia couldn't conceive. Probably if she stopped being Mr Joyce's right hand, there wouldn't be any competent Miss Ker, only a shabby and crumpled Celia trudging round the labour bureaux, or whatever they called these dreary places.

She was entering Mr Joyce's room when she heard footsteps behind her, then a voice: 'Miss Ker, have you a minute? I'd like to speak to you.'

She turned round and regarded the young man standing in the doorway. In the dim light his face had the unhappy expression of one whose hidden fears are on the point of realization. It was an expression she had not surprised hitherto on Charlie Wren's face, and it sent through her nerves a queer tingle of apprehension. She was conscious at the same time of a feeling of eagerness, the eagerness of a person about to be admitted into an intimacy with someone desirable but hitherto unknown.

'What is it?' she said, and was surprised to hear her own voice sound so quiet and unconcerned.

'Have you heard anything? Will you tell me honestly?'

'Heard anything? What about? I don't understand.'

'Sorry. I thought you'd guess. About Joyce's.'

Celia's fingers fell from the electric switch which she had been on the point of depressing. Uneasy subjects, she may have felt, are best discussed in the dark.

'No,' she said. 'Why?'

'You knew I was with Fuljacks', didn't you?'

'Fuljacks'? Who are they?'

'India merchants. One of the best-known firms at one time in the country. Safe, you'd have thought, as the Bank of England. The Fuljacks themselves – splendid old boys. Pompous as maharajahs, yet shrewd as Jews. They're living, I believe, on a thousand or so a year now in retirement in the country.'

'Why? What happened?'

'Bad trade. Bad debts. They went "phut", and I've been wondering . . .'

'You don't think that we – Joyce's . . . Oh, but that's absurd!'

'It isn't. When you were out old Jacks rang up to speak to Mr Joyce. The bell tinkled after a bit downstairs. I picked up the phone, thinking they'd finished. I heard a few words; enough.'

'You're sure . . . ?'

He nodded grimly, and at the expression in his eyes Celia averted hers. The tingle which had warmed her a minute ago had given way to a creeping chill. Her eyes, so quick and bright with life, were dull, as though a cloud had fallen upon her brain. Her body quivered with trepidation.

They stood in silence for a moment, the man's face pale with foreboding, Celia's hot with the flush of an unexpected blow. And then he drew closer to her and put his hand on hers to comfort her, so lost she seemed, so pitiful, trembling in the shadows. She looked up at him, glad to rest her eyes on the living warmth of his face. Her lips parted as though to speak, but before she could utter a sound their sense of intimacy was cleaved by the rasp of the telephone bell.

Celia's voice dragged as she spoke into the mouthpiece.

'Hullo, yes! Mr Joyce's secretary speaking. Oh, about the roses I ordered some hours ago? . . . You've just got them in? A shilling each, did you say? That's all right. We'll let the original order stand. Mr Joyce won't mind. Send six dozen, as arranged, to Madame Adèle Elberstein.'

CHAPTER V

An explorer questing the source of the city's wealth would easily enough pass by the building containing the offices of Joyce and Son. He might, indeed, mistake the Square wherein those offices are situated for a burial ground, with its wilted grass plots, its tombstone statues. And if, for a moment, it occurred to him to question the advisability of having a cemetery in the centre of the city, he would attribute, doubtless, its presence there to the lugubriousness of a people who, or so it would appear, found pleasure in recalling the obsequies of the dear departed in the intervals of rushing for trains and snatching meals at the hotel opposite.

Probably the wayfarer, adventuring farther east into a region of mean, narrow streets, would retreat hastily and push downhill until he saw the masts of ships emerging as though from hiding beside the arch of a bridge. Here, he might be forgiven for believing, the glittering treasure lay. For to him, invoices and ledgers and rooms full of diligent clerks would have no significance. Even the name of Joyce and Son, held in high esteem by many a reverent seigneur overseas, would indicate nothing at all.

To Mrs Humphry, conversely, the 'offices', as she called that maze of corridors, of stone stairs, of rooms guarded by doors of frosted glass, represented the Palace of Plenty. To her thinking, those rows of desks, those piles of heavy books, contained a magic writing which mysteriously conjured riches out of the air. Riches piled up in the locked safes, whose protruding brass handles recalled to her mind those on the test-your-strength machines you see at the seaside. You pop a penny in the slot, and if you are strong enough and pull hard enough you get your penny back. Mrs Humphry never had any pennies to risk on this ploy. But she often thought about it when she ran her grimy duster over the maroon paint on the safe in Mr Joyce's room. Pull hard enough, and you get all you want – motor cars, as much mince collops as you can eat, clothes that keep out the rain . . . My, Mr Joyce must have been a nailer at pulling in his day!

Her own husband had never been a nailer at anything. At a time when jobs were plentiful he had lacked the will to work, just as, latterly, he had died because he lacked the will to live. The professor at the infirmary had put a fancy name on it. But she knew better. Partly out of pride, partly as an outlet for her anger at his inertia, during Joe's lifetime she had loudly preached the Gospel of Work . . . 'For my part, I'm never so happy as when I'm working. For my part, I don't know how some folks can thole to be idle . . .' This when she was down on her knees at night, scrubbing the kitchen. (She cleaned the 'offices', and 'did' for a lady, Mrs MacGregor by name, during the day.) This when she was sending up clouds of dust about her husband's head, or causing him to raise his feet to the spars of his chair to escape little runnels of soapy water. Then, dragging her tired limbs over to the sink, she would proceed to wash up her cloths, her brushes, in water that sent a chill through her swollen fingers; and the tale in a different form would be retold . . . 'Nothing like work for keeping you healthy. Mrs MacGregor, she's down with the 'flenza again. "I never catches nothing," I says. "And how do you contrive to avoid it, Mrs Humphry?" she says to me the day. "Jist because I've no time for to be ill," I says. There's nothing like work for to keep you well . . .'

There was a grim touch of irony in the fact that it was upon this gospel young Joe, her son, had from his earliest years been fed. Joe, who at the age of twenty had never done a full day's work in his life. 'Read! Read!' gibed his mother. 'You'll never provide for your old age that way. For my part, I'm never happier than when I—' But one night, quite suddenly, he stopped her there. Unlike his father, Joe wasn't worn out by internal suffering. Although a grey film blurred his personality, clouding his eyes, his skin, the colour of his hair, through his veins the blood still coursed lustily. He seized a chair and held it threateningly over her head where she knelt beside her pail.

'If you keep on yammering like that,' he said in a terrible voice, 'I tell you, I'll – I'll . . .'

She stared up at him in horror. This wasn't Joe, this stark-faced youth. His eyes were blazing. The corners of his mouth were twitching.

'Joe,' she whispered, 'Joe!' And the brush fell with a thud from her fingers. At the sound he started, set down the chair. Irresolutely, he shuffled over to the sink. She stooped to pick up the brush, but her hand was trembling so that she could hardly grasp it. She knelt there, looking at it, lost in a fierce reverie. Work. I'm never happier than when I'm— Oh, what a lie, a damned lie! What she wanted was to stop in bed, like Mrs MacGregor, and have her breakfast brought in to her, toast and marmalade, and tea, and ham and sausage, all curly brown. And the offices could go to pot. Old Joyce and the clerks and— God! What was that?

She scrambled to her feet, went over to Joe. He was bending over the sink, sobbing in agony. She touched his arm. Like a splint of bone it was, so bare of flesh, so thin.

'Wee son,' she besought him caressingly, this child of hers who only a moment before had threatened to brain her, 'wee son.'

It was not until later, when the storm of his emotion had abated, that he talked to her, talked as he had never done before. His tears seemed to have washed away all his natural reticence. From the abyss to which his spirit had descended during that moment of unbridled passion when he had almost surrendered to the impulse to murder the stupid, self-righteous creature at his feet, he had arisen with a strange feeling of liberation.

He talked and got tangled up in his own speech, contradicting himself, saying the same thing over and over again. But his mother did not care. She sat idle, for once, listening. It was the first time since he was a child she had got so near to him. She wondered what it was that had been dividing them; his silence, or her tongue.

When she rose at last reluctantly – fegs, but when you sat down and took your ease, you were sweirt to rise again! – Joe shuffled to his feet.

'What'rr you goin' to do?' he grunted.

'Feenish up,' she said, and looked about her for the brush.

'Och, you sit down. I'll easy do that.'

He found the brush in a slaver of soapy water. While his mother sat back in her chair nursing her swollen hands, he fell on his knees and scoured the floor. There was no thought in his mind that by taking over her task, he was making amends to her for his ill temper. His action was not animated by generosity, but by blind instinct alone; that instinct which impels man when he is suffering to grip something with intensity, lest the pain close in upon him and stifle his soul.

'There!' he said when he had finished. 'There!' And he set down the brush and went to dry his hands.

'My! What a fine job you've made!' said Mrs Humphry, roused from a dream of having a girl to work for her the same as Mrs MacGregor, and seeing her son installed at a desk in Joyce and Son's.

He never scrubbed the floor for her again, but from that night things were different between them. Mrs Humphry gave up the pretence that she rose at five and went out in the biting cold to do the 'offices' because she liked to work. Joe gave up pretending he liked 'mooching' around. 'By God,' he raged, 'every man born has a right to his job. It's those —— capitalists that's doin' us out of ours. The world's like an excursion train. Nobody's any business to more than his own seat. But there's some wants a whole corridor to their own cheek; some thinks they owns the – train, and they're squeezin' the rest of us dry; dry, I tell you. But it'll nutt last. We'll be on top some day.'

'Then it'll be your turn to squeeze the underdogs dry,' Mrs Humphry thought. 'Well, if I was Mrs MacGregor, I expect I would be for wanting a compartment to myself right enough. Them that's on top always does. Same as they always sing "God Save The King" the loudest, because at the back of their minds they're hoping that after He's seen to His Majesty, He'll save them that's next to His Majesty – meaning themselves, the ones that's on top.'

Spurred by a recognition of her son's need, Mrs Humphry spoke to Charlie Wren one morning on the stairs. She spoke humbly, because, to her, Wren in his well-brushed suit, his eyes and skin glowing with health, was a grand gentleman; one of those, doubtless, who had never known what it was to lack his meat.

'It's a fine day,' she said, 'but cold for the time o' the year.'

He assented: 'Very cold,' and wondered for what reason this poor work-worn creature had stopped him now.

'My son,' she went on, twisting the end of her coat between her fingers. 'I suppose you couldn't be makin' a way for him here? He's nutt done a stroke of work for long enough. And he's awful clever at his books.'

Wren's heart constricted with pity. Poor devil! Clever at his books. The city was full of that sort. Oh, damn Fuljacks', damn all the craven firms that hadn't faced the Depression, fought it out!

'I'm sorry,' he said. 'I've no influence, really. I'm only a junior here, a newcomer at that. But I'll speak to Mr Joyce, although I doubt if it will be any use.'

It wasn't. He told her so next day. She thanked him humbly. After that, he did not see her again to speak to, only sometimes he caught a glimpse of her disappearing down the street, her long, shabby coat flapping grotesquely behind her.

On the morning Mr Joyce arrived at his momentous decision, she was late for the first time in her life in coming to the office, so late that she was still kneeling in the passage when Celia came along. She looked after the girl and thought, 'That's a nice hat.' Then her mind, averted momentarily from the burden of worry which overlay it, grew heavy with apprehension again . . . Joe was that reckless when he got excited. And the police were always ettling to get their hands on somebody. 'It's only wearin' out your shoon, son,' she had pled with him.

'Ach, what's shoon compared to my immortal soul?' he had retorted.

She sighed. You couldn't argify with Joe, not when he started quoting Scripture at you. And if he'd made up his mind he was going out with the hunger marchers today, nobody would stop him. She flipped her duster about, shifting tiny particles of grime from one place to another the while anxiety gnawed at her breast. By the time the processionists reached the Square, she would be at Mrs MacGregor's, threepence-worth in the tram away.

She put on her hat, her coat, slowly, aware of a queer, shaky feeling in the pit of her stomach. The day, so dark, so cold, was making her feel quite done.

A solitary policeman on horseback was touring the Square. She stared after him in loathing. Then she raised her eyes to the black range of cloud blotting out the sky.

'God save Joe,' she entreated. It was like the National Anthem the way she said it, the thought occurred to her afterwards when she was in the tram . . . Well, if He wasn't too busy saving them that was on top, He'd maybe take a thought to them that was under.

CHAPTER VI

Three hours after his mother set out for the offices, Joe swung his legs out of bed and sat hunched on it, staring into space. The blind was up, and through the window he could see a scoop of darkness and the broken stonework of a tenement chimney. Because the building in which the Humphrys lived stood on the top of a sloping tract of ground, they could see, if they craned their necks a trifle, the sky above the houses opposite. As a child, Joe had thought the moon a great white bird when he watched it emerge behind the black crest of the tenement roof. Today, in the half-light, the roof's ferrous line resembled a scab on the sky's dark sheen; and Joe pictured the town below, smoking vaguely in the strengthening light, as a place of peace and plenty, were only these black scabs erased from its sides.

Actually the city Joe's groping mind conceived was no modern cosmopolis of ferro-concrete, but the over-coloured seascape of the railway poster, the child's picture of Jerusalem with the magnificence of Hollywood thrown in. His brain, confused by indiscriminate reading, was like a sheet of blotting paper which had absorbed the ink of a hundred letters written by persons of varying creeds and temperaments. Thus he was at once moral and amoral, at once militant and pacifist. All he had read lay heavily on his mind, a mass of undigested matter which, sooner or later, if he were to retain his mental balance, his system must rid itself of by some means or another.

Joe was one of those unfortunate beings who touch life only on one side. His outlook might be said to have been circumscribed by the slant of the tenements opposite. It was not until he was adolescent that it widened, that some of the tags of Marxian writers, of Communist agitators, gathering together in his mind, illumined it with a sudden burst of light. After that, any stray orator had only to utter the words 'tyrants', 'capitalists', to touch the little live switch which lit up the boy's brain.

That switch had been pressed by no uncertain hand last night, when Nimrod delivered a series of five-minute addresses to men in different parts of the town.

Hitherto, to Joe, Nimrod had been a mere name, a name which stood for justice in the same way as the name of Joyce stood for tyranny, for a grinding down of the poor. It stood for tyranny because Mr Joyce was known to be the owner of fine motor cars, large offices, safes full of riches. And no man has a right to all that while another man lacks bread . . . So Joe argued, keeping his mother awake with his excited talk.

And now she was off to her offices, and he had to get breakfast for himself. God knew where he would get his dinner. In the lock-up maybe. No, not there, he told himself violently, for he'd kill any —— cop that tried to lay his dirty fingers on him.

As he dressed, Joe recalled the meeting of the night before. In an old rat-haunted shed near the river it was. You could see the dark flow through chinks in the rotten wood.

It had a faintly putrid smell, that place. As the men crowded into it, their faces gleaming whitely beneath the light of the primitive lanterns suspended from the roof at either end – as they crowded into it, converting the space between the gaping walls into a confused and distracted zone, it was as though sedition were a passionflower sprouting from corruption's black stench.

There was a big crowd, men for the most part; only here and there a woman whose shapeless body and pinched features seemed to have shed the distinction of sex. One of these women stood sideways crushed up against Joe, a girl with a shawl huddled about her shoulders and a mob of light-yellow hair. The colour, so gay, so unexpected in that grey place, fascinated him. He could not take his eyes off the girl's averted head. At that moment he was vaguely aware of a cleavage within him. There were two Joes, one strung up with excitement, waiting in this hubbub for a man called

Nimrod, who would paint for them a picture of a future state when all men should live in brotherly love and equality; the other Joe, isolated from all these fellows in mufflers, away from the stench and the smoke, staring in a kind of sad, happy trance at a woman's hair, and wanting nothing so much in the world as to dip his fingers into its yellow tangle.

Nimrod was late in coming. The shuffling figures separated as word went round that he had been nabbed by the police. The fringe of a shawl slapped in Joe's eyes.

'What the hell are you starin' at?' said its owner. And Joe shrank back into himself at sight of the blotched and evil face. He pushed towards the door, but was held back in the press of a sudden commotion. Someone was hauling in a chair. A man mounted it. His features were not distinguishable in the obscure light, but whenever he spoke, a shout went up.

What happened after that was blurred. Joe's heart was a box that rattled in Nimrod's hand. One moment it was leaping in exaltation, the next its beats flagged, apprehensive of disaster. Now it was knocking against his ribs wildly, jubilantly, at the vision projected by the orator, a vision of Authority despoiled, of palaces blazing, while all the belfries in the world rang out their song of joy.

'A great f'la, Nimrod,' someone said at his elbow in the crush going out. 'You're right,' he rejoined, and pulled his cap farther down over his eyes lest anyone descry the tears in them. When the others went on in little groups, he lingered behind, looking down at the river.

In the darkness of the night it seemed young again – a waterway of romance reaching out to sea, sentinelled on either side by constellations brighter far than stars. Presently, one of those constellations drifted aloof from the rest, swam slowly into midstream. Joe's heart swelled with a sense of wonderment. A ship going out to sea. Hundreds of souls sailing into the Unknown. It was like death, going away like that, a triumphal death with the fume, the noise, the terror of the city left behind. And before you all the glory of the moon-streamed sky.

A woman plucked at his arm, stared at him for a second, then hurried on. She had no time to waste on one so bemused as he. His eyes were bent on the quivering arrow of light cast on the water by the disappearing vessel. A moment, and it was swamped in blackness, and the river lay quiescent as a backwater whose deeps have never been stirred by the passage of a lovely ship . . . Oh, to leave behind all the hopelessness, the mess; to start afresh in a new country! Start – Joe interrupted himself, shuddering. Me that hasna ever begun!

He stared at the little low puffs of cloud floating across the deep pool of the moon, and thought of far-off lands – America, India, Canada. He had seen posters of Canada with vast yellow fields of wheat – or was yon stuff corn? There were rolling hills behind; and a sun like a ripe watermelon in the middle of a blue, blue sky. The heat of that sun would warm your very blood.

Dimly he felt that warmth might release in his body some secret virtue, some hidden spring that would redeem it from this senseless waste. Dimly, he believed that in a younger country, where the life-stream flowed faster, his mind and body might achieve that springtide of which they had been starved.

He pressed closer to the river's edge, peered down upon the water as though, here and now, he were fain to cast upon it the bright new galleon of his dreams. But there was no outward swell, no scatter of fine spray, to bear them out to sea. There was only this stagnant flow, with its cold background of streets and sterile lights scooped out of the hollow of the night.

Canada, he said again under his breath; but this time there was execration in his voice. They were pouring back from Canada every day, the lads that had emigrated after the war. Canada was done; the Colonies were done, they said, the same as Scotland. Done! Ach, why had he been born at a time when everything was decaying, coming to an end? Why hadn't he been born when the Scots had guts enough to fight among themselves, as well as to keep the English on their own side of the border?

He turned his white, tragic face towards the bend in the river. On either side, constellations still burned; but he no longer thought them brighter than stars. He knew them for what they were – ships at anchor, ships preparing to set sail for Canada, or some far-off port to fetch back more folks to swell the sum of the country's unemployed. Home, sweet home, they'd be thinking over there. Ay, they'd be thinking that until they saw it, this city of theirs – saw its empty wharves, its deserted yards, its rotting sheds, its streets full of idle men – and then they'd sing a different tune. The 'Red Flag' most like.

'A great f'la, Nimrod,' someone had said. And, by Gees, he had spoken like a god tonight. In that dark shed, you had felt the waves of excitement rising in a flood. You had felt the soul being drawn out of your body by the intensity of a strange new force.

Joe had not got near enough the speaker to see him clearly, but he pictured him straight-limbed and splendid-looking. Because he knew himself for a weakling, Joe worshipped strength. And he recognized that quality in Nimrod, recognized it and exulted in it.

It was of Nimrod he talked to his mother that night, and of Nimrod's plan for a mass demonstration in the Square next day. Secret instructions were to be issued to intending marchers at stated points in the city at noon, and, Joe added glibly, his inventive powers quickened by the sound of his own voice, arms most like as well.

Mrs Humphry's face blanched. She stayed up till after midnight pleading with him to stay at home, to let the marchers gang their ain gait without him. In the end, she retired to bed, not to sleep, but to brood and battle far into the night. These politics were as bad as a woman. They took her son away from her. They vexed him, made him restless . . . Revolution. What was it but a fine-sounding word, empty as a drum? They'd been beating at it long enough, yet nothing had come out of it, and nothing was likely to, not in her time. Just a lot of laddies they were, these marchers, beating at their drums because they had naught better to do with their hands. But them that was on top didn't see it like that. Instead of letting the poor souls be, they sent for the police. Mrs Humphry was not an imaginative woman, but that night before she slept she saw her son mixed up in a bloody scrimmage; she saw that which made her clutch the bedclothes in fierce anxiety.

He was asleep when she rose next morning. She moved on tiptoe lest she should disturb him. She was opening the door to go out when, on impulse, she turned back and went over to where her son lay. His head, cradled childishly on his outflung hand, was half covered by the blanket. Only his brow and his downcast lids were exposed. The bedclothes outlining his thin form moved gently with his even breathing. While she stood looking at him, a deep sigh seemed to shake itself out of his very heart.

'My bonny,' she whispered pitifully, and leaned over him, hoping he might awake.

But he did not stir, and she had to slake the passionate mother-love that brimmed up in her by laying a finger lightly on his hair.

Something seemed to have gone dead inside him, Joe felt, when he went out into the street that morning. He felt less assured, half afraid. The high sky of the night before was masked in cloud. The streets were full of shadows. Looking ahead was like looking into a dark haze. You couldn't see the housetops, the trams, anything. The man who was posted at a corner to issue instructions to a section of the marchers was shivering. His voice was so husky he could scarcely speak. Joe wondered if he had heard aright. Incredulously he repeated the words.

The man nodded. 'Nimrod's orders.'

Joe moved on. He hadn't liked the feel of the morning earlier. He liked it less now. Round the corner he halted, considering matters. It was too early to go to the meeting place, and he had no wish to return home. After a moment's hesitation he decided to make for the Square. He might as well wait there as anywhere. It would be livelier. He'd see what was doing.

He trudged slowly along the drabbest street in the city, a street possessed of not a single redeeming feature, but which falls mercifully away on either side at the end to permit imprisoned eyes to escape from the squalor of shambling buildings, to enable those who have deemed themselves lost in chaos to see a way out. Today, the river lying lifeless on either side of the bridge's gentle arch held no promise of clear skies beyond. The anchored ships were distorted shapes in a vale of shadow. Joe leaned over the parapet, looking down on the soundless stream. Last night, for a brief space, it seemed to him a noble waterway leading to a new world. Now he knew it for an inky sludge sunk between the ridges of empty lumber-sheds and old warehouses.

He was crossing the Square when a wayfarer approaching from the opposite direction collided with him.

'Hi! Mind your feet,' said Joe.

His assailant grabbed him cordially by the arm. 'I implore your pardon, signor. Me – it is my fault. I run, and so I do not see where I go. A thousand pardons, signor!'

'Ach don't mention it, Frenchy.'

'Italy,' the other corrected him. 'I was born in Milano. You have heard of Milano?'

Joe scratched his neck. Milano, Mussolini. The Black Shirts. He'd heard of them, all right.

'You'll nutt be one of the Fascisti, are you?'

A tremor went over the features of the Italian. For the first time in his life, Joe understood the meaning of the phrase, 'he shook in his shoes'. This foreigner was shaking in his. Worse, his head was shaking, shaking horribly, grotesquely, like the head of Punch when the hangman's rope encircles it.

'I do not speak of them,' he said at last.

Some obscure instinct of cruelty prompted Joe to query why. 'Feart, are you?' he gibed. 'And for what?'

'I do not speak of them,' reiterated the Italian. Then suspicion sharpened his voice. 'Why do you ask this? What are you, signor?'

What indeed? A 'moocher'? A supporter of the 'buroo'? Ach, you couldn't explain that to a foreigner. Joe thrust out his chest. Inspiration had come to him.

'I'm a Communist,' he said. 'You'll see by and by. Here in the Square if you wait long enough.'

'What do I see?'

'A demonstration such as you never seen in Italy. A march your Fascisti themselves couldna beat.'

'You mean – there will be a great-a fighting?'

'Fighting!' Joe flung the word from him in scorn. 'Fighting's nutt the word! Afore many hours is by you'll see—'

But he was talking to air. The little foreigner had gone. Joe saw him diving hurriedly into the basement door of a hotel across the street.

CHAPTER VII

Belowstairs, Carlo halted, leaned against a wall. His mind reeled in panic. His breath came short. *Santa Maria!* And he had thought that here he was safe. Only a minute ago he had posted a letter to little Giovanna telling her so. In London he had never felt secure. There were too many of his countrymen. And the arm of the Fascisti is far-reaching. He had never dared to linger to speak to any of his compatriots in those narrow winding streets of Soho where on national fete days the flags fluttering from the windows on either side formed a ragged, gaily coloured archway. Always he had worked in the extreme east or west end of the metropolis. In disreputable cafes where the rats fought in corners in the basement and shady customers talked in whispers upstairs; in ultra-respectable private hotels where scrawny maiden ladies donned chiffon scarves over their black dresses to dine off tomato *farciés*, cold-storage mutton, and tinned pears.

He had never stopped more than two months in one place. Six weeks here, two months there; that had made up the sum of his existence since he left Italy a year ago. In a way, it seemed longer, much longer. A whole lifetime lay between now and that night when the Fascisti burst into the Cafe Antonio and murdered its owner. They found documents, firearms, in a press which Carlo had believed to contain wine alone, and while still the Black Shirts rampaged through the cafe, in a frenzy of fear he had fled for his life. It was the harbour master, a cousin of his father, who smuggled him aboard an incoming vessel sailing next day for the Port of London.

Carlo remembered little of the voyage. He spent most of the

days at sea lying in his bunk in a kind of daze. When he disembarked, the clangour of London's streets unnerved him. The sound of the traffic resembled, to his thinking, the shouts of irate men.

Driven by his nerves, he kept moving from place to place; from dubious nightclubs to frugal temperance hotels where the high colour of ginger ale in a glass caused the other diners to glare suspiciously at the supposed tippler; from so-called Italian cafes to so-called old English tea gardens. And always jagging his peace of mind was a dread of political meddlers, of Fascists, of all who dare authority and dabble in affairs of state. It was a noisy demonstration in Hyde Park that sent him scurrying to take a ticket for the north. The natives of Scotland were cold, slow to ire . . . So he had been told. So he believed until today.

He stood now in the stone passage of the hotel and trembled. Within an hour two people had given him warning of impending trouble. The pleasant signor in the lounge who had gone upstairs to visit Madame Elberstein, the queerly spoken young man with whom he had collided on his way from the post office in the Square. Two persons – *Santa Maria!* That was enough. It was time for him to go.

But he had no money. A man could not travel without money. Pff! He had been careless. Why had he gone to the cinema these last few nights? Why had he drunk so much red wine in that stupid cafe? It was not good wine either. Nor were the films he had seen good films. Why had he sent that money to Giovanna? Of course, she needed a fur, the *povera bambina*, to keep her warm. The other girls at the class wore furs, and it was not fitting that Giovanna alone should go with her shoulders unprotected. His wages? No, not for another week according to his agreement were they due. All he had in his pocket now was a few shillings gleaned in tips. The Scots were not ungenerous, but they had a queer, graceless way of bestowing their tips. They slid a coin shamefacedly under a plate instead of pressing it warmly into your hand with a, '*Mille grazie*.'

He slipped off his overcoat, hurried upstairs. He would go to the manager; and the manager would give him money to take him back to London. The manager would lay a hand on his shoulder and say, 'Carlo, it is with the deepest sorrow I see you go.'

But the manager's room was empty when he knocked, so he took up his customary stance in the lounge outside the dining room until that gentleman would return.

The dining room was already crowded with the broad, dark backs of businessmen. It always astounded Carlo to watch them eat, those solemn signors; so fast and with so huge an appetite, but with so little real enjoyment. At one o'clock they came – a black surge that sucked the colour from the room as a swarm of crows swooping down on a field blots out the green. If one among them so far forgot himself as to flap his wings, to laugh out loud, the others looked up and stared. Eat and drink – yes, that was permitted, but not to be merry. *Ma*, no! *Aie*, how serious they were today, bowed over their plates! Did they grow gayer when they returned to their wives at nights? Did they sing and hold *festas* in their tall grey houses? Did they dance their children on their knees? Or did they sit solemnly round their great cold rooms, hands folded across their middles, and brood on the business of the morrow – the morrow that would be just like today? But would it be like today? If out there, in the Square, there was fighting? Ah, no, the world – their world – might fall about their ears today.

He had an impulse to warn them of their impending end, these heavy-jowled signors gorging themselves with such grim precision on cooked meats and cheese. But his tongue clove to his palate, his throat felt closed as by fire. Fear – that was what made his throat feel like this . . . Oh, Antonio, Antonio, what a furnace must have burned in yours when you leapt from your bed that night!

The click of the door made him turn round. The lady receptionist, Miss Smithers, was leaving the manager's office. The manager, then, must have returned. Timidly Carlo asked for admittance.

Mr Valley gazed at him as he entered, fluttering his thin hands. He explained volubly that he must leave, leave today. It was necessary for him to return to London. He had many regrets. He hoped the signor would excuse him, but . . .

He talked on while the manager drew from a drawer a large sheet of cardboard intricately scored.

'Your name?' he asked.

'Carlo Amorelli, signor. I come to you three week ago – you remember? From the Cafe Amerique in West Kensington. I think, perhaps, I go back there.'

'You may go where you like when you leave here a week today. Meanwhile, according to the timesheet, you should be on duty in the lounge. Get back there, and look sharp about it.'

Carlo felt his knees giving way beneath him. His head wobbled on his shoulders. Regarding him, Mr Valley wondered what had induced him to take on such a weak-looking fellow . . . Ah, he remembered now. Fergatti had to leave in a hurry, to have his appendix yanked out, and this man had appeared providentially, or so it seemed, that same morning.

He turned his back on Carlo, took a cigar from a newly opened box which stood on his desk, and lit it carefully. Savouring the fine flavour, he had almost forgotten the Italian when a voice, staccato with emotion, rose in his ears.

'Signor, signor, I beg of you – you do not-a understand. I must go today, now, this very instant, back to London. I must have my money. I beg of you to give it me. It is my money, I tell you. For the time I have worked and worked.'

The manager suppressed a sigh. God, these foreigners! And yet you had to employ them. You couldn't do without them here. The Scot was the world's worst waiter. Too proud to 'wait' on any man. Too steeped in the porridge-haggis tradition to appreciate good food and the ceremony with which it deserves to be served.

'You get back to your post, and no more talk about it,' he said good-humouredly. 'A week today you clear out. A week today – no sooner – you'll get your wages.'

Carlo's hands flopped to his sides. This gentleman – he was not human. You could not make him understand. He was a wall you would only hurt yourself by hurling against. *Aie*, he was not made of flesh and blood. He was – ah, he had it now – he was part of a system. A system for reducing people to puppets on a string. It was all down on that big paper, the names of the puppets, the hours at which they must dance, at which they must go out, come in. He was like a god, this man, ruling his little world. You go here, go there, according to the timesheet. At ten in the outer lounge, from one till three in the inner, and look sharp about it. It was all set down on the paper. But one day, if a man – he disappear, he die and disarrange the system, what would this god in a frock coat do then?

Carlo was in the act of leaving the room when Mr Valley's voice recalled him.

'Here, you might dispose of that somewhere.' And pointing to his desk, he indicated some blackened slices of burnt toast.

When the waiter had gone, Mr Valley flicked the crumbs delicately from the polished surface and leaned back in his chair. As the fine savour of his cigar filled his nostrils, he pictured a future existence when by some fortuitous circumstance he would be permitted to tell people precisely what he thought of them. No need for finesse, for preserving the absurd illusion that the client is always in the right; no need to play the courtier, to live up to the boiled-shirt tradition night after night. 'Such a gentlemanly fellow – Mr Valley.' That was the general verdict. Gentlemanly – if they only knew as they listened to his deferential accents the number of good round Elizabethan oaths that were languishing through enforced disuse in the waste ground of his mind!

He thought grimly of Mrs Ferrell and her burned toast. An over-pampered stomach was what was wrong with the woman. He would liked to have told her so at the end of her tirade. 'Write to the directors, if you like, and show yourself up for what you are – a doddering old she-devil who has got every blurry thing out of focus, a crawling worm on the face of the earth who dares to think the dirt it feeds upon of any importance. Write – write, by all means, to the directors! They'll stop, doubtless, in the middle of a shareholders' meeting to read your letter; they'll hold up the draft of their next report; they'll keep their auditors and their lawyers and their secretariat waiting. They'll wire their departmental chiefs to sack the lot; they'll shake the walls of their hotels to their very foundations and then flee in terror from the consequences of their own acts. And all because – because your breakfast-toast, Mrs Ferrell, was burnt! Oh, write the directors, dear lady, by all means!'

He sighed, profoundly bored by his own eloquence, and stared fixedly at the gloss on his neatly trimmed fingernails. The varnish was at odds with the broad thumbs, the fleshy palms, even as he himself was frequently at odds with his job. It wasn't the clients alone, his thoughts ran on, but the staff as well. There was Miss Smithers, as bad in her own way as any Mrs Ferrell. Always itching to make some change to 'humanize' the place. As if it weren't hotching with humanity all the time! He had heard it said that asylum attendants were apt to go potty in the end themselves. Perhaps it was the same with hotel-keepers. Smithers, quite definitely, had a bee in her bonnet about numbers. Still, she'd got the right manner. Soothing syrup. And she dressed cleverly. Just well enough to make hard-up visitors realize when they arrived that here they must wear their best clothes all the time, and yet not well enough to raise the envy or the suspicions of the sophisticated.

He sighed again, glanced at the time. He had just five minutes to spare before he was due at a conference with the cellarman. That last consignment of white port hadn't come up to expectation. Like Mrs Ferrell, he would have to write to the directors about it.

But instead of drawing out a sheet of paper and a pen, he rose and unlocked a drawer in his private desk. From it he produced a sporting leaflet. Tonight at eight sharp, Pat M'Lintock versus Joseph Aherne.

Mr Valley's heart glowed as he pored over the lists of events. Boxing in these parts wasn't invested with the glory that it was in the south. The contests took place in a dingy hall in a filthy neighbourhood, and in the kind of atmosphere in which a boiled shirt was unknown. But you saw as good footwork as you did in the Holborn Stadium. And you could let yourself go – by Heaven, you could let yourself go!

He shoved the leaflet back in the drawer as a tap fell on the door. It was one of the porters ready to go on duty.

'The police say there's likely to be another big unemployed march today, sir. Will you want the main doors closed if it looks lively, and shall I let people out at the side?'

Mr Valley nodded. 'I suppose so, Sanders. Bad for business, that sort of thing. If only these marchers could exhaust their superfluous energy in some other way! The young ones would be better having a go with the gloves.'

CHAPTER VIII

At the same time as Mr Valley was holding consultation with the cellarman, Mrs Humphry lay crouched on the floor polishing the linoleum in Mrs MacGregor's hall. It was comparatively new linoleum – Mrs MacGregor had only been married four years – with a lovely luminous blue pattern which merged into black at the edges. A sunlit sky bounded by threatening breakers. When you put some pith into your rubbing, the pale, glossy surface shone like glass. Today, it didn't seem to Mrs Humphry to be taking on the usual shine. She reared back on her knees, regarding it – regarding the translucent waves which didn't seem like waves any longer, only a series of irregular curves sprawling over a pallid surface that was constantly showing up streaky patches. She blamed her cloth and the polish time about. Not so good as it used to be, that stuff; and she took the tin and shook it vindictively. Kind of gritty, her duster. She turned it over in her hand and stared at it as though expecting to descry in its folds something strange and untoward. But there was nothing, so she spat on it vigorously, then, stooping again, proceeded to rub the moistened cloth on the floor. Say what you liked, there was nothing like your own spit for polishing. There was nothing like elbow grease.

She was on her way, with a pail, to scrub the doorstep, when Mrs MacGregor called out to her from the landing to be sure to say she was not at home if anyone came asking for her.

Mrs Humphry nodded. It was funny, she reflected, the glib way gentry with their fine houses desired themselves 'not at home', while those that hadn't a home worth calling one never dreamt but to say, 'Come away in,' when anyone came chapping at the knocker.

Mrs Humphry was no philosopher, or she might have recognized a subtle distinction here between her own class and the class above her. The class above her, living in security, can afford to hold the outer world at arm's length. Those who belong to it are rarely dependent for their interests, their entertainment, or their livelihood upon chance encounters. They are making their way through a realm that is policed and protected at every turn; and the fear of chaos, of disaster, is remote from their minds. The poor, on the other hand, cannot afford to hold potential friends at a distance. To the Mrs Humphrys of this world, existence is only rendered bearable by embracing every opportunity for widening the narrow circle of their affections, for fulfilling the dictates of their social consciences. This conscience it is which bids its owner call out, although there is scarce a crumb in the house, or a chair to sit down on, 'Come away in.'

Upstairs, Mrs MacGregor dressed in a flurry. If she had known earlier, she reflected for the twentieth time, she was going there, she would have put on fresh 'unders' in the morning. She shivered a little as the cold silk of her cami-knickers, just back from the wash, brushed the skin of her thighs. She scrutinized her legs, rummaged in a drawer for stockings. Light-hued, yet not too light, or they'd make her limbs appear nude under the brown of her coat. There! She drew out a pair only to thrust them back again at the sight of an incipient ladder. Her rummagings grew more agitated, less controlled. She beat through her drawer as though she were beating sugar and butter to a cream in a pudding basin. If she didn't light on a decent pair soon she'd be obliged to send Mary hustling off to the nearest shop, and then as likely as not she'd get the wrong colour! At last! She examined the sleek bronze silk for flaws, and sighing with relief at finding none, set about clothing her legs. Men always looked at legs. Or was that an old-fashioned belief dating from the days when legs were never visible?

She pulled her shoulder straps taut, glanced at herself in the mirror, very slim and straight in her pale-pink tights, her ecru lace bodice. A pity, she thought, one couldn't go out to lunch in one's cami-knickers. One looked so dowdy in a dress in comparison. She wriggled hers over her head, glanced this time with profound dissatisfaction at the mirror's reflection. Odd how clothes – even good clothes! – made one look ordinary. It must be glorious to go to the Lido, to Florida, and to bask all day long in a sun-bathing suit. A series of pictures as exhibited in *The Tatler* of lovely ladies displaying their charms at Palm Beach flicked before her eyes, making her mouth thin with envy. A little shiver of excitement rippled her flesh. Supposing this telegram of Monty's meant something! Supposing it meant . . . ! Her heart swelled happily. For a moment she stood tingling with a delicious sense of power, of abandon – a handsome enough young woman when the mask of boredom slipped from her face.

She picked up the telegram and pushed it into her bag. It was a mercy George was away before it came. George hadn't liked Monty. Male jealousy, of course. She recalled one night in the Mediterranean when, coming late into their cabin, George had flown into a rage and accused her of 'carrying on' with Monty. She had flushed slowly, painfully, for the accusation was untrue. And it humiliated her, steeped as she was in the best novelette tradition, to admit it. Yes, it was untrue. Monty Bagshaw, the most popular man on the ship, had favoured her with his company for long hours on deck, but he hadn't breathed so much as one word of love in her ears. It was disgusting. A moonlit night, soft music, waves lapping gently, a jealous husband waiting downstairs – everything but the lover. Shaken with anger, she had burst into tears. For there must – there surely must be something lacking in her, some essence of femininity, or else Monty had had her in his arms. True, she had had enough femininity to attract George four years ago. She still attracted him, or he would never have showed himself jealous. But George was one of those unromantic souls who take everything for granted – even his wife. He never gratified her passion for scenes, nor did he deem quarrels worth while for the sake of tender reconciliations. Yes, there must, she argued between sobs, be something lacking in herself – what the novelists call sex appeal. Accordingly, she set out next day to cultivate that quality – she who had really no need to cultivate it at all – and to subjugate Bagshaw. It was easily done. He had only been biding his time. But long practice had rendered him discreet. Consequently, although George had now real cause for jealousy, he never again accused his wife of philandering with Monty. And because, now her self-esteem was reinstated, she was thoroughly enjoying herself in the role skilfully limned for her by Monty of a lovely wife with a husband who neglected her, she had no desire to make George jealous. Life held quite enough 'thrills' without that.

These 'thrills', however, ended with the holiday cruise. Back in their own home, from a sense of power, she fell upon a knowledge of futility. The humdrum hemmed her in – the irksome necessity of catering three meals a day. George liked what he called a 'solid breakfast', while she toyed elegantly with tea and toast, and enjoyed a square 'tuck in' at eleven. There were days when her nerves warned her of danger, days when she felt the desire rise up in her to wreck the neat breakfast table with its dish of smoking bacon and eggs and, having left them trickling in a horrid mush on the carpet, to slam the door and run out of the house. That would rouse George, surely, startle him into taking some notice of his lovely wife! He had taken lately to calling her 'my dear' in an absent-minded sort of way, as though they had been married for years and years. 'All right, my dear, I'll remember to be back early tonight . . . Can't rise to a car this autumn, my dear; maybe next year, if we make do with a cheaper holiday; a little house for a month would be quite jolly.'

Quite jolly, my dear! . . . Oh, she wanted to scream and tear out of his hands the newspaper behind which he screened himself each morning! She wondered as she adjusted her hat what he would say if she brandished this telegram before his eyes. 'From Monty, George. He's coming north especially to see me; travelling three hundred miles.' Of course, Monty hadn't said all that in his wire. Words counted for something in a telegram, but he had expended an extra copper, she noted with gratification, to include the word love. That was one of the things George would never have done.

She shut her drawer and bestowed a glance round the room. It was untidy, but Mary could easily put things to rights after she had gone. For a moment, as her eyes swept her surroundings, it occurred to her to wonder how she would feel if she were about to leave them for good. Supposing Monty . . . She sat down suddenly on the bed and stared at the tortoiseshell brushes ranged on the toilet table. The picture of herself in the role of a lovely neglected wife wavered before her eyes, and as its plaintive outlines grew blurred and dissolved, another figure paraded triumphantly in its place. Monty's wife – surely George would divorce her – Monty's wife with the world for a playground. Palm Beach, the Lido, Eden Roc. But it wasn't very real, that figure. It was like a woman in a book whose course was all mapped out by the writer. Her course wasn't mapped out at all. Monty might not ask her to go off with him. He might be in one of his casual off-taking moods when her blandishments were no more than dissolving dew on the crystal of his mind. But if he wasn't in one of those moods, if he were serious and wanted her . . . In a fit of abstraction she slid the rings off and on her thin fingers. If he really wanted her – she drew a quick breath, feeling something melt within her. With a rush, her days, so bare recently of lovemaking, of the savour of romance, seemed to recede behind her. The future loomed ahead, all glamour and sparkle like the bronze-and-amber pattern of her tortoiseshell where the sunlight brushed it.

A tiny sound penetrated her dreams. She looked down and saw her wedding ring wheel in a spinning circle along the floor at her feet. Was that an omen? She rose almost reluctantly to recover it. The platinum struck a chill to her warm flesh.

Mrs Humphry was engaged in polishing the letter box when she went downstairs. Mrs Humphry, who always prided herself on being what she called sociable with her employers, gave her a friendly nod.

'You'll be for out?' she said.

'Yes; I'm going into town. I shan't be home for lunch.'

'If I was you, I wouldn't bother the town the day.'

Mrs MacGregor did not reply at once. She was engrossed in a last-minute study of her features in the hall glass. Her face was rather narrow, her eyes very blue and extravagantly calm. She rejoiced in their size, their expression of baby innocence almost as much as in the pallor of her skin. In an endeavour to enhance that pallor, she added a further touch of powder. As she replaced her puff in its gilt case, she recalled what Mrs Humphry had said about not going into town.

'Why not?' she said. 'Is there fog?'

'No, not what you'd be calling a real fog. Just a . . .' Mrs Humphry stopped helplessly, smoothed out her duster. 'It's they marchers,' she said. 'They'll be blocking up the Square. My son – he's started going with them. Jist wearin' out his shoon, I tell him. But he'll nutt listen to me. This Nimrod's everything with him the now.'

'Nimrod should be shot,' said Mrs MacGregor with conviction. 'A man with his views is a danger to the community.'

She turned on her heel and went off down the path which intersected the miniature lawn of her garden. It was queer, she reflected, how everyone was conspiring to stop her from going into town today. You would almost think they *knew*. First George with his prophecy of fog in the city; then Mary with a reminder that the man about the new gas cooker was calling, and would she be sure to be back to see him at two? And now old Humphry with her bogy of marchers blocking up the Square. It was a pity, all the same, that Monty had fixed on the hotel there. If it had only been the other one . . . She advanced to hail a bus swaying round the corner. It was empty, and the seats, newly cushioned, were springy as those in a private car. She leaned back luxuriously, responsive to the comfort of the new upholstery. In this atmosphere of ease, of speed, she could yield again to the fine mists of her dreams.

'Fare, please!'

She sat upright, stared at the cheeky features of the young conductor as she might have stared at those of some Peeping Tom who had violated the privacy of her toilet. Then because, in her excitement, she had come out with nothing less than a ten-shilling note in her purse, she realized she must smile on the man, try to propitiate him.

He repaid her politeness by stopping beside her, discoursing upon the disagreeable nature of the weather in town.

'Not a regular fog, mind you. Not when we left, anyway; but it'll not surprise me if it's come down thick by the time we get there.'

Another person entering into the conspiracy! But she wouldn't be browbeaten. Fog or no fog, she was going to meet Monty today.

Mrs Humphry was standing gazing thoughtfully after her employer when a voice from the kitchen reached her, bidding her come and have a cup of tea. Tea, she thought gratefully, that'll cheer me up. But the scalding-hot liquid, drunk in conjunction with a thick slab of hot buttered toast, only added to her sense of discomfort. She leaned her elbows on the table and let her head rest on them while her thoughts trailed dismally back to the time when Joe was born. She hadn't wanted a child for fear it should be ailing like its father, always complaining. She had never given Joe justice, she realized now. She had brought him into the world unloved, and then instead of trying to make up to him for that, she had visited upon him the sins of his father. At the moment, the fact that she had worked for him all these years seemed to amount to nothing. In some far inner part of her heart she knew she had failed her son. That hurt her most of all.

She dragged herself to her feet. 'Hech, sirs!' she said.

Mary regarded her with some concern. 'Is the toast comin' back on you? Would you like a tick o' baking soda?'

Mrs Humphry shook her head. She went into the hall and picked up her pail, her polishing duster . . . Them that were on top didn't like these shouting laddies. Hide poverty up the closes! Don't wash the town's dirty linen in public, let it fester instead in the middens! That was their cry. So Joe said, anyway. Poor Joe! God, save Joe . . . don't – don't let anything happen.

PART II

AFTERNOON

CHAPTER I

Adèle Elberstein lay back in her big chair, purring. Little over two hours ago she had been stamping about the room raging at its awful emptiness. No flowers, no deputations from musical societies awaiting her. No cards from unknown friends, no throng of admirers clamouring for *entrée* to her presence. No newspaper representatives, only a solitary reporter, and one of your stolid, stupid Scots at that! No chance to make fresh conquests, to exploit her vivid personality. Nothing to do but to sit and twiddle her thumbs until night, or to look out at the deadly gloom of the Square. Heavens, what a city!

Apart from a passionate desire to impress, apart from her unbridled egoism, Adèle had a genuine hatred of solitude. Having no resources within herself, her nature was frankly gregarious. Had she lived in a three-room-and-kitchen house, she would always have been running in and out of her neighbours' homes on the pretext of lending or borrowing; of conveying some piece of quite unwanted information. She would have been constantly on the common landing, laughing, gossiping, relating some tremendous happening which on investigation would prove not to be tremendous at all.

It was this furious longing of hers to be close to her fellow creatures, to identify herself with their lives, that accounted for her association with all manner of incongruous persons. By birth a child of the people, even in her most exalted moments she hankered after the people. The splendid isolation of the star, while it gratified her overweening vanity, roused in her a sense of real unhappiness. Alone in this strange city, she felt uneasy, neglected. The dun-coloured sky, the stark high buildings, filled her with foreboding. Had it not been for the concert at night, and the convention imposed on her by Elberstein, she would have flung on her hat and rushed out into the streets. She would have walked the town until she found some glittering emporium, some fancy-goods shop to plunder; until she encountered some friendly saleswoman to whom she could chatter freely, some shopwalker whom her magnificence would impress. She would have bought countless extravagant powder boxes, and feathered furbelows, and useless pieces of bric-a-brac. She would have roamed the place, collecting interested glances, admiring murmurs with the same zest as a small boy collects stamps; and then she would have gone on her way rejoicing, her sovereignty recognized and firmly established.

'That's Adèle Elberstein, the famous singer . . . I say, d'you see who that is? Adèle Elberstein, looking exactly like her picture in the *Wire*.' . . . And because she adored her fellow beings, she would bow and smile to those of them who recognized her in the same way as the ruler of a reigning house acknowledges the salutes of his subjects. She would have gone even further and engaged them in conversation had it not been for the rule of silence, which was another of the conventions imposed upon her by Elberstein. Oddly enough, although she had left her husband years ago, she still paid tribute to his wisdom. Albert had got to the top. What was more remarkable still, he had contrived to stop there. Oh yes, he was wise, she allowed. It was unfortunate that his dictates were so often at war with her inclinations.

She tried to strike up a conversation with her maid; but Marie, instead of being properly flattered by her mistress's graciousness, was uncompromisingly short. A trunk which had been stood on its end in transit, and was consequently in need of tidying, was engrossing Marie to the exclusion of all else. It was a porter, bringing in coal to replenish the fire, who saved the situation.

'What's that building over there?' he repeated in the indulgent tones of the native who cannot wholly conceal amazement at the newcomer's shocking ignorance. 'That's the City Chambers . . . No, not all that. That's offices over there, business premises. Arnolds', the wool people. You'll have heard tell of them? And of Arthur Joyce's?'

Arthur Joyce! She clapped a hand to her mouth like a delighted child. Heaven be thanked, she had one friend in this God-forgotten city! Bursting into the bedroom like a hurricane, she besought Marie to stop fiddling about and to come and find a number for her on the telephone.

And now, restored to confidence, raised to her throne again by the warming knowledge that here was at least one fellow being who admired her, she sat talking after lunch with Arthur Joyce, creating for herself a kaleidoscopic background which grew more colourful, more blatantly unreal, with every word.

'Since we met, I've been to Africa, to South America. The President of Patagonia sent a squadron of cavalry to escort me to the frontier. The adventures I had there!'

In a trice, she had drawn him into that rose-coloured sphere where most of the people were a shade unreal, like players in a film. She was piloting him through a maze of mad adventure, in and out of courts with crenellated walls, gardens full of cypresses beneath whose shade the eyes of swarthy men flashed fire and swords crossed in defence of her honour. In one breath she described a silent camp on the fork of a deserted river above which gigantic hummingbirds hung poised by day, and the flutter of movement, the hubbub of excited applause, in a crowded concert hall. Her landscape was dotted with fierce-looking peons following a trail guarded by great white cactus, with the hooded figures of horsemen slumbering on the hillside, and with the scarlet uniforms of the National Guard assembled in state on the steps of the Opera House. Thronged all the while in the background, like an ever-ready chorus, were love-sick officials, petty presidents, rebel leaders, jealous tenors, chorus girls, nuns – more than once on her travels she had slept within convent walls – and banditti.

'Did you give the bandits half a crown to capture you so that you could relate the story of your adventure afterwards to the press?' interjected Joyce, thoroughly enjoying himself.

She slid a hand in his. 'Wicked! You do not believe one word of what I say!'

He made no motion of denial. Of course, he didn't believe one-third of her tales. It was obvious they sprang, most of them, from the astounding lottery-bag of her mind, which was lined with dragonfly colours and contained all the rich loot of the far-travelled adventuress. But what matter? Her talk amused him. She amused him, this international vamp whom he had met in the staid precincts of a girls' school. And today, when the whole grand structure of his existence was toppling, he was doubly grateful for the beguilement she offered. He made one attempt, however, to cut through the rose-clouds of unreality enfolding them.

'I'm poor company this afternoon,' he said. 'Business worries. In fact, things have come to such a pass I've decided my place must close down.'

Adèle lit a fresh cigarette and regarded him nonchalantly. 'So you will be free, a slave to business no longer, eh?'

Had he ever been a slave to business? He thought not. True, business had served as a buffer he had interposed on occasion between his person and the outer world. Like the moon at nightfall, it had been a definite object in a vague windy space. You steered the ship of your existence according to it, as the first navigators steered their vessels according to the stars. But a slave – no, he had never known the weight of chains.

'You never felt your chains,' pursued Adèle rather surprisingly, for he had not uttered his thoughts aloud. 'No, but when you are rid of the shackles you will know the difference. There are but two ways to live, my friend. Rooted always to the same spot, with your interests growing narrower and narrower, or wandering the world over, calling no one house your home.'

He had not been rooted to one spot, he felt tempted to remind her, when they had met at Hathdown in the long ago, nor when they had spent that week together on the *Alcasar*, nor on the subsequent times when they had travelled in company. But she was talking on in that warm contralto voice of hers, outlining her own immediate plans.

'A tour of the English provincial towns, ugh! All smoke and dust and sweaty labourers. Aren't you sorry for me, Arthur? Leeds, Bradford. I have four clear days between here and Leeds. Listen, I've an idea. Why not join me for those four days at some quiet little place on the Yorkshire coast?'

Joyce shook his head. Inwardly, he queried, why not? Tonight, if he didn't go to the concert, but kept closely at work in the office, he could clear things off and leave the necessary papers in Jacks' hands. At the end of a short respite from business, he would return refreshed and in a better frame of mind to tackle what would be required of him. The dismissal of staff could be effected well enough by letter should he decide not to come back at the end of four days. Deep down in him, he knew that it was unlikely if he went off with Adèle tomorrow he would return so promptly.

Artificial and dissatisfying as her mode of life was, it appealed to him momentarily. Wandering the world over, calling no one roof your own . . . Well, it was possible his interests had grown narrower and narrower, but if he hadn't had those interests to engross him – very vividly he limned an exaggerated picture of himself as a middle-aged bar lounger, one of those freshly tubbed but rather unpleasant individuals you meet on ocean liners, imbibing cocktails at all hours, and bragging royally between drinks of their card winnings, their adventures with the other sex. There were no stars in the heavens of these gentry; they had nothing to steer the barques of their existence by, but they were free, free as air. An exhilarating thought that!

'I'll come,' he said. 'Tomorrow morning? I don't suppose you'll make an early start. D'you know, I believe life is going to be good after all.'

'Life is good,' she said with emphasis, forgetting that less than two hours ago she had sworn it to be intolerable in this God-forsaken city. 'Don't I know it? What d'you want, *garçon*? I did not ring.'

Carlo stood on the threshold, fluttering his hands, his face ghost-white.

'Madame Adèle Elberstein,' he said. 'Madame, I have heard you sing. At Milano.'

She gave a little screech of delight. Homage from however humble a source never failed to excite her.

'You come from Milano? You have heard me sing, then, in my great roles? You have heard me sing many times?' She recited rapidly the parts she had played, the names of the exalted witnesses of her triumphs. Then, oblivious of the little waiter quaking by her side, she turned to Joyce and was starting to retail with tremendous gusto a scandalous story concerning a rich old Jewish merchant and a royal princess who occupied adjacent boxes, when Carlo, growing frenzied, interrupted her.

'Madame, madame, it is because I have heard you sing, because I know in Italy, my own country, that they love you, that I am come to warn you. There is to be a great-a demonstration in the Square. I know. I, Carlo Amorelli, I have warning.'

The anguished voice stopped. Joyce, observing the man closely, saw that his head was trembling on his shoulders, his features were writhing as though with pain. Mental, poor devil, he said, and hoped Adèle would recognize the futility of holding further converse with the fellow.

'A demonstration here in the Square?' Turning her back on the two, Adèle went to the window. The idea of a crowd beneath it, even a belligerent crowd, thrilled her. Through her mind floated a beneficent picture of herself stepping out on to the balcony as she had done in Paris, and singing to an acclamatory throng all she could recall of the Internationale.

'*La-la*,' she hummed, something in her blood leaping to the memory of that sea of upturned faces, of waving arms. For a second she was outside herself. She was not Adèle Elberstein, née Mitchison, any longer. She was one of the mantua-makers who brandished their shears in the face of the Empress herself. She was a sansculotte leading a ribald chorus in the inner courtyard at Versailles. Then her glow faded. The stage wasn't set for heroics. There was no balcony here.

With an air of passionate resentment, she turned to Joyce and proceeded to upbraid him for the hotel's architecture. He did not reply. He was saying something to the little Italian. He was shepherding him determinedly out of the room. The door shut, he turned the key in it.

'That chap's not responsible,' he remarked. 'The Council Chambers are just across the Square. There are often crowds, demonstrations, in front of them. But they mean nothing. Just a little hot air.'

She smiled provocatively. 'I am not afraid.'

They stood together for a moment at the window, looking down on the Square. The leaden sky, closing in on the high stone buildings, seemed to Joyce almost malignant in its immensity. He felt that by some means or another one ought to be able to reclaim those walls, those sooty plots, from gloom; to prevent the stone buildings retreating into their native rock, to arrest the approach of this unnatural night which threatened to extinguish the Square. It had meant a good deal to him, this corner of the city, for the last twenty years. And now he was withdrawing from it vanquished. He, and along with him Joyce and Son, was being blotted out.

He gazed across in the direction of his office. A light shone in his private room. Miss Ker, doubtless, back from lunch, was clearing away the litter on his desk. In the darkness, that luminous window was curiously bright. By the light of it, he saw the little bluff-bowed ship which had been the first of Joyce's to set out for the Indies. He saw the East like a gaily painted fan expand before his eyes; a maze of milk-white bridges girdling blue waters, of pagodas whose painted roofs twinkled like peaks of flame beneath the sky.

His forefathers had beheld that vision of the East and it had inspired them. Alone in their dingy offices, they had brooded on the glitter of the countries overseas. By the flicker of a solitary candle they had pored over maps, pressing great thumbs on uncharted waters, and breathing heavily while they pondered ways of discovery. They had visualized ports where none existed. They had pictured sweet bays where currents crossed and the sea churned in a fury. They had anticipated friendly natives on peninsulas where only wildfowl lived, and their emissaries had encountered pirates and cannibals in unexpected places.

But they had known deep triumph, these old merchant adventurers; and in the end the content that comes of a great achievement had been theirs. The content and the fine omnipotence of those who can look around at their fellow men and with every justification say of them: 'They know nothing because they've ventured nothing. They never will know anything, for they've always trimmed their sails for safety; whereas I – by God, I've taken risks!'

Standing there, he gathered up all the memories of the daring trade exploits in which the firm had engaged since the year following

Trafalgar – memories of those first voyages across uncharted waters, exploratory voyages, many of them, daring as that of Columbus; memories of gunrunning when war fever ravaged the Indies, and of the gamble of essaying to establish with a horde of gibbering natives the beginnings of a regular and legitimate trade. There was no law to protect them; no officers with sheriffs' warrants to inculcate fear of a debtor's prison. It had meant going on in blind faith, hoping that a dusky skin would prove as amenable to reason as a white. Not infrequently, there ensued disappointment, a morass of muddled accounts – it was rare to discover a captain who could steer a straight course, use both a ledger and a cutlass. There had been wild scares of plague, queer superstitions to fight . . . The Scotsmen were bringing sorrow to the island – next time we must not let them land. And in place of a welcoming people there would be ranged on the yellow sands a hostile array, weapons blazing in the sun.

While Joyce stood musing, his eyes on the window across the Square, the light in it went out. So it would all go out, he reflected. And there would be nothing left. He would have no star to steer his barque by. He stood for a moment very still, as a man might stand by the grave of a friend. Then he turned instinctively to Adèle.

She was buffing her nails against a pad of chamois leather, but as though aware of his need of her, she looked up and flashed upon him the brilliance of her smile.

'Why so melancholy, friend Jacques? Aren't you coming on holiday with me tomorrow?'

'When do you plan to start?'

'Any time. About midday. Look, there are the mounted police coming across the Square!'

While she stood, her arm linked in his, gloating on the horsemen, Carlo was hastening up the back stairs to his room at the top of the house. It seemed to him a terribly long and perilous journey, this ascent. He dreaded lest he reach the sanctuary of his room too late, lest screams such as had escaped Antonio's lips that night rend his ears before he could silence them.

CHAPTER II

Before crossing the Square, Joyce lingered for a moment on the pavement in front of the hotel. While he had been with Adèle, the unnatural dusk had become tangible like smoke. It enveloped in its shallow flow the statues in the Square, so that they looked to him like supermen trembling on the brink of materialization.

It threatened them all, he thought, that shallow flow; the living as well as the dead. It was as though the molten light which glittered on the fringe of the town, silvering the frost-white trees, splashing with rainbow waves the icy slopes, was powerless to scale the walls of the city. On its very threshold, the smoke – or was it, in reality, the emanation of a great despair? – had quenched the ardour of the sun. It had sullied its brightness, so befouled its rays that in place of light there was this streaming darkness. A darkness not warm and consolatory, but consciously cruel; a black flame which did not wholly consume its victims, but laid upon them the shadow of doom.

While he stood there, awaiting a chance to cross, little groups of people, converging into clots, blotted the pavement momentarily, then dissolved into units. Cars, flowing from the five streets leading into the Square, met and mingled in a continuous stream. A trades lorry, thundering down a cobblestoned incline, set up an unseemly racket amid all these smooth, silently moving vehicles. The horse, treading clumsily, sweat glistening on its great brown flanks, seemed to have stepped out of another world, a lustier world of ploughed fields and windy skies. Beside the big clamping beast, the gleaming bodies of the cars looked meaningless. A conglomeration of machines with no fixity of purpose, only some inner spring of motivation.

Watching them, Joyce asked himself if modern civilization were at the root of it all, of this rot which had set in. Or did the cause lie deeper still – in the divorce of Man from Nature? Did the fruits of the soil no longer sufficiently nourish the body of Man, did the sun and the wind no longer nerve him for conflict, inform with power his limbs, because between himself and Nature, Man had raised so many artificial barriers? Skyscraper buildings, rabbit-warren tenements, subterranean passages, railways that scarred the lovely face of the earth.

For his own part, he had no nerve for conflict. With Jerry's death, something in him had died too; died or dissolved. He did not know which. And there was nothing left of the deep sea-wave of his being but the surface froth of a few fleeting passions and desires.

He stepped into the roadway, causing a car to halt abruptly with a hideous squealing of brakes, and then, without hurry, he gained the opposite pavement. Inside the passage the lift attendant, a one-armed man and an ex-soldier, saluted him. As he entered the lighted cave, shot upwards, he thought, 'Another barrier. What's to hinder us using our legs?' And smiled wryly to himself.

He encountered Charlie Wren on the landing.

'A bit of a fog coming down,' he said.

'A fog coming down and you are doing nothing to prevent it,' Wren retorted inaudibly. 'How can you come in looking so sleek and well fed, dripping with self-satisfaction, knowing what you have in mind? Why is it only the ghosts of the past who haunt us? Why don't the ghosts of the future, the ghosts of those we have yet to slay, swarm in a hungry battalion about us? Can't you see them, the ghosts of clerks, of typists, of merchant seamen, of dock labourers? Can't you hear them pleading with you, hurling insults at you, crying shame upon you – Joyce's putting up the shutters, Joyce's, who have traded with the East since Trafalgar?'

A faint discomfort stirred in Mr Joyce. Perhaps, for the space of a heartbeat, he may have felt the chill breath of the wraiths of his subordinate's imagining. As he passed on, he asked himself if it were possible the youngster suspected anything. He had regarded him queerly. Of course, it was confoundedly hard luck for the lad. First Fuljacks', now Joyce's.

'It's turned quite dark outside, Miss Ker,' he said; then asked himself sharply, was his imagination playing tricks with him, or was his secretary, too, regarding him queerly?

'There was a message from Mr Jacks,' she reported. 'He said to tell you he would be here at the appointed time.'

'Good ' he murmured.

'Good,' she echoed under her breath. 'Oh, God!'

Macfarlan, a junior clerk, handed in a batch of letters which had just come by post. As she dealt with them, setting aside those inscribed personal and ranging on one hand those she deemed important, and on the other the bills, the circulars, her mind buzzed with arguments and counter-arguments.

'Dear Sirs, In reply to yours of the 1st inst., we beg to state . . .' Important, that. Oh, it was absurd! Joyce's couldn't close down after all these years! . . . 'Dear Mr Joyce, Thank you for your communication of . . .' From the head of a big firm, that one. Important, too. And this and this. Oh, it was ridiculous with all these enquiries pouring in for anyone to suggest closing down. Did a shop bang its doors in the face of intending customers? Did it put up the shutters when the public was clamouring for admittance? And yet there was no denying Mr Joyce had been preoccupied for the last few weeks. Even the juniors were speculating whether liver or some unfortunate speculation were the cause . . .

'Dear Sir, In accordance with your request of July last, we beg to advise you that the shares in Celver Bros., which you bought at 18s. have now risen to 84s.' No, an unfortunate speculation wasn't likely. Money begets money. Her father used to say that, her father who never had a *sou* to spare. Mr Joyce wasn't the type to take risks. He would always bet on a certainty, and be contemptuous of those who took chances. Yes, he would lie back in his armchair in the gathering twilight quite oblivious of the battle raging elsewhere in the sun.

She stopped short in the act of lifting the last envelope. What was she saying a second ago? That Mr Joyce wasn't the type to take risks. Herein, perhaps, the true explanation lay. In these days of fluctuating markets, business was chancy; you had to take risks. But Mr Joyce wasn't having any. He was going to get out, to cut clear now that he could no longer be sure of banking on a certainty. He was going to get out without giving a thought to other people. Oh, the skunk! The black-hearted skunk!

She tore open the envelope in her hand with a jerk that slit in two the sheet inside. It was a communication from a 'bucket-shop' in Liverpool – an invitation to get rich quick! Odd that it was always to those who were already rich that these invitations were addressed. She never recalled her father having received any. Appeals for charity had made up the chief part of his slender mail.

As she disposed of the rubbish in the wastepaper basket, and heaped in a neat pile the communications she accounted worthy of her employer's consideration, her anger cooled. After all, Charlie Wren might be wrong. Business was going on as usual. Everything seemed quite normal in every respect . . . Charlie, you're a wicked scaremonger. Nerves probably. Having been with Fuljacks' when they came down . . . it was natural after that to go about scenting disaster, spying it even where it didn't exist. Just like a man travelling for the first time in a train after he had been in a railway accident. And yet Mr Jacks was coming at five-thirty. Just when the office was closing. An odd hour that . . . For her life, Celia couldn't help feeling there was something ominous in the lateness of that appointment.

While the sky poured gloom and black shadows wound themselves about the Square, the brightly lit room was an eyrie of white fire that excited the glances of street-corner loafers. Seen through the smoky greyness produced by this admixture of soot, of grime and chemicals which was enveloping the city, the lighted offices of which it formed a part loomed like a maze of Babylonian palaces starting up suddenly in a desert place. Instinctively the wayfarer, shivering in the raw chill air, envisaged a warm sensuous stream of life flowing behind those gilded windows. Men and women happily at work, pursuing mysterious occupations in a luxurious atmosphere, juggling with coins amid a profusion of gold and silver, so that without effort, bewilderingly and beautifully, the piles of shimmering roundels mounted into pinnacles so tall that it were easy, at a distance, to mistake them for the towers of a new temple to Mammon erected on the crumbling ashes of a lost civilization.

Of the state of tension impeding the stream of life in these lighted rooms, no one outside could have any inkling. And yet everyone inside the office was dimly conscious of it, from the junior clerks, working sporadically at their entries in the intervals of debating which was the likeliest winner of the Manchester Handicap, to Celia seated at her desk within a few paces of him who was the cause of it all. She tried to recall something Jimmy had said to her the other day at lunch. She had been engrossed in debating what she would order. Yes, she had been so absorbed in contemplation of her 'eats' that she'd let Jimmy's comments pass unheeded. What was it again he had said? Something about a rumour that Joyce's would be the next big firm, if things didn't look up, to find themselves in Queer Street.

Why had she let that slip by so carelessly? Why hadn't she recalled it at lunch today, recalled it and bombarded him with questions, instead of blethering on about Adèle Elberstein? As if Adèle Elberstein really mattered! She was only one of those fabulous beings whose whole existence is bounded in luxury. She had merely to open her mouth to have everything a woman could want chucked at her – gorgeous clothes, expensive cars, opulent furs, suites in grand hotels, flowers at a shilling a head. Surely – ah, surely, if things were really bad, desperately serious as Charlie made out, Mr Joyce wouldn't be fallaling with Adèle Elberstein. Surely he wouldn't be giving a thought to flowers.

Flowers. Roses; exquisite waxen white blooms exuding a faint sweet aroma she associated vaguely with sickbeds, with wreaths for the dead. Red roses, gleaming brightly on the smooth sheen of a light evening dress. The thought of them tore at the portals of Celia's wrath. She banged a letter-weight down on the table with such a clatter that Mr Joyce started, glanced at her in surprise. Either it was the light, or the girl was unusually pale this afternoon.

'Got headache, Miss Ker?'

'Yes,' she said sullenly, and stared at him – at this quiet-voiced, rather distinguished-looking man who had apparently such a queer sense of values. The odd thing was, he didn't look like a person whose perspective was all agee. Nor had he struck her as lacking in imagination, in human sympathy. Perhaps that was because she had never looked at him closely enough, analysed him as she was doing now. Hitherto he had been Mr Joyce of Joyce's, and unconsciously she had endowed him with the integrity, the steadfastness upon which the reputation of the firm was builded. Now she recognized in him a fellow creature whose subsequent actions might render him despicable in her eyes, as a man whose motives she could no more hope to probe than she could those of any criminal who commits murder or wrecks happiness without a qualm.

It struck her for the first time that he looked very tired. The lines of his chin were sagging. The wrinkled leather of his forehead was deeply scored. Perhaps beneath that cool exterior, beneath that surface languor there was a strong current of goodwill which fatigue had momentarily clogged. If that current could only be released again, if he could be made to see the consequences of his act . . .

She had an overwhelming impulse to vault the wall separating employee and employer, and then, having once gained equal ground, to demand of him without preamble if it were true what they were whispering – that he intended closing down Joyce's. And, if it were true, had he considered what it would mean to all those people who had trusted him, all those who had worked under him, and with him, who had flung their hearts, their souls, their interests into Joyce's? Oh, she would put up a tremendous fight for them; for them, and for herself! She would remind him of the achievements the firm had gained in the past, of its growth, its harvest of prosperity. Since Trafalgar . . . She was only a paid secretary, but the thought of that had kindled a spark in her from the very start, a spark which had burgeoned in this hour of trial into a bouquet of fire.

If that failed to move him then she must shed the last remnants of her pride. She must force her lips to the utterance of a different kind of appeal. An appeal which would, of a certainty, shock him, for he could have no vivid realization of poverty's effects, this man who in an hour of crisis could think of flowers for Adèle Elberstein. She would be constrained to speak of things she had never before dared to contemplate. Evil things: hunger, cold, horrible surroundings. Oh, they were bad enough, but not so bad as the mental anguish arising out of the knowledge rubbed into you day after day, rubbed in not gently, but brutally, with the salt of insults, that on God's earth there was no niche for you. You were only a cumberer of the ground.

With a sudden inconsequent jump, her thoughts went back to the old days at home, careless, harmonious days when money had never seemed to matter. Oh, it wasn't fair that she should have been cast out of that old enchantment into this hellish muddle! They had offered her a home, certainly, some of her father's relatives, when her penniless condition had been revealed after his death. But they had offered it so grudgingly, and with such slighting references to poor Tom's improvident ways, that Tom's daughter had jumped on her high horse and ridden straight to a commercial college in the nearest town, where she had paid away for class fees and lodgings all the money in her possession.

At the end of the course, it was with a heart bursting with pride that she had written to her aunts announcing her appointment to the staff of Joyce and Son's. 'The well-known India merchants. Their business was founded soon after Trafalgar.' Yes, she had bragged about that even to them. To their letter of restrained congratulation she had not troubled to reply, since when there had been silence between them. It occurred to her now that, lacking the shelter of Joyce's, she would be terribly alone.

She looked over at Mr Joyce. His face in profile had a certain nobility of expression, a fine dignity which must surely augur a corresponding degree of nobility, of fineness of mind. She gave a little inaudible clear of the throat. Better plan what she meant to say – no, better not, for if she hesitated long enough to do that she might end by saying nothing at all. Best to blurt out what was in her mind, to trust to luck, or to God – she didn't know which.

'Mr Joyce,' she said, 'there's something I'd like to ask you.'

'Just a moment, Miss Ker.' He finished reading the paper in his hand, then raised his head. 'Yes, what is it?'

Her hands trembled in her lap in an agony of shame. During

that moment of waiting, her high-spirited impulse had wilted. All the bloom of its earlier gallantry was shed.

'Do you wish me to stay late when Mr Jacks is coming?' she brought out at last.

'No, just you go off as usual.' So that was what had been worrying the girl! Afraid she'd be asked to stop late when she had some jaunt to a picture house or dance hall arranged. He pushed to a side the paper he had been studying, drew another from out a drawer. 'Lord,' he thought wearily, 'I wish all my troubles were as easily disposed of as that!'

CHAPTER III

While Celia sat upbraiding herself for a coward and a weakling, and Mr Joyce pored over his papers, preparing them for the captious eyes of Jacks, his legal adviser, and Carlo in his attic bedroom tugged frantically at the rope encircling his trunk, a vast stream of humanity was converging on the Square. To occupiers of window tables at the Palatial, and to those of the staff who had time to glance outside, it was as though a teeming deluge had engulfed the cobblestones, the pavements. It was as though the collapse of some great dam had released a torrent, and from the deepest deep of Nature there now gushed this living flood.

Driven from the rear, without pause, without fluctuation, it surged on – Black Care, Hunger, Revolt, shambling between stately frontages, between rows of lighted shops agleam with the tempting fruits of a luxury trade. Fine fabrics, velvet cushions, bedspreads of exquisite lace, bathed in the tropical sunlight of amber glass and roseate shades. Muscatel grapes, cantaloupes and oranges, cool-gleaming and richly coloured. Pink fondants piled in gilded baskets, multicoloured cakes and crisp brown pastries rising in pyramids behind an expanse of glass that glowed with the reflection of a fountain of crimson fire. Regarding that fire, you pictured a gargantuan oven opening to reveal on its vast shelves dozens of fowls richly browning and sizzling with slices of fat bacon disposed generously on their breasts; the flanks of sirloins exuding their fine warm aroma, gigots like rocky islands surrounded by seas of succulent brown gravy, and steak-and-kidney pies decked with the luscious diamonds and squares of flaky paste.

A citadel this of food, a palace built for its sale, its consumption, and reeking of affluence, of a careless profusion from attic to basement. A place worthy of plunder, you might think, worthy of being the objective of this ragged throng; but Dull Care, Hunger and Revolt appeared as though they saw it not.

Nor did the women among them give heed to the extravagantly apparelled dummies staring out at them from behind adjacent plate glass; to these queer freaks in gilded composition, their senseless arms swathed in furs, their inanimate limbs silk-clad, their bodies encased in all the ravishing garments which lend ease and contentment to the feminine mind. They gave no heed to them – these shivering creatures jostling in the raw air of the street; they gave no heed to the gilded freaks, in their soft warm setting, who wore on their lifeless backs all those things which human flesh lacked.

It was, in truth, as though the shuffling figures, male and female, composed one vast distorted body which no force on earth could disintegrate or divert; squalor embodied in the form of a dinosaurian monster before whose snapping jaws culture must vanish, frivolity must doff its tinsel, and in whose maw whole tracts of civilized country might conceivably disappear.

Lost in the midst of the crowd, helplessly isolated, were two tramway cars, and a few paces distant from them the elongated body of a draper's delivery van. Glossy with varnish, exhaling feminine elegance by virtue of its fresh paint, its sheen, the commercial vehicle suggested the pale glow of powdered faces amid a rabble of desperate men.

Halfway up the street, where another thoroughfare cut sharply across it, a resolute line of traffic brought the rabble to a standstill. Caught momentarily, or so it appeared, in a trap extending from the bend of the street where a shop sign glinted luridly to this barrier of double-decker tramcars, the crowd seethed and muttered. From the shufflings, the swirls, isolated voices detached themselves, grating noises. It were easy to snare the smaller animals, but not this mammoth specimen of the Atlantosaurus.

Frenzy will out, not in lawful actions, articulate speeches, considered gestures, but in a fierce untrammelled outburst, pregnant with sincerity, that seems to spring from the very soul of

Nature herself. Regarding it, you felt if this shambling monster were held in bondage much longer it must stretch forth its great limbs, break loose and storm the buildings on either side. And for a space you saw Chaos rampant. You saw the outposts of civilized order tottering, the Citadel of Food overrun by swarms of human rats, the gilded dummies stripped of their clothing, and the shiver of broken glass falling like deadly rain upon the street.

Then aware, apparently, of the danger of holding human volition in check, the barriers ahead went down. Into the clear space the marchers poured until there was no space at all, only a dense mass of moving figures.

The draper's van emitted a low chortle of triumph. Slowly it nosed its way through the last stragglings of the crowd. Clothes, women's clothes. Once more they were of paramount importance. As the shining grey vehicle slid northwards, window-gazers inside the Palatial felt a pang at the disappearance of this symbol of wealth and luxury. It was as though in the battle for supremacy, the black swarm had won and the aristocrat had been driven off the streets.

Vaguely uncomfortable, the late-lunchers, the tea-drinkers, asked of one another why Somebody didn't do Something About It. It was terrible to see all these men going idle. Of course, the real sufferers didn't advertise their woes. There was such a thing as good Scots pride. They left that to foreigners . . . They said there was a steady stream of Soviet money coming into the country these days, that Russia was behind all the disturbances. Really, the police shouldn't allow traffic to be disorganized the way it was. Spoiling trade, keeping people out of the shops. Supposing a fire had broken out, and the brigade had wanted to get through? . . . Disgraceful to allow a mob to control the streets . . .

By the time they had devoured a few more pastries, the majority of the tea-drinkers had veered round to quite a different viewpoint from that to which they had subscribed at the beginning. Apparently, in the process of eating and drinking, the fear out of which their pity had originally sprung had hardened into indignation, a two-fold indignation directed against the authorities for permitting the gaunt spectre of poverty to stravaig the streets, and against themselves for having yielded momentarily to panic, to the fear that even their bodies might be swept into the dark flood and cruelly buffeted.

Fanny, the plump waitress, casting a glance in passing out of the window, hurried back from it to receive a complaint from an even plumper lady than herself that the hot buttered toast was cold, and an order from two smart young things at an adjoining table for a pot of China tea and some iced cakes. On her way to the speaking tube to give the order, she shivered suddenly. Losh, it wasn't right – all these women stuffing themselves with cakes and tea and these poor devils outside starving . . . Well, maybe not as bad as that, for, of course, there was the dole. But you couldn't live comfortably on that. She knew. It took her all her time to keep her sister and herself on her salary.

'Two China teas. And send up some more iced cakes, Jane.'

When they arrived, a pile of pink-and-white squares intersected with marzipan and decorated with glacé cherries, she was visited by a wild desire to throw open the window, to call out to those below to hold out their hands and catch. She pictured the cakes spinning like tiny coloured rockets through the murk, and hungry mouths closing on the dainty morsels, then clamouring for more. More! She would have liked to strip the tables for their benefit, to snatch the mutton pies, the fried fish from under the very noses of the smug eaters.

She would have liked to wreak havoc on the whole of the vast plateau of tea and cakes, to create an uproar in every corner of this overheated, food-surfeited place. Instead, she walked very quickly back to the two China Teas. She set the little floral pot and the big stand of fancy cakes down on the table before them with a murmured: 'That everything you require?' Then without waiting an answer, for in her opinion they had all and more than they deserved, she drifted over again to the nearest window.

'It shouldn't be allowed, that sort of thing,' a thin, wheezy voice complained. 'D'you know, John, I was held up nearly an hour in Marylyn Street? I got quite worried. I thought I'd be late for my tea with you. I'm sure and I don't know what the world's coming to!'

'I'm sure I don't know either,' echoed Fanny, her heart thumping uncomfortably in her side; but in the clatter of cups, the murmur of many voices, no one heard the fat waitress speak.

As the crowd rounded the corner, Jimmy watched it from a doorway. His eyes raked the irregular ranks in search of Nimrod. It would be hopeless to try to spot him in such a mob, but for the fact that his compact figure would be distinctive among all these slovenly knit fellows. A kind of sick disgust froze in Jimmy's breast as he regarded the grey, witless faces, the shuffling limbs. Slum rats, most of their owners – dark shapes casting their shade on the bright lamp of world prosperity. It was those fellows and their like who were responsible for the whole ghastly mess. But you couldn't approach a chap and tell him to drown himself to make way for another man. Almost it looked as though war were the only solution to the problem, a world war when that portion of the population which was unwanted could be served to the enemy guns as fodder.

Jimmy had often before watched the hunger marchers, but today he felt there was something different about them. They walked with a more dejected gait. Hardly any of them carried a stick or any kind of weapon. No bands accompanied them. They were moving only to the depressed rhythm of their own shuffling feet . . . What was the bright idea? Had they been foreigners, you would have expected to behold, at a given signal, the flash of hidden weapons dramatically disclosed. But things like that didn't happen here. No, not even on days such as this, when the sight of the sky lying like a coffin lid on the housetops, and the stale odour of smoke pent in a narrow place laid open the mind to a host of sinister fancies.

As he stood there, watching the marchers sweep on, he thought the newly lit street lamps above their heads were like little stars spread above a vast floodwater. The fume of the town was vanquished by it. There was nothing below these steadfast stars but this dreadful current, this dragging silence.

It dawned upon him then that it was this silence which made the marchers seem different today. On those other occasions when he had seen them, they had created an atmosphere of spurious excitement by shouting, by waving sticks, by shrilling of fife bands. Today, walking quietly and without their music, they seemed a part of the premature night enfolding the city, a part of its stillness and its terror.

'Nimrod,' he said to himself. 'This is your idea, I'll wager. The two-minutes silence prolonged. A gesture of respect not to the dead but to the living.'

Well, he reflected, if only the men could stick it, the march as a spectacle would outlast all the others. It would be like that procession of silent khaki-clad figures in *Cavalcade*. In a moment, those figures had wiped out all the melodrama of the earlier scenes, lifted the play on to a higher plane. War. You realized the grimness of it, the futility, as that pitiless line wound on and on, a dark frieze of moving figures blotting out everything until you were fain to scream, 'For God's sake stop!' To scream, or to shut your eyes upon the spectacle of men caught up in an inexorable machine.

Jimmy drew his cap over his eyes, glanced at his reflection in the shop doorway. He had gone home after lunch and changed into his oldest clothes. He wore his coat turned up round the neck to conceal the absence of collar and tie.

'I wish my mother could see me now!' he chanted, then insinuated himself into a gap on the pavement and swung on to the roadway. He had not gone more than a few strides with the marchers before the sound of their shuffling feet, their deep breathing began to chafe him. There was something so intense about it all and yet so hopeless. Like the clang of waves on a level shore. He wondered if it were the close proximity of these men, the nearness of their heads to his, that was causing his thoughts to flow perversely. Or was he one of those human chameleons who take on the colour of their surroundings? Whatever the cause, here, trudging with his fellows, he saw things differently. He felt different. Perhaps that was why they rigged out fighting men in uniform even in the new armies where expense was a consideration. Probably they realized a coloured jacket lent you courage just as the absence of a collar and tie made you feel as though you were about to be hanged. It was a wretched feeling – enough to make you say to yourself, 'Well, it doesn't matter what I do. I'm for it, anyway – doomed.' Did all these fellows feel like that? And if they did, why in the name of thunder didn't they break loose, raise Cain? Why did they mooch along, so mealy-mouthed, so mum?

He forgot, for the moment, there were flashes in his blood that were not in theirs. He forgot that in an ill-nourished body passion does not readily catch fire. Nimrod – he wished he could speak to Nimrod now.

He enquired of the man nearest if the leader were to be in the Square. The man grunted in response, compressed thin lips, and turned his head away. 'I'm suspect,' Jimmy said to himself, and wondered why. Perhaps he was walking too jauntily, with too much of a swing for a man about to be hanged . . .

It was queer, he reflected, to regard the shops from this angle. Deep in obscurity, their lighted windows were full of colour. 'Great reductions. Come inside', white lettering on red strips of paper pasted on the glass of one invited the multitude. Higher up, outside a touring-agent's office, was the suggestion in gigantic letters, 'Why not go a Mediterranean cruise this winter?' And below it, from a luxury tea shop, came a warm whiff of hot scones. How did all this strike the man whom no great reductions could tempt for the simple reason that he hadn't a bean? What were his reactions to that proposed Mediterranean cruise, that picture of blue-eyed Amazons, of bronzed youths in elegant white sweaters lounging against a deck rail?

But there was nothing to be gleaned from the faces of his companions, Jimmy realized. Each face wore that peculiar shut-off look of the very poor.

Well, he knew how he would feel if he were in the shoes of any one of those poor devils. He would feel – he would feel revolutionary. No other word for it. He would be ready to fight like a demon for his rights.

They were nearing the Square now. The high buildings rose out of the gloom like cliffs. Almost, as you advanced, you expected to hear the whisper of the sea.

The man next him was grumbling to his companions, 'The same ruddy round.' That was the burden of all their plaints. So the same procedure was to be adhered to, the procedure honoured by custom and observed on every occasion by the marchers of circling the City Chambers while the councillors held their meeting. But the great ring their shambling bodies created had no real pressure in it. It could never close in and squeeze the life out of those within. It could never reach those urbane wearers of robes and chains, those arbiters of a people's destiny. It could never reach them, because they were all-powerful. They represented Authority, and you might as well hurl a stone at a statue in the Square as at the stately frontage, the high walls and frosted windows enfolding Authority's sacred person.

As he moved mechanically on, he saw the marchers as a pitiful multitude over which Christ Himself might have sorrowed, a multitude made up of the lame, the halt and the blind. True, none of his immediate companions lacked either limbs or sight. But his instinct told him they lacked that which was even more essential to their spiritual welfare. Dried up within them was the inner fount from which joy bubbles eternally on the stream of hope. Stagnant, too, was the source of their dreams. With an odd little constriction of the heart he heard his father's voice repeating from his country pulpit the words of Christ's message to mankind: 'Come unto Me all ye that are weary and heavy laden and I will give you rest.'

But there was no vestige of Divine light on the clouds overhead. There was only this cold, forbidding darkness.

He started as a hand touched his arm. Turning, he looked into a known face.

'You here,' said Nimrod. 'Well, what d'you think of us?'

Jimmy stared at him stupidly. Then his brow cleared. Of course, Nimrod didn't know that since he had joined the procession he had deliberately identified himself with the marchers. Nimrod didn't know that for the time being he was one of 'us'. He was having no truck with 'them'.

CHAPTER IV

At the same time as Adèle Elberstein and Mr Joyce were lunching upstairs, Mrs MacGregor and Monty were sitting opposite each other in a corner of the big white-and-blue grill room. Privately, Mrs MacGregor would have preferred the table d'hôte. It had more style. The service, too, in that room was better – not so slapdash. Still, grill room or no grill room, there was no reason why she shouldn't preface her remarks for weeks to come with: 'When I was lunching at the Cavendish . . .' There was nothing to prevent her sunning herself in the aroma of opulence which clung to the hotel.

It was the consciousness of this aroma which was sustaining her now, for Monty's greeting had proved disappointing. His conversation, too, was lacking in the proper sentiment. As they waited what seemed to her an interminable time for their *petite entrecôte*, an awful blankness descended upon her. There were frequent pauses in their talk, terrible pauses which, if Monty had only been sensible and had the table d'hôte luncheon, would have been nicely filled by a discussion of the hors d'oeuvre; or, if they were consumed and the soup was long in coming, an appraisement of the people at the other tables.

Here there was no one worth turning your head to look at, no one smart at all. Only a lot of carnivorous-looking men and women devouring steaks and chops as though their lives depended upon their dexterity and speed. Mrs MacGregor regarded them with a sweeping disdain. There wasn't a hat in the room. She touched the brim of her own provocatively, tilting it a little lower over her eyes; but Monty wasn't looking at her. He was fiddling with the French mustard, his eyes on the table.

She hated him then suddenly, hated him for having raised a tumult in her breast, for having cheated her into believing that she had heard again the low sweet chords of romance. As she sat there, very erect and conventional in her high chair, she felt as though her heart were contracting. And the process hurt. It hurt so much that she wanted to hurt somebody in return, to hit out at Monty whose big soft eyes had no message for hers today. But before she could command a weapon deadly enough for her purpose, the waiter had returned and a silver dish was set with some ceremony between them.

A familiar odour rose in her nostrils. Steak. So *petite entrecôte* was nothing exciting after all; it was just steak, common steak, and revoltingly undercooked at that!

'Done to a turn,' declared Monty with a relish she thought should have been reserved for greater things. 'Mustard, Elsie? '

She played with her knife and fork, slit open her roll and buttered it carefully from edge to edge, then set it back on her plate again. She felt too sick to eat. Monty regarded her solemnly.

'I say, you're not in form. D'you remember that day we lunched at Casablanca?'

Remember! How dared he ask her that? It wasn't she who had forgotten. Again there rose in her the savage desire to wound.

'Did anything come of that scheme of yours – the chemical amalgamation you were so keen about? I remember you talking about it that day.'

She remembered, further, that he had promised to wire her from London if he succeeded in bringing off the deal. The telegram had never come, and it gave her a little sadistic thrill to taunt him with his failure.

He smiled across at her. 'Imagine you recalling that! By Jove, Elsie, that's been a lucky thing for me. As a matter of fact, that's what brought me north today. I'm an idler no longer, my child. I'm a hard-working businessman. I've to see Flatterty of the dye works, you know, this afternoon. To us they're proving a little gold mine.'

So he hadn't come north to see her – oh no! She was only filling in his time till he could get a train to Dunledin to see Flatterty, the dyer. A stifled little laugh burst from her lips, a harsh uncontrolled sound in an atmosphere decorous in the extreme. She bowed her eyes on her plate, praying for some inspiration whereby she could account for her sudden lapse. But Monty had not noticed it. He had thrown back his head and was talking in the tense, passionate way that had fascinated her when the subject of his discourse had been herself. Now that it wasn't, her attitude was more critical. 'Vainglorious,' she murmured inwardly. Blowing about the new plant they were installing at the factory just as, three months ago on board ship, he had blown about his visits to Palm Beach and the Lido!

It disgusted her when he spoke of the future and its possibilities for his firm, to see his eyes light up as they had done when he was dancing with her on the upper deck and whispering, under cover of the band and the general babel, words of love in her ear. She was filled momentarily with a deep contempt for all men. They belonged without doubt to a lower order than the members of her own sex. They had no fastidious instincts, no fine sense of discrimination. Eating and drinking, bargaining and making love, laughing and shouting and kissing women – to them it was all part of the day's work. She glared angrily at a noisy group at a table opposite. 'Here's hoping, old girl!' one of the men was saying as he raised his glass and made sheeps' eyes at his neighbour, a big blowsy woman with untidy brown hair and bright red cheeks. She giggled delightedly, and Mrs MacGregor loathed her for fostering with flattering noises the unbridled egoism of the male.

Quivering with an irritation which she knew to be utterly without reason, Mrs MacGregor withdrew her gaze from the offending table and turned it again on Monty. He was good-looking, of course, in a showy sort of way. But his skin which had been bronzed and glowing on board ship was now pallid and flabby. His eyes had lost some thing of their clarity, but they still retained that melting wistfulness which had been one of his attractions for her. Dogs' eyes, she now thought suddenly, sometimes looked like that. Set a biscuit down before an animal you had trained to the trick, and say severely, 'Don't touch,' and its eyes immediately filled with that expression of wistful pain and desire. As a respectable young married woman with a husband in tow, 'don't touch' had doubtless been writ all over her during the cruise. It was still writ all over her, thank goodness, she reflected in a flash of self-righteousness, choosing at that moment to forget that the ticket might have been promptly and unprotestingly removed had Monty's demeanour towards her today been different. As it was . . .

'Tell me,' she said abruptly, 'why did you wire me to meet you today?'

He shifted imperceptibly in his seat. Had Elsie turned thought-reader? That was the very question he had been asking himself. Why had he expended a perfectly good shilling only to land himself in for this dismal luncheon? He might have known better. Ship-mates never seem the same on dry land. Over and over again, he had been taken in that way. Seen here in these surroundings, Elsie lacked glamour. She was just an ordinary little provincial bit with no 'go' about her at all. Too smug and respectable for words. That other woman at the next table, overblown though she was, had more to her than Elsie. She could laugh, a fine big rollicking laugh, and let herself go, and give her man back sally for sally, whereas Elsie was so damned afraid of seeming common that she *was* common.

Conventionality oozed from her at every pore. No social nous either. Who but a simpleton would have hurled at him this question now? If he answered it honestly: ' Because I thought you'd help pass a couple of dull hours for me, and by a lucky chance I found your letter in my desk with the address'; a letter, incidentally, he had never troubled to answer, nor, for that matter, to destroy – if he answered her that, she would be bound to rise and go off in high dudgeon, without finishing her sweet. And by all the rules of decent behaviour he would be obliged to leave his too, and accompany her at least as far as the hall door. If, on the other hand, he lied to her, said soothing, flattering things, she might start simpering, turn coy. And he couldn't bear that. Not in this hearty atmosphere of tobacco and cooked meats. In any case, that hat of hers was never meant to be worn by a coy young thing. It was sophisticated as its owner was simple. In his eyes – and he knew something of women's headgear – it was a very devil of a hat designed for wear in a rackety restaurant by some bold bad woman.

'Don't trouble to reply,' Elsie's voice cut sharply in upon his reflections. 'I know quite well why you telegraphed. It doesn't matter. Isn't this pudding dreadfully uninteresting? I'd like some sugar and cream with it.'

In the few seconds he had been ruminating, she had taken what she called a pull on herself. She felt better now – capable of feigning light-heartedness. There was no use telling Monty what she thought of him. In any case, her desire to hurt was lessening. It was unlikely she would ever see Monty again. She regarded him thoughtfully and wondered how she could ever have endured the pressure of those coarse lips on her own, how she could ever have felt excited, delightfully self-important, at being singled out by him for special attention from amid the crowd of undistinguished women on board. She stared at his nose, rather red and shiny and inclined to hook; at the sinews in his neck, showing above the starch of his collar. And again that distaste for the whole male sex possessed her. Ugly brutes, men – every one of them.

The sight of Monty placidly chewing, those obtrusive sinews of his working like so many rope pulleys, irritated her so much that she wanted to scream. Instead, she thrust her elbows on the table and essayed small talk. It was easy once you got started. There were lots of interesting places to recall. Nevertheless, it was a dismal lunch, as Monty had realized earlier. Neither of them was sorry when it was ended and they could repair for coffee to the lounge. Mrs MacGregor felt happier in its spacious atmosphere. There were more of her own kind here. Some really smart people. One or two quite fashionable hats.

With an effort, she put away from her the inclination to pose as the heroine of a broken romance. She set about with commendable good sense to glean what entertainment she could out of this luncheon at the Cavendish. She must get George to bring her here sometimes. George, in common with many of his countrymen, was dubious about hotel food. He was in the habit of asserting that he enjoyed far better what he got at home than what he had for his midday lunch in town. That was all very well, of course, for George. He didn't have to cope with meat in the raw. That reminded her, she'd meant to give Mrs Humphry the end of that cold roast. But she'd be gone most likely by the time she got home.

A little later, Monty pushed back his chair after a hurried glance at his watch.

'D'you know it's train time already? I'm sorry. Come along and I'll get the porter to call you a taxi; then I'll nip into the station by the other door.'

But when they looked out into the Square, it had grown curiously dim and unreal. A great mass of moving figures was sweeping from the far end across it.

'Unemployed demonstration,' said the hall porter. 'Afraid there's no hope of a taxi just now, sir. Even the trams get hung up in these crowds. Wouldn't the lady be better to wait a bit till the Square clears?'

So this was the bogey Mrs Humphry had tried to scare her with, she thought, as from a window in the drawing room upstairs whither the porter had conducted her she watched the marchers envelop the Square. She was glad Monty had gone and she could watch them undisturbed. A hurried, half-shamefaced sort of leave-taking theirs had been. A slight pressure of hand – hands that had once clung together lovingly, now shying uncomfortably from contact with the other.

'Goodbye, Elsie. Thanks awfully for coming. Hope you'll get home all right. Daren't miss my train or I'd have waited and seen you safe myself.'

'Goodbye, Monty. Don't fuss about me. I'm all right. Goodbye.'

And she was all right, really and truly all right. She wasn't feeling a bit hipped now, or unhappy . . . that had only been wounded vanity, that funny feeling she had experienced earlier. Actually, she told herself boastfully, she didn't give two straws for any man, unless, perhaps, George. She was used to George. George wasn't a 'blow'. Even if he'd been to Palm Beach a dozen times, he wouldn't talk about it for fear of making the other man, who hadn't been, feel inferior. George was like that. Oddly enough, from the first George hadn't cared for Monty. 'My dear, it takes a man to judge a man.' And, of course, George was right. That was the most tiresome thing about him, his liability always to be right. She sighed profoundly, then forgot all about both George and Monty as she regarded the passing figures outside.

Mrs Humphry's Joe would be among them. What a pity she had forgotten to tell her to take that end of cold roast! They looked awful, some of these marchers, just like the people you read about in stories of the French Revolution. *À La Lanterne*, and all that sort of thing. But they weren't threatening anybody with a rope and the nearest lamp post, these processionists outside. They weren't singing or shouting or waving their arms menacingly. They were walking quietly, row upon row of them, all dark-clad. They were walking soberly, silently, like mourners at the funeral of some great king.

A frightening thought took possession of her mind, stripping it momentarily of its sensuality, its foolishness.

Were these men mourning the demise of the city's trade? Were they on their way to dig a grave for all those who had helped to kill it – the slackers, the idle rich, the braggarts, the mean-spirited, the advocates of the trend to the south, the women who, like herself, had done nothing to help?

For the space of a second she trembled and wished Monty were back beside her – Monty guzzling underdone steak, or talking with his gay, confident gestures.

CHAPTER V

Joe joined the marchers when they entered the Square. As they passed beneath the offices of Joyce and Son, he looked up at them, at the lighted windows illumining the Palace of Plenty, wherein his mother spent so many of her working hours. Would she still be there, he wondered, bent double on her knees, scouring and scrubbing? 'I'll lay,' he said to himself with a queer little flick of pride, 'she works harder than any of them. And she doesn't ride in her motor car to her work either!'

For the first time, it struck him that his mother's lot had been a harsh one. Used from infancy to seeing her always at it, he had never thought of her in possession of ease and comfort, he had never pictured her in fine clothes. Now it occurred to him she couldn't always have looked as she looked now. There was a faded photograph of his father and her taken just before they were married, sitting in a garden shelter outside a boarding house at Dunledin.

They had been able, seemingly, to afford holidays at the coast then. They had had money for such luxuries as railway and steamer fares, food and lodging in other folks' houses, even for photographs. In this one, his father had worn the slightly foolish, rather nervous yet boastful expression of a man who is intimidated by the camera and flustered by its operator's injunction, 'Smile, please.'

His mother had appeared natural enough, a merry-eyed girl with an engaging smile dimpling her rounded cheeks. That photograph in its red plush frame had stood for many years in a place of honour on the mantelpiece. It was gone from there now. Joe couldn't recall having noticed it anywhere lately. Perhaps his mother couldn't bear the sight of the girl she had been; the girl who had loved little outings and enjoying herself at the seaside; a proper picture of a jolly girl proud as Punch at the prospect of having a home of her own.

It wasn't matrimony that had worn her down. Her one great boast now was that she had had a good husband. Sometimes Joe thought she said that meaningly, bitterly, as though she wished she could say as much about her son. But he had done nothing to account for the change in her. It wasn't his fault her face had lost its brightness, her body had shrivelled, grown so thin. It was the fault of the tyrants who ground them down; of the capitalists like old Joyce who had commandeered for their own use the whole train, when, by rights, no man is entitled to more than his own seat.

For a time Joe's mind writhed in the maze of tortuous argument, then, wearying of its intricacies, he became personal again. It was Joyce, Arthur Joyce, who had robbed his mother of her youth, her gaiety. It was Joyce and his like who had worn her out.

He saw the Palace of Plenty in a new light – a storehouse crammed with rich treasure which it was torment to look upon and not be permitted to touch. And all these years his mother had endured that torment, endured it without saying a word.

As he stared upwards, the faces of two youths appeared above the frosted-glass rim of one of the windows. Two of the young gaffers, he thought angrily. Two of them that wore fancy-coloured shirts, drew a big pay and did deil all. And as like as not they'd look down on his mother; they'd put on fine 'haw-haw' voices when they spoke to her, so as to make her feel the difference between them. Difference – Gees, and there was a difference. All the difference in the world between a decent working woman and a pair of parasites.

'Nimrod's orders, tach!' A voice rose in his ears, a voice harsh with the force of a bitter grievance. 'I'm tellin' ye what it is, lads: Ramsay's got a grip of him, and he canna deny it. "We've got to make ourselves felt," I says to him, "and you used to say that yince yourself, Hamish Nimrod. It's nutt making ourselves felt to mooch about as though we was feart. I'm nutt feart. I'm nutt feart for any man born, nutt even for yourself, Hamish Nimrod. So I'll tell ye what none of the others will tell ye. I'll tell ye what they're saying ahint your back. That the Government's got a hold of ye, that—"'

But in the confusion consequent upon rounding the corner, Joe was separated from the braggart. He was thrust into a group of sullen elderly men, several of whom appeared to be breathing hardly, as though they felt the air to be poisoned. They all looked dreary, disconsolate. The silence which frustrated a part of their normal activity was stifling them. But none of them dreamed to break that silence. They were old soldiers, these men, and orders were orders. Besides, Nimrod *knew*. He was no foolish Jack-in-office. In his heart's privacy, each man acknowledged Nimrod's power, his right to dictate.

Above the frosted rim of the window, the heads of the junior clerks in Joyce and Son's wavered, then withdrew. The faces of the two – More's pimply white pudding, Macfarlan's countrified white oval – froze into the sort of resentful immobility which overtakes most faces when a show suddenly and prematurely comes to an end.

Without the exchange of a single word, they lounged back to their chairs, stared at the neat little rows of figures they had been adding. Pounds, shillings and pence. Never for a moment did they think to translate these terms in their minds. Never for a moment did they become masters of millions, titillating Wall Street and the London Stock Exchange by violent speculation. No necromantic visions salved for them the monotony of existence. Joyce's from nine till five. The 'pictures' at night with, for More, who was city bred and tarnished, the adventure of making up to some strange girl in the dark. He was in the habit of boasting next day of his conquests to Macfarlan. He embellished facts until, for a brief space, he saw himself a veritable Don Juan, creating havoc with feminine hearts in the fourpenny seats . . . Such Men Are Dangerous. In furtive whispers, to the pulse of his sexual vanity, he painted a portrait of himself in the role of dangerous male. It was his chief form of recreation, this portrait-painting. It almost compensated him for the snubs he had received from independent young women the night before. He thrilled to the enjoyment of 'making Mac open his eyes', and Mac, who had a habit of staring fixedly at whoever was addressing him, listened quite unperturbed.

Nothing perturbed Mac. Born in a cottage near Rannoch, a cottage which crouched so close to the grey earth that it seemed to grow out of it, Macfarlan had absorbed into his system part of the impassivity of the silent moor. If excitement ever broke over his stolid young body, he veiled it instantly, as though ashamed of a bared emotion. Actually, external things touched him very lightly. Although it was over three years since he had come to the city, he had adopted none of its airs, its ways. He carried his home on his back like a snail. His background, the background from which he would never become wholly detached, was the dark moor.

Because of this, he had a way of staring at people when they spoke to him, staring because for him it was always an effort to wrench his mind from things that were at a distance, such as the moor and the cottage with his mother framed in the big chair by the window, to those persons and things that were near. The intensity of his regard flattered young More. It increased the spate of tall-talk which gushed from his lips when none of the elder men was about. Today, the seniors were in the adjoining room with Mr Wren. There was something in the wind, it was whispered. The result was that the two junior clerks had been left pretty much to their own devices since morning, and More had exhausted more energy in inventing tales than in totting up columns of figures.

A middle-aged man put his head inside the door in search of someone, then went away again. A door slammed along the passage. Young More swaggered over to the window, a pen behind his thick red ear.

'Hi,' he said, 'come along! The marchers are coming back this way again. Crikey, what a mangy-looking lot! There was a girl I met on Monday, not at the pictures, but in the lounge at the Palatial. Did I tell you about her? Her father used to be a plater in the yards down at Greengarth. He's out of it, of course, now. They're all out of it. They say the grass is growing down there already. Anyhow, he's one of that lot.' He nodded at the processionists. 'A regular Bolshie, spouts all over the shop. Never does a hand's turn. She told me she was keeping the old boy and the whole blinking family. Mannequining in a West End shop. Said it was funny parading in finery for the benefit of the nobs most of the day, and then going home at night to hear her father's mind of them. A real top-notcher, she was, all the same. Blood-red nails, lipstick and "perm". You know the style.'

In his exuberance, he forgot about the procession passing below the window. He forgot that, close as he was to the glass and focused in the strong white light, all his animated gestures, his facial jerks, were clearly obvious to anyone looking up from the street.

His white-pudding face resolved into a revolting smirk as he gave a rapid outline of his amatory advances, as he mimicked the girl's agitated but encouraging, 'Oh, re'ely, Mr More, you shouldn't do that,' the while Macfarlan, close to the window likewise, and wrapped in silence, gazed at him intently. Thoroughly reckless, More was striking attitudes, leering repulsively, playing the dandy one minute, the helplessly subjugated maiden the next, when Joe, struggling on the outer edge of the procession, cast his eyes upon the lighted windows of 'the offices'.

Through his tired body swept a red wave of heat. The dark clouds above his head trembled. He tried to move on as though nothing had happened, but his feet felt like blocks of wood, clogs his limbs couldn't control. He stopped dead, stared up at the two young 'gaffers'. One of them, it was plain to see, was imitating the marchers; he was taking them off, jeering at them. They were both jeering, those —— fools sitting up there in their fine soft jobs!

As he stood there looking towards them, Joe's heart listened so intently that, down here in the crowd, it caught the echo of ribald laughter, the grating sound of 'haw-haw' voices. Those voices clutched at some sensitive chord in his brain so that it twanged suddenly, hideously, upon his taut ears. He started as though an arrow quivered in the flesh above his heart.

He pushed a way through the crowds on the pavement into the stone close leading to the offices of Joyce and Son. The lift attendant, seeing him pass, looked up from his paperbacked novel to say to himself, 'There's a bloke in a hurry,' but made no move to intercept him. He pounded up the winding stair, and along a narrow passage where, by chance, he encountered Macfarlan, who had been summoned, a second before, to take some books to the seniors' office. Unconscious of the clatter of footsteps, Macfarlan raised his eyes from the ground, was fixing upon the intruder his profound gaze when, to his vexed surprise, the passage became a place of chaos, of gathering twilight and pain.

As Macfarlan went down below his whirling blows, Joe had the impulse to scream out loud in triumph. His soul was a bead of gold glancing in the light of the fire that enfolded him. He felt like God dealing out retribution to the unjust, levelling to the dust the occupiers of high places.

In striking down this unknown youth, he had struck down old Joyce – Joyce who had robbed his mother of her youth, her gaiety. He had struck at all those who think they own the earth and take a corridor to their own cheek. Looking down at Macfarlan's limp figure, he saw Capitalism laid low, Liberty flaunting her scarlet cloak in the dim stone archway of the Palace of Plenty. He saw a world transformed, a luminous world which the workers could control as easily as a child controls a coloured ball. And then, quite suddenly, the golden bubble of his vision burst, leaving no glimmering splinters behind.

From the stone where Macfarlan lay, terror rose up and clutched him. He came to the surface of himself as he had come that night when he had threatened his mother with a chair. Now, as then, remorse savaged him. A dry cry breaking from his lips raised a shocked echo in those staid precincts. The sound startled him into action.

He slipped down the stairs, passing so softly that this time the lift man failed to observe him. The last straggle of the procession on its way back to encircle the Council Chambers still mottled the roadway. He thrust determinedly into the ranks, driven by the feeling that close to his own kind he might lose the horror which, like a noose about his neck, was choking him. But every face he looked at seemed akin to that stark oval lying motionless in the stone passage of Joyce's offices. Every hunched pair of shoulders, every averted head, seemed to resemble those of the man he had murdered . . . Murdered. He turned the word over in his mind, examining it. At every turn he disliked it more, disliked and distrusted its lurid aura. Murder – you associated murder with villains in penny 'bloods'; with Saturday nights at the pictures, where, on the screen, before your eyes, toffs in boiled shirts with pink carnations in their buttonholes, or desperadoes on bucking horses, thought nothing at all about doing one another in. You associated murder with tales of old crimes in the Sunday papers – with Madeleine Smith, and Burke and Hare, and those ones; you associated it with police-court reports of awful brawls, with visions of blanched men with evil countenances and bloodstained hands, with the limp figures of flashy women lying prone on fine sofas. You associated it with fierce, exciting events, with political intrigues, with pitch-black nights and bleak, lonely houses, and ancient feuds and loud, passionate quarrels, not – God, not with a lighted passage in a city office, not with this trundling round a murky square.

He had an imperative desire to break the monotonous round, to stand still and to shout out loud. Murder – he would like to have put the question bluntly to the marchers – was it murder to smite the unworthy, to aim at the bloodsuckers, to drag down the capitalist from his gilded throne?

He was still brooding over this strange word, regarding it with spellbound eyes, it and the queer deathlike images it evoked, when he became aware that the marchers had almost completed their circle. They were nearing again the offices of Joyce and Son. Already the reflection from their windows was creating in the darkness a little funnel of pallid light on the heads of the foremost of the demonstrators. He pictured the stone passage in an uproar, peopled with police, with detectives and doctors and ambulance men. He visualized a dozen jigging heads in the frame of each of the lighted windows. He had the impulse to stare up at those heads, to defy them to find him – the man they were looking for, the murderer, amid all this jostling throng. But overlaying this desire was the creeping chill of a mortal fear.

He fell out of the ranks before the circle was fully completed. He slunk down a side street which seemed strangely deserted after the hubbub in the Square. A stray cat, licking dirt with its long pink tongue at the kerb of the pavement, raised its back aggressively at sight of him. As he drew near, it streaked across his path in panic, tore headlong into a nearby opening. He stared after the flying animal. Was it possible, even a cat— But he couldn't conclude his question. The flow seemed to have stopped in his brain. No thoughts came.

He walked on mechanically until he reached a thoroughfare where the traffic was normal. To an observer he looked just like any ordinary young man going home from work for his tea, and planning, if he could afford it, to take his girl out to the pictures afterwards. He did not halt until a bus overtook him and stopped at his side to permit a couple, who were waiting at a red post, to step aboard. Then he stepped aboard too.

As the vehicle sped out of the city, he sat shivering in a corner. When at last it reached its terminus, instinctively he raised his head to the light.

CHAPTER VI

Joe's limbs were stiff when he stepped out on to the road. While the driver and the conductor fraternized, and the other passengers set out purposefully, he stood gazing about him with the air of one who has arrived, all unexpectedly, and with no effort on his part, in a strange place.

He found himself staring at a great sweep of frost-bound country, at a stark-blue sky. It spanned the world from rim to rim, that sky; and no cavernous black arches, no ferrous ridges, shut out one speck of the radiant blue. The immensity of it stunned Joe. He forgot himself momentarily, lost in this world of quivering light. A creature of city streets, with the reek of fog, of germ-haunted places clinging to his person, he felt, as he stood there gazing, as though he were being uplifted by some force in the strong clear air. Into his cheeks, blanched by poverty and fatigue, by resentment and longing, crept a sharper tinge. His shoulders braced themselves to meet the wind. It swirled up the valley, a salt-laden gust that broke on the ear like the crying of a deep-sea bird. It frolicked across the fields, the frost-girt places, before hurling itself against the hard, white glitter of the hills. When it retreated, whimpering, from their fastness, its lilt was that of little waves lipping the scattered rocks of an ungracious coast.

In this vast scallop of open country, the hills were the dominant feature. They emerged from behind the slatternly village on the right, their shining serenity a reproach to broken piles and irregularity in stone. Below them the valley dipped to the river, but you could not see it from here; you could only divine that somewhere between those wooden slopes, those untidy villages, were the black wharfs, the washed edges of a great waterway.

Close to where you believed it to flow, the square tower of a church thrust itself into the sparkling air. By some freak of the frost, its outline had escaped the diamonded white tracery. Grimly black in a realm of transfigurated light, it was a giant cairn that challenged passing ships with its antiquity, that reminded man of his ultimate doom. As though to correct the effect on the mind of this sombre pile, the chimneys of commerce belched smoke behind it. From a bevy of abrupt ochreous stalks, the wind blew crape-like wisps that formed into a grey gauze which floated lightly, then disappeared, in the shining sky.

Joe ignored these stalks. They did not flaw the panorama spread out before him, but he disliked them because they were a reminder of all he had left behind. He found himself staring at the hills, at their sharply chiselled sides, the deep clefts where shadows lurked; shadows so transmuted by the clarity of the light that they resembled gossamer clouds, grape-blue and purple-veined.

'Pretty,' he said to himself, unaware of the mawkishness of his adjective. 'Pretty.'

His eyes were on those rainbow shadows when a step behind him, a voice, caused him suddenly to *remember*. From a vast white platter brimming with divine peace, the sweeping countryside became a place terror-haunted. Whirling past his eyes, blotting out the hills, went a crazy frieze of prison vans and courtrooms, of grim-visaged warders and black-capped judges, of hangmen and newspaper headings: 'Last Minutes of the Square Murderer. Accused Takes a Hearty Breakfast.' They always said that.

He turned to the man whose advent had evoked all this, and recognized the uniform of the bus conductor.

'What?' he asked fiercely.

The conductor, a north-countryman by his speech, blinked his eyes. 'I was only saying we would be after starting in a minute if you was wanting to come back with us.'

Back – back to that blasted town? Joe found himself trembling with rage at the thought. He shouted at the conductor, who went off in a huff. As the bus lurched away, Joe leaned against a wall and cursed himself passionately for a fool. He had done the very thing to arouse the fellow's suspicions, to fix himself on the man's mind. Why couldn't he have shaken his head, marched on, instead of letting fling like that? 'Accused Traced to . . .' What did they call this place? 'Bus Conductor Reports Conversation with Suspect.' That would be the outcome of it. Oh, why hadn't he held his tongue?

The tide of his anger subsiding, he fell into a black depression during which he stayed motionless while the wind died down and the glowing pool of the sky grew darkly blue. It was a queer numbness followed by the sharp pain of a chilled member that roused him.

He wriggled a dead leg in panic. 'Gees, am I paralysed?' he cried inwardly, and stooped to flog with his hand the deadened limb.

As the life in it came back, a horror of death filled him. To go numb all over like that, never to feel things again – his soul recoiled at thought of his body's extinction, at thought of the end of pain and poverty, of hunger and humiliation. Shot through them all, he realized, had been something finer, something richer, a sort of blind faith which irradiated even the blackest-seeming thoughts, so that in the end they turned to hope and confidence. Some day something would turn up. A job, a fortune, a revolution. You went on, hour by hour, building on that, dreaming of it, letting it ease for you the awful sinking sensation which inevitably followed snubs and short cuttings. The darkness of the present only threw into brighter relief the possibilities of the future – when the dictatorship of the proletariat was established and every man occupied his own safe seat in the train. The thought of that, and of lording it a trifle over the displaced princelings of commerce, never failed to afford him a little secret thrill.

On that instant, Joe, looking back on his life, knew that in the main it had been good. Fragmentary recollections, vital pictures, took shape before his eyes, an absurd jumble so vivid, for all its chaotism, as to set his heart knocking fiercely against his ribs. The moon swimming like a great yellow bird above the tenement ridge; his father's face, sharply drawn, the features shapeless, as though anguish had robbed his mind of its reason; the conical white hat, the blobs of rouge on the face of a shore performer he had loved, at a distance, one Fair holiday; Nimrod's figure erect in the crowded shed, his voice a drum that beat your blood to a ferment; the maze of hunger marchers in the Square, and that face – that upturned face lying so still in the dark stone passage.

Joe wiped the moisture from his brow. He would never escape that, seemingly; never be able to close his eyes but what that face would insinuate itself between his lids.

A couple of tinkers, trudging citywards, passed him. The woman, a ruddy-cheeked young matron with a young child in her arms, stared at him curiously. She said a word or two to her companion which caused him to turn round and devour Joe with his insolent blue eyes. Joe's colour rose. First the bus conductor, then those two. There must be something about him which made people remark him. He had never felt noticeable before. He wondered if what he had done had in some queer way altered him, given him an air of importance.

He knew now he hadn't done what in the first sharp minute of exaltation he believed he had. He hadn't smashed Capitalism, he hadn't raised the Banner of Liberty in a forbidden place. He hadn't even finished old Joyce. He had only done in a youth who jeered at the marchers as the Jews had jeered at Christ on the Cross. Gees! What put that in his head? Was this ruddy business going to make him turn religious?

He rubbed the side of his neck with his hand in a gesture of self-disgust and perplexity. His eyes, roving the hillside, rested on a tree on the summit, its bare branches outspread against the pale primrose of the sky. So still and black were those branches that they might have been carved out of stone and set there at the world's beginning.

'The crucifix,' he said; and something within him trembled.

Round the world night was sweeping, shedding waves of ebon cloud on wind-whipped waters, undulating woods and clotted streets. It swept the pale lake of the sky, dimmed the lustre of the valley. Only on the frost-white fissures of the hills it seemed to hesitate and wane. Behind Joe, the slatternly village dissolved. In its place was a grey blur, starred here and there by a single glim. Above it, the sky, narrowed down to an islet of gold floating amid a sea of turbulent cloud, showed streaks of red. A bloodstained sky. Joe's eyes reverted from it to the Gethsemane tree on the hilltop. It still braved the flood of the oncoming dusk. In the very lap of horror it remained inviolate, a symbol of enduring courage and grace.

He sighed heavily. If only he could believe in Christ as he believed in Nimrod! Christianity in the beginning had been a kind of Communism. There were bits in the Bible about Christ feeding the starving multitude and succouring the weak. There had been no side about Christ. He was all right. It was the Church, the Church stinking with riches and the pomp of landowners, that had raised the barriers; the Church that looked askance at you, or its elders did, if you went in of a Sunday night just as you were, in your working clothes. Like a swell entertainment the service was, with a paid choir and dressed-up women in light gloves, and a silver collecting plate thrust at you half-time in case you'd slip away, as you did at the pierrots, before the plate came round. Yes, they thrust it at you – you that had more need to take than to give. But the Church gave nothing nowadays. Not like its Master, who gave bread. Small wonder they had done away with the Church in Soviet Russia. It was the Church that raised the barrier between God and man. There should be no such barrier, he reflected passionately. The Cross should be there before you, clear as it was now.

He gazed at the solitary tree, and saw its bleached branches lift before the wind. From where he stood, it was as though Divine arms were being raised in supplication to the sky, as though they were essaying to ward off from the world the swiftly gathering shadows.

While he stood there watching, his heart formulated a challenge. If the clouds stop short of the crucifix, if they don't blot it out, I'll believe – I'll believe in you, Jesus Christ, and do your bidding.

But as he so vowed, in a sudden panic it occurred to him that a life for a life was one of the awful exactions demanded by the Lord. If he were to obey the Divine Law, he must go back, give himself up to justice. And what had he, Joe Humphry, done, that he should be sentenced to death? He hadn't struck intentionally at a human being, alive and palpitating like himself. He had only hit out at Capitalism, at cruelty. And they would hang him for that . . . His mind seethed with apprehension; from his heart sprang little conflicting cries as the cloud-wraiths grew blacker and up the crest of the hill crept the intangible smoke of dusk.

It hovered at the bark of the tree, and once again a tremor shook its branches, a gentle movement that seemed to stay the progress of the oncoming dark. Overhead, slaty-grey clouds hung motionless, leaving untouched a strand of faded gold that formed a halo about the tree so that it stood out as though set in a crystal heart.

At that moment, Joe was perhaps nearer to happiness than ever in his life before. He had called for a sign, and he had been accorded one. The image of the crucifix set high against the sky filled his whole being with a sense of exquisite pain.

'God, I believe,' he avowed, and in the flush of a pure emotion was confident that his belief would nerve him for whatever lay ahead.

Slowly, feeling tired and shaken, he turned his face towards the town he had left. Best get it over quickly, he thought; and decided he would give himself up at the first police station. He would knock at the door and say, 'I killed a man an hour or two ago in the town. I've committed murder. Take me.' Maybe they wouldn't believe him, for he had no signs of guilt about his person, no bloodstains, or rusty weapons. Maybe they would think he was mad, or drunk. But he'd tell them to ring up Joyce's in the Square. They would tell them quick enough. He was in two minds as to whether or not he should give his real name. His mother wouldn't like to think of him in the dock. She would feel it a disgrace. But she'd have to know sooner or later. There would be those pictures in the paper. It was a pity about that.

He was entering the village when from the lighted doorway of a squatly built house, which he guessed to be the district constabulary, a police sergeant emerged. He emerged reluctantly, in the manner of a man loth to leave a warm fire and congenial company. He turned to say a parting word to someone behind, and as the door swung farther back on its hinges, in the flush of the gaslight within a smiling young woman in a blue, flowered overall was clearly revealed. For the space of a second, officialdom shed its austerity. Joe saw a man about his own age chaffing a girl from whom he was loth to part. Then the door shut on the picture of domesticity with a tiny bang. The police officer, alone in the darkness, pulled down his helmet-strap, and, with the slow determined gait of his kind, tramped down the path leading from the house to the roadway. At sight of the familiar uniform advancing towards him, the outline of the crucifix which still wavered before Joe's eyes dissolved. He drew back into shadow and waited to see which way the sergeant would go. But he too halted, looking about him, until Joe could stand the suspense no longer. He turned on his heel and ran swiftly back along the road.

It was only when he had gained the shelter of a tiny thicket in the valley that it occurred to him to wonder if the tree on the hilltop still stood untouched by cloud. He peered upwards, but in the enveloping dusk he could see nothing but the skeleton tracery of nearby branches.

CHAPTER VII

Wrapped round in her furs, Adèle Elberstein sat at the window of her sitting room looking down on the marchers and silently condemning them for a dull-looking lot. They lacked the audacity, the vigour of the foreign mob. The crowd she had sung to from her balcony in the Paris hotel, the crowd led by her friend, Comrade Imerinsky, had been instinct with devilry to its finger-ends. A seething, restive crowd fermenting that which must almost immediately explode. These men looked too apathetic to nourish revolt in their breasts. They were part of a dull mass that rolled on and on. No fight in it, no spleen. Differently attired, these people might be guests trooping to a grand party which it was compulsory for them to attend, but at which they had no hope of being happily entertained, or even cordially received. Bored, they looked to her thinking, and utterly weighed down. No flashes of anarchy there, no hidden bombs. Only a sort of dogged determination that bound them together, engendered as that determination was by the same dimly formulated desire. Top dog. I want to be top dog. I've been under long enough. Roughly, she translated the Socialist doctrine into this demand. She did so readily enough because it was the sort of demand she herself would have shrilled had she still been under. Yes, she would have shrilled it, shrieked it at the pitch of her voice. No silent suffering for her, no uncomplaining endurance of hardships!

Oh, she had no patience with a people who didn't seize what they could, who emitted no terrifying threats as they marched by. Even the little midinettes, when they struck for higher wages, had more spunk than that. They paraded the Rue de la Paix flashing their scissors, threatening to chop the nose off any intrepid customer who made to enter a shop door. A demonstration – bah! This wasn't worth the name. It was as dull as ditchwater. What had the little Italian waiter been talking about?

She rang the bell, demanded of the page who answered that Carlo should be sent to her. Where are your fireworks? she would ask him. They do things better in your country. They have a flair for spectacle in Italy. Were you in Milan three years ago on the Duce's birthday?

She had almost collapsed on the stage that night, so strong had been the scent of flowers banked up on the proscenium, so unbridled the waves of emotion rippling through the house. All day they had been militarist, these people, holding themselves in check, parading, saluting, cheering, keeping on a straight white line. Now they had broken free. They were above themselves like children released from school; voluble, reckless, ridiculous children impossible to keep within bounds. But the music held them. She held them, although at the start her nerves had been poised in suspense.

She was standing again on the flower-banked stage, reassembling in her mind the notes of her final duet, when a knock fell on the door.

'Come in,' she called, and turned to find the manager on the threshold.

'You wanted someone, Madame? If there is anything I can do . . .'

She shrugged impatiently. It was the Italian waiter she wished to see. He had been here only a minute ago.

Mr Valley's eyebrows jigged upwards. Here in Madame's sitting room? Surely she was mistaken. Carlo's place was downstairs. It was not his duty to attend the private rooms.

She tapped the floor with the toe of her satin shoe. Blast rules and regulations!

'Maybe, but he was here a minute ago – or it may have been an hour ago. Anyhow, I wish to see him again now.'

Mr Valley edged his way to the telephone. 'If Madame will permit me,' he murmured. 'That you, Henri? Send a page to the lounge for Carlo . . . What? Send the boy upstairs to his room, then.

Tell him Madame Elberstein wishes him. Number seventeen.'

He laid down the instrument. 'Carlo will be here immediately, Madame. There has been some mistake. Usually he is on duty in the lounge at this hour, but . . . I trust you are comfortable, Madame; that everything is to your mind.'

She smiled graciously, focused her dark brown eyes on his face. After all, even an hotel manager was a man.

'You are coming to my concert?' she asked. And the effect was as though claws had been sheathed. Mr Valley's eyes brightened. His shoulders relaxed gracefully. He knew nothing about music, but he flattered himself he knew something about women. And this was a fine-looking creature; not just a voice encased in layers and layers of fat like most of the singers who came to the hotel. You wanted to look at them out of the wrong end of your opera glasses, the narrow end that reduces everything to a minimum. Adèle Elberstein was different. She could bear close scrutiny. Plenty of style and sex appeal. Not very young, certainly old enough to have seen a bit of the world, to know what was what. He wondered if she had any interest in the Ring. She was the sort, he'd be bound, who would appreciate a good contest. Nothing squeamish about her. Had she been in Paris by any chance last month when the nigger met the Italian?

Within a few minutes he had succeeded in diverting the conversation from Stravinsky to Carnera – Milan, naturally enough, suggested the famous boxer – and he had made the astounding discovery that she had actually been present at the recent Paris event. On that instant his heart lifted. While the shuffle of the marchers filled the Square, he leaned against the mantelpiece a magically contented man, immune for the time being from the worries of staff, from the irritation consequent upon the temperamental outbursts of foreign hirelings.

He was discussing the prospects of a young local boxer he had seen the previous week when a page burst into the room. The boy's face was scarlet. His eyes were wide with terror.

'C-Carlo!' he stammered. 'Carlo!' But before he could bring out another word the manager hustled him out of the door.

Wildly curious, Adèle went after them. She stepped in their

wake on to the lift. They were shooting upstairs before Mr Valley, engaged in hurling questions at the trembling youngster, became aware of her presence. He addressed her gravely, the dignified functionary once more.

'I fear, Madame, something unpleasant has happened. I must beg of you to return to your own rooms.'

But ignoring his protestations, she pushed after him to the door of a little dark room where something, something in the shape of a man, hung from a rope suspended from a hook in the skylight window. She fled at sight of it. She sat down on the topmost rung of the stone stairs because her legs were shaking so that she feared they could not support her. The lift had disappeared. She looked down on the carpetless steps, up at the sloping ceiling, the walls papered in ochre yellow. They were familiar to her. She had been here before, often before. But never had she dreamed that behind any of these closed doors horror lurked. She had imagined the narrow rooms to be peopled by persons of her own kind: artistes, businessmen who for professional purposes must have what is known as a 'good address'. The Ritz-Carlton. The Grand-Majestic. Who, seeing that on your notepaper, was to know you weren't occupying a luxurious suite, or, at least, a comfortable third-, or fourth-, floor bedroom? Who was to guess you were skied in the attics, a sparrow on the rafters?

Top floor, typical top floor. That was why the steep stone stairs, the sloping ceiling, the hideous wallpaper, were so familiar. For years they had formed her background. She shut her eyes and shuddered. 'God,' she cried in her soul, 'I couldn't come back to this, I couldn't!'

She rose, walked unsteadily towards the well of the lift and pressed the bell. There was a responsive movement in the cables on either side. The huge cage sped upwards, stopped at the floor immediately below. It stayed there for a full moment. Furious at the delay, she held her finger tightly on the button. Then, relaxing, she drew her furs closer, preparatory to stepping on the lift. But it slid downwards. She saw the shadow of its roof disappear. Oh, but that was typically top floor! You rang and rang and nobody came.

Standing there, she smarted at thought of the old humiliations, the petty affronts put on her by the most snobbish class in the world – hotel servants. You might act the duchess downstairs, dress up to the nines, but somehow they knew. They knew you for one of the sparrows, and so you had to hang about for ages before they'd condescend to give up your letters; you had to scan the noticeboard for your own telegrams and telephone messages. There were never any eager porters thrusting them before your eyes, offering to carry your cloak upstairs. You could carry it, and coal for your own fire, for all they cared! Even your tips they accepted condescendingly, although out of sheer bravado you gave more than the swells. Yes, you threw half-crowns about and then boiled an egg and made tea on a spirit lamp in your room to save the price of a meal in the *salle à manger*. The tea leaves and the shells were the very dickens to dispose of next day. They composed a sloppy parcel you daren't let the chambermaid catch sight of, and that was liable to lower your prestige – what little you had – were you seen carrying it downstairs. And if you had the bad luck to drop it . . . She laughed outright at the memory of her chagrin when a grinning concierge at Monte Carlo had restored to her with a bow her dripping property.

The sound of her mirth shocked her. How could she laugh when behind the door in that little room . . . ? Oh, she must get away from the horror of that hanging figure, the sordidness of these upper reaches!

She looked down on the stone steps, clutched hard at the handrail. It wobbled in her grasp. Shaky, needing repair. Oh, but that, too, was typically top floor!

She felt as though she were regaining Paradise when her feet trod crimson carpet again. Her maid stared in alarm when she entered the room.

'Madame, you look ill. Where have you been?'

She shook her head. She wouldn't say where she had been. Marie wouldn't understand. And the less said about Carlo's suicide the better. They hushed up these things in hotels. They deemed death, even a normal death, a little inconsiderate. Hotels were meant to live in, to eat and drink in, to dance and make love in; but you mustn't die in them. It wasn't done.

She sat, when Marie left her, brooding with her head on her

hands. Her life, she realized now, had been one long struggle to attain to first floors, a struggle during which she had used men as stepping stones. First Elberstein, then Aristide the pianist, then Brutling the American Senator. They had all served in their turn, they and others, to edge her into this atmosphere of spiritual steam-heat. So used to it had she become that she had all but forgotten the cold outside.

Yet the greater part of humanity was enduring that cold. For the first time for many years it occurred to her to contrast her own vivid life with the lives of other women born at the same time, and in the same social stratum as herself. Household drudges, most of them, or drapers' assistants clocking in each day at a given hour. Tired out and fretful, many of them, nursing a grievance against a fate that had seen fit to stunt them of pleasure all their days, that had given them nothing in return for all their youthful ardour, their high-spirited vivacity, but a husband who wasn't much good, or a job that wasn't great guns either – only a defence against starvation now, and in their old age.

Yes, life yielded precious little for some people. It had proved too much for Carlo. It was trying to the uttermost the mettle of the demonstrators outside. She wondered if they were still there, or if they had passed on to that uncongenial banquet they were bidden attend, that banquet at which the boards were bare and there were no lights burning. She shivered at the image of want conjured up by her mind; but even as she did so, she realized she was play-acting. Her pity wasn't poignant enough to pierce right through.

She went to the window and looked down. Police were keeping a clear space on the pavement, but the roadway swarmed with moving figures. A group of men were shouting in a corner, waving a red flag. They were calling out for justice; justice, she reflected dispassionately, in a world where there is no justice at all, only sex and a queer kind of crafty cunning. She had wielded the sex weapon for all it was worth. Without it, she might still have been out in the cold.

She leaned back in her chair, preening herself on her own cleverness, basking in the sunshine of the prosperity that cleverness had brought her, while the beat of footsteps rose like a dull tide from the far end of the Square. The sound invaded her consciousness presently. She raised her head and stared at the gilded leaves adorning the mirrored mantelpiece. Those thick gold leaves, wreathed at each of the four corners like the headpiece of a Bacchanalian god, represented in her eyes the crown of her own success. She had gone forward and won. These men had gone under and lost.

Suddenly, before her eyes there was projected the hanging figure of Carlo. They were correlated, she felt, in some strange obscure way, the hunger marchers and the dead man. She pressed her hands to her eyes as though by so doing she could erase from them the recollection of those dangling limbs. It might be as well, the thought came to her, to make some propitiatory gesture to the fate that had aided her in her escape from the horrors lurking on top floors, to the lucky chance that had guided her footsteps to stardom.

'There, but for the grace of God,' she murmured unctuously. But she did not mean God. She meant Elberstein, and Aristide, and all the others.

Obeying a superstitious impulse which prompted her to act quickly if she would avert from her person the consequences of suicide's evil eye, and ensure for herself a continued share in the world's riches, she made up her mind to write a cheque for the city's unemployed. That would placate the jealous gods, and at the same time please her publicity agent. She would communicate with him right away. 'Prima Donna's Generous Action'. She nibbled the end of her pen as she asked herself just how much would she require to give to justify the use of the word 'generous'?

She signed her name with a flourish at the same moment as a threatening roar mounted from the Square. So engrossed was she in contemplation of her own beneficence that she heard nothing at all. If she had, she would no doubt have translated these shouts of execration into the enthusiastic 'bravos' of a grateful people.

CHAPTER VIII

Jimmy never rightly knew what started it. Perhaps from the first it had been inevitable. You couldn't let loose a flood and still keep it under control. There was bound to be damage done somewhere. A woman's scream, tearing the air, sent a shiver through the closely packed ranks. A bruised silence followed, pierced by the shouts of irate men.

Nimrod swore aloud. Jimmy, hearing him, was astounded at the foulness of his language. As the din grew louder, the leader pushed forward, enjoining silence. But his voice would have needed to be as powerful as Jehovah's to have soared above those swirls of fury, those recondite currents now coursing across the Square.

The modern battlefield, Jimmy thought grimly. According to the League. All done by kindness. No screaming of shells, no thunder of guns, only this close, hard pressure of human bodies, this desperate push of starving men. No, not starving, he corrected himself. In this Christian country of ours, none need starve. A man may be stifled in the insane pressure, trodden down by hooves in the Gadarene rush; but he need not starve. Not so long as he had strength to drag himself out to draw his dole. On it, he could live like a lord on a diet for obesity. But did he ever stop to think, when he was drawing his dole, what he was and what he was doing? Did it ever occur to him he was the unwelcome guest of the white-collar brigade, that his needs were draining its resources, choking like a heap of filth a strong clear stream?

The white-collar brigade . . . But by what right was it cock of the walk? Its business was to distribute the goods made by the masses, and a right muck it had made of the job of distribution. The workshops were so cluttered with machinery and goods that there was no stirring room. That was what was wrong with the world. Not enough clear spaces open to the sky.

At the moment, tight-packed in a wedge of shifting figures, Jimmy would have welcomed a thunderbolt, anything that would have stemmed this homogeneous spate of flesh. It was pouring towards the Council Chambers, a desperate current hurtling itself against granite rock. And all to no purpose. There was the tragedy. You cannot pit flesh against stone.

As though aware of this, a yowl of pent-up rage broke from the foremost portion of the mob. Above its colossal and distorted body circled a dark-blue line.

'The mounted police,' said Jimmy, and blasphemed whoever was responsible for their presence. Why couldn't the authorities realize they were the Aunt Sallies of democracy, these 'mounties'? Sitting up there so cock-a-whoop, they positively asked for it. You wanted to shy something at the one nearest just for the fun of seeing him duck, or, if your shot were lucky, of seeing him drop. Great sport, laying low the mighty. No prizes, though, for successful competitors. If they were wise, the successful would show a clean pair of heels.

Sweating, jostling, pushing, the great press of men swept forward. The menace of the wheeling lines of blue grew more sharply defined. You had the fear a truncheon suddenly revealed would strike you in the stomach, send you sprawling amid this crush of scuttling feet. You felt more and more oppressed by the awful futility of it all. Nimrod, Jimmy wondered, where was Nimrod now? Not that he, or any man born, could do anything. No one could stay this gargantuan rush. The mob would do its worst. Gosh! Where, oh, where was the jolly old League now? All done by kindness – brutality, you mean.

A sudden clout on the head cut short his ruminations. Someone had unfurled a red flag. They were fighting round it, trying to uphold it. They were screaming, cursing, like wild beasts vomited out of a primeval forest. Their distorted faces, black with frenzy, were mouthing threats . . . 'Stand back, there, or as shair as death

I'll brain ye! Back, there, you – or . . .' But the words were lost in the mad uproar. It rose in waves around the flag, a banner now high above the bobbing heads, now ludicrously tilted to a side and flapping in the hands of its agitated bearer like a woman's red petticoat hung up, still limp from the family wash, in a breeze to dry.

The uproar grew louder and louder as the thin wedge of mounted figures, drawing nearer, separated the noisiest of the combatants from their comrades; as it closed in upon them, isolating them and their banner from their kind. The warm breath of a horse fell on Jimmy's cheek. He put out a hand with the intent to push the animal's face away when something – he never knew what, the heel, perhaps, of another man's boot – tripped him up, sent him sprawling to the ground. He fell on his knees in a heap. During the second he lay there, his consciousness, like that of a man in desperate peril, gathered intensity.

An underdog literally for the first time in his life he saw things from the underdog's point of view. He saw despair like a current-whorled river enveloping the people until, buffeted and exhausted, their sense of perspective ran mad. He saw the old accepted creeds, the decent conventions, discarded and scattered like wreckage on the face of the waters. They were meant, these old shibboleths, for gentle living, not for those fighting death, fleeing destruction . . . 'Christ,' he groaned, 'give us a new religion of brotherhood! Help us, or we perish by one another's hands in a world of hate!'

He struggled to his feet, clutching instinctively for support at the arm of the man nearest. He was unhurt, but he felt slightly sick and light-headed. Something, he realized, had happened to him since he had joined the marchers. A force that was too strong for him, a sense of a looming Presence, had swept on to his mind, overweighing it. He had lost a grip of the old scale of values, the accepted angle of vision. One thing only he knew – he couldn't go back to the office and write up a lot of slosh about Adèle Elberstein, and ignore, as was the policy of his paper, the happenings here in the Square.

True, nothing with a 'news' value had happened, and, pray

heaven, nothing would. A few, doubtless, like himself had looked a police horse too closely in the face and sustained minor injuries, but that was all. No, nothing that mattered a tinker's curse had happened, and yet he knew life had altered, had assumed for him a new shape. He looked round anxiously. During the instant he had been down, the pressure had miraculously lessened. Satisfied, apparently, at having given convincing evidence of their ability, if need be, to throttle, the horsemen had eased their grip.

Perhaps they had made off with the Red Flag as a trophy. There was no sign of it now, or of its bearer. The men round about had stopped shouting. They were muttering to themselves, the incontinent mutterings of those who smell defeat. Poor devils, they were born to be defeated. They were defeatists themselves with their sharp, animal-like features, their narrow foreheads and their poor addled brains.

Jimmy's one desire now was to get away from them, far enough away so that the fiery emanation of their thoughts should not scorch the dim raw material of his. The office was no good. There was no sanctuary within its steam-heated corridors where a man could stay quiet and think. Not, really, that there was anything much to think about. Only, he felt impelled to examine the nature of this spiritual force which had invaded his consciousness, this force which forbade him waste words on Adèle Elberstein when there was so much that was of real import to be written.

But once in the midst of this throng it was not easy to break free. Men glared at him as he tried to elbow his way to a side, suspicion in their eyes. Did they guess he was not really one of themselves, he wondered? Did they recognize his clothes, despite their shabbiness, to be a cut above their own? Did they resent his possession of a strength that was wanting in them?

He was nearing the fringe of the crowd when a fresh uproar broke out behind him. He looked round to see a familiar face amid a welter of struggling figures. Nimrod, by gum! The police had nabbed Nimrod!

In the flame of an unreasoning fury, he threw himself into the thick of those who were fighting to release their leader. He was hitting out bravely, swinging his army like flails, stopping suddenly to rain a series of well-directed blows which caused his victims to crumple up, when he was violently pinioned from behind.

Nabbed, the same as Nimrod, the thought went through him; and in his pride at being in such good company he let out a blood-curdling yell. A thousand voices answered it. Before the savage onslaught of sound his ears thrummed.

'Oh, hell!' he said disgustedly, for he had been set upon getting away somewhere quiet by himself. 'Oh, hell!' he repeated again in tones so disgruntled that the tall policeman constraining him could not refrain from making response.

'Hell, and youse was the boys that raised it,' the big fellow hissed. 'Youse was the ones.'

Meanwhile, at various points round the Square a deep line of illuminated fortresses had sprung into being. The sight of them, crowded with people, looming brightly through the darkness, raised no alarm in the hearts of the marchers, only a little thrill of pride, for they recognized these fortresses for what they were – lighted tramcars which they, by sheer weight of numbers, had brought to a standstill.

In one of the farthest back, a white tram which barely a second ago had been swinging briskly downhill, Mrs Humphry sat stiffly between a benign old gentleman with twinkling eyeglasses, who smelled slightly of brandy, and a handsome young woman, very fine in dark furs and light gloves. Mrs Humphry gazed out of the opposite window, but her thoughts tore on ahead. They walked in the wake of the marchers who would have left the Square by now, and who would be holding their meeting on the Green. It was about this hour the meeting was timed for. Even if he stayed on till the last, Joe would be home before her. He would maybe have the kettle on and, if he were hungry himself, the tea set. There was a nice tin of salmon ready for the opening.

But even as she pictured it all, cheerfully tinted like a grocer's Christmas calendar, she knew she was only fooling herself. Some deep mother-instinct, lending her prescience, gave warning that her homecoming would not be so arranged. Joe would not be waiting for her when she got back. Maybe he would never wait for her there again.

'What's up, conductor?' The testy voice of the elderly gentleman startled out of his benignity cut sharply across her forebodings. 'What's keeping us? Breakdown or some accident in front, is there?'

The young lady in the dark furs and light gloves leaned forward anxiously to hear the reply. When it came, everyone in the arrested tramcar contributed their mite in the form of an irritated exclamation, or a sigh, to the general chorus of vexed annoyance; everyone save Mrs Humphry, who sat bolt upright, her fingers clenched tight, her eyes on the reflection in the opposite window of a bird-fancier's shop.

. . . Trouble with the unemployed in the Square. The mounted police called out. All the trams held up. Joe – God, save Joe! Send him safe home!

CHAPTER IX

It was while still the marchers processed silently through the Square that Mr Joyce chanced to look out of the window and to observe them.

For two hours or more he had busied himself with files and documents. He had absorbed the faint musty smell they exhaled, and wearied his eyes with their faded lettering. While they lay piled in heaps upon his desk, earnest of his forefathers' proud activities, or spread out in full before him, no visions inspired by their ancient agreements rose before his eyes, no voices from the past intruded upon his calculations.

He was working mechanically, doggedly, half resentful of the fact that he should be obliged to do so. What he would have liked to have done was to have shut the door of Joyce's one night without saying anything, to have turned the key in the lock – the key he had once regarded as a proud talisman, a link between the West and the East – to have turned the key, cast it over his shoulder and then to have strode off, knowing the business was ended. That, he felt, would be a proper finish. This preoccupation of facts and figures went against the grain. It was too much akin to the fuss of a grand and costly funeral. Well, it was his funeral. The end of an epoch in his life. You stepped over the borderline from boyhood to manhood without feeling anything save a pleasurable increase in power. You could hardly hope to get over the next jump so easily. There was bound to be a wrench sooner or later. There was bound to be a sense of dwindling interests, a slackening of one's grip on affairs. It was odd, it occurred to him suddenly, he was taking it for granted that the instant he retired he would develop into a doddering old idiot. He had seen lots of men run to seed the moment they downed tools; but surely to the Lord, he need not necessarily be of their company. Better join the bar-loungers – they were lusty enough fellows most of them – than the imaginary invalids, the garden potterers. He would be happier trotting round the globe at Adèle's heels than going to bed early at nights with a mustard plaster on his diaphragm, or rising before breakfast to plant tulip bulbs upside down.

He switched off his desk lamp. What with blinds drawn and lights blazing, the room was becoming airless, or was it the reek of those old papers that made it so stuffy? He hauled up the blind, looked out. There was something strangely mournful about the Square today. Like distorted cliffs, the buildings on every side, rock hacked and indented to form lighted caves which glowed in the dark above the roadway's shadowy chasm. There was a sense of silence outside as well as within. A dead day, Mr Joyce reflected, the kind of day upon which it was fitting things should come to an end.

There was a movement behind. Celia had entered – Celia trying to look very brisk and businesslike in the endeavour to convince herself that the competent Miss Ker was not yet down-and-out.

'The London post, Mr Joyce,' she reminded him in her soft voice. 'Have you anything ready?'

He regarded her for a moment without answering. It wouldn't matter although he never caught another post. No, it wouldn't matter a single damn.

'No,' he said loudly; so loudly that the curt monosyllable shot into the mild sadness enfolding the room startled Celia. Her flesh shrank as though on that instant a bolt aimed at her heart had found its mark. She stood motionless, quivering inwardly, then through force of habit she turned to her own desk to collect the letters there. Shooting out an arm blindly, she sent a ruler clattering to the floor and felt the ceiling press down on her head as she stooped to reclaim it.

'I believe I'm going to faint,' she thought dizzily. A long breath – that helps. Get out of the room somehow – it was the competent Miss Ker now who was in charge – get out. You can walk well enough without falling if you keep close to the wall . . .

She hung on to the door handle when she reached the passage outside. She leaned her cheek against the cold stone and felt as though she were drawing strength from it. Charlie Wren, coming along presently, found her standing there.

'Hullo!' he exclaimed. 'What's wrong?'

She essayed a smile which didn't quite come off. 'Nothing, nothing,' she said.

He took a step nearer, alarm in his face. Nothing – then why, in heaven's name, was the girl all white and shaking? Why was she looking like this? He forced himself to speak lightly, jocularly.

'Liar! Why keep it dark? There's something.'

'It's only . . .' She stopped short, emotion welling up in her throat so that she feared she was about to disgrace herself by bursting into tears.

'Only what? Has Mr Joyce said anything?'

She shook her head. 'Not a word. It's only – there's no London mail.'

'You've been in for it?'

'Yes. He said there wasn't anything.'

'What was he doing? Poring over books, or what?'

'No. That was the funny part. He wasn't doing anything. Just standing at the window, looking out.'

'Looking out! I hope he looks long enough to see the hunger marchers circling the Square.'

The savage irony in the young voice awoke in her a shy stirring of compassion. It was worse, far worse, for a man to have to face the loss of his job than it was for a woman, she told herself. More humiliating somehow. Girls from their infancy were used to doing without things, to making shift; not like men. Girls could run up their own dresses, they could retrim their hats, cut quite a decent figure without expending a cent; whereas men . . . She remembered how her father used to bemoan the expense of a new suit. And he would never have his overcoat silk-lined. She used to feel quite cross when affluent patients came and left their grand coats hanging up in the hall. Oh, it wasn't fair that men like her father and Charlie Wren should have to worry over little things like coat linings and the price of collars laundrying.

A dreadful pang went through her as she pictured Charlie dispossessed of his position in Joyce's, poring, as she had seen seedy-looking little men in tramcars do, over the advertisements for men wanted in the pages of the daily press. It was such a meagre little list always. The one above it – the one inserted by applicants on the lookout for posts – was invariably three times the length. Like a horrible torturing game of musical chairs it was; but instead of only one person being left out at the end, there were hundreds and thousands left out every day.

It wasn't so bad for a woman, she told herself again. There were so many things a woman could do without loss of self-respect. She saw herself alternately gliding about a tea room in a skittish uniform, embroidering lingerie, polishing antique brass and silver filigree in a dim old Georgian house, and growing rich in the process. Then from a sense of power, she fell suddenly upon a knowledge of utter incompetence. She couldn't 'wait' for nuts. She couldn't clean or polish as well as poor old Mrs Humphry, and look at her!

She averted her eyes from the image of that grotesque figure in the flapping coat, the coat someone had given her but which was far too large for her scarecrow body. She looked up at Charlie, and again her lips essayed that travesty of a smile.

'Here's hoping,' she said with the air of one drinking a solemn toast.

'Here's to Joyce and Son's,' he said quickly. 'May it never— Right you are, More; Miss Ker has the letters.'

Still lost in abstraction, despite the incident of the dropped ruler and Miss Ker's noisy exit, Mr Joyce sat at his desk beside the unblinded window and looked out into the Square. By putting up the shutters now, he could perhaps save it from being the scene of another failure. Better empty caves, desolate and unlighted, than offices overrun by angry creditors.

He hoped rather anxiously Jacks wouldn't be late. He would be glad to get this over. He would be free then to escape into another existence which, wherever it led, would be exempt from the responsibilities, the particular heartbreaks of the present. Of late, the office and all it spelled had not meant much to him. There were days when he felt like a disinterested onlooker. That youngster, Charlie Wren, was keener far than he. You could see young Wren positively expanding, looking pleased as Punch when things went well. Jerry had been keen like that, keen as mustard. There would have been no putting up of the shutters had Jerry come through. He would have cut the cobwebs, rid the atmosphere of its staleness long ago. He would have sent a new current charging through the place, a current richly stirring and adventurous. In the Slump, he would have seen only another obstacle to be cleared as his forebears had cleared the obstacles that rose in their day. Yes, regarding every transaction as vastly important and exciting, Jerry would have carried the whole concern forward on the crest of his unflagging enthusiasm. There had been no holding back with him ever, no thought of sparing himself. All his days he had lived intensely. It was not only at the last that he had stood poised like a young god in the fierce white fire of danger.

Looking out now on the Square, Mr Joyce saw the dusk rise in great puffs like the smoke of guns. He saw the slow eddying traffic as part of a vast turmoil that involved men of all classes, of all nations. Grey-bearded German professors, middle-aged French manufacturers, Italian poets, long-haired Hungarian musicians, Rumanian peasants, passionate Serbs, Irish agitators and Jewish moneylenders, English clerks and commercial travellers, American gentry and Australian diggers, Scots miners and crofters from the Outer Isles; and boys, boys of all nations, a host of pink-cheeked, confiding youths like Jerry, ready for the sake of the wingéd dream conceived by their ardent minds to run their breasts upon a spear.

While still this strange congress possessed the four ways, he saw it break, swerve closely to the sides. It was as though the world had suddenly emptied itself; and there was nothing left but a void and this immense dark silence which reached up to him, pressing him down. There were visible no small shadows whose passage might have released imprisoned sounds. There were no travelling glims.

On that instant, Mr Joyce passed through one of those lost

spaces of time when reason stands suspended and the passing moments are of no account. The years that had slipped by since Jerry's going seemed little more than the flash of a swallow's wings. Somewhere, quite close to him, here in this office whose atmosphere had gone stale, Jerry was holding out eager hands to him, Jerry who had yielded up everything for the sake of a dream.

He leaned forward at the bidding of a Voice which, even as he obeyed, he knew to be silent as the passage of a cloud over the bright face of the moon. He leaned forward, his eyes on the shadowy space below at the same moment as out of the blackness, filling the void, there poured a long line of haggard men. He stared at the advancing legion, in his ears a dull throbbing like the mutter of distant drums. On the edge of the Square, the illuminated fortresses were already springing into being. The glitter of their lights was a menace, threatening the spectral figures who walked so draggingly, their clothes the colour of calamity itself.

He stared and saw in the deep narrow pool of the darkness, Youth and Gallantry and Joy extinguished in the roar and flash of gunfire. He saw Death and Destruction like a blood-red film roll over and enfold the earth so that the golden harvest of the fields was laid waste, and the gleam of the towns was blurred. He saw Want and Hunger and Revolt like jeering imps spring out of the destruction of factories and streets and shops; he saw the three imps straddle the capitals from end to end, invade the countryside, causing men to quail at their approach and women to lie tossing, sleepless, in their beds at night.

He saw those things, but only as though they were remote and distant from him, as though, indeed, they hovered on the dream-fringe of his existence. Nearer to the core of his being, so near that it was as though a hand clutched at his heart, awakening its blind veins to unaccustomed sight, a more awful vision lay: the vision of graces riven open by dead men who could not rest in peace, of a Legion of the Lifeless assembling on Flanders fields, of the throbbing notes of a strange inaudible reveille breaking upon ears upon which no earthly sound would ever break again.

Quick march . . . The words had the import of sublime music. Quick march – a march of phantoms drawn from eternal tranquillity into worldly stress again, drawn by Divine pity, by anguish, by anger; anger against a people who had forgotten so soon, against the faithless who had failed in their vows. Quick march – on through roads where the guns once lumbered and the Verrey lights flashed crimson, on to the base where the rest camps lay, to the ports where the big hooded liners nosed softly across the Channel. Dover – ghostly white in the slow November dawn. Dover, town of many memories, first glimpse of home. Into a deep hollow hallowed by a pallid radiance, their ship comes slowly to anchor. And then, like a snow hill melting in the sun, they overflow its sides. They step ashore – these ghosts of Flanders, and before the tremor of their drums the sounds of the morning are muted . . .

They swelled, the sound of these drums, in Mr Joyce's ears as he gazed down into the fog-ridden square, gazed at the apparition of those youths who had set out so bravely, in all the proud panoply of khaki and brass, and who were now returning so draggingly, clad in the vestments of mourning and despair.

'Jerry,' he whispered aloud, and a grief far sharper than any he had yet experienced rent his breast. 'Jerry, what brings you, my son?'

But out of the living gloom there came no answer back, only louder and louder in his ears rose the mutter of martial drums.

'Jerry,' he said again, and bowed his head in agony; for as the sound broke from his lips, he knew the vision which had lain at the very centre of his being to be lost. The limitations of time and space were closing in upon him again. Jerry had gone from his side; and he was alone in a darkening world.

He stayed for a time motionless, seeing that world as a dreary waste in which he was no more than a small shadow driven by the winds of Fate; a shadow which would soon fade and be forgotten, as such shadows are. But something of him, by God's grace, should live on, that part of him which was a part of Jerry. Jerry whose sole memorial was vested in two monosyllables: 'and Son'.

'And Son' . . . The words blazed in letters of fire before Mr Joyce's eyes. They were bright grains set high like stars in the firmament. They were banners of glory recalling the pride of battles hardly won. He felt a glow steal through him at sight of them. No victory, after all, was worth acclaiming a victory unless that which followed a fight which was hardly won.

He rose and, going close to the window, drew down the blind. But before the green baize could blot out the Square, he recognized the procession for what it was – a march of the city's unemployed. No phantoms of the mist, these fellows swarming on the pavements, but suffering flesh and blood. Hunger and Want and Revolt embodied in sharpened features and furtive eyes, in weary hearts and daunted spirits. Was it, indeed, upon these selfsame men he had looked a while ago, looked out of the aching vision lent momentarily to the veins of his heart? Perhaps by some miracle, for a brief fraction of time, the ranks of the hunger marchers had thinned, and in place of these human derelicts a heavenly host had walked, a host composed of the war dead, risen from their graves to implore man's compassion upon man.

Very slowly, Mr Joyce sat down again at his desk. He looked, as he stooped over it, a tired old man. The taut chord which kept his features under control, his shoulders erect, seemed to have snapped. He leaned forward like one nursing an internal wound. As the clock struck, he started up. Another hour before Jacks was due . . . I wish to God, he thought anxiously, he were here now!

CHAPTER X

Celia regarded the scene in the Square with apathetic eyes. Ready as a rule to absorb through every bit of her consciousness the happenings out there, today she had her blind side turned to the marchers. Like a sufferer racked by pain, she was isolated in a world of her own. She was aware only of her own personal pangs and reactions, and of the swelling sense of something impending which filled the air.

That there was aught of drama in the conflicting elements never occurred to her. Nor did she dream that darker threads than were visible to the eye might be woven into that strange shifting pattern. She would have been frankly incredulous had anyone told her that the events in the office, and certain happenings in the hotel opposite, were all a part of the web being woven by Destiny in the Square. She would have maintained that what went on within these four walls had naught to do with the shouting outside. Loud as it was, the voices seemed to her far away and unreal. Not for a second did they impinge upon the sharp edge of her consciousness.

Seeing her own face in the mirror, she marvelled at its immobility. She had expected to see it shaken out of its usual cast, showing some sign of the panic into which she had fallen, instead of which it was precisely the same as it was when she had washed it with soap and water in her bath that morning and dusted lightly over with powder before presenting to the world. Not by so much as a quivering eyelash was it any different. She realized with a little shock of surprise how far removed the palpitating entity inside, the 'I' which is one's self, is removed from the flesh. And the realization, sharp as is every rejection of the romantic convention in favour of truth and self-knowledge, made her feel strangely humble. She looked down at the keys of her typewriter and thought: 'I'll never judge anybody by appearances again . . . I'll never, never call people callous or unfeeling because their faces aren't all white or tear-stained.' She recalled saying to her father of a woman in the village whose child had been run over and killed by a motor car: 'She's taking it very calmly.' Now, looking back, she knew her own ignorance to have led her astray. In her youth and simplicity, she had expected the bereaved mother to answer her facile emotion with her own. Instead, the woman had remained tearless in face of her visitor's flow of sympathy. It was only now, with the image of reality pressing in on her heart, that Celia understood what torments of grief, of pity, of self-reproach surged behind the woman's calm exterior.

It occurred to her to wonder then what manner of thoughts were passing through Mr Joyce's mind. He had not shown the slightest sign of perturbation. He had looked merely tired. But for all that, behind those quiet eyes a battle might be raging; all sorts of fiery arguments might be rending his mind. You couldn't tell. Maybe he had not yet arrived at a definite decision. Maybe his brain was cluttered up with whole lists of pros and cons, counter-columns ranged like hostile forces on opposite sides, one from the other. That, perhaps, was the reason for his appearing distrait. When she had been last in his room, he had been staring out of the window. Engrossed in his thoughts, he had probably failed to notice the presence of the hunger marchers. They had been orderly enough then. It was only a few minutes ago they had started shouting.

Pressing her hand to her forehead, she wished they would be quiet, much in the same way as she might have wished a dog would be quiet whose howling disturbed her in the night. She wished they would clear out of the Square, and make off to the Green, or wherever their leaders delivered their final orations; and then she turned to respond to More's voice, upraised on a note of unwonted excitement, calling her name.

'What is it?' she said shortly, for she didn't like More. His rather full blue eyes had a way of appraising her person too closely. She had a vague suspicion that his over-nice manners – More was always charming to ladies – concealed habits not so nice.

'I say, Miss Ker, have you any eau de cologne or smelling salts handy? Mac's had a fit or something. I found him lying full length in the passage. I was going to call for help, but he sort of waked up when I spoke, and got up and came into our room. But he's still looking a bit queer and dazed.'

Macfarlan smiled sheepishly when Celia entered. From the day he had first come to Joyce's, she had inspired him with an admiring awe, an awe which had ripened gradually into an almost reverential affection. Despite the fact that she was country-bred, he linked her in his mind with the things of the city. She appeared, to his thinking, to embody in her person all that was finest and most beautiful in this roaring, sprawling town. The fleetness of movement distinguishing the high-powered cars that glided across the Square was reflected in her grace, her carriage. The rich aroma of luxury surrounding the gilded picture houses with their henchmen tricked out in crimson and gold was repeated in the faint sweet fragrance emanating from her person. The sense of distilling light in the darkness which was achieved on a black dismal day by the advent of a splendidly lit bus – all this he associated confusedly in his mind with Celia's entry into the office.

Seeing her now, he gathered together his scattered senses as a man must do in the presence of his idol. He murmured some sort of apology which she did not hear.

More fussed around him like a clacking hen with its chicks. 'Come to now, aren't you, old man? That's great!' he cried affectionately. 'My word, Miss Ker, if you'd seen him when I did, you'd have thought he was a goner. Stretched out there, white as a sheet. A pity, Mac, when you felt it coming on, you hadn't the gumption just to squat down in the passage; but I suppose it was too sudden for that, took you all of a heap.'

Slowly, Macfarlan removed his eyes from Celia. He focused his absorbed stare on his friend's face. 'But I never felt anything coming on,' he said in his precise way. 'I tell you, the fellow had me down before I had time to feel anything.'

Celia and More exchanged puzzled glances. Then More's face

lightened as recollections of the detective yarns he had devoured before he discovered that, for him, *rara avis*, the sex novel rushed in on him.

'D'you mean to say you were attacked by an – an assailant, Mac? What was he like? Had he any distinguishing features – any birthmarks, warts or anything?'

'I tell you I never had time to see. If I had, he wouldn't have got me down, not, at least, until I'd had a skelp at him.'

'Seems to me,' said More, looking mysterious, and speaking in a hushed voice, as though he feared conspirators of the unknown assailant might be lurking in every corner – 'seems to me as though it was a case for the police. Detectives, you know.'

A slow flush of colour overspread Macfarlan's pallor.

'Police your granny!' he retorted. 'The chap was either daft or drunk. And I couldn't identify him if I was paid for it. Besides, it would be a nice story to go spreading over the town that a man of my size went down without getting in a single blow.'

That settled it. Even More, who was obtuse and coarse-grained, realized that Mac's pride was smarting. Reluctantly, he relinquished his vision of Joyce's as the centre point of an exciting detective drama, of seeing his own portrait in the daily press: 'Mr Thomas More, Who Discovered The Body.' Well, of course, they mightn't have put it like that, he admitted, seeing the said body had got up and walked away. Injured Man – that was probably how it would have run. But here was Mac, in reply to Celia's solicitous enquires, declaring himself unhurt. Stupid mutt to insist he was all right when a pretty girl like that was ready to make a to-do about him. For a second, More found himself wishing that he, and not Mac, had been the victim of the attack. He would have known so much better how to capitalize it. He would have had the fair Celia stroking his forehead, and holding his hand by this time!

The bell from the seniors' room clanged loudly. Macfarlan rose.

'I'll go, More,' he said, and walked slowly, carefully, out of the room. If there were any unknown dangers lurking in the passage, he preferred to face them here and now. He drew up the cuff of his right sleeve to free his arm in case of need. He wasn't going to be caught twice, he told himself. This time he would see and get in a few before he went down. But to his disappointment the passage was empty. The only sound was that of his footsteps striking the stone.

More stared after him as he went. 'Funny go, that! I wonder, now, if anyone really rushed up and hit him, or if he's suffering from a hallucination, a hallucination of the brain.' He repeated the word because he was proud of his aptitude in producing it on the spur of the moment from the archives of his mind; but Celia, to his chagrin, appeared unimpressed.

'Dear knows,' she said, and went back to the next room.

It was the kind of day, she felt, to breed hallucinations. Perhaps it was all part of a vast hallucination, the uproar in the Square, the sense of impending doom in the office. Perhaps the strange unnatural dusk was responsible for the release of a host of troubled fancies, fearful dreams. Perhaps when the fog lifted, and the stars shone out, they would all vanish, like smoke clouds in the void.

But she knew well enough as she sat there staring at the black letters on the keyboard of her machine that they would not do that. She saw herself tapping out endless letters beginning: 'In answer to your advertisement in this evening's paper, I beg to apply for the post of . . .' secretary or bottle-washer – it didn't matter which. Anything rather than: 'Dear Aunt Jane, You'll be sorry to hear Joyce's has closed down and I am out of a job . . .'

'No, never,' she told the little black imps who ducked, then rebounded so blithely beneath her fingers, 'never shall I write to the aunts in that strain.'

'Better starve,' the motionless letters threw back at her mockingly; 'rather starve, would you?'

'Rather street-walk!' she shrieked at them, and grew hot then cold at the thought. Charlie Wren, entering at the moment, put an end to her silent argument.

'They're kicking up Dublin down there,' he remarked, nodding towards the window.

'Are they?' she said indifferently. Then when he had picked up a jotter and was proceeding to make some notes she interrupted him. 'I wonder if it was one of the unemployed who attacked young Macfarlan?'

'I shouldn't be surprised. When a fellow goes berserk, it's all one who he hits so long as he hits someone. That's self-expression in its lowest form.'

The blood rushed to her face. Poverty reduced everything to its lowest form. There was – what she had been thinking about a moment ago when Charlie came into the room. She shielded her cheek with her hand in terror lest that which was in her mind should reveal itself in her face. Then faces, she remembered, are nothing but wooden blocks. Her heart might be scalded with pain, yet her lips would show no trace of suffering. She would go on looking the same until she was old and played-out. Perhaps then she would write to Aunt Jane.

She turned the lever of her machine, inserted a sheet of paper.

'Dear sir,' she was beginning, when she paused, attentive to the telephone bell shrilling at her elbow. 'Yes,' she said into the mouthpiece. 'Oh-h! Ask him to wait a minute. I'll enquire.'

White-lipped, for the end was threatening to come more quickly than she anticipated, she turned to Charlie.

'That's Mr Jacks. There's been some mistake about the time of the appointment. He's here already, waiting to see Mr Joyce.'

CHAPTER XI

At the same moment as More was ushering Mr Jacks into Mr Joyce's private room and the processionists were being driven from the Square, the long line of tramcars suspended on the edge of it began to advance.

On that instant, the bird-fancier's window upon which Mrs Humphry's eyes were set gave way to a panorama of little shops whose dusty glass squares reflected alternately butcher's meat at its crudest; crusty brown loaves and the bright squares of cakes; mounds of apples soaring above the solid phalanxes of biscuit tins. Tight-wrapped in the cloak of her anxiety, Mrs Humphry saw none of these things. Her thoughts were set on the picture of her son which she had carried all day in her breast. Even when she had been scrubbing and washing, she had kept on regarding it, a feeling of apprehension increasing in her heart each time his features rose before her mind's eye . . . Joe, I wonder where he is now? Poor Joe!

Why she pitied him, she could not have told, only obscurely she knew he was deserving of pity, not so much because he was unemployed – she had always been able to supply his needs – but because there was some dark strain in his blood which rebelled against life as it was. Joe wanted to destroy things, to smash them for all the world like a wee laddie who has no more sense than to break up its toys.

As the tram gained speed, she found herself sitting back heavily in her seat as though by the weight of her altered position she could stay its progress. She was terribly tired, but she did not want to get home quickly. So long as she wasn't there, she could comfort herself with a picture of Joe stripped to the waist, washing himself noisily at the sink, or of Joe with his head on his breast poring over a book. So long as she wasn't there . . .

A deep sigh escaped her. Another half-hour at this rate, she reflected, and she would be home; home to whatever awaited her there. Subconsciously, she braced herself for disaster.

When presently, the car, gliding down the incline into the Square, stopped dead, the hard lines of her body relaxed. While the benign old gentleman leaned forward, inveighing loudly against the shiftless good-for-nothings who were the cause of all the delay, the young woman in the dark furs and the light gloves turned her head in another direction to harken to a loquacious voice in the corner laying off to all and sundry a long story about a five-thousand-pound contract which had been lost – lost, mind you – to the city, owing to the failure of the representative of a local firm to turn up in time to meet a Big Pot from London at the Cavendish Hotel; a failure due to the said representative being held up – held up, mark you – by a demonstration of the unemployed, by those very fellows, in fact, who would have benefited most by the signing of that contract.

Throughout the hum of angry comment this story invoked Mrs Humphry sat with limp hands folded in her lap. She was not listening, but even if she had been, she would have shown no resentment. Her excuse for those folk whom in old-fashioned parlance she still called the 'gentry' was that they did not understand. She neither blamed them nor reviled them for their lack of comprehension. She simply accepted it as she accepted most things that occasioned her discomfort, such as the cold and the fog. While the other passengers fretted at the delay, she beguiled herself with dreams of a perfect homecoming.

She was hardly conscious of the precise moment when the car began to advance again, although its forward swing was exhilarating after the enforced stop. The accustomed rhythm of it restored the confidence of her fellow travellers. They sat back, lords of the city again, obliged no longer to bolster up their courage by loosening their babbling tongues.

In a kind of stupor, Mrs Humphry passed in the tram beneath

the windows of the Palace of Plenty, and never thought to bestow on it a single glance. She passed through the Square without ever being conscious of the swirls of discontent, the shallow currents of greater seas, surging there.

Ahead of the long line of released tramcars the marchers swarmed. Ousted from the Square, thrust into bottleneck ways, they were driven like refuse before the brush of the oncoming traffic. The pavements were mottled with bobbing caps, with jostling bodies. Street lamps poured light on the broken ranks of a civilian army fleeing in disorder before a line of illuminated fortresses, a line which advanced upon the laggards with a loud triumphal clanging of bells, a mocking blast of hooters.

Above the rabble glittered the lights of the Palatial, a spangled fantasia in food and plate glass. An outpost on the frontiers of luxury, it was an ally of the advancing citadels, a part of the whirling sky-signs, of the golden sheen of the shops. With its niggling turrets tricked out with lights like sequins on a man's top hat, and its lower windows ablaze, it arose at the corner, a shining symbol of plentitude in a world of starving men.

Fanny, the plump waitress, looked down on the scattered ranks and shivered. So many lost dogs in the world! It didn't seem right somehow. Swells rolling up here in their cars to grand banquets at night and so many of these men just skin and bone. She shivered again, thanked goodness it was her time off for tea. As she drank the hot, sugary liquid and licked the butter left on her fingers by a hot toasted scone, she felt warmer, more comfortable. The grudge her mind had harboured all day against the Palatial and its well-fed patrons was superseded by a sense of drowsy content. She rose presently and threaded her way back through the crowded rooms to her own stance. A stolid-looking young man wagged his fingers at her. She went over to the table where he and his companion, a flushed young woman, were sitting.

'What'll you have?' the young man asked his companion, for all the world, thought Fanny, like one chap to another in a pub. Apparently he wasn't in the habit of standing a lady her tea. Fanny thought she had better give him a lead.

'Tea?' she murmured. 'Tea and fried fish? Or would you like

some scones and nice cakes?' And she gave the menu card a little edge towards him so that, without seeming too anxious, he could get a good squint at the price list. 'Tea and fried fish, bread and butter, 1/6.'

But the pair were not to be hurried. They consulted in whispers, the girl all fluttery, as though he had just proposed, the man rather sheepish, as though already he was beginning to wish he had not been so rash.

As it chanced, Fanny's summing-up of the two was not very far out. Not that Mr Joyce's chauffeur, Burns, had proposed to Flora, nor had he any intention of doing so, but at the back of his mind he had an uncomfortable feeling of having been netted like a fish that had made no show of fight. And yet Flora, to do her justice, hadn't connived at the meeting. It had been chance, pure chance, plus the hunger march. On his way back on foot from Purley's, where he had gone, at Mr Joyce's request, to see about a new rug for the car, he had run into the retreating marchers. He had stood in a shop doorway out of the crush, smoking a cigarette and watching them pass. He was in no particular hurry. Mr Joyce wasn't leaving the office until late. So he lingered, leaning his shoulders against the glass, regarding the passing crowd as disinterestedly as he might have eyed a crowd of Bacchanalian revellers in a film. It was not until he observed a girl, on the outskirts of the crowd, being carried forward by it, a girl who was obviously trying to win clear of the crush, that his attitude become less impersonal. He drove forward, caught her by the arm. It was only when she was standing in the shop doorway beside him stammering her gratitude that he recognized in the excited young woman by his side Mr Joyce's haughty young parlourmaid, Flora.

'These aw-ful people!' she said, her singing cadence heightened by her agitation. 'I'm sure and I don't know where I was after going with them. I was just coming out of the station and starting to cross the street when they came down on me. And I couldn't see a policeman nowhere. It is my afternoon off, and I came into the town to go and see my sister in her place in the South Side.'

'You'd best wait till the streets clear a bit before you try getting on a tram or a bus,' he advised.

She sighed, pulled her hat forward off the back of her head, where it had lain like a big flat scone. Then she looked up at him out of her big, soft eyes. 'And me so wearied for my tea!' she said.

Burns never knew how it came about; whether he suggested a cup at the Palatial, or whether to avoid the crush and to get warmed up a bit after standing, they went there by mutual consent. Anyhow, before he realized what he was doing, he found himself pushing her in front of him through a busy brightly lit room towards a tiny table which was so narrow that he could hardly move a foot without coming into contact with that of his companion. He found himself, once the complicated business of giving their order was accomplished, and the waitress had set before them a little stand with a puzzling array of fancy cakes and a pot of tea which he admonished Flora, 'You go on and pour out. Strong and four lumps for me' – he found himself harkening with a peculiar pleasure to her soft, slow accents, and saying in the fiercely urgent tones of one who wishes to impress upon his guest that she may eat as much as she likes, for expense is no object: 'Here, try another tuppenny cake. Or what do you say to a sangwitch, one with ham?'

But all the while he was listening to her pleasant drone and to the delicate aria of the string quartette threading with tremulous ecstasy the clatter of teacups, the murmur of voices, he was ruminating at the back of his mind upon how it would end – his encounter with this young woman who only a few hours earlier had slammed a door in his face. His instinct told him she would never do that again. But he had better be careful, he adjured himself, and not go putting Ideas into her head. This tea might mislead the girl, cause her to think he was making up to her. And with her in the big house, and him in the chauffeur's lodge only a few yards away, that would be awkward. They were too near to each other for any shufflings, any backing out. Yes, he would have to be careful, mind his step. But when they rose to go he realized suddenly that he had no wish to part so soon with this big, pleasant creature.

'What about the pictures, Flora?' he said boldly. 'I've not to go for Mr Joyce for quite a bit yet. Or would you rather be getting over to your sister's?'

She took a step nearer to him, so that her arm lay against his.

Beneath the candelabra on the staircase, her cheeks were very bright, her eyes lustrous, as though stung by excited tears.

'Och,' she said with a simplicity that charmed him. 'I'll not be saying but what I'd like to go with you to the pictures, Mr Burns, but my sister'll be looking for me. On my next night out, I will come if you please. On Thursday, that is, at seven o'clock.'

CHAPTER XII

At the time of his mother's tram ride home, Joe, in hiding in the thicket, was wondering anxiously what to do. He had a vague notion he was near the river, and that if he went straight on along the road he would strike a port of sorts with outgoing ships. Very carefully, he turned out his pockets to retrieve such coins as might be lurking there. Usually he knew to a nicety the amount of his capital, but today was different. He couldn't recall what coin he had proffered the bus conductor at the start, and what change, if any, he had got back. He only knew that he had been called upon on the way to render up more money. And he had been so thankful that he was able to produce it, and that he did not have to stumble out on the roadway for lack of coppers, that once again he had failed to count the cost.

He surveyed his capital now, uttered a rueful 'Huh!' For a fellow can't go far on the sum of tenpence farthing. No more buses for him. This decision arrived at, he emerged cautiously from the shelter of the trees and set off along the road which his instinct told him must eventually find the river. He was swinging along briskly when a little group at a crossroads in the hollow below attracted his gaze. In the gathering dusk, the light of a street lamp outlined two shining sickles at the level of the blackened hedgerow. They quivered incessantly, bright-edged curves chained, apparently, to one spot and yet afloat in the soft white glow.

They broke, suddenly, from the black blur of the group around the lamp post and rushed at full tilt up the hill towards him. As they drew near, he recognized the curves which the steadfast light had transformed into shining sickles to be handlebars of two motor-bicycles. Before they could pass, he had dived like a frightened rabbit into the wooded glade on his left, his heart leaping in his side. Motor police, by Gees! He had spotted them just in time. He ran wildly on through the frost-white undergrowth, his feet cracking thin ice, his face lashed by the whips of frozen twigs. He stumbled blindly over old roots and broken branches, barking his shins, bruising his knees. He had lost by this time all sense of direction. He was obeying blindly the panic instinct which bade him flee for his life.

He paused at last in a little clearing, not because his panic was allayed, but because his wind was giving out. He leaned against the bark of an immense low-spreading beech and gasped for breath. But even in his stress his ears strained for every sound. Once he jumped in terror only to discover that the hissing he had believed behind him was that of his own harshly indrawn breath. If he had not been racked by fear, he would have rejoiced, his struggling consciousness told him, in the cool quiet of this secluded place. After the rabble of the tight-packed tenements, the stillness, stretching like a shaft of tender light between this colonnade of ancient trees, would have seeped into his soul and tranquillized it.

Disturbed as he was, and with every sense alert, he felt as though in his wild onrush he had fallen over the brim of things into a mystic white world peopled by trees alone; a world low-vaulted and dim, remote alike from the vengeance of God and man.

He stood quite still until his breath came back to him and the dizzy drumming of his head had ceased.

He proceeded then to look around, his senses sharpened by the necessity, which in the last few minutes seemed to him to have grown more urgent, of making good his escape. The stony bed of a frozen stream wound in and out between the trees sloping downwards. If he followed it, his reason told him he would reach the river. But for all his anxiety, he felt loth to leave this new-found sanctuary. He lingered absorbing its peace until that peace was shattered.

He drew close to the great beech as the whistle of voices rose in his ears. Within a few paces of him a man and a woman passed, their arms intertwined. Lovers, thought Joe, and a gust of rage swept him. For poverty shut you out from all that. It froze a man's natural instincts, turned a part of him to stone.

He forgot to keep close to the beech's outspreading branches; forgot to hold himself rigidly so that his feet might make no noise, and some fragment of sound indicating that they were not alone in this quiet spot must have reached the lovers, for they stopped, unloosened their hold upon each other, and looked back. There spread thereat in this mystic world the hateful taint of earthly things. The gloating voices of the newsboys rose amid the stilly trees, their voices and the din of traffic in a city miles away. 'Square Murderer Seen Skulking in Wood. Suspect Reported by Lovers to Local Police.' So real were these voices, so loud, shrieking in the hollow of his head, that they drove from his mind all thought of caution. He crashed out from under the friendly tree-shelter, cast one glance at the intruders, who now stood staring at him in open-mouthed surprise, then hurried on. This time there were no sleuths at his heels, there were only voices, but it was not until the hum of blood in his ears grew loud as a drum that he escaped their menacing cries.

He was clear of the wood by then. He had attained the road which skirted the river. The sight of it winding sweetly just where he had expected to find it soothed him. That way, he felt, lay escape.

The plan which was slowly taking shape in his mind was to seek some little harbour and to find amid its clustered shipping a coal-brig on the point of sailing. He had an idea that in the bustle of departure it would be an easy enough matter to slip on board and to conceal himself until the vessel was well out to sea.

He got no further with his plan of the future, for the words 'at sea' sang in his imagination like a great wind which, purified of earth's scents, free from the let of mountain peaks and tossing pines, circles the ocean to all eternity. He saw the river at his elbow widen to meet a waste of lustrous waters. He saw his past slip from him as familiar shores receded, and only the pursuing waves gave chase. Once lost in the immensity of night at sea, and he would be safe – safe for a space at least from all those things he had struggled all his life in vain to free himself from.

A private car, racing along the slippery road, passed him with a warning hoot. The lights of a village showed round the bend. They were scattered inland, these lights, he noted with regret. Not yet had he reached his little harbour.

As he neared the first of the houses, a large white villa from which the blare of a wireless band was issuing, he decided that it would be unwise to expose himself to the glare of street lamps, to the possibility of casual encounters. Accordingly, followed by a blast of crazy negro music, he turned up a steep lane which ran at right angles with the village, and which he hoped would take him past it by devious ways. But the lane so writhed and twisted that when at length it looked on to what appeared to be a main road, he could not be certain in which direction to turn. He stood for a minute, scratching his head, and debating whether to go on or to turn back. After that sugary music, it seemed very still up here. His mind swayed vaguely to the lilt of the remembered tune. He was almost tempted to retrace his steps so that he might hear more of it. The crooner's voice, cleaving the darkness, had conjured up for him the same sort of pictures as the shipping companies' posters of Canada invariably did – pictures of contented labourers working under blue skies, of vast yellow fields of corn swooning in the sun . . . The sun! It warmed you to think of it on a night like this.

He stared at the road ahead as though he could pierce it with his gaze. By rights, he argued, it should run parallel with the one he had just left. By rights, it should link up sooner or later with the road near the river. Comforting himself with this assurance, he started to walk on; but the stiff climb uphill had tired him. The increasing chill in his limbs warned him that his pace was slow. He had eaten nothing since breakfast, he remembered then, and judging by the light it must be getting on for five o'clock. He began to regret he hadn't braved the lights of the village, that he hadn't gone boldly up to the back door of the house whence the music was issuing and begged for some food. He had never begged from anyone in his life, but it might have been safer to ask a 'piece' from some serving-maid in the dark than to have gone into a shop in the main street.

Turning a corner, he espied a light ahead, a light he recognized to be the rear lamp of a stationary vehicle. He could hear sounds of a motor engine spluttering, of a man's voice cursing lustily as the engine failed to function. Joe halted at the back of the lorry, considering matters. The chances were it would start in a minute or two. If it did not, to slip off again would be only a matter of seconds. He was thus debating when the driver let out a shout of triumph, and a loud throbbing filled the air. The man spat on the hardened ground, mounted to the driver's seat at the same moment as Joe swung himself up on the boards behind. They were ice cold and smelled of tar. When the lorry set off, roaring and plunging into the night, Joe threw out a hand to hold on to the surrounding ledge. As he did so, his fingers closed on something that crumbled between them, something in a thin paper bag. Drawing it towards him, he tore it open. Pies. What luck! He balanced himself very carefully, then, without stopping to consider how they came there or for whom they were intended, he dug his teeth into the solid slab of paste and mincemeat.

As the lorry throbbed on through the frosty air, he lay back contentedly, his mind and body at peace.

PART III

EVENING

CHAPTER I

The lorry flew on through the empty countryside, past lamplit villages sprawling in the hollow, and solitary farm steadings. It thundered beneath high walls overgrown with ivy, past little grey lodges guarding the entrances to great estates. Instead of swooping down to the river as Joe had confidently expected, the road wound steadily on the level until it reached an expanse of open moorland, where it soared and soared.

Joe's heart rose with it, swinging upwards to meet the stars with which the sky was now aglow. He lay on his side, absorbed in the beauty and mystery of the night.

This was almost as good as being at sea, he thought. The rush through the sharp clear air had given him a sense of being lifted above the world, of having left behind all that was evil in the past. The pulsation of the engines drowned in his ears the newsboys' cries which had haunted him in his solitude. The frosty air, entering into his lungs, drove the fever of impatience from his blood. As he lay there outstretched on the hard boards, his mind wandered back over the day. It seemed to him now that the Joe who had risen late that morning and joined the marchers in the Square was someone he had known slightly, but not really well. He knew himself better now. Yes, although everything was still so confused that he could only gather together his impressions in broken pieces, the picture of himself that emerged was crystal clear. A murderer not because his mind was evil, and his fingers itched to destroy, but because – because . . .

But his mind baulked at confining too closely the swiftly travelling current that flowed through it. He only knew, obscurely yet deep down in him, that he was a part of the city he had left. He had been conceived and bred amid its endless din and confusion. Its torrid midsummer heat had scorched his limbs. Its dust had gritted in his throat. He had groped in the black tunnels of its fog-bound streets, stared at its tenement walls, shared in its common life. So close had he been to the city's heart, so many of its melancholy secrets had he shared, that a part of it had soaked into his blood. And he had come to feel, inextricably entangled as certain fibres in his nature were with it all, that the city owed him something even as a mother owes something to her child. But the city had repudiated her debt. He could wrest nothing from her ungrateful breast. And something within him had turned sour . . . A murderer, not because his mind was evil and his fingers itched to destroy, but because his own had gone back on him. True, it hadn't let him starve. It had yielded him food and shelter. But it had denied his right to existence.

'Gees,' he thought, 'if it was me now driving this motor-lorry!' And his brain reeled at thought of finding release for his fervours in the nervous task of guiding this cumbersome vehicle through dizzy lines of traffic, of steering her lovingly round looped corners, or urging her to scale dangerous heights, and then to glide easily, and without undue haste, downhill.

Joe had never ridden so fast in a vehicle before, and the effect upon him of the rapid motion was akin to the effect of champagne upon the temperate. His spirits bubbled up. The clanking of the wheels seemed to him one long sustained shout – I'm free – free!

He had no notion where they were going. He had only caught uncertain glimpses of villages dropping to the river, villages to which he could affix no names. And now he was high up, cleaving the frosty air, flashing past wooded cliffs, twisting in and out of shadows cast by great heights, skirting moorland wastes where the coarse grass, rippling in the wind, suggested the movement of a restless sea.

Joe stared about him entranced. He did not know how far he had travelled, and for the moment he did not care. As the lorry lurched strongly on, he felt like a spirit floating through space. The stars seemed nearer than the occasional festoons of artificial light draping the valley. Dreams visited him, new ambitions stirred in his mind. To drive on and on like this, with the wind singing a challenge in your ears, to see night drop down from the sky, turning the land into this dim white mystery – the wonder of it filled him with a new taste for life, a vivid apprehension of its magic.

While he was savouring his happiness, turning it over in his mind as a child turns over a sweet in its mouth to make it last longer, he became aware that the rhythm of the engine had changed. There was a beat missing. An intrusive discord grew in volume until, in obedience to its jarring demand, the lorry stopped with a convulsive shudder.

The driver got down slowly. Joe could hear his heels striking the hard ground. Suppose, he thought, the chap comes round here hunting for his pies and finds them gone, and me stretched out here instead. The idea struck him as so irresistibly comic that he had much ado to keep from laughing out loud.

But the driver was too much concerned with his refractory engine to give a thought elsewhere. He belaboured some part of it with a sharp instrument which sent echoes ringing through the night; he pottered about with a petrol tin, but apparently without success.

While he was thus engaged, the moon rose from behind a thin network of frost-white trees. With her rising, the sea of waving grass was transformed into a molten sheet of pearl. The blurred hills were revealed in sculptural masses, and groups of nearby shrubs glowed sombrely, enmarbled façades in black and ivory. Ahead the road stretched like a silver trellis cast haphazardly across the moor. Joe stared at it fascinated, and burned to go on. Despite the miracle evoked by the moonlight, the cold and the enforced inactivity were beginning to chafe him. He had an impulse to jump down, to make his presence known to the driver and to engage him in friendly discussion, as he had often seen men do in similar cases. It would be heartening to hear his own voice again, cheerful to exchange views with another fellow, interesting to come to close quarters with the intricate machinery of a big lorry like this, fine to gaze knowingly – he who knew nothing at all – at its piston rods or whatever they called the things. Then perhaps the driver would produce a fag or two and they would stand contentedly puffing and regarding it – this great powerful brute you couldn't whip into action, which set its black teeth at you and refused to budge despite all your coaxing and cursing.

He could not make up his mind whether it would be wiser to stroll along casually from the rear as though he were a stranger who had emerged from a nearby house, or whether to own up frankly that he had enjoyed a free meal and a free ride, and to offer in return to lend a hand. Quite absurdly, H. M. Stanley's historic words in the African wilds recurred to him – his father had been a deep admirer of Blantyre's famous son – 'Mr Livingstone, I presume?' He was smiling in the darkness when a faint movement sent his hopes sky-high. Encouraged, apparently, by the slight tremor, the driver proceeded with a great display of renewed energy to send sharp splinters of sound ricochetting through the stillness. With a quick turn of the wrist, he cranked up the engine. It responded this time with a roar, whereat he leapt into his seat. Joe's heart bounded. They were off! He gripped hold of the sides in readiness for a resumption of the bumping swaying motion of an hour ago; but despite its show of ebullience, the lorry advanced limpingly, as though reluctant to adventure farther into the unknown.

With the noisy grinding of shifting gears, the driver coaxed her forward until, turning sharply down a road at right angles from the one they had been traversing, she seemed to gain fresh impetus on the hill and to need urging no longer. Joe sighed and lay back, but try as he might he could not wholly recapture the glow of his earlier mood. Reaction had set in, and he was aware of a sensation of weariness which even the spectacle of the moon-silvered landscape failed to dispel. He cradled his head on his arm and closed his eyes. Could Mrs Humphry have seen him then, his face ghost-pale in the moonlight, her heart had been wrung with pity. Such a boy he looked with his hair pushed back off his forehead, his limbs outstretched like those of a tired warrior, his sensitive features exposed to the moonbeams' searching glare.

He awoke with a start as a car, travelling in the opposite direction, flashed lights in his face, then hummed past. Almost immediately came another blinding glare, the snort of a throttled engine, and then a whole chorus of humming sounds, an intermittent frieze of lights, crazy, meaningless. Joe pulled up erect, stared about him. They were switchbacking up and down a tree-lined road which their engine was flooding with a dull booming roar. Apparently they were nearing a town of sorts. A port, Joe assumed it, for no better reason than that a port was what he willed it to be; and although he could catch no glimpse of water, he fell again to picturing the sleepy harbour with its clutter of little coal-brigs, on one of which he would set sail. But at the top of the road the trees lining it fell abruptly away, leaving a clear space on the right side. Below it, a vast sheaf of outspread lights flung its challenge to the sky. The glare strengthened as the lorry groaned onwards until it seemed as though this lighted sheaf was but the outflung arm of a net of bodies held together by hundreds of golden streamers which criss-crossed endlessly in the continuous city below.

Gazing at this fantastic cosmopolis, Joe wondered if it were a freak of the moonlight, the reflection of one of those radiant cloud-cities which hang suspended for a space in the sky before their imponderable grey pillars, their ladders of flame, their rose-walled palaces, dissolve into a mist of rain. And then the sinuous curve of a hill on the opposite side of the valley twanged in him a chord of memory, a chord that jarred hideously through every fibre of his being. He stared, caught his breath, surely that was . . . No, it couldn't be. God, but it was – it was! On that instant he could have screamed aloud in agony at the knowledge, suddenly borne in upon him, that he was travelling back to the city from which only a few hours ago he had so desperately fled.

He sat hunched, too stunned to think calmly. Like a horse nearing its home stable, the lorry was gaining rapidly in speed. It raced downhill, surmounted a bridge at a dizzy rate, then rushed between rows of lighted houses with a discordant expression of joy. These houses with their smouldering lights terrified Joe. They were models, each one, tiny grotesque models of the Palace of Plenty. Roaring past them, he felt the chill of the stone passage close in upon him again. He saw the huddled figure on the ground. Above it, no banner of liberty waved to and fro amid the splendid acclamation of the crowd. Only within his head something set up a shout of murder, and he shuddered like a man fain to escape from himself.

A sudden jerk of the lorry made him struggle to his feet. Withdrawing his eyes from the whizzing palaces, he forced himself to contemplate the roadway swimming by. What he must do was to leap on to it, he told himself. A second's fear, a quick effort, and he would be free of this lurching vehicle. He would be free to turn back, to get clear of the city.

He stood poised, nerving himself for the jump, his heart thudding in unison with the clanking wheels. 'Jump, jump!' they screamed at him as the villas gave way to the encroaching arms of the tenements. 'Jump, you coward, jump!' the motor-buses, thundering this way and that, bellowed in his ear. 'Jump before the city has smashed all your fine dreams of freedom, before the crowds envelop you, and you are lost in the din and the glare. Jump, man, jump!'

But Joe crouched, shivering like a frightened dog, on the trembling boards. He held fast to the surrounding ledge as they swung past the broad leafy avenues of the suburbs and dived deeper and deeper into the glaring hollow of the town. The fog of the day had gone. With dusk had come a clear luminosity which lay like a velvet sheen above the jungle of the streets. Such narrow pens with their jagged chimney stalks, their openings wrapped in shadow, they seemed after the windy heights – so close and mean and earthbound. (Jump before they get you down! Jump!) Even the moon seemed robbed of her radiance. She sailed remote in a sky which held aloof from the garish, light-spangled world below.

A crossroads hove in sight. The traffic slowed. 'Now,' thought Joe, 'now,' and crept close to the side. Below, the cobblestones glinted like slabs of ice. The tram-rails set up a shower of sparks as a car sped by. Pedestrians scurried to and fro – women in shawls, thickset men in warm coats and coloured scarves. In and out of the slackening stream newsboys wriggled, shouting their wares. 'Jump,' their hurried antics seemed to say to him; but he waited until he could see a clear space. No use jumping right into a policeman's arms – that would be asking for it, that would! – or on to the step of a swell Rolls-Royce – it might be one of old Joyce's for all he knew. He waited, and then it was too late. The driver had spied the clear space too. He had spied it, and without a second's hesitation he had shot into it with his swaying lorry. 'Jump? Gees, I dare not,' Joe whispered, and held on for dear life to the quivering ledge.

He was half numb with cold and fright when the lorry backed cautiously between the narrow brick walls of a garage in the centre of the city. The driver, peering into his engine, called for a mechanic to come and see what was up with the blasted thing.

'Well on my way there, I was, and had to turn back,' he grumbled. 'I was feart to risk the climb up the Rest in case she'd stick altogether and I'd be proper stranded.'

While the two were talking together and the mechanic, a burly youth with a shock of dark-red hair, was doing mysterious things to the unresisting engine, Joe slipped down. The driver would never know he had conveyed a passenger halfway there, wherever 'there' was, and back again. He might come hunting for his pies, wondering where on earth they had gone, but that would be all. Lurking in the shade of the lorry which had carried him closer than he had ever been in his life before to the Mountains of the Moon, he was conscious of a sense of flatness, of grey depression. He regretted now, although not with much conviction, that he hadn't had the courage to jump at first sight of the city. He regretted, but with even less conviction, that he had ever mounted the lorry, ever left the river road. If he had gone on straight through the little village, past the lighted house where the wireless negroes were crooning, he might have been on board that coal-brig and at sea by now. At sea . . . Deep down in him, he realized that this sea-lure was all part of a dream induced by the shifting scenes, the excitement, of the night. Even had he reached a port he would have hung back, fearful of taking a decisive step, just as he had hung back, clung to safety a little while ago. Yes, he would have hung back; he would always hang back. He knew that now.

He bowed his head in his hands and wept. The city had got him down. It didn't matter where he went, or what he did. The city had got him, the city whose child he was, the city which despised him, had no place for him.

It was the red-headed mechanic on his way for a spare part who espied him.

'Hi!' he cried. 'This isn't a howff for loafers. Out you get!'

Joe went humbly without a word.

CHAPTER II

There was a little crowd at the close-mouth. Mrs Humphry saw it whenever she got off the tram. Instinctively she started to run as fast as her swollen feet would let her. But by the time she drew near, the group of anxious women, of idle grinning men and gaping children was breaking up. The curious were turning away. From vacant faces, the flush caused by an unwonted excitement had ebbed.

'What's up?' she asked of a youth who still loitered. 'What's up?' And dared him fiercely to speak Joe's name.

He looked at her for a moment dully, incapable apparently of summoning up sufficient energy to answer her question.

'They've lifted Smith,' he brought out at last, and there broke over his face that slow reflection of vindictive glee to which the sight of other people's misfortunes sometimes gives birth in the breasts of onlookers.

'Smith?' echoed Mrs Humphry impatiently, for who cared about Smith? 'Have you seen Joe?' – the question trembled on her lips, but she bit it back. She couldn't bear the suspense of seeing that dense face go blank while its owner dived in the meagre store of his memories for some derogatory scrap. She couldn't bear to hear the note of malicious triumph which would inform that slow voice had it aught of ill to retail.

'She shouted for the police,' it was saying now. 'And then she raised Cain when they took him away.'

Mrs Humphry nodded and passed on. Ahead of her, up the winding stair, a woman trailed, her shoes shuffling on the stone. She turned round as Mrs Humphry overtook her, a dull, apathetic-looking creature. For a second, the two women eyed each other in silence, then, moved by a sudden twinge of compassion, Mrs Humphry laid a hand on the other's arm.

'Come away up,' she said, 'and I'll get you a cup of tea'; and then instantly regretted her hospitable impulse. For if Joe were there, what would he think of her bringing in this dishevelled-looking woman? Joe, obedient to her training, believed in keeping himself to himself. They had never had truck with their neighbours, least of all with the Smiths. Smith, like Joe, was out of work. That was nothing against him, save that he employed part of his leisure in belabouring his wife. The noise of their quarrelling filled the close. Mrs Humphry, fresh from the chastened atmosphere of Mrs MacGregor's house, bitterly resented the obscene uproar. Apart from the fact that it kept her from sleeping, she felt it in some obscure way to be humiliating. She always prayed Joe might be asleep and not hear it, but she knew with a sickening hopelessness of spirit that the same sounds which awakened her must have awakened him, that they were dinning into his ears on the other side of the wall just as they were dinning into hers. What she did not know was that he translated them in his own way, not as might have been expected into some hideous leitmotif of sex, but into a discordant measure that had compressed into it all the heterogeneous elements of the tenement – the disorderliness, the dirt, the grinding poverty, the whimper of infants, the cases, the sudden eldritch cries, the mutterings and whinings and reproaches. Welded together, those elements composed a fine marching tune for revolutionaries. With that in his ears, a man might fling a bomb into the innermost ring of the capitalists and harken unafraid to the roar of its bursting.

These nocturnal disturbances occurred with maddening frequency. Joe's laconic, 'Smith's had the drink again,' was always a prelude to an uproar which lasted well into the small hours, for Mrs Smith was no silent sufferer. She would shriek out for help, declare she was being murdered in her bed at the same time as she was standing, fully dressed, in the doorway for all beholders to see. And then she would yell loudly upon her neighbours to go for the police – 'if there's a man among you that is a man'. Apparently, such a man had at last revealed himself, a man who had taken her at her word and gone.

'Tea?' she said in answer to Mrs Humphry's invitation. 'I feel more like throwing myself over the stairhead the night.'

She leaned against the railing, her eyes sullen with the weight of unshed tears which lay behind them. Mrs Humphry stood by her side, reluctant to leave her, and yet anxious to get away.

'Aye, they've got him,' Mrs Smith broke out at last. 'But they needn't be thinking they'll get me to say a word against him. Nutt me! They'll have to go elsewhere for their evidence, as they calls it. And if one of youse here says a word against my man . . .' Her features writhed in a sudden spurt of passionate malevolence.

Mrs Humphry took a step back. Again that vague feeling of humiliation stirred in her. When she spoke, it was with an air of dignified reproof that would have done credit to Mrs MacGregor herself.

'I, for one, have never been in the way of taking notice of my neighbours, of interfering in their concerns. And it's fine, Mrs Smith, that you know it.'

'Oh, you don't need for to tell me. You've aye looked down on me.'

Mrs Humphry's lips tightened. It was true. And she wasn't going to deny it.

'Aye, you've all looked down on me because I yell for the police when Geordy has the drink and starts hammerin' me. I suppose you think I should keep nice and quiet, and just put up with it the same's the rest of you. But there's nutt one of you has a man like Geordy. He could strangle your Joe and wee Sandy Fellowes up the stair and never look over his shoulder. You should have seen the way he went for the police the now! There's more than one big sumph away with a pain in his neck, I can tell you.'

Mrs Humphry drew back, affronted at the trend the talk had taken. The woman was actually bragging about her husband's strength. Her eyes blazed with pride; but only momentarily. Her face drooped as remorse surged up; she drummed her fists on the handrail.

'Oh, and I should have held my tongue,' she reproached herself. 'I shouldn't have cried out, for it only angers him. And he's enough to bear. It's preyed on his mind, going idle so long. And he's nobody to let out on but me.' She sighed, raised a hand to her bedraggled locks. 'Tell your Joe from me if it was him as went for the police—'

'Joe has never been one to interfere in other folks' affairs,' retorted Mrs Humphry. Then, her patience exhausted, she went on up the stairs. But before she had advanced many steps she stopped to listen to what Mrs Smith was doing below. It would be terrible, she reflected, if the woman went and threw herself over the stairhead while she was calmly going into her own house to make her tea. For the first time, a vague sense of the responsibility which proximity imposes stirred a fresh uneasiness in Mrs Humphry's mind. It was queer, but being under the same roof knit you all together whether you willed it or not. You were responsible for one another here in a way that Mrs MacGregor wasn't responsible for the people on either side of her. Mrs Humphry stopped ruminating to listen intently for any sounds below. No, Mrs Smith hadn't gone into her own house. She was crossing over to the door of the people opposite. She was banging on it with her big fists, a fierce rat-tat which gave way suddenly to her irate voice.

'Here! I want to tell you, if it was youse that went for the police—'

Hurriedly, Mrs Humphry went on. She shut her door on the sound of the noisy argument. The little kitchen was very quiet and cold. There was no sign of Joe. And the fire wasn't lit, nor was the table set for tea. The dirty dishes that had lain since his breakfast were at one end. Mechanically, with the sure instinct of the housewife, she got to work to put things straight. At any moment, she told herself, Joe might be in, wanting his tea. Well, he wouldn't have long to wait for it.

In a trice, the kitchen was full of the smell of new-kindled wood, of bread crisply toasting. On the hob, the big black kettle steamed slowly. Mrs Humphry took a sharp implement from the shelf and prised open a tin with a cut of bright pink fish pictured on the outside. She set the contents on a plate in the middle of the table as though it were a flower.

'There,' she said aloud, 'there!' And then she started at sound of footsteps outside. But they passed on, up another flight of stairs, and she guessed it must be Geordy Fellowes on his way home.

She sighed almost unconsciously. Eh, but Mrs Fellowes was lucky. She had her son at work. He brought home a regular pay each week. Mrs Fellowes knew when he would be coming in, when he would be going out. A nice regular life just like at Mrs MacGregor's. Meals at set hours. Breakfast, dinner and tea. Oh, Joe was regular enough as a rule. He wasn't one that ever went on the batter. It was just since he had taken to attending these meetings.

She rose and drew the kettle to a side. It was boiling, and she supposed she had better take her own tea and not wait much longer. She had a lot to do after it. The sink was in a mess, and there was the floor to give a good thorough scrub. No use slithering about too long. But her hand shook as she poured the hot water into the teapot to warm it, and she set it down again without reaching up to the mantelshelf for the tea caddy.

'I couldn't put a mouth on it,' she said to herself. 'Not until I know what's come over Joe.'

She stared round at the familiar walls as though asking them to tell her what to do. She couldn't go staving into the police station to enquire of a gaping young officer, 'Have you got my son in the lock-up?' She couldn't go round to the neighbours asking, 'Have you seen Joe?' as though she feared he had gone off on the batter. She could only sit here and wait; wait for him to come home. Oh, she had done that often enough before, and he had been later than this often; but today was different. Today she felt so closely bound to her son that she irked to have him with her, to hold him, as she had done when he was a child and venturesome, closely by the hand.

She could not bear that distance should separate them. And at this moment she realized there was a whole world between them – an unknown world she knew not how to plumb. She wouldn't care, she told herself anxiously, if it wasn't for this feeling, this certainty that something was wrong. She couldn't get over the feeling; no, not even here where she had lived all these years, where she had sat so often with Joe.

She crossed over to the window and opened it. The fog had cleared, and the wind blew in with a gust that set the blind-cord striking noisily against the pane. She felt intensely old as she stood looking up at the stars with the cool air on her face. There stirred in her a memory of Joe, her husband; not of the Joe she had fretted over, treated like an ailing child at the last, but of Joe the lover, whose first embraces had released in her a current of fierce delight. And now he was gone. All that was over and done with for her.

There was left instead this vague hunger, this aching desire to interpose her body between that of her son and those who threatened him. Oh, it was a pity he had grown up, got away from her! If he could have stayed helpless always, close to her side, this would never have happened . . . This— She took herself sharply to task. What? Nothing had happened, nothing. But something in her blood told her differently. She drew back from the window, too miserable to look any longer at the starlit sky. Without thinking what she was doing, she drew on her coat, her hat.

On the threshold, she hesitated. Maybe Geordy Fellowes might have met Joe. Maybe he could tell her something. She gazed up the winding stair, hoping, as though in response to her desire, Geordy might suddenly descend. If only he would, she could ask him quite careless like if he'd seen Joe, say something about his being extra late. That wouldn't be making any fuss, not like going up and knocking specially on the door and bringing Mrs Fellowes out in the middle of her tea. She tried to rehearse what she would say to Mrs Fellowes, but she couldn't think of anything that would do. It seemed all wrong, somehow, for her to question a stranger about Joe, her own Joe.

As she went on down the stair, she heard sounds of hilarity in the close. Someone was playing a fiddle. There was dancing and 'hooching' to the strains of a Scots reel. She was not surprised to discover that it was from Mrs Smith's house these shouts of merriment were issuing. Apparently Mrs Smith was having a party to celebrate Smith's removal. Or maybe it was just her way of trying to get through the evening wanting her man. Women were like that, Mrs Humphry reflected; glad to do anything to make the time pass when they got upset. She went on downstairs, the jigging notes echoing in her ears. On the pavement in front of the tenement she stopped short. She didn't know which way to go. She didn't know what she was going to do.

A wave of unreasoning terror broke over her. Without Joe, she realized she was nothing. It didn't matter to anyone what she did. It didn't matter whether she went to the offices tomorrow or not. Nothing mattered if Joe didn't come home.

She wandered off down the street, her big coat flapping about her scarecrow figure. She passed through the press of people unnoticed, a solitary being who, in stripping life of externals, had stumbled upon its great loneliness. Nearer now in spirit to her son than she had ever been before, she believed him lost to her. And her lips, tight-drawn over her teeth, showed wonder and resentment at the hurt.

CHAPTER III

Mrs Humphry would have been surprised and scornfully incredulous had anyone told her that at the same moment as she was recalling the exclusive atmosphere of her employer's house, and dwelling a shade enviously on its regular routine, her employer's mind was engaged in wondering, and not for the just time that day, what sort of home Mrs Humphry possessed. For this unwonted exercise on Elsie MacGregor's part, the hunger marchers must be adjudged responsible. The fear which the first sight of their restless files had aroused in her breast had been superseded almost immediately by a morbid curiosity. Where had they come from, all these people? Were they tools, every one, of ranting politicians, or had they assembled here of their own free will with the object of displaying, as Eastern beggars do, their sores to the world? What manner of women were the mothers of these shambling youths? Had these dull faces ever known vividness or colour, or had they from birth conformed to the same drab pattern? What kind of homes did they come from – evil-smelling dens of vice, or decent little places bleached to the bone by poverty?

Her mind descended to a fantastic underworld of her own creating, an underworld ridden by mean hovels in which the yowling of pampered greyhounds, of these luxurious animals which miners working only two days a week are reputed to feed on prime beefsteak, mingled with the sobbing of neglected and starving infants. She tried to whip up a righteous indignation against men who squander their wages on betting while their offspring go without, but somehow her indignation failed to function. Instead, it struck her that to these people, greyhounds, and the chance of gain they proffered, represented all the world of joy they knew. Chance! For the fraction of a second, she saw it suspended high above the narrow dismal track of their days in the form of a rich cluster of golden fruit which any minute might yield to their grasp. Forbidden fruit, frowned upon by the moralist, sneered at by the middle classes, but all the sweeter, the more tempting, for that. Chance – glittering and luscious, offering at any moment to change the face of the world for him who seized it, promising to reveal it as an enchanting place instead of the wilderness he had hitherto believed it.

Were there any greyhounds lying snugly on cushioned beds in Mrs Humphry's kitchen? Elsie MacGregor wondered. She didn't for one instant believe it. Looking down on these men, the pampered greyhounds seemed the absurdest of myths. Like the introduction of a Punch and Judy show in the midst of a desperate battle.

Her eyes ached as she watched the human mass. It was almost a relief when it broke up into segments, and the mounted policemen came on the scene. She felt as though she were watching a mob in a play, a drab sort of play, in which nothing very dramatic ever happened. She became aware presently that she was not the only spectator in the room of the happenings below. A middle-aged woman in a tight black satin dress, who had entered a minute ago, was standing at the next window, looking out.

Moved by a friendly impulse, Mrs MacGregor turned round. When she spoke, her voice was rather shrill.

'Isn't it awful?' she said.

Miss Smithers hastily assumed her placated smile. 'Awful,' she agreed feelingly. 'And in a civilized country. They ought to be ashamed of themselves.'

'Who?' Mrs MacGregor pondered. 'Who ought to be ashamed of themselves – the Mrs Humphrys' sons who can't get work, or we who don't do a hand's turn to help?'

'Yes,' she said hastily; 'they certainly ought,' and glared at two policemen who were hustling an old man to the pavement.

Her gaze was straining after them when the door behind was thrust open. 'Miss Smithers,' called out an agitated voice, 'Miss

Smithers, I've been looking for you everywhere. Mr Valley wants you. You're to come at once.'

Miss Smithers turned a cold eye on the intruder. 'That's not the way to speak to me,' she said in a reproving undertone. 'Have you no manners, boy?'

The pageboy's body quivered. The muscles of his mouth went slack. His features writhed. He looked as though he were going to be sick at any minute.

'It was me that found him,' he whimpered, 'hanging from the ceiling with a rope. They've cut him down now. He's dead.'

Miss Smithers jumped – a funny little springing movement that sent the staid lines of her black satin frock dancing. 'What nonsense!' she said; but she scurried from the room, her face very red. The inhumanity of the hotel numbering system was conducive to suicide. She had always known that, preached it at every turn. It was conducive to suicide in that it tended to stifle the ego, to shrivel natural self-importance. But would they listen when she told them that? Well, here was proof, further proof! She wondered which of the guests it was, and if the police would make a terrible fuss.

As she went along the corridor, she saw Madame Elberstein cross the passage to her suite – Madame Elberstein not looking like a famous operatic star any longer, but just like any other frightened woman. Miss Smithers felt she would have liked to stop to speak to her, to reassure her that this demonstration meant nothing at all. Probably Madame Elberstein, who was a great traveller, had seen some of those dreadful Nazi riots in Italy – or were they in France? But Miss Smithers had no time to spare. Moreover, she required reassuring at the moment herself. For if by any chance it was George Judge, the actor, or Lord Elbon, the motor-racing peer, who arrived yesterday, and it might be; there were rumours that he was insolvent and that a divorce suit was pending – if it were either of these two, then publicity was inevitable, and publicity of that sort was fatal to business. She hoped to goodness, as she descended the stair to Mr Valley's room on the ground floor, that it was only one of the commercials whom she didn't know by sight, one of the 'single-nighters' who passed in a steady stream in and out of the hotel all the year round, leaving behind no trace of their presence other than the sixpence the chambermaid usually found on the toilet table of their deserted room next morning.

Left alone in the stately drawing room with its plastered Venuses set at either side of the mirrored wall, Mrs MacGregor sat with her hands clenched, staring about her. In this strange place she felt ringed round with horror. There was the mob outside, and now here, here where she had felt safe and warm and comfortable, this awful tale of cutting down someone, someone who was dead. Of course, the woman had exclaimed, 'Nonsense!' but you could see by the way she scurried out of the room that she knew it wasn't; you could see from the boy's face he was speaking the truth.

Mrs MacGregor sprang to her feet. She wouldn't stop here another second. She would rather be out there amid the crowd, hustled by policemen, than wait in this silent room. But at the door she hesitated, casting a frightened glance back at the stucco figures whose ghostly limbs were alive with shadows reflected by the fireglow. If she went into the passage now, she might run into some worse horror – they might be taking him away, the unknown him.

She came back and stood warming her hands at the leaping flames. If the fire had been lower, she might have made that an excuse for ringing the bell and getting into communication with someone. She thought longingly of the friendly porter who had brought her up here, saying the drawing room would be quieter, nicer for her when she was alone than the lounge, and she'd get a rare view of the Square. Nicer! Her nerves screamed the word. If only she had heeded what they all said to her and kept away from town! If only she had never had that wire from Monty! Monty – Monty was the cause of it all. And by now he would probably be immersed in talking business with some beery old man and have forgotten all about her. Men were like that. Well, perhaps not all men; certainly not George.

A sudden thought struck her. She would ring, and ask whoever came to telephone to George. No matter what he was doing, if she wanted him he would come straight to her. You could depend on George. He wouldn't care although he had to fight his way through the Square. He would get here somehow. But before she had pressed the white electric button, she knew that wouldn't do. She couldn't appeal to George now she was stranded; she couldn't do that after having contemplated, not so many hours ago, leaving him altogether.

A fresh discomfort stirred in her breast. She felt like a child who has spurned its playmate, and then who is obliged to beg that playmate to rescue it from the ditch into which it has fallen. George – she had despised George because he wasn't smart and witty and gay like Monty, George who was worth a dozen Montys, George who was far too good for her. She fell to lauding her husband, to lauding him until he assumed the dimensions of a superman bearing no relation to the decent good fellow without any pretensions to looks or charm that he really was.

And then presently she realized that she was very tired and that her head ached. There floated through her mind the comforting thought of her own cosy fire, of a tête-à-tête dinner at home. She determined on her way there to buy something special to celebrate, something George particularly liked, such as oysters or cantaloupe. Of course, George wouldn't know it was a celebration. She wouldn't tell him anything about Monty. If he asked where she had been today, she would just say vaguely, 'In town.' No use worrying the old dear with jealous doubts. That was all ended now.

She went over to the window and looked down on the Square. The marchers had gone, and it was flooded with long lines of traffic which had been held up earlier. She stood for a time watching the coils of light and the people hurrying past. Then quite boldly she advanced to the door and opened it. There was no one in sight, but as she walked down the wide stairway she met a man with a very snub nose coming up, a man whose face she knew she had often seen before. She glanced at him sideways, doubtful whether or not to bow; but the man looked her straight in the eyes without recognition, and it was only when she had reached the last step that she recalled who he was. Lord Elbon, the famous motor-racing peer. She had never seen him before, only his pictures in the papers. A tiny pang went through her at the thought that she couldn't tell George, when she got home, that she had seen Lord Elbon in the flesh.

The friendly porter ignored her as she went out. She walked quickly through the Square to a greengrocer's near the Palatial. As she was pricing the expensive fruit, the recollection of the marchers suddenly came back to her. And she astounded the shop girl by buying a pennyworth of parsley instead of the cantaloupe she had originally asked for. Feeling very virtuous, she awaited the advent of her tram.

She responded to her husband's kiss that night with a fervour that so much surprised him, accustomed as he was to her perfunctory salutations, that he caught her closer and kissed her again; 'For luck,' he murmured half shamefacedly when he released her. She blushed and felt a little shy too. Then she turned and ran upstairs to put some more powder on, and to give her lips an extra touch. She wanted to look nice tonight, specially nice, just as though George hadn't been George, but the Monty of her morning dreams; as though the Laurels were a strange hotel which, thank goodness, it was not!

As she applied her lipstick and eyed the features which her quickened blood had imbued for the time being with the glow of beauty, she reproached herself for having been such a screw as not to have bought that cantaloupe. The girl's face had been a study when she said, 'No, I won't have it,' and then added, not liking to leave the shop without buying anything, 'A pennyworth of parsley, please.' But the girl probably hadn't seen the hunger marchers . . . Mrs MacGregor wondered if George had, and what he thought of it all, of this queer old topsy-turvy world. Most of all, she'd like to know – but he was too great a dear ever to tell her – what he thought of women like her who hadn't realized until now how bad things were in the city, and who had never done a hand's turn to help.

CHAPTER IV

It was queer, Charlie thought, when he left the office, to look back at it and to see the light still burning in Mr Joyce's room. Normally, the chief went off about half past four, often earlier. Maybe, if he hadn't always left so darned early, if he had put his back into things a bit more . . . For the life of him, Wren couldn't help blaming his employer, he couldn't resist hurling at his unconscious head an occasional backhander.

After the turmoil of the afternoon, the Square seemed strangely empty, a windy quadrangle drained of life and colour. Only the buses tended to destroy the illusion that the fume of the day was over and tranquillity had descended upon the city. They tore east and west, their bright eyes scanning the human stream darkening the pavements. They put to shame, with their snorting engines, their magnificent semblance of stress and hurry, the quietly dawdling trams. In a corner of the world that was threatening to slow down, their loud-voiced hooters were a savage slogan extolling speed: 'Get on, or get under!'

'Lord,' said Charlie to himself, 'don't *you* start yapping about it! We're going under fast enough.'

He decided to walk home instead of taking a tram. That way he might sweat out some of his misery. Incidentally, he would save tuppence. And he would have to begin counting the tuppences again. Thank God he had nobody but himself to fend for. Fellows who married young these days were fools; fools or selfish swine. No wonder so many women were marrying men old enough to be their fathers. Decent-minded youngsters didn't dare to propose matrimony, and those who weren't decent-minded the girls rightly disdained. Result: photographs every day in the papers of twenty-year-old brides assisting doddering old grooms of eighty down the church steps. Oh, it was the day of the old men right enough. Youth was down-and-out. The elders were carrying off all the prizes. It was a pity that, especially when you thought of a girl like Celia Ker. It made you sick to think of her honeymooning with some lascivious old brute old enough to be her father. And yet for anyone like her, marriage presented a fairer prospect, on the whole, than an office career. Typing and all that was a blind alley that took you so far and no farther. And out you go at fifty! He tried to picture what Celia would be like at fifty, but it was no use. He could only see her as she was now – very sweet and gravely responsible and utterly unfitted for the rough and tumble of ordinary business life. She was all wrong in Joyce's, really, as much out of her element as a blush-rose. And the way that little tick More at times eyed her . . . !

He shook his head in answer to a taxi driver's solicitation. A taxi tonight? No fears! He watched the cab crawl slowly along the kerb, touting for custom. That was something new in the city. A sign of the times. Nobody was taking taxis these days. It was as much as most folk could do to scrape up coppers for the tramcar. There was a little crowd at the next stopping place waiting for a yellow one. When it came along, it was already half full, and a miniature scrimmage ensued. Among those who were worsted in the fray was a girl in a green hat. Charlie, recognizing it in the forefront of those struggling to gain the footboard of the car, was in no way surprised to see its owner ousted and thrust back. Quite evidently, her tactics were not vigorous enough to enable her to hold her own with burly men and fur-coated women holding arms and sharp-edged parcels akimbo.

'Hullo!' he said. 'Got left?'

Celia smiled ruefully. 'Looks like it. And this is the second time. I'm no good at pushing.' The competent Miss Ker was in abeyance at the moment. Besides, when it came to the bit, even the competent Miss Ker, Celia was bound to admit, was no heavyweight.

'Tired?' Charlie asked her.

'No. Why?'

'We might as well walk on a bit, then. You're going home, aren't you?'

She looked at him sideways and flushed. 'To tell you the truth, I wasn't. I was going right on to the terminus.'

'At this hour? Whatever for?'

'You won't understand.'

'Try me. Even after today, I've still some glimmerings of sanity left.'

'It isn't your sanity I'm doubtful of. It's mine. I just couldn't go back to my room tonight, and sit there listening to the girl below practising scales on the piano, the same scales over and over again.'

'Lord, no! Of course you couldn't. It isn't scales in my place. It's a chap with a typewriter. Authors' manuscripts.'

As they walked, and she drew closer to him when the pavement at parts became congested, he felt she had brought her own atmosphere with her, and was stirred. She was too simple to be contemptuous of the world; nevertheless, she did not belong to it, not to this nervous, hustling world that was all agog, now the day's work was over, to get home. It disturbed him to think of her harried by it, trying to hold her own in the insurgent tide.

She was nearly as tall as himself, so he had no need to modify his stride to suit hers. Oddly enough, neither did he feel it incumbent on him to furbish up conversation with which to fend off silence. He stayed quiet, content to share with her the spectacle of the stars looking down upon the flickering sky-signs – signs whose jerky, nervous movements seemed to reflect the heart-throbs of the crowds below.

When a crossing place brought them to a standstill, she looked up at him, and their eyes met in intimacy and candour.

'I keep on wondering what they are talking about,' she said. 'I keep on picturing that interview.'

'It won't last long. "Get me out of the blasted concern, Jacks, as best you can."'

A note of bitterness crept into Celia's voice. 'No, I don't suppose Mr Joyce will waste much time. He'll be in too big a rush to get home to dress for the concert.'

'What concert? . . . Oh, Elberstein's. I say, would you like to go to it? No, I don't suppose you would,' he added, realizing even before Celia's gesture of dissent that she had a score against Adèle Elberstein, feeling her, in some vague way, to be responsible for Mr Joyce's decision.

He hesitated for a moment; then, 'Maybe we're mistaken; maybe things will be all right,' he was beginning to murmur, when his half-hearted attempts at consolation were checked by her candid young eyes searching his face. She saw through him, of course. No use lying at this stage. 'Try not to worry too badly,' he concluded lamely enough.

Her gaze fell. Upon her cheeks, the colour flamed up. 'I feel lost,' she said, and he realized that for all her childlike looks she had already had glimpses of the uncharted world of the unemployed, a world immune from the necessity of being anywhere from nine till six.

Were there visiting her, too, he wondered, dreadful pictures of how she would employ those gaping hours – trudging from free libraries up long, tiring stairs to top-flat offices where indifferent eyes would stare at her, careless voices would say, 'Post's already filled,' and doors would be slammed in her face? Looking at her now, he was certain she was already detached from Joyce's. The portals of the India merchants had closed on her and on all the rest of them for ever. She was a solitary unit wandering through space, fleeing the fear that lurks at such times around every corner, the fear of having your incompetency, your craven weakness, discovered by a jeering world.

'Take a pull on yourself,' he admonished himself silently. 'You're infecting the girl with your pessimism.' Aloud he said: 'What I think we both need is a good square meal. Let's go and have dinner at the Du Barri.'

She gazed at him in surprise. 'The most ruinous place in town! Are you crazy?'

'No, eminently sane. It restores your nerve when you've taken a toss to mount again quickly. I thought it would rehabilitate my self-respect to go there and be awfully lordly with the waiters, and toy with the wine list even although I did end up by ordering a bottle of ginger beer and tumblers for two. But if you don't like the notion . . .'

'I don't. Unless you let me pay for myself.'

He shook his head. 'Let's say the Palatial. That won't break me, And we might do a picture house afterwards. Anything to delay the scales and the authors' manuscripts.'

But the picture they chose was an unfortunate one. The figures that flickered on the screen, assuming goliath-like proportions as they came and went in unison with the music's quick, excitative notes, were those of forgotten men and their daughters, kings of finance broken by Fate, dollar princesses reduced to penury by the Slump.

In the darkness, the heroine's anguished features seemed to Celia to reflect her own. The tears spilling from those eyes rolled down her own cheeks. The sobs rending the air burst from Celia's own lips, although she made no sound. She averted her head, but the music pursued her, forced her to turn from the semicircle of darkness in which the only thing familiar was the outline of her companion's profile. Unexpectedly pugnacious, he looked, sitting there with arms folded, almost fleshly in comparison with the wistful young financier on the screen whose sinuous grace repelled, rather than attracted, because of its unmanliness.

Celia had a momentary feeling, glancing at Charlie, that there was some granite quality beneath the surface of which she had been hitherto unaware. And, womanlike, she thrilled to the discovery. Reluctantly, her eyes went back to the life-size figures on the screen. Across it, the traffic in one of the lowest quarters in New York passed in an endless chain. The raucous noise bludgeoned her ears. 'Look, look, look!' the nasal voices, the grinding wheels, the clanging overhead railway insisted. 'This is the street of forgotten men. Here abide the down-and-out, here amid the decaying garbage of the city.' As fleetly as the lid is raised from a box, the fourth wall of one of the tall houses liquefied, revealing fetid apartments piled one on top another like cells in a honeycomb, and buzzing over with humanity. Old men and young women jostled each other in the narrow confines; in one a child was born, in another a youth lay dead. Overhead a dope-fiend screamed out in frenzy; next door to him a young mother sat nursing her child. A woof of life, this dreary film into which was woven all the misery of the world; a tragic scroll epitomized by the moans of the young woman in labour, by the insensate ravings of the drug-fiend.

Celia shrank closer into herself. She wanted to get away from the desperate complexities of these fabulous people, to look at the lovers who sat on her right hand, to watch the attendants with their little guiding-star lamps combating the darkness. Above all, she wanted to look at Charlie, to gain reassurance from his confident pose. It was awful of her, she told herself tremulously, but she would have liked to have slid her hand within his arm. It would have comforted her to feel, while all these dreadful happenings were filling her eyes, that he was there, close beside her, closer than any of the tragic figures darkening the screen. They were so huge, these figures, that they bore down on you like giants, mutilating your mind, making things appear out of perspective, all aslant. You saw the world lost in darkness, peopled by shadows among which you moved, a shadow yourself.

Her heart beat harshly in unison with the music's strident notes. It beat so loudly that she felt they must hear it, the lovers sitting in a trance at her side, the quartette of giggling children in front, the attendant standing near, guiding an old man with her little flashlight bulb. Charlie, she knew, heard it, for he turned and looked down at her, a strange expression on his face. She never knew whether, instinctively, she made the first movement, or whether it happened quite simply, and of mutual accord, but on that instant she felt her hand gathered in his and drawn within the warmth of his arm.

The tension was heightening on the screen. In that street of forgotten men, the torrid midsummer heat was invoking the torments of hell. The rabbit warren of the apartment house steamed with humanity; with humanity degraded to the level of brute beasts by the insensate glare, the scorching heat. They sprawled about, these exhausted men and women, in varying attitudes of stupor and fatigue. They lay outstretched on tumbled beds, on bare boards, snarling in one another's faces like mad dogs on the verge of a fight. They sat hunched with their knees touching their chins, brooding, while all about them rose wave after wave of stifling air. If a bolt of lightning had descended from the blue and destroyed them, one and all, the onlookers had felt it to be the act of a merciful Providence. But the drone of the music, which was set to the tempo of their lives, dragged on. No release here for the suffering, no way of escape save by the furtive back alleys of crime, lit by the flame of a lecherous torch. No room there for soft visions of the past, for sentimental dreams of the might-have-been, no room for anything but the deadly grains of hate – black and implacable hate.

On that instant, Celia's hand trembled in Charlie's.

'Shall we clear out?' he whispered.

She nodded, struggled to her feet. She was shaking all over, he noticed, and cursed himself for not having suggested leaving before. The difficulty was where to go. Another meal so soon was out of the question, and they had had their fill of pictures for one evening. What, he pondered, did people do, where did they go in a case like this? It was no night for a pleasure stroll, nor for a tram ride. By this time the picture galleries would be shut. The only places he could think of that offered free shelter were the railway platforms, or one of those dubious little amusement arcades that spring like arrows off the long, broad stretch of Marylyn Street. But he couldn't take Celia there. Better make for home and be done with it.

He glanced at her pallid cheeks and pictured her alone in a room whose rafters rang with the deadly cacophony of ill-played scales. Tee-tee, tee-tee. It didn't bear thinking about. Authors' manuscripts were nothing to it.

'It's too soon to go home, isn't it?' he said. 'What about coming along for a bit to my flat?'

He had a sudden apprehension as he proffered the suggestion that she might spoil his lovely conception of her by turning on him a steely gaze. To his relief, but not, really, to his surprise, she gave a little sigh followed by a quick nod of assent.

'Thanks, I'd like that,' she said, and the colour came back to her cheeks as they stepped out of the glare of the portico and stood waiting on the pavement for a car.

CHAPTER V

For over an hour, Mr Joyce and his friend Norman Jacks had sat talking. Contrary to Wren's belief, Mr Joyce had no wish to make short work of the interview. He wanted to verify the exact position of affairs, to have before him a statement of facts so lucid that any lingering doubts which might still be lurking at the back of his mind would be swept away forthwith.

As he lay back in his chair, smoking, Jacks thought he had never before seen his friend so much in earnest. And earnestness became him. He looked younger, more alert, than he had done for many a day. Jacks broke off in the middle of a sentence to remark on the fact.

'I believe it's the prospect of an unbroken holiday that's cheering you,' he said chaffingly. 'Quite obviously, you are going to enjoy the next few years, old man.'

Mr Joyce fiddled with a ruler, shifting it from place to place without aim.

'You bet I'm going to enjoy myself during the next few years,' he said grimly. 'A change is always enjoyable to a man of my temperament.'

'Not that you've exactly ever overworked, have you?'

'That's where I made the mistake, Jacks. It simply never struck me as being worth while. I had enough. There was plenty for Constance. That seemed to me to suffice. I forgot there was something owing elsewhere.'

'You mean . . . ?'

A slight quiver sped across Mr Joyce's weathered face. He did not answer immediately. When at length he spoke, his eyes were not upon those of his friend, but upon the darkened blind of the window.

'The rent of my room in the world,' he said. 'That's not original. I don't know who said it. But I'm beginning to see we owe it, not only to the past generation, but to the present, to pay that rent. When I think of those forebears of mine – old "Blowhard" Joyce, who started the concern; and my father. You won't remember him. He was one of the godliest men I've ever met; they don't breed his type nowadays. He had hellfire on the brain; but would he sacrifice any of his dubious undertakings out of fear of it? Not he! Church twice on Sunday. Sharp practice – and some of it *was* sharp, by heaven! – on the Monday. Yes, I believe he would rather have sold his soul to the devil, for all his dread of the hereafter, than have sacrificed the smallest contract on his list.'

Jacks flaked the ash off his cigar and regarded his friend in silence. Joyce turning garrulous. Joyce raking up the past. It was odd, he reflected, very odd. Something must have occurred to shake Joyce out of himself. He had been cool enough, almost casual, when this question of giving up the business had been discussed. There had never been the faintest sign of any kind of emotion. It wasn't the prospect of the firm's demise, he could swear, that had riven Arthur's composure. It must be something nearer, more personal. Was it possible there was a woman in the case? Through a cloud of smoke, Mr Jacks studied the other with renewed interest. No doubt about it, Joyce was still physically attractive. A man of the world possessing that peculiar distinction which Scottish blood and an association with the sea, however remote, sometimes bestows upon the favoured. Oh, yes, Constance might come home any day to find a stepmother installed at Craighfast House, and serve her jolly well right! In common with other of his friends, Mr Jacks resented Constance's frequent absences. Instead of gallivanting all over the globe, he considered she should have stopped at home and attended to her father. That he might not have benefited much from her ministrations was a point of view which never occurred to Mr Jacks, who was himself the centre of an adoring circle of female relatives, each member of which subscribed to the belief that the man of the house should be waited upon hand and foot, in order that his strength be conserved for business and his Jovian detachment remain unimpaired.

While he sat there, smoking in silence, Mr Joyce could feel his friend's thoughts searching his own. Old Jacks was too sly a fox to say, 'What are you playing at?' but that was what was in his mind all the time. For without a doubt he was sensing obstacles, he was cognizant that some change had taken place. Actually, Joyce asked himself, what had occurred? Adèle Elberstein had come to town for one thing. Her voice had stirred in him a wealth of old memories, echoes of forgotten sensations. And out of these he had compounded for himself a drug with which he hoped to dull the first sharp shock of rupture. Yes, like a man about to rub his hand upon a knife, he had looked about him beforehand for something to staunch the bleeding. But he hadn't found it, and now he didn't need it. There was to be no bloodshed, no rupture if he could help it. With an effort he roused himself to address Jacks.

'Let's get down to brass tacks. You've gone into everything thoroughly?'

'I have, and I think you'd be well advised, as I said before—'

'Yes, I know you did. I don't query for a moment the wisdom of your counsel. Don't worry, Jacks. I've made up my mind. I know exactly what I am going to do. All I want to get absolutely clear are the facts and figures. If I shut down tomorrow—'

'Here you are. Is that plain?'

As they pored over the neatly typed statement, a faint vibration passed over the telephone bell. A second later it rang out loudly, jarringly. Mr Joyce glared at the instrument in annoyance.

'You take it, Jacks. Say anything. I'm not in – busy, in conference. That's the great phrase today, isn't it?'

'At this hour? I'm afraid that would hardly . . . Hullo! What? Yes . . . No. Yes.' A slow, beatific smile overspread Mr Jacks' round, fattish face as he listened, the fatuous smile of a man engaging in conversation with a woman whom he knows to be attractive and sought after, and with whom he is secretly elated to find himself in contact.

'Who is it?' demanded Mr Joyce irritably. 'Somebody for you?'

With elaborate care, Mr Jacks placed his hand over the mouthpiece. 'No, for you. Madame Adèle Elberstein. I didn't know you had such distinguished friends, Joyce. I couldn't very well tell her you were in conference, could I?' He handed over the telephone. 'Er – like me to clear out for a bit?'

'Don't be a fool. Hullo, Adèle, hullo! What do you want? What's up?'

So there was a woman in the case, and a celebrity at that! Adèle Elberstein no less. No wonder Joyce looked flustered. With a parade of discretion, Mr Jacks buried his head in a newspaper. But while his eyes scanned the market reports, his ears were on the alert for every changing inflection in his friend's voice. Adèle Elberstein, by Jove! Arthur Joyce was a picker all right. No small fry for him. Adèle it was who dazzled the Aratarian princeling, wasn't it? Joyce, incidentally, sounded none too cordial, not like a man conversing with his lady love. Of course, he was giving nothing away before him, Jacks reflected. His presence doubtless accounted for that touch of taciturnity.

'Very generous, I must say.' A bit dryly said, that. 'I should make it payable to the Lord Provost, and send it over to the Council Chambers right away . . . Concert? Sorry. I'm too busy. But you'll have a packed hall. One enthusiast won't be missed . . . What's that? I'm not so sure. By tomorrow I may not be in a position to afford myself the luxury of a holiday. I may be— Oh, sufficient unto the day, Adèle. I'm busy. Goodbye.'

He hung up the earpiece, and Jacks, surprised and a trifle shocked at his brevity, brought his head out from behind the covering newspaper. As Mr Joyce turned round, he could feel his companion's eyes probing his own. He could feel Jacks throwing out silent tentacles of enquiry which courtesy forbade his putting into words. And then Jacks' eyes, passing from his friend's face, came to rest on a framed photograph of a youth in khaki which stood on the mantelpiece directly beneath the hanging picture of old 'Blowhard', the originator of the firm.

'If your son had lived,' he said musingly, 'one might have looked at things differently.'

Joyce started up, a victim to the fear that the solitude which was a part of his very essence had been laid open by some unguarded gesture on his part to invasion. But Jacks' gaze was on Jerry's picture, a picture as unsatisfying to his father's mind as are all such pictures to those who seek to find behind the glass protecting them the tender flesh, the ardent gaze, the tireless mobility of youth whose generous impulses are still unspent.

'It's strange,' he wanted to say, 'your speaking of Jerry just now, because—' But his lips refused to formulate the words. He recoiled as he might have recoiled from a hand pressing down on a wound. For the life of him he could not speak out that which was in his mind. Not for a few minutes yet. So long had he schooled himself against the mention of Jerry's name that it would take a time before he could bring himself to utter it easily, without a betraying flush of emotion. And it would be well-nigh impossible, he reflected regretfully, to convey what he must without mention of Jerry and of all those others who had been his companions at the last. In any case, he thought, excusing his weakness, it was too precipitate. He must get things clear first. Constance had to be provided for, whatever happened. She wasn't likely to marry, but if she did, he had no mind that she should go to her future husband other than handsomely endowed. In these days, it was not enough for a woman to be prepared to love, honour and obey a man. If she were to hold her own in an unequal contract, she must be prepared to contribute her share. Constance had nothing to offer – neither brains nor beauty. She hadn't even what is commonly known as a loving disposition. It behoved him, therefore, to ensure that her bank balance was sufficient to outweigh her personal deficits. Instead of mentioning Jerry, he spoke again of Constance.

In his element now, Mr Jacks laid down his cigar, produced his spectacles and a pencil, and proceeded to do some juggling with figures. Jotting down the result, he pushed it over to Joyce.

'There!' he said. 'Whether you carry on or clear out, this sum remains; a sum which, if you settled even a third on Constance, would be large enough to attract the pot-hunters.'

Mr Joyce lay back in his chair, ruminating. 'Yes, a third invested even as low as three per cent – you're right, Jacks. Con is safe enough. Now, in case I take to drink or worse in my old age, I want to settle that on her now. I want it made secure so that I can't touch it, so that her husband, if she picks on a wrong 'un, as she probably will, can't lay a finger on a single penny.'

Mr Jacks wriggled in his seat. He didn't at all approve of the turn things were taking. In his opinion, it wasn't too well-considered an act of Joyce's, handing over so much to his daughter. In the first place, what did a single woman want with all that money? With nothing to keep up, she couldn't possibly spend it. And if she married – hang it all, no man wanted his wife lording it over him because she possessed a bit more in the bank than he did. And you never got a woman with money to sing dumb, to be subservient. She was so stuck up about her ability to pay the piper that she tended to parade her prowess all the time.

Constance was just that sort. One of those thoroughly objectionable females who wanted to have her wings clipped and not strengthened by a sudden access of riches. If she had been a nice womanly creature likely to accept a man's guidance, he wouldn't have said a word; but Constance . . . He cleared his throat, folded his spectacles preparatory to voicing a solemn protest.

'You know, Joyce,' he began, 'I do not think you are altogether justified in settling so much on Constance. That's a large sum, a very large sum, even in these days. Of course, I recognize what your aim is. Avoidance of death duties and all that, and in the natural course of things . . . But to go back to Constance. She's a very capable girl and far-travelled, but she's still young and' – he paused, cleared his throat again, this time with a view to emphasizing a platitude – 'money, you must remember, is a grave responsibility.'

Joyce looked up at that. Unconsciously, he clasped the arms of his chair. Behind the litter of papers on his desk, behind the massive brass letter-weight made in Benares, the inkstand cut out of a solid piece of Malayan teak, a vast, dark world arose, a world connected to his desk by the little wavering blue lines, like threads in a spider's web, that curvetted delicately across the map. Trade routes, these lines were called, but they were in reality tendrils springing boldly out of the seeds of male enterprise, male initiative, here in the Square and stretching out of sight to take root in other countries overseas.

Joyce pictured them disrupted, rotting because of some canker at the root. And on that instant he let his fist fall with a thud on the table by his side.

'By heavens, Jacks, you've said it. Money is a grave responsibility.'

But in his heart he acknowledged that it was only now, this very afternoon, since he had seen the hunger marchers in the Square, that he had come to realize how grave.

CHAPTER VI

Adèle Elberstein was quivering with rage when she set down the telephone. She had cleaned the powder off her face preparatory to applying a fresh make-up for evening, and on her cheeks the angry blood rose up between the folds of sagging flesh like tiny weals. As she stood there in her elaborate negligee, lace falling in cascades from her neck, her arms, she looked like a street virago, a female Sly masquerading in the elegant garb of her betters. In place of the red plush and marble, the veined oak and gilt mirrors with which she was surrounded, the stone floor and scrubbed wood of some riverside bar had provided her with a more fitting background, for in the violence of her untrammelled emotion she had stepped back a decade. She was Addy Mitchison, raging because the butcher's boy who lived next door had gone off to the circus without her; raging not so much because she adored Teddy and wanted to be in his company all the time, not because she was dead set on the circus – a bit mangy it was, nothing to get excited about – but because she hated the feeling that she had been left.

'Sufficient unto the day, Adèle. I'm busy.' The cheek of him to speak to her like that! Even although the old buffer who answered the phone was listening, even if he were in the room all the time, what did it matter? She didn't expect any 'dears' or 'darlings', only a little common gratitude. Wasn't she, a stranger to the city, sending all that money – her own hard-earned money, too, not like his, derived almost entirely from the exertions of others – wasn't she sending all that money to the local unemployed? 'Very generous, I'm sure!' She mouthed the words vituperatively. It didn't matter a damn his not coming to the concert; he'd never be missed in the crowd, but he ought to have been flattered at her taking the trouble, when she should have been resting her voice, to ring him up. Yes, he ought to have been flattered by that instead of having the cheek to shut her off before she had rightly begun. And yet, for all that, as like as not he'd turn up tomorrow smiling, expecting her to register delight at sight of him. Men – that was men all over. At the moment, she hated the thought of them, resented their presence on the earth.

Still hot with animus, she darted into her bedroom and began to apply cold cream to her face the while she disparaged Arthur Joyce much in the some way as, years ago, she had disparaged the butcher's boy who went off to the circus without her. Who was Arthur Joyce, after all, that she should waste her smiles on him, submit to his cavalier treatment? Only a merchant of sorts, and an unsuccessful one at that. A provincial, too, and the father of a grown-up daughter, of one of those little brats in uniform who had nearly stared their silly eyes out at her at Hathdown in the long ago. It wasn't as if he had been an artiste like Aristide, whose very fingertips oozed temperament, and who tore the heart out of you with his playing, or a man of influence and dignity such as Senator Brutling, or a charming youth like Egbert of Aratania. She ceased operations at this point, her face a mask of chalk-white grease, to reflect on the Prince's charms; or rather – for in reality His Highness was a gawky youngster, singularly lacking in personality and possessing none of the grace and intelligence of his beautiful mother – to recall the satisfied pride that had been hers when she was in the position to refer in public, quite casually, to her companion as 'the Prince'.

In the act of removing with her little finger an infinitesimal blob of cream that was clinging to an eyelash, she wondered a trifle sentimentally if she would ever see him again. He was married now, of course, but that needn't make any difference to their friendship. His mother had chosen his wife for him. No man in his senses would ever have chosen the Princess Sophia as his bride. It gratified the spark of the malicious that was in Adèle to recall the Princess's lumpy features, her mottled red arms, as she had seen them many a time framed in the royal box at the opera. Poor Sophia!

Floating once more on the rich, exciting tide of an old romance, with courtiers bowing down before her, and rose leaves strewing her path, she could afford to look down from her diva's throne and pity poor dull Sophia, who had never been Egbert's divinity, only his wife.

'I shan't wear black,' she said to her maid, who stood warming a pair of flesh-coloured stockings between her hands at the fire. 'Put out my new blue, with the pailettes. And all my jewels. The Russian tiara, too, Marie. I want to look like a queen tonight.'

She was trying the effect of yet another ornament on the shimmering corsage of her gown, when Marie, summoned to the door by an urgent knocking, returned in a flutter after a lengthy colloquy with someone outside.

'I'm sorry, Madame, but it's the hotel manager. He says he must see you for a few moments, he and another gentleman. I told them you never saw anyone before your concert. I tried all I could to make them go away. But they are still there, waiting. The manager said to tell you it was about Carlo, and most urgent.'

She let the jewelled spray slip from her hand on to the floor. Carlo, the little waiter who had heard her sing at Milan – Carlo. Was she never to escape from the horror of that dangling figure? In a sudden spasm of fury she wished she had never set eyes upon him; she wished she had never gone up to that top floor. She wished— 'Oh, bring them in, Marie!' she cried. 'Then go away and shut the door.'

Mr Valley's propitiatory manner was in marked contrast with that of his companion, whom he introduced as a member of the local police force. In point of fact, he had done his best to avoid this invasion of Madame Elberstein's privacy. He had urged that she should not be disturbed by the discussion of this unhappy business before such an important event as her concert. He had contended that her knowledge of the deceased was no more than that of any other guest in the hotel; but without avail.

Standing in the room now, he felt vaguely unhappy that he should be here as one of a pair of unwelcome intruders, and he endeavoured by the excessive courtesy of his tones to emphasize the gulf between himself and the blunt-spoken young plain-clothes man by his side. By word and by gesture, he tried to convey to Madame Elberstein that their being here at this time was at odds with his sense of what was due to a lady of her standing.

'My most sincere apologies, Madame, for this intrusion,' he murmured. 'Just a few inquiries, merely a matter of form. As it happens, you were the last to see the deceased alive.'

'I wish to God I had never seen him, dead or alive,' she burst out, then realizing the stranger was regarding her with some surprise, she subdued her voice, assumed the chastened manner of the virtuous heroine who is wrongly suspected of evil-doing. 'I never saw him until he came to my room today to tell me he had heard me sing in the opera house in Milan.'

The police officer sat down suddenly. Diving into his pocket, he produced a notebook and pencil, an action which gave her the feeling she was being interviewed by a disagreeable and rather ill-informed reporter who, out of sheer spleen, would describe her as portly and middle-aged, and credit her with sentiments which she had often entertained in private but always had the wit to refrain from disclosing to the public.

'On what pretext did this man, Carlo Amorelli, come to your room? Merely to tell you he had heard you sing at Milan?'

She fingered the sapphires at her wrist and thanked heaven she had on her blue satin. Assuredly, this man with the fierce brown eyes, the scowling expression, would have tried to browbeat her had she been arrayed in anything less imposing.

'He came,' she said, 'to warn me about a demonstration in the Square. He seemed very much alarmed about it. I don't know why.'

Mr Valley drew a quick breath of relief. He nodded proudly at the police officer as though to say: 'My trick.' 'That coincides with what I told you he said to me,' he remarked gravely. 'It also coincides with the evidence of the staff.'

But the plain-clothes man was not to be put off. He fluttered the leaves of his notebook determinedly. 'Did he speak to you of anyone called Giovanna? There are some letters in his pockets bearing that signature.'

She shook her head. 'No,' she said wearily, 'but Giovanna is a common name in Milan. There is at least one Giovanna in the corps de ballet at the opera there.'

'If you ask any more fool questions, I shall scream,' she added inwardly. Then remembered she must do no such thing for fear of straining her voice. Her face, too – she must not let herself become excited, or she would have to make up all over again. 'God, what it is to be a woman!' she groaned; and from reviling them, swung round to a momentary envy of men who have no need to curb their emotions in order to retain their good looks. Men, men! They had the best of it all the time. They grabbed what they wanted, and were applauded for their strength. They fought for their deserts, fought for them cleanly, straightforwardly, whereas women, in order to attain their heart's desire, were obliged to seek roundabout roads, to grovel, to grin and fawn on some silly fool they despised – a mental picture of Prince Egbert, smiling fatuously, his pale eyes watering, his weak mouth gaping, flashed upon her mind.

When at last the two men went – Mr Valley murmuring polite regrets, smiling apologetically, the police officer curt, as though dealing with a common criminal – she felt as though she had been dragged into a sordid case in a public court. Opening the door, she called upon Marie to come and spray the room with perfume. She had the feeling there lingered in it some faint odour of putrefaction. Had it not been too late, she would like to have laved her face in scented water, to have let it trickle over her skin until her nostrils were full of the fragrance of roses, and her nerves were soothed by the cloying scent of midsummer blossoms. Instead of going to sing on a concert platform to a lot of old fogies in semi evening dress, she would like to have gone forth herself splendidly arrayed to some new and colourful ballet. She would have loved in her present mood to have watched a maze of twinkling figures unfold the theme of some fantastic story, a story of super-beings, of gods and goddesses emerging on tiptoe from a mock palace decorated with gold leaf, and dancing to the piping of a great green bird perched high in a willow tree.

As she went downstairs, she wished herself back in Paris. A swift drive along the Boulevard and the bright glow of the lights, smouldering beneath the trees, would have brought a stream of cheerful images into her mind that would have restored her confidence, raised her to her throne again. The faint silver of the sky, revealed here and there between a crack in the melancholy black buildings and the uncertain lights of the side streets along which the car was gliding, were not vivid enough to transmute her thoughts. She sat back, feeling lost and rather lonely in the dark little sphere of the slowly moving motor until it stopped outside a door inset in a large building. From that moment, the lonely woman ceased to exist. There stepped from her car and swept over the threshold a graciously smiling personage, scattering radiant glances upon delighted onlookers who flushed and drew stifled breaths, as though unexpectedly they had received some mark of royal favour.

Marie, trudging in her mistress's wake, evinced no surprise at the sudden transformation. She was used to seeing publicity serve as the match that kindled Elberstein's flame. She was used to seeing the real woman replace the reigning queen whenever the shouting was over.

Tonight it went on and on, a dull, almost sullen roar intersected now and then by the high-pitched note of hysteria. Listening to it, Marie, waiting in the dressing room with a knitted scarf round her shoulders, her feet close to a sunken fire, saw a great bay in which faces like white coins, bodies like black lobes, nodded and leapt in an atmosphere pregnant with an electric brilliance . . . The glancing arms were beginning to tire now. Between the outbursts, the intervals of stillness were growing more prolonged. Quick, Madame, quick, Marie's nimble brain urged, or there will be a scraping of feet, there will be a rustle of cloaks, and you will forfeit your last encore . . . Ah, there it was, the first notes of the piano imposing silence upon the restive with their promise of yet another interlude of bliss. There was the rapturous din of a populace childishly delighted by its own perspicacity in recognizing the first bar of a hackneyed tune. Like a silver ripple in a black corrie, a cool, clear sound in a turgid undergrowth, the singer's opening note. As it lengthened and grew more insistent, Marie clapped her hands to her ears.

'"Home, Sweet Home",' she groaned. 'Gawd!'

But over the great bay a tide of quietude had lapped. The rows of white faces were transfixed. Their owners had swum clear of the sterile glitter of the lights. They were bathing in familiar waters, sweet, sun-flecked waters.

And she who had granted them this respite from the nervous course of their lives was aware only of the uplifted pallor of her accompanist's face, of his eyes watchful for the first diminuendo of her trill.

She released it at last lingeringly, reluctantly, as though unwilling to surrender her dream of an unworthy paradise. Then she stood quite still while for the fraction of a second the wings of silence rested within the great bay.

While they were receding rapidly before the challenging blare of applause, Marie rushed out of the waiting room, in her arms the cloth-of-silver wrap in which Madame was wont to make her final obeisance to the audience. But Madame Elberstein did not wait for it to be cunningly arranged about her shoulders tonight. Snatching it from her maid, she drew it across her bare arms as casually as though it had been a bedraggled feather boa. The din broke out afresh when she swam across the platform wreathed in smiles. But even as she bowed delightedly, blew kisses, extended her arms in fervent protestations of gratitude which rather surprised the more provincial-minded of her audience, her brain was full of feverish plans.

If that newspaper she had caught a glimpse of in the artistes' room spoke truth, Egbert would be in London tomorrow. Egbert – there had been no word about Sophia. Poor Sophia! Probably she had been left at home; Sophia who with her big red arms looked so like a good, respectable laundrymaid. Egbert would probably be stopping at the same place as he used to do. It was fortunate the restaurant there was a favourite of her own. Everyone knew that. 'Among the well-known people to be seen lunching in the Italian Room at the Hotel Riche yesterday were Madame Adèle Elberstein.' Every other day, when she was in London, paragraphs to that effect, sent in by her press agent, formed part of her mail. Assuredly Egbert, who was fond of the place, would dine there sometimes also. He couldn't always be out at parties . . . 'Oh, a wonderful audience,' she broke off to agree with an old man with a straggling white beard and a monocle who was plucking anxiously at her sleeve. 'Such darlings they are here. Not an audience in the world to compare with them.' . . . There was no reason now why she should go to a quiet seaside place, no reason at all. Arthur Joyce had defaulted; in any case, when it came to a choice between a prince and a bankrupt merchant . . . 'Oh, perfectly lovely. Too, too sweet of you all really. I'm dreadfully spoiled, wherever I go.' . . . No, there was no reason why she shouldn't go right back to London. She had four days before the Leeds date, four precious days. Eight meals, if need be, at the Hotel Riche. Lingering meals, for he might come in late. Thank heaven, her usual table was beautifully conspicuous. And in her blue dress – a pity now she had worn it tonight; still, Marie could send it to be pressed the instant they reached London. The décolletage was perfect, so deep and yet . . . 'No. I never wrap up. I rarely catch cold. Of course, it has been rather chilly today, but I've simply loved every minute of my visit here.'

In a swirl of compliments and thanks, she was escorted to her car, at the window of which she stayed for a second, a radiant vision in blue and silver, to wave her hand and to smile at the little crowd of enthusiasts fluttering handkerchiefs on the pavement. As they passed from view, she lay back in the darkness and let her thoughts leap on ahead. London tomorrow. Perhaps Arataria next month. Poor Sophia! But then, she reflected, Sophia always had this satisfaction, that in the eyes of the world, by letter and by law, she was Egbert's wife.

CHAPTER VII

Coming into Charlie's flat, Celia thought, was like coming into one of the innermost rungs of the tower of silence. The top flat of the house, it was approached by the common hall and stair, but separated from them, and from the furnished flats below, by a thick green door.

The room into which he took her was one of those friendly rooms which, in company with the woods and the fields, admits even newcomers to a sense of kinship. A little brown room that bore sign of common usage, it was littered with books and papers lightly filmed with dust. A tawny carpet gave out its faded colours, and between the dark curtains draping the prodigiously high windows, and the ledges of thick wall, a seam of starlit sky escaped.

Although the house was the last in a terrace clambering up a steep incline, it was not really high up, or very far from the centre of the city; nevertheless, Celia felt as though the room stood on an elevation of its own, so detached was it from worldly confusion. 'If I could only stay here always,' she thought, 'I could garner up each night peace enough to carry me through the day.'

'Like it?' asked Charlie, aware that her gaze was travelling over the room, and seeing it change as purely personal possessions have a way of doing when subjected to the appraisal of alien eyes.

'I love it,' she said, and instantly the defects he was silently deploring swam out of sight, and he heard himself admitting that for him the place had a value quite beyond its worth. His first niche outside the family circle, he had furnished it gradually, selecting each item with care, because his income was not such as to permit of any mistaken purchases, any shoddy misfits he might wish next day he had never bought. That was why he had concentrated on reproductions of the antique. It had stood the test of time. Cubes and triangles were jolly enough, stimulating to the imagination, but within a year you might be itching to get rid of them, longing to replace them with the mellower, less attenuated lines of the Jacobean period, or the spindly elegance of Chippendale. There were no pictures, no ornaments, only a little Tanagra figurine on the mantelpiece. His first year's salary hadn't run to extras. It was out of that salary he had furnished the place. It had, indeed, in those days seemed to him redolent of Fuljacks', of that tincture of trade and romance which overhung the maze of offices in Leyden Street. And then suddenly that tincture had gone sour. All the dreams he had gathered up in the place had been betrayed. He had stayed on in it during the brief interval which intervened between the old job and the new. He had stayed on because the rent had been paid in advance and there was nothing else to do. And then quite unexpectedly a gate had been opened to him – Joyce's. And instantly, in a flush of gratitude, old loyalties had given way to new. Within these walls fresh dreams had been formed; high expectation had resumed its old sway.

It was uncertainty, a queer kind of constraint, induced by her presence here in his rooms, that set his tongue racing. Some intuition warned him that she, too, was conscious of it, and he desired above all things to draw her into friendliness and ease. As she stooped, warming her hands in the heat-waves vibrating above the newly lit radiator, the curve of her shoulders, the gleam of her fair hair, were caught and framed in a circlet of yellow light. From the circlet there flowed through the room, as there flows from a strand of fanciful tapestry hung on the wall, an impression of delicacy and fragrance. You couldn't translate that fragrance into scent, he told himself, only into sound. The chiming of bells, perhaps, on a starlit night; certain phrases of Bach, challenging and very stilly.

They rang in his ears as he sat back in his chair, facing her. She was the first woman, he reflected, who had been in his rooms. Mrs Haggart, the caretaker's wife, didn't count. It was difficult to believe that she and Celia belonged to the some sex. There clung to Celia's person, even now when she drooped, relaxed, over the stove, a sense of speed suspended, a grace that was akin to light. He had noted it before in the office, but there, where she was always strung to action, it had seemed more a quality of the mind than of the spirit. Now he realized that this supple alertness was instinct in her as in a fawn, that it persisted in solitude and was not brought into being by the exigencies of the commercial world. It angered him to think of her exposed to the changing winds of that world, exhausted by the fret of it, buffeted by its elements. Beauty, he told himself, was like genius. It should be set aside in an enclosed place and tended by sensitive persons such as poets and artists and musicians, whose minds would be keyed to a true perception of its worth. Porcelain on cobblestones at a street corner! His fists clenched at thought of it.

'A penny for them,' said Celia. 'You look as if your thoughts were worth that and lots more at the moment.'

He flushed as he met her gaze. 'I was thinking – you won't be offended if I tell you the truth? I was thinking how out of place you are in the world of commerce. It's not your lay somehow.'

She nodded ruefully. 'I know. But I try awfully hard to pretend it is. I'm sorry you've found me out. I'm always trying to pretend I'm cool and calm and competent – the competent Miss Ker.'

She looked down suddenly at that, hot with embarrassment. He did not know it, he never would know it, but she had let him into a secret. She had lowered a veil and let him look inside. She had introduced him to one of her closest intimates – an imaginary one, but none the less dear for that.

'The competent Miss Ker,' he repeated. 'Yes, I believe I know her best. She comes to the office sharp every morning, leaves it punctually each night, or doesn't she leave it? Does the real Miss Ker emerge then – the real Miss Ker, whose natural background isn't a city office, but a sylvan landscape, with birds and trees and a lake or a shining river in the background?'

A startled little flush dawned on Celia's cheeks. She gazed at Charlie with round, eager eyes.

'It's funny your saying that. You see, I was born beside one, a river, I mean, when the birds were building in the trees.'

'I was sure of it. You don't fit into Joyce's somehow.'

They fell silent at that, seeing Joyce's dissolve as an office scene in a film dissolves and is merged in a succession of other pictures. It was with an effort Charlie roused himself from contemplation of them.

'Tea,' he said. 'Let's go and make some.'

While they were getting it, she commented on the quiet of the place. 'Where is your friend of the authors' manuscripts tonight?' she asked.

'Out on the binge probably or you'd have heard him. We share this top flat together. I couldn't rise to a bathroom for myself. We share that, and the kitchenette, otherwise our rooms are our own.'

She admired the kitchenette, a compact box, very neat and shining, every inch of which she longed to examine. In one corner stood a gas cooker with up-to-date gadgets over which she brooded in delight.

'Do you use this for grilling, and for making toast? Oh, and you can boil two pots on one jet with the use of this. That's right, isn't it?'

He shook his head. 'Blessed if I know. I never boil two pots at once. Try them and see for yourself.'

She did so, then turned on him eyes bright with vexation. 'If I'd known you had this perfect stove,' she lamented, 'why, we could have bought things, and I could have cooked the nicest mixed grill instead of going to the Palatial.'

It struck him suddenly that, in women like Celia, there is a streak of domesticity which not even a preoccupation with commerce can wholly eradicate. Apparently this streak was more than a mere veneer with her. It was ingrained, causing her who looked so queenly, so ethereal, to itch for commonplace objects like pots and pans and gas stoves. He laughed out loud. To his delight, her laughter mingled with his.

'I know what you're thinking,' she said, 'that it wouldn't have been the nicest mixed grill if I had cooked it. I'm horribly out of practice, of course. You can't cook much in one wee bed-sitting-room over a fire that keeps on continuously smoking.'

Soon, with teacups and biscuits which she was too polite to tell him had gone prematurely stale because they hadn't been kept carefully in an airtight tin, they were back in their chairs beside the fire. They were talking with an ease, an abandonment that overturned such barriers as arose between them before either of them became aware of the barriers' existence. It was as though there was in the tea some warming fire that promoted intimacy, that united them so that their minds were now attuned to the same exciting rhythm. And yet, despite this sense of nearness, Charlie felt as if she were ringed off from him, a being apart, secure in her own reticences, weighed by a wisdom to which he could never attain.

They talked of Joyce's, and of what the future might hold. They spoke of the 'old days', when they were young, the days before this shadow had fallen upon them, as though they were bearded patriarchs nearing the end of their days, instead of fledglings peeping fearfully between the tree leaves at the whirling spectacle of the world. And always their hopes reaching out, as do the hopes of youth, wildly, extravagantly, met and mingled. In a moment they had girdled the earth with the ships of commerce; they had set on fire all the waterways of the world. They had created new trade routes, new alliances between hostile nations. And while they talked passionately of external things, things with little or no bearing upon their own personal problems, the strand of intimacy between them waxed stronger and stronger.

As she spoke of Joyce's distant connections, Charlie's eyes were caught by the moving pulse in the cup of her throat. As she listened, she was profoundly conscious of his nearness. She had never felt so near to any human being before.

Intuitively, he recognized that she must pay with unhappiness for that limpid vitality of hers. In those glimpses she had afforded him of her life at home with her father, and of those self-righteous women who, incredibly enough, were her only surviving relatives, he had seen something of the curiously mixed influences which had been brought to bear on her. He applauded in silence her rashness in cutting aloof from these uncongenial females. Better face the wind than be tangled up in old-wifieness. He had a fleeting vision of her, sparkling with wayward pride, setting her face to the gale, and defying a ridiculous row of bonneted old women crying out upon her for her stubbornness, her selfishness; a row of old women willing her, with all the venom that was in them, to come to grief because she had escaped them, because they knew now they would never batten, in the years of their increasing frailty, upon her youthful strength, her grace.

Breaking in on their talk came the sound of footsteps on the stair, of a door opening, then banging shut. A flicker passed over the transparent clarity of Celia's eyes. She drew herself erect. To Charlie, watching her, it was as though she were withdrawing herself, as though the real Celia were on the point of taking shelter behind the competent Miss Ker.

'Old Lewis,' he answered her unspoken enquiry. 'You'll hear his machine going in a minute.'

And almost immediately it began, an insidious tapping that created a sense of disturbance in the quiet room in the same way as the beak of a sparrow, perched on the windowsill at early morning, creates a wild din in a world of chastened light. It ceased presently, and there fell on the door a loud rap. Charlie glanced doubtfully at Celia, whereat she flushed and, rising, drew aside. He nodded approval, not so much at her action as to being admitted into a conspiracy with her, and went to the door.

'Hullo, Lewis,' he said pleasantly enough. 'Sorry. I'm busy tonight. Can't ask you in . . . Oh, cigarettes? Sure. Here you are. No, keep the packet. I've got more in my case.'

As he stepped back from the door, he turned to Celia, and their eyes met as those of gay conspirators do – smilingly, confidingly. He put a hand on her arm.

'Come and sit down,' he said.

She shook her head. 'I ought to be going,' she said, but without much conviction. 'I must go.'

She reached out for her coat, and he held it open for her arms. But instead of relinquishing his hold on the garment when she had slipped into it, his arms stayed about its folds, so that the warmth of her person communicated itself to him. She made no effort to step away, only while still he hesitated on the edge of a discovery – or was it the edge of a dream? – her eyes came round to him, lingered on his face.

At sight of her parted lips, her shining eyes, the breath of expectancy quickened in him, and a wave of inexpressible delight, breaking over him, burnished the instant with the lustre of a deep enchantment. It enfolded them both, that momentary ecstasy, sealing them together as any profound emotion which is shared seals together its participants. Aware, instinctively, that the same flame which pulsed in him was that which kindled her to radiance, he bent his lips to hers.

Tap-tap-tap! The throb of the typewriter across the passage awoke again. But this time it seemed to them that the sparrow perched on the windowsill was no noisy intruder, but a harbinger of joy proclaiming the advent of a perfect dawn.

CHAPTER VIII

When they stepped apart, her body was tremulous, like the branch of a tree responsive to the caress of a gentle wind. Her hands fluttered to her face, as though by their pressure she could erase the lovely flush which had invaded it. For a time neither spoke. It was enough, he felt, to let happiness possess them, to rest hand in hand in the little harbour, set apart from the outer world, that happiness had builded for them.

Beyond that harbour lay darkness, disturbance. Both the world and its fear belonged to another life which he had left behind. When he went back to the world, it would be as one renewed. It would be with an armour rendered invulnerable by another's confidence. He wanted to cry out loud in the fullness of his new sense of power, but the sound that trembled on his lips dissolved into the syllables of her name.

'Celia,' he said, his fingers tightening on hers. 'Celia, my sweet.'

She met his eyes shyly. She had a childish impulse to hide her hot cheeks, to steal away as long as this gladness encompassed her. So precious a possession it was that she wanted to hold it closely, to thank God for it on her knees and in solitude. Unlike Charlie, she neither looked back nor forward. An invisible orchestra was flooding her being with its music, and so steeped was she in the aerial chords that she could not recall a time when they had not vibrated in her mind.

And then, dissipating her illusion of celestial sounds, disrupting her vision of a sweet harbour, there arose the insistent bell of a typewriter harshly driven. Apparently its user was becoming disgusted with the flow of another's eloquence; he was venting his spleen on the hapless machine.

'Fancy typing a love story like that!' said Charlie. Then, out of the depths of his new-found knowledge, he added pityingly: 'The poor chap doesn't know what love means.'

'What does it mean?' she murmured, not that she had any need to ask, but because the sound of his voice was a fitting substitute for the flood of celestial music.

He hesitated, groping for words. To his thinking, no phrase could express the rushing of wings, the sense of power, the restive delight which this strange new intimacy induced. It were easier to define marriage. Marriage today was intended not for the procreation of children, as the Church still had it, but for the protection of man and woman from that terrible loneliness inseparable from life in an overcrowded realm. It was a defence against stress, against that struggle to communicate, one with the other, from which only the closest of human relationships partially releases one.

Like children linking hands to cross a busy thoroughfare, a man and woman joined together were exempt from the worst terrors of the crossing. The current of adversity did not catch them unawares. They moved on through the roar and the turmoil as steadfastly as a ship which had cast its moorings at darkling moves out with the tide. They moved on unerringly, confident despite the wiseacres who have robbed the Hereafter of its heavenly attributes, reduced it to a scientist's vision of hell, that something of their love must survive, some imperishable spark born of the flame within them.

Celia, listening, realized that her mind was not wholly responsive to his thoughts. While she agreed in soft monosyllables, she sat lost in a trance through which the sound of his voice reached her as a sound from the mainland reaches one on a distant isle. Time and space alike were withdrawn from her now. For a brief interlude, she was possessed by that sense of eternity which imbues the passing moments with such intensity as to make it seem impossible they will ever slip away.

'I understand now why men marry,' said Charlie. 'It isn't so much that they aren't alive to their responsibilities as that instinctively they are grasping at a lifeline.'

She had to laugh at that, not because what he was saying was funny, but because of the feeling of lightness in her heart. They were laughing together, foolishly, irresponsibly, when the whir of a telephone resounded from the passage. Reluctantly, he disengaged his fingers from hers.

'Probably his girl for Lewis,' he said. 'But he'll never hear. He's making such a din.'

He left the door ajar as he went out. She could hear his voice elevated in surprise. 'Yes, Mr Joyce . . . Tonight? Now? Certainly. I can go right away . . . You what? I beg your pardon. I don't quite— Oh, changed, I see. You'd like me to look through them tomorrow. Yes, sir, I will. Good night.'

His eyes were blazing with excitement when he returned to Celia. 'That was Joyce,' he said. 'You heard, didn't you? He wants me to go down to the office right away. He's left some notes on his desk he doesn't want the char to find when she goes in in the morning. I'm to take them home with me, look through them, and – he spoke of changes, Celia. But he didn't speak as though they were . . . Oh, either he's bluffing in a way I cannot believe him capable of, or else I'm mad, quite mad; but I believe – I do, on my soul and conscience, believe he's carrying on.'

Celia experienced a little pang when they stepped together into the street. The rhythm of her emotion still continued, but the spell of silence woven by that quiet room was lost to them now in the stir of the city. It encroached on her peace of mind, filled her with foreboding. Mr Joyce wasn't given to bluffing, but she knew, perhaps better than Charlie did, his habit of shirking the unpleasant, of occupying himself with trifles when important matters were afoot . . . Flowers for Adèle Elberstein. The thought of those roses still moved her to ire when she thought of them.

While Charlie talked gaily, confidently, of the notes he was to retrieve from Mr Joyce's desk, she had a stark conviction that what he would find there would be a brief intimation of the business closing down, directions, perhaps, for the dismissal of the staff which Mr Joyce had funked giving by word of mouth himself.

Rather to Charlie's surprise, she refused on the plea of fatigue to accompany him to the office. She hated to oppose him, but she desired, with all the force that was in her, to increase to the stature of his imagining of her. And she knew she dared not risk being with him when he examined Mr Joyce's notes lest at sight of his disappointment she give way altogether, reveal herself for the weakling and coward that she was. And she was committed now and in the future to heroism. Love gave, but love exacted. In the first sparkle, she had not realized that to the delicious game any penalty was attached. No, penalty wasn't the word. Privilege was better. For it would be her privilege, if she could transcend her mood to lend him courage, to restore, when the blackness of self-distrust was upon him, his belief in himself.

She said good night to him at the corner of the house in which she lodged, a grim, forbidding house whose unpainted walls and unlit hall contrasted with the gaiety of the other private residences in the neighbourhood. There was no telephone, Celia explained, save for the use of the owner who lived on the premises, and she dared not have a visitor at such an hour – the place, Charlie thought impatiently, was hemmed round with needless rules and regulations – so it was arranged that after leaving the office he would walk back that way along the terrace. From her window, which was at the front, she would be watching out for him, and he would wave a handkerchief if all was well.

'And if it isn't?' she countered.

'I'll wave my hand. No, I'll stand and howl on the doorstep till you are obliged to let me in. But truly, darling, I know – I feel it's going to be all right.'

But his confidence ebbed when he left her and strode downhill towards the city. A full moon, yellow and sullen, hung over the terrace gardens. Below it, flickering and spluttering, was a watchman's fire set at the base of a fan of high houses out of which, like bright flecks, shone little squares of light. As the roar of traffic came up at him, he recalled the hunger marchers. He thought of them now as a vast section of humanity feeling its way blindly, almost aimlessly, through endless space, reaching out arms to some will-o'-the-wisp – reaching always upwards for something better, something finer than their own lives could ever show; an endless procession revolving below the moon. Perhaps one day the masters would throw down their pens, their chequebooks, and join in too. They would all join in, every man jack of them, from the storekeeper in the basement to the slater on the roof. They would join in a vast hunger march against God, against a God who had put them into the world and then left them to fend in it for themselves, helpless as tiny ears of wheat against the wind and the rain. And so great would be the press that as the march revolved round the globe, the tail end and the head of the procession must inevitably collide and a bloody war would ensue. A war that would be a thousand times worse than any other war, for in it all the people in the world would be involved. But despite the confusion each man would know full well what he was fighting for. He was fighting neither for nation nor for party; he was fighting neither for supremacy nor for riches, but simply to gain a foothold in an overcrowded world.

The Square was quiet when he reached it. He opened the outer door leading to the offices and left it ajar, knowing all the doors inside to be separately locked. On the threshold of Mr Joyce's room he hesitated. The aroma of cigar smoke clung to it, and the faintly musty smell of old parchment, an intriguing mixture suggestive in its potency of Big Business.

. . . Big Business? Oh, yes, it still existed, for all the pessimists might say. If ultimately it dwindled and disappeared as the gold standard had done, it was because the stature of man had dwindled too. Charlie switched on the light and saw the eyes of old 'Blowhard' Joyce, gimlet eyes, watching him from the wall. Beneath them, from his frame on the mantelpiece, Jerry's face smiled out at him. Slim and boyish in his neatly fitting uniform, Jerry looked as though he were holding a brief for the younger generation. For the first time Charlie studied his features attentively, the features of old 'Blowhard's' lineal descendant, Mr Joyce's only son. If he had survived . . . But had it never occurred to Mr Joyce that although his son had fallen, others of his generation had come through, others were holding out chill hands to the fires of life?

With an impatient sigh, Charlie turned his back on Jerry and advanced to the desk where a few sheets of pencilled matter lay outspread.

He sat down heavily and began to read, thankful all at once that Celia wasn't here, and that he was alone. For the figures shown were proof of adversity. By no twist of imagination, no gift of optimism, could you construe them otherwise. The graph alongside told a similar tale. It sloped steadily on the downgrade. Followed some notes, some queries in Mr Joyce's neat, fastidious handwriting. As he perused them, the swelling tide of Charlie's despondency was arrested. He turned the page, his face lightening, his eyes growing limpid as he read on.

And then, breaking in upon a room which seemed, when he entered it, almost as silent as the grave, came the echo of footsteps in the distance. For a time Charlie paid no heed to them, accustomed as he was to the coming and going of people during working hours. Then his nerves awoke. He threw back his head, listening intently, and as he did so he caught young Joyce's eyes. 'We've won,' they smiled at him; but Charlie was too startled to grasp their message. He sprang to his feet, made for the door. Could it be Celia? the thought occurred to him; but it was a man's figure that loomed in the darkened corridor, a man's voice that gave answer to his challenge, 'What are you doing here?'

Charlie stared at the intruder, a pinched-looking youth who leaned helplessly against the wall.

'Look here,' he said, 'this is private property. You can't stay here. If you're stuck for a night's lodging, here's something.'

But the youth made no move to take the extended coin. He stayed motionless, as though too exhausted to do anything else. Then he raised tormented eyes to Charlie's face.

'I suppose you're from the police station. Well, if you want to know, I can tell you. It was me that done it. Just where you're standing now.'

Done it – done what? A light broke on Charlie's mind. He recalled the strange incident of Macfarlan's fall in the passage, his statement that he had been knocked on the head, his insistence, when they doubted him, that it was no swoon, but an assailant's blow that had knocked him out.

'You mean you attacked someone here?'

Joe nodded sullenly. Beneath his apathy, Charlie fancied he could detect a covert note of pride.

'Yes, it was me. I did for him just here.'

CHAPTER IX

It was force of habit, strengthened by a sort of blind instinct, that turned Mrs Humphry's footsteps towards the Square. The Square had been the objective of the marchers, and she cherished a vague hope that some of them might still be loitering there. It was not likely Joe would be among them – he had never been a street lounger – but you never knew.

She was pale with fatigue by the time she reached the bridge and crossed the river into Marylyn Street. The lights of the Palatial, rising like a conflagration in the dark cocoon of the city, seemed to cast their hot breath on the crowds below. Usually, an incursion into these crowds at this late hour would have savoured to Mrs Humphry of a pleasure jaunt seldom enjoyed save at Christmas or the New Year. But tonight, the magnificence of the winking sky-signs, of the gay shop windows and the glittering trams signified nothing to her at all. Everything she saw spoke to her of Joe. That grand young fellow in uniform standing at the door of the Palatial had a job that would suit Joe down to the ground. Joe would look quite the gentleman in that nice light green. The couples hurrying in and out of its portals whispered to her of an experience Joe had never known – going with a girl. No, so far as she could remember Joe had never had a girl. He had never walked out with anyone, never hurried off to picture houses, or cheap dance halls, to return at night flushed and bright-eyed. Vaguely, she knew that Joe had missed something, and she hated those couples who brushed past her, hanging on to each other's arms, smiling into each other's faces. She hated them because they were enjoying some secret rapture denied by Fate to her son.

She felt weak in every bone when at last she neared the Square. As she entered it, she saw the moon-streamed sky like mother-of-pearl above the throng of the high buildings. For the space of a second the Square was very still, as though these buildings were the gnarled trunks of ancient trees, and the space they guarded a deep enclosure set aside for a Druidical rite. And then the thunder of the traffic broke out afresh; round the far corner glanced a maze of lively sparks – the bright foreheads of buses, the eyes of hurrying cars. Like monstrous offspring of a Machine Age, these hooting vehicles rushing by, jeering and hissing at the ancient stone which with its air of dignity and calm soared above them. Almost it was as though these sneering moderns were defying the spirit of the past to rise up and condemn them; as though they were calling upon ancient ghosts to emerge from behind the cracked mortar, the peeling window frames, to behold the marvels of the present day. Houses on wheels that tore through space; trains that ate distance; lights that flooded roadways at an unseen signal; factories with smoothly working cylinders and steel hands that took the place of human labour. 'Look, look!' the hooters seemed to shriek to the shrinking spectres of old merchantmen. 'Look at what we have accomplished today! Behold the wonders of the Machine Age!' 'Yes, look,' the ghostly voices would make reply; 'look at the terrible trail of misery you have left behind you!' But in the din, no one could hear the muttering of those poor ghosts, not even Mrs Humphry, whose ears were attuned tonight, as never before, to the dark theme of the world's travail.

She passed the doors of the big hotel without glancing up, and threaded her way across the roadway. The statues, bleached by moonlight, were like waxworks she had once seen in an alley off Marylyn Street. Joe, a small boy then, had wept angrily because one of the figures whose looks he fancied would not speak to him when he wagged a finger at it. She halted to avoid a tramcar which rushed by, splashing the buildings with stars of lights. It was a reflection of those stars, she told herself, that was shining in a window of the 'offices'. Nobody was ever there at this time of night.

She stood at a little distance from them, looking up, her mind immersed in the perplexities of a new problem. That light, surely, wasn't a reflection. It couldn't be a reflection, for the tram was out of sight, and still the light remained. She tilted her head to one side, nodding it a little as she calculated which room it would be. Not Mr Wren's, or the boys' (as, to their intense annoyance, she called the junior clerks). No, it was none of theirs. It was more like Mr Joyce's own room. She drew herself up in triumph. Yes, that was Mr Joyce's own room, and the light was a real one. It was the big centre one, she'd be bound, with the white shade with the wee crack in it which she dusted from the top of the steps every Monday morning when the offices got their thorough clean.

Acting on a sudden impulse, she sped across the street. At the door of the offices, she hesitated, doubtful what to do, for the door, to her surprise, was unlocked; it was gaping ajar, showing plainly that someone was inside. Supposing that somebody was Mr Joyce himself, she'd feel a pretty fool if she summoned the police, kicked up a fuss. But she'd feel worse to go staving in herself. Mr Joyce, if he was there, might think she had sneaked in to nab something – they were awful suspicious-minded, the gentry. She stared at the open door, her brain in a ferment. It was a funny-like hour for a gentleman to be at work in his office, and she had overheard them saying that Mr Joyce didn't fash himself overmuch with business. Certainly he had never come in early, not in her day. No, it wasn't likely to be Mr Joyce or any of the staff. It was much more likely to be someone trying to break in; someone desperate with want, or maybe one of the kind you read in the papers about, one of the 'smash-and-grab' ones.

A little shiver of apprehension went through her. She stood peering along the passage, twisting between her fingers the fringe of her long, shabby coat. She pictured the rabbit warren of rooms upstairs invaded by men in dark masks; she pictured the dirt of men's feet she would have to clean off in the morning, the muddle of torn papers, of things thrown about. And then all at once, she recalled the great safes, with their 'pull hard' handles, in whose locked drawers so much riches lay. Forgetful from that instant of her own safety, obsessed only by a fear that anything should befall the objects which she had regarded with such awe and reverence, and kept shining all these years, she hurried along the passage.

As she mounted the stairs, the sound of voices, male voices, met her ears. She pulled up short, hung back to listen, for if the speakers were by any chance two of the boys, or Mr Joyce himself and Mr Wren, she would beat a retreat. If, on the other hand, they were strangers . . . She drew a quick breath at that, her heart seeming to turn over in her side. For one of the voices, or worry had taken her brain, was Joe's – Joe's strung up to such a pitch of weariness that she yearned to snatch him up as she had done when he was a child, to give him ease and comfort in her arms.

Without thinking what she was doing, she faltered into the room where the light was shining, Mr Joyce's room. Joe was lying back in the big leather chair beside the desk, the chair she always gave a special dust to each morning because she associated it in her mind with Mr Joyce himself. It seemed strange to see Joe there, enthroned in the Palace of Plenty. Mr Wren was standing beside him, saying something in his resolute voice which she was too bemused to comprehend. He jerked round with a quick exclamation as she entered.

'Hullo, Mrs Humphry! Where on earth have you sprung from?'

She clutched his arm, pressing her thin bony fingers into his flesh. 'Oh, sir,' she cried, 'oh, sir,' and looked at her son. 'What has Joe done?'

Charlie smiled wryly. 'Nothing, nothing at all. But I believe he's a little bit hipped at the discovery that he hasn't.'

An expression, half sullen, half sheepish, flitted across Joe's face. The while he pondered the other's words he gazed at the criss-cross pattern of the rug at his feet; an Eastern rug with a design as subtle and baffling to the eye as the complex motives of mankind. His eyes were still upon the mellow blur of green and bronze and scarlet, a blur which time had robbed of its rich enchantment, dusted over with a fine film of soot, when he heard Charlie, following his mother's tearful demand for an explanation of her son's presence here, proffer it with commendable brevity.

Thereat the tiny bubble of self-importance which, despite all his fears, his tremors, his hunger and his fatigue, still floated at the back of his inner consciousness, was pricked. He saw himself momentarily through another's eyes – no fiery free thinker scaling the heights to storm a capitalist stronghold and wreaking havoc within it, but a poor fool who had lost his head, flung out without result. An idiot thrusting his body against a barrier and injuring no one but himself. For the space of a second Joe regretted that he could not bolster up his pride with the reflection that with his own hands he had taken a life.

He rose with a careless ruffling of the rug at his feet. Instinctively, he irked to get away from the scene of his humiliation. Charlie turned to him anxiously.

'Feeling all right now? He went a bit faint in the passage, Mrs Humphry. That was why I brought him in here, gave him a nip of brandy. I don't think he has bothered much about food since breakfast.'

Mrs Humphry tucked her hand within her son's arm, just like a girl, Charlie thought, going off delightedly with her young man.

'There's a nice bit of salmon waiting at home,' she said. 'We'll away down and take the tram and be there in a tick.'

But Joe hesitated. He wanted to be off, but before he went he had a feeling he would like to shake this young fellow by the hand, say things to him. He stood silent, revolving the most obvious in his mind. 'If all gaffers were like you—' But how did he know they weren't? He had never talked, as man to man, with one before. For that matter, he had never emptied his mind to anyone as he had done, sitting here in this room, tonight.

The relief mingled with chagrin which had suddenly flooded his being when he realized that all day he had been fleeing nothing more tangible than the phantom of his own fears, had caused some axis in his brain to whirl, so that for a time he hadn't known where he was. When he came to himself, it was to find the young gaffer whom he vaguely despised supporting him in his arms.

Joe had let go after that. He had answered questions without animus; and Wren, roused to excitement by the happenings of the night, and seeing in the shrunken figure before him a shadow of the crisis which had so nearly touched his own life, talked to him as one absolved temporarily from the rigidity of mind inherent in those of his class. He had expressed interest without curiosity, proffered sympathy without condescension; and for a brief space these two alien minds had captured between them a mood of friendliness which neither would ever wholly forget.

To go now, Joe felt, without saying *something* didn't seem right. And yet how say what he was minded to before his mother? She'd only think he'd gone soppy, and maybe he had. The colour rose in his face. He made a little noise in his throat, and advanced towards the door.

'Good night, Mrs Humphry,' Wren said. 'Night, Joe.'

Joe looked back at that. He looked Charlie right in the eyes.

'Good night, sir,' he said in a low voice, for never before in his life had he brought himself to call any man sir. But with *him*, he thought, it was different. He deserved it. As Joe tramped down the stair in his mother's wake, he hoped Mr Wren, as he'd heard her call him, would understand. A second later, on the pavement outside, he gripped his mother's arm with a fierceness that surprised her.

'For any favour, now you've got me to yourself,' he said, 'don't you be starting asking any questions.'

She looked at him sideways and sighed. She had always been a one for asking questions, she knew. Not that she was curious, she told herself. Not really. It was just that she wanted to know things. And tonight there were an awful lot of things she'd like to know. Mr Wren had told her a little, but not very much. Just that Joe had gone off thinking he had done for young Mr Macfarlan, and Joe was no sooner away believing himself a murderer than Mr Macfarlan had risen, none the worse. It was kind of funny, that, when you thought of it. The kind of story some folks would laugh over; but somehow she felt nearer tears.

She snuggled her fingers over his, drew them close to the warmth of her heart. Then with a sudden movement she averted her face.

'Here's the tram comin',' she said in a voice thickened by emotion. 'Eh, but we'll be glad to get home again. Just you and me.'

Charlie stood for a second in silence after they had gone. 'I wish I could do something for that poor devil,' he murmured, and decided next morning to sound Mr Joyce. Then, putting the papers into his pocket which he had come to collect, he clicked off the light. As he turned the key in the door outside, he recalled how he had found Celia leaning against it that afternoon looking like a ghost. To each second of our lives, he reflected, is attached some fleeting emotion which creates an image of its own. It isn't time that passes, goes on from hour to hour; it is we who continuously process, leaving time, in the likeness of a clock, ticking on and on.

With this thought in his mind, he saw again, as he went out into the Square, the gargantuan hunger march he had envisaged earlier, revolving endlessly beneath the moon.

Meanwhile, Celia, her breath dimming the windowpane, watched a dozen lover-like couples stroll by and separate beneath the sprawling branches of the frost-girt trees. Twice over she heard the chimes of a clock drive through the silence, pronouncing doom. Half past ten . . . eleven. Oh, he should have been here ages ago if he had gone straight there and back again! She pictured him finding on Mr Joyce's desk a curt notice of dismissal and plunging into the gloom of the Square, walking round and round, until he had shed something of the blackness of his mood.

And then the glitter of headlights advancing along the terrace drew her eyes. She pressed her cheek to the window, looking down. Perhaps he couldn't bear to stand waiting for a tram. Perhaps, in the exuberance of his heart, he had taken a taxi . . . But the glossy flash of the enamelled roof slid on beneath her window. In a second, there were visible only two elements of gold swaying on the roadway as the car swept on through the dusk.

She stood erect for a moment, chilled and depressed. The moonlight beating on the street and transmuting the housetops with its pallor was threatening as a drawn sword. 'If I could look at a book,' she thought, 'I could perhaps beguile the time away.' But she had no book at hand save an old volume of poetry which she had read and reread, and even if she had, she knew she dared not raise her eyes from the terrace, lest she forfeit the first sight of her beloved striding up the hill. She must stay here, growing colder and colder, waiting and watching, for all the world like Mariana in the Moated Grange. As a child she remembered hearing her father ascribe the words of a sentimental old song to these pouting pre-Raphaelite lips the owner of which hung in a cheap frame above the dining room mantelpiece at home. 'For men must work and women must weep.' But they mustn't weep. Not nowadays. They must work too, if they could find work to do. If they couldn't – still they must not weep. Men depended upon them to strengthen their bluff . . . Was that Charlie now coming at the double up the hill? . . . Oh, what an insult! How could she, even at a distance, have mistaken that scrubby little youth for him?

She drummed her fingers on the pane. 'God,' she tapped out, as though beseeching the Almighty through the medium of her typewriter, 'bring him quickly, quickly! I shall go mad if I've to wait much longer!' But the terrace remained deserted, save for a hurrying servant-maid who had stopped out after hours, and a tall policeman who walked with leisurely gait as though taking the air for the benefit of his health.

And then at last she saw him coming. He came so quickly that she feared he would be past before she could look on him long enough. And whatever his news, be it good or bad, she wanted to let her eyes rest on him, to fill them, rim to rim, with the image of his face.

He stopped a pace or two from the window, and his searching gaze found hers. A white handkerchief fluttered in the air, and then a wafted kiss.

'Gone case,' muttered the policeman standing at the corner, and wiped his lips with the back of his hand.

CHAPTER X

'For obstructing the police in the pursuit of their duty.'

To Jimmy, this seemed a totally inadequate reason for his being kept overnight in a prison cell. It struck him as an astonishingly childish punishment, rather akin to pushing a small boy into a corner because he had been obstreperous, and making him stay there until his limbs were so cramped, his mind so numbed with contemplation of the same patch of wallpaper, that he was ready to yield up his will to his elders even to the extent of committing himself to the ridiculous promise, 'I'll be good.'

Good? Jimmy's lips tightened. He was damned if he was going to be good. This – this had absolutely torn it. He had always despised the men who kept their noses to the grindstone, the plodders who knew their jobs and did them from nine till five without let or hindrance. They were the bulwarks of the nation, these fellows, he admitted cheerfully; the pegs who held up the tent. But today that wasn't enough. There were Big Things to be done, things that could only be achieved by sacrifice of routine, by rebellion. Nimrod might not be one of those destined to change the trend of a nation's history, to cause it to substitute a new political creed for one that was already worn thin; he might prove merely to be a member of a rash band marked out for ultimate failure and ridicule. The two, Jimmy reflected, were inseparable. Once break away from the herd, try to scale the heights, and you are a being apart. A superman if you attain the peaks, and applauded as such by the populace below; a figure of fun nailed to the cross of your own overweening ambition if you falter halfway.

No, Nimrod himself might be nothing at all; merely a bubble

on the surface of the world's discontent; but behind him, behind all this vague unrest, this groping for betterment, was a force which no power on earth could curb.

Recalling his sensations in the Square, and the conviction which had come to him there of a Presence above all this rushing to and fro of little men, it was borne in upon Jimmy that it was less a political than a spiritual need the people were craving to assuage. They were not hungering after power so much as after a beauty unattainable save to those existing within the inviolable sanctuary of saints, or to those whose attributes had become like unto the attributes of saints. Brutish fellows, waving flags, were blackguarding politicians for keeping from them that which, never so long as their natures remained unchanged, could they hope to attain. Others, caught in the mesh of their own humility, were trudging on and on with their eyes on the ground, never thinking to raise them higher – to raise them above the seats of the mighty, as high as the sky.

While Jimmy sat there, his gaze fixed on his own small square of grey wall, his mind stumbled from thought to thought, his eyes conceived vision after vision. 'A country fit for heroes to live in.' That had been the old post-war tag. The Depression had inspired a simpler motto, less high-sounding. 'A country fit for human beings to live in.' Ah, but that meant a lot. It meant far more than a land fit for heroes, it meant a land fit for gods; for in every man a spark of the Godhead burns.

He brooded over that land till he was back again, a child, in his father's old church. He was looking through the bevelled glass window behind the altar out upon the blur of fields beyond. Diamonded with sunshine, seen through the fret of the glass, those fields had seemed to him then a veritable entrance to that land of milk and honey of which his father often preached. It was a part of the mystery that, when he left the church, he could never find that englamoured land he had beheld so plainly through the glass. In its stead, there was a sea of waving grass, or, on winter evenings, a vast cobweb of rising mist.

And then, his thoughts leaping onward a decade, two voices sounded in his ears. 'You'll be going in for the Kirk the same as your father and your grandfather, eh, Jimmy?' And his own, shrill, boastful 'No fears!'

Lord, what a fool he had been! In his ignorance, he had thought going in for the Church would impose upon him a mode of austere living at an age when he desired, of all things, to be free. Now he realized that freedom of the spirit has nothing to do with one's way of living. It persists, even as the plashing of a stream persists, day in and day out, no matter what assails it. He sighed, not unhappily. 'This ends my career as a newspaper man,' he thought. And wondered if it were the effect of his recognition of the fact, or of the picture of himself setting out on a new and adventurous quest, that was sending this tingle of excitement up his spine. He had a ridiculous impulse to cheer the figure that was starting out so unconcernedly on this lifelong journey, and with no watchword on his shield, no slogan on his lips. Everything as yet was too confused. Only one thing, Jimmy mused, he saw clearly. That no kind of political readjustment, no state of Communism, or of perfervid Nationalism was going to save the country. A country such as this, parched and resentful of the marauding spectre of famine, no man born of woman was capable of saving. There was only Christ.

Jimmy drew a long breath that was almost a cry of the heart. 'My grandfather and my father . . . and now me. But I've no wish to wag my head in a pulpit even if they'd let me. I want a wider audience. I want to lead a Revival; a Revival of the Spirit of Universal Brotherhood, with the Almighty as Chief Patron, and the saints as Associates. That's the sort of Communism we've got to establish in this country, if the country is to survive . . .'

And then quite suddenly he remembered Celia. Where did she come in in all this? Could he be ruthless and set her aside as the disciples had set aside their women and their responsibilities towards them? Even as he thought of her, she seemed to recede farther and farther from him. The memory of his association with her was no more vivid than was that of any of his early companions. The only one who walked with him tonight was his father. His father, who had died sorrowing because, for all his passionate endeavours, he knew he had left his flock almost untouched by the religious faith for which he would have given his life . . . 'Come Unto Me All Ye That Labour.' He had never laboured as his father had laboured, Jimmy reflected sombrely; no, neither at school nor at college; and least of all on the staff of the *Wire*. The *Wire* didn't want labourers. It wanted men ready to reflect the vacillating moods of the politicians who called its tune. It wanted puppets to dance at the bidding of the public, puppets to drug that public with soft promises, to satisfy its passion for salacious gossip, to treat it like a puling infant instead of a lusty adult capable of digesting strong meat.

As he sat there alone in this narrow space, Jimmy knew beyond a doubt that the missionary spirit which burned in the breasts of his forefathers, turning their thoughts aside from worldly gain, had kindled to life in him. There could be no looking back now, no evading the challenge that had awaked his soul to the lofty emotion martyrs know, but which normal folk can only sustain for a brief period of grace. With every nerve in his body alert to his mind's fierce intentness, he dedicated the rest of his days to Labour – a vague enough vow, but one that satisfied him and endowed the remainder of his nocturnal musings with glory, as though whatever of evil lurked in the cell had been driven from it by an angel with a flaming sword.

Within a short distance of Jimmy, Nimrod, locked up for the night, sat on his bed looking into space. So near they were, those two, that their thoughts, meeting and mingling, might have set up a strange current, a tumult of conflicting and exultant dreams in that sterile place.

How long, Nimrod was asking himself, would it be before the authorities recognized the value of the work he was doing? How long would it be before the capitalists started kowtowing to him, acknowledging his red banner as part and parcel of the insignia of a civilized state? They dubbed him a dangerous revolutionary, but in reality, it was he, and his like, who were saving the country from a second revolution. Actually, the first was over long ago. It had passed quietly and without bloodshed. Only a few had noted its advent, and those few had been laughed to scorn when they foretold that trains would run over a track of human bones, that dynamos would drive prosperity from the land, and with the grinding of wheels would arise the groans of the unemployed. The capitalists, strangely enough, had not been responsible for that revolution, nor the bankers either. It had been brought about by the Clever Men, by those who worked in laboratories and dark places, who dreamed of motes and atoms and miracles wrought by steam. So absorbed were they in their abstruse calculations, so blinded were their eyes by the malodorous fumes of their own creating, that they forgot to reckon with the needs of the human race. So long as the piston rod functioned, they gave no thought to stomachs that might go unfilled, no thought to that new race of weaklings, known as the unemployable, which must inevitably spring into being when men are obliged to go unfortified by the joy which labour with the hands bestows.

Yes, it was he and his like, Nimrod reflected, who were saving the country now. If the people were not encouraged to blow off steam occasionally, there would ensue such an explosion as would set not only the British Isles rocking, but every other country in Europe as well. They were ignorant of mass psychology who would silence the people by force. He smiled grimly. He had tried to silence a few of them for a time today, and the experiment hadn't been a success. Better let them blow it all out at the start next time – fifes and drums, shouts and curses. Then there would be less fear of a row at the finish. He thought of that row with relish. Given more room, he could have sent a few of those heavy-jowled policemen spinning; he could have sent the Highland sergeants well on the road to the Isles. In the press of the crowd, one hadn't a chance.

He lunged out with his arm, drew it in again with a sigh of regret. If only you could fight with your fists as men had fought in the old days, if only you could close with your enemy, wear him down with your skill and weight, instead of letting your strength run to seed while you lashed out with your tongue. Words! Words! Words! Impotent at the best and ephemeral. They amounted to nothing in the end, nothing at all.

Hugging his knees schoolboy fashion, he sat dreaming of old battles when claymore met claymore, and the colours of the great chiefs emblazoned the air. While others in adjoining cells dropped off to sleep – petty pilferers, wife beaters, drunkards, dozing uneasily – he stayed awake, brooding not upon the possibilities of tomorrow, and the projects nearest to his heart, but upon the happenings of the distant past.

It was his way of escape from the perplexities of the present, this incursion into another age. It was the private retreat he sought when he could not reconcile his soul with its environment. And always he emerged from his romantic fastness refreshed, revived by the brave spectacle of valiant deeds, of deathless devotion to a forlorn cause. He returned from the shining glory of old battles to the world again to regard its yawning pit with no shudderings of disgust, but in his heart the conviction that the root of the contest lay in men's minds, and that pacific action was the only weapon with which you could influence thought today. But while you were searching for the right weapon, employing it deftly, subtly, there was the mob outside to be kept in motion; to be kept in motion because less danger accrues from a mobile than from a stationary body. But could he persuade those fools in office to recognize this—?

Again and again he damned them as he sat there – this leader of men who longed to fight cleanly with his fists, but who was condemned alike by his reason and his generation to stem the flow of his fiery blood, to let his tongue reveal that which leapt up in his mind and burned there.

CHAPTER XI

At the same time as Nimrod was reflecting upon the past, and Jimmy was eagerly anticipating the future, Mr Joyce was engrossed with the things of the present. After he had locked the door of his office, gone out to his waiting car, it struck him that the stone building might almost have been a sentient creation, responsible to his mood, so grave and resolute did its grim bulk appear in the pallid confusion of electricity and moonlight.

He glanced back at the Square, a casual thoroughfare now, whose strange secret life ended, as a rule, at nightfall. The bottleneck exit jutting out from it was emptier than he ever remembered seeing it. Perhaps that was not surprising. At this time last night, if it had occurred to him to notice it at all, he would have thought of this narrow street as leading out to life, pointing to the children of the pavement the way to freedom. Now in its desolation it seemed to be evading the glare of the city, to be fleeing the risk, the gamble, the adventure of affairs.

Sitting alone in his home that night, and recalling the conflicting emotions of the day, he felt as though his moment of union with Jerry had brought to his being the beneficence which great music sometimes bestows, the sense of being soothed and enfolded in shadowy waves of harmonious sound before which all that is jangled and unworthy recedes and dies. But they were not languor-giving, these dim celestial chords. They had not plunged him into a lotus-land that turned the will to water. Rather had they induced in him the sensation of a newly acquired strength; a conviction that with all the foolish trappings stripped off, the accumulation of worldly wisdom and one's own little store of personal prejudices discarded, it were possible to start clear again, possible once more to wield a burnished sword in a murky world and to see misfortune and evil suggestion go down before it.

Midnight had struck before Mr Joyce rose to go upstairs. As he moved about his room, he was conscious that he was walking with a buoyant step, that he was anticipating the morrow with an eagerness he had not known for years. He would have to start and be up with the lark, he told himself. It would be like beginning business all over again, only this time he wouldn't have his father to drive him, he wouldn't have his father to cry, 'Ca' canny,' when he was on the point of spending money, of launching some wildcat scheme. Would his father, would old 'Blowhard' have disapproved this scheme he had in mind now, this scheme for developing Joyce's which seemed to him to be the only way of keeping the place going? Jacks hadn't liked the look of it on paper at all. He had raised his eyebrows, pressed his handkerchief to his nostrils as though there had suddenly been released in the room a bad smell. Later he had come round a little. He had laid off for quite ten minutes on the folly of taking risks. And in these bad times. They are so bad, so damned bad, we've got to take risks, Joyce had countered. But Jacks had shaken his head. To risk money these days, precious commodity that it was, represented to his cautious mind little less than a crime. Eventually he had conceded a reluctant admiration for his friend's courage. He had risen to his feet, stood with his hat in his hand for a second without speaking, then, 'By God, Arthur,' he had said – and it was only when he was stirred to the core that he was wont to invoke the name of the Deity – 'by God, Arthur, you're what I call a real sportsman.'

Extinguishing the light over the toilet table, Mr Joyce pulled up the blind, as was his custom before going to bed. Below the line of the house, the garden fell away like a mystic forest steeped in a silver sheen. Below the tall trees, the steel blade of the river cleaving the landscape separated the silvered sward from the little loopholes and chains of flame which guided the eye towards the distant glare of the city. Like a sunset submerged by some freakish jest of the Olympians in a bucket, that distant glare – a sunset which, once the jest was ended, would send forth streaming splinters of flame that would kindle the whole world to a blaze.

Mr Joyce's mouth was set fast as he regarded the distant glow of which the Square was the innermost speck. The offices would be nothing now but a black hulk in the moonlight, one of a chain of grim bastions bitten by the chemicals that infused a faint foul odour into the cloud of the city's smoke. Tomorrow the secret life they sheltered would be quickened anew. It would be almost as though behind the crumbling mortar the spirit of old 'Blowhard' himself had come to life again, old 'Blowhard' with one of his splendid, fantastic projects which he was wont to vow no power on earth should prevent him carrying through. For the most part, he had kept his word. He had kept it, and as it is not in human nature to refrain from speaking about an achievement whose wisdom others have doubted, he had bragged about it until the very wails had rung with old 'Blowhard's' Jovian boasts.

He would never get even with his forebears, Joyce reflected. In these times, the full flavour of adventurous enterprise was nullified by science. No uncharted routes, no encounters with thieving tribes today. And yet a fight of sorts, a fight with the fate of human hopes, if not of human lives, hanging in the balance. He thought suddenly of the members of his own staff. He saw their faces, like those of men and women in a dream, flit past him – anxious elderly faces with misty, care-laden eyes, ardent young faces defying misfortune to molest them. He saw the owners of those faces form into a sorrowful procession that poured down the stairs of the office and out into the Square. But instead of turning towards the bottleneck exit which led to life, they loitered, these broken children of the pavement, waiting for death. And it was he who had almost betrayed them . . .

He let go the curtains, and, obeying an imperative impulse, he fell on his knees beside the bed. But it was not to the Almighty he lifted up his voice in prayer, but to one who was very near to him then, one who was of his own flesh and blood.

'You didn't plead for them in vain, Jerry. You didn't plead in vain . . . Give me strength and wisdom to keep going. I dare not fail those who are left behind. For your sake, Jerry – Jerry . . .'

*

Meanwhile, the Square had taken on a new aspect. With the stilling of the day's turmoil, it had shed its covering of fog and smoke, and in the process achieved a significance hitherto unrecognized in the stress and bustle; a significance and a brooding sense of peace. Exempt from the clash of opposing wills, from the strain of competitive effort, the offices contained in the high stone buildings rose like a solid black shield warding off evil from the city.

In place of a sunken enclosure, a seething cauldron within steep cliffs, the Square was now disclosed as a moon-silvered place of grassy plots and statues; statues so uncouth as to give character to what otherwise might have seemed a mere pleasance set in a maze of streets. With the lights in the surrounding windows extinguished, and only the glitter of the street lamps outlining them, these plots composed a little sanctuary where dreams might be born, fresh hopes conceived, hopes high enough to scale the walls of the enfolding offices, hopes brave enough, if a tithe of them were realized, to increase to a splendid diapason the dwindling heartbeats of the city's trade.

Soon after midnight, a blustering wind sprang up which swept the streets like a zealous scavenger determined to leave behind no trace of the day that was spent. It shrilled through the narrow bottleneck, blew in wild gusts about the Square, and battered loudly against the tall buildings. A late car, gliding round the corner, met the clamour of the gale with the triumphal lilt peculiar to a lightly weighted vehicle of its kind. On that instant, the Square resolved into a dim harbour for this golden galleon whose bow wave, spreading to the frost-white grass, shone in the darkness. Then, the arrogant splashing of its lights lost to view, the moonshine lapped again the space within the dark stone ring, a space no longer vibrant with the emanation of conflicting hopes and fears, but invested with the serenity of an ancient bulwark.

For a space, the windows looked down upon a deserted square. Where the hunger marchers had walked, there was now not a single living creature. And then, almost at the same moment as the sound of approaching traffic arose, a sound symbolic in its deepening excitation of the cross-currents which alter men's hearts, take hold of their minds and shape their lives anew, the chimes of a church clock struck one.

As the solitary note reverberated through the city, the moonlight cast a trellis of crystal upon the building containing the offices of Joyce and Son; and the wind, changing its direction, ceased to whimper as it swept strongly across the Square.

THE END

APPENDIX I

Journalism and short stories by Dot Allan

a) *Glasgow Herald*

1922

July 29	The Greyhound
Dec 30	Tanaka's New Year

1923

Jan 27	Spring Flowers
Mar 29	Sarah Bernhardt: personal recollections
Dec 29	McClintock's New Year Cold

1924

Jan 26	First Grief
Feb 23	First Fear
Mar 29	Chanticleer in Hyndland
Apr 19	The Gypsy Mother
May 17	The Price of a Cocktail
July 19	A Shilling in the Slot [short story]
Aug 2	The Trip
Sept 13	Reverie in Ayrshire on Burns
Oct 4	Forest Fear
Nov 15	2d [twopence] and a Blessing
Dec 29	Christmas of a Marionette

1925

Feb 28	On an Answer to an Advertisement
Apr 18	His Own Home
July 22	The Return
Sept 19	Green Soap
Nov 7	J. Nelson Smith

1926

Mar 6	The Sewer
Mar 20	Crepe de Chine

June 19	Wild Beasts
July 3	The Studio
July 31	The Hat Shop
Nov 27	The Taxi
Dec 24	Santa Laughs at Life

1927

Feb 5	Song of Sixpence
Apr 9	His Inheritance
May 7	Before and After
Jun 11	The Mannequin
Oct 19	The Artist
Oct 29	The Spae-Wife
Dec 24	Christmas Eve

1928

Jan 14	Going into Town
May 19	Pixie in the Park
July 14	Bluebells and Barbed Wire
Aug 11	Happy Memories
Sept 22	Humiliation
Dec 22	Christmas Eve in Star-town

1929

Jan 9	Henry Arthur Jones
June 22	Making Toast
Aug 3	Shut Houses
Oct 5	The Book Folk
Dec 21	Christmas Eve

1930

Jan 25	In Portman Square
Apr 5	Exiles
July 12	In a Garden
Aug 23	Choosing a Pension
Oct 25	Ten till Six
Dec 20	Christmas Eve

1931

Mar 21	Snobs
Mar 30	Arnold Bennett
May 2	Our Mr Podkin
Oct 31	The Post

1932

Feb 13	Wildfire at Night
Mar 8	Recollections of Sousa
Mar 19	Dinner Gong at Miss Buxtrode's
July 16	The Lost Tickets
Oct 1	Things don't Matter, it's People who Count
Nov 12	Gods into Men: Olympians of cranes and concrete
Dec 24	Christmas Eve: a lady looks back

1933

Jan 10	Personal memories of Pachmann
Mar 25	Great hours in Glasgow's history
Apr 1	– do –
Apr 8	– do –
Apr 15	– do –
Sept 9	Meeting in the Crypt
Dec 23	Santa's Dream

1934

Jan 27	New Hotel
Feb 24	The Other Room
Apr 28	The Three Fates [short story]
June 23	First Night
Oct 1	Tribute to Annie S. Swan
Dec 22	One Christmas Day

1935

July 13	Invisible Mending [short story] *[see Appendix II]*

1936

Mar 14	The Second City's Castle

Dec 19 Mr Smithers's Christmas Hamper

1937
Dec 11 Memories in Bottled Honey

[No contributions during 1940s]

1953
Sept 26 The Modern Jehu

1954
Feb 6 Pilgrimage to Epworth

1955
Feb 26 An Evangelist Comes North
July 30 Overheard [short story]
Dec 3 Stained Glass Window [short story]

1956
Oct 13 Life Down the Well

1957
Feb 16 The Triple Mirror [short story]
Oct 26 Vienna Express

1958
Jan 11 When the Ship Stopped [short story]
June 7 Required, One Exit Permit
Dec 27 Who were the Bradleys?

b) *Scotland's SMT Magazine* short stories

1929
'The Lone Inn' (vol. 3, November 1929, pp. 76–80)

1930
'Unlucky Ground' (vol. 4, April 1930, pp. 64–6)

1933
'The Old Ladies' (vol. 11, December 1933, pp. 67–71)

1939
'The Last Deal' (vol. 23, July 1939, pp.24–7)

1940
'Up, the Bonnet-makers!' (vol. 26, October 1940, pp. 19–22)

1950
'On Such a Day' (vol. 45, January 1950, pp. 55–6)

APPENDIX II

Invisible Mending

Dot Allan

Published in the *Glasgow Herald*, July 13 1935

The room was very small, very hot, and draughty. The warm air, blowing in through the open windows, rose from the pavements in gusts. It was like the hot breath of the monster that was fuming and screeching and champing below, the monster of modern traffic made up of lurching 'buses, of cars, and scurrying pedestrians undulating along the Edgware Road.

The faces of the girls bent over their work were fine-drawn with fatigue. Their lips, pursed or pouting or wearily sucked in, alone showed colour. Their bowed heads and moving fingers framed by the sloping ceiling and faded walls composed one of those pictures from which the minds of more fortunate women shy distastefully, so grey is the background compared with that of their own variegated lives.

A dozen stocking-legs, dangling from a stand, flapped in the draught as Miss Eddicot, the proprietrix, came from the office next door. She was a tall, thin woman with a high, thin voice which sounded a perpetual reproach. 'Still at that ladder, Miss Lane?' she said, whereon Miss Lane sniffed apologetically, feeling herself unaccountably slow. 'What about you, Miss Grey?' whereat Miss Grey's needle, glancing aside, drew a spirt of blood from her thumb. 'And you, Miss More? Just finishing? Well, take a look at this. It belongs to a special client. Of course the ladder is above the knee or she'd never have worn it again. And you'll need to be quick. Miss Lyndon wants it for tonight.'

'Not Olivia Lyndon?'

Miss Eddicot inclined her chin. 'The same,' she said shortly, as though annoyed with herself for having launched that glamorous exciting name upon this stagnant backwater. It created a stir sure enough which manifested itself the moment Miss Eddicot had departed, almost as much of a stir as though, from the pearl-grey stocking, the lovely, laughing little lady herself had danced.

'My, isn't she a treat? Did you see her in her last play? Sweet she was as the ole man's daughter.'

'No, I saw her last year, though, in Piccadilly, goin' into that new restaurong. Mink coat, little tight hat – you know, one of them that looks like one, eleven, three, and costs – Oo, I don' know how much!'

'Sheer silk this,' said Miss More, smoothing the laddered surface across her shabby blue skirt. 'A two guinea pair, I shouldn't be surprised.'

She sighed as she took up her thread and regarded the skin of her hand, gleaming rosily behind the delicate mesh. The feel of the silk afforded her a wonderful sense of wellbeing and affluence. What it must be like to walk the world in hose like this! As her needle flew in and out simulating the close-woven pattern, she was not Carrie More any longer, but Olivia Lyndon. Instead of strap-hanging in a 'bus she was travelling in the smoothest of cars; instead of tidying up the house when she went home and getting supper ready for her father, who was on the night-shift, she was sallying into one of those high-style flats with a cocktail bar and cushiony seats all over the place. She was shedding her mink coat and that little tight hat with the sublime indifference towards worldly possessions which money breeds. Instead of waiting about and wondering if Joe would pop in and suggest the 'pictures' – fourpenny seats and a bag of peppermint creams in the interval – instead of washing up her own tea dishes and, if Joe failed to appear, going off to bed because her back ached and her eyes burned with poring all day over other women's stockings, she was dining with some nob at a ritzy restaurant. She was toying with caviare or oysters – whichever was the most expensive – and listening to the flattering voice of her escort, the while there surged about the table at which they sat that rich exotic stream of life which springs spontaneously from the flower-banked entrances of grand hotels.

Then, unexpectedly, surprisingly, a bead of perspiration rolled down her nose on to her hand. She jerked erect like a slumberer who had suddenly awakened. In a fit of spleen she rent the stocking she had been so carefully stitching and burst into a fit of sobbing. For she wasn't Olivia Lyndon, she never would be Olivia Lyndon, only Carrie More. And she was dead sick of sitting stooped from morning till night in this stuffy place; she was dead sick of the noise and the heat and the sight of the other girls' faces. She was dead sick, too, of going home night after night to a mean little house that was for ever needing cleaning and scrubbing, and of cheap seats at the 'pictures' and all the rest.

'Ssh-ssh!' warned the girls in chorus, crowding round her and glancing apprehensively at Miss Eddicot's door. In whispers, they shot sympathy and enquiry at her bowed head. 'What's wrong, dearie? Is it the heat? I bet there's thunder somewhere … Still feelin' queer, are you? We could all be doin' with a nice cup of tea … D'you know, I've felt something awful myself all day.' Then, 'My goodness!' exclaimed Miss Lane, picking up the pearl-grey stocking. 'Look what she's done!'

The cold horror in her tones dispersed the mist of hysteria clouding Carrie's mind. She dried her eyes and gazed at the silk mesh she had rent between her nervous fingers. She gazed at it, and heard Miss Eddicot's thin, high voice condemning her. There were no half-measures with Miss Eddicot. Menders, she was wont to say, were two a penny. A mistake, and you were in the street.

As Carrie looked round the cluster of friendly faces, the concern expressed in them drove the chill from her heart. Wrapped about in kindliness, her confidence came back. But only for a second. Undermining it was the awful conviction that tomorrow she would have lost her foothold on security. She would be cut off from this world of generously minded companions. Instead of sitting here at peace, high above the roar and hustle of the street, experiencing a glow of satisfaction at seeing jagged holes rendered invisible by the deft manipulation of her needle, she would be down there, job-hunting in the soulless bustle. Either that, or she would be hanging about at home. Even though Joe took her to the 'pictures', she wouldn't enjoy them – not really. In the hot dark, she would only sit and think … Not pleasant thoughts. Calculations mostly that came out on the wrong side. For with Dad only making a pittance, and herself out of a post … 'What am I to do?' she said in a small voice, looking round the little circle. 'What am I to do?'

Miss Lane picked up the mutilated stocking. She smoothed the ravelled edges torn asunder by Carrie's frenzied gesture of revolt. She pressed together the ruffled silk with her big, capable fingers, on one of which a cheap ring shone obtrusively.

'D'you know,' she said reflectively, 'd'you know I believe I could mend this so's you'd never be able to tell?'

'Could you?' breathed Carrie. 'Could you?'

Mary Lane's candid gaze travelled from the lacerated stocking to the girl's anguished face. Carrie was a nice kid. Life wasn't too easy for a sensitive soul like her, and the heat today had been enough to try a saint. But Miss Eddicot never made allowances. Of a certainty little Carrie would get the 'push' for this, unless –

While Mary still hovered on the brink of a decision, Miss Eddicot's door opened.

'What on earth are you doing, Miss Lane?'

Miss Lane sniffed slowly, apologetically, but under cover of that aggravating sound she had made up her mind.

'It's not what I'm doin', it's what I've done,' she declared dramatically. 'And to Miss Lyndon's stocking, of all people's! Miss More felt kind of queer, so I said I'd do it. Tore it before it was a minute in me hand! I suppose I'm a bit excited today. My gentleman friend and me – we fixed things up last night. A month today's the wedding.' She raised her eyes to Miss Eddicot's, hoping to surprise in them that gleam of sympathetic interest which the disclosure of one woman's romance invariably invokes in another. But her employer's face was twitching with anger, so with scarce a pause she rushed on. 'I can put this right though – re'ely I can. I'll work late, finish it so's Miss Lyndon'll never can tell. … Oh, I know I'm a fool and a disgrace to the firm, but you'll not 'ave me to trouble you much longer.'

'Why ever didn't you tell us? Congrats, Mary … A month today, but that's the 13th! Wot an unlucky day!' The room buzzed with voices when Miss Eddicott disappeared. Only little Miss More sat silent, hugging her rescuer's arm in an ecstasy of silent gratitude.

'Unlucky!' retorted Miss Lane grimly. 'I should say it was. You don't catch me getting married on the 13th of any month. No, I jus' thought I'd risk it, tell her I was leavin' so's she'd say to 'erself, "It's not worth while getting' rid of 'er. She'll soon be gone anyway." By the end of the week she'll 'ave cooled down, and the chances are, when I tell her the nuptials are postponed, she'll never even 'int at my going. I know my work, and she knows I know it, what's more. Now I must get on with this ... Oh, Carrie, Carrie, dear, stop cryin', and stop callin' me an angel-saint. If you don't dry your eyes this minute, I'll use such langwidge that you'll be callin' me – Oo, I don' know what you'll be callin' me then!'

The sun was high over the trees in Hyde Park when Carrie went down the stairs into the Edgware Road and turned the corner into Oxford Street. It looked very beautiful, she thought, sunk in a purplish haze with the traffic undulating between the high white buildings. Near the New Cumberland Hotel a bevy of newsvendors displayed posters proclaiming the latest happenings. As Carrie handed her fare to the conductor a familiar name caught her eyes, 'Olivia Lyndon for Hollywood'.

So Olivia Lyndon was going to Hollywood. Well, let her! She, Carrie More, still of the Eddicot Invis. Mend. Company, was content merely to be going home.

ASLS ANNUAL VOLUMES LIST

THE ASSOCIATION FOR SCOTTISH LITERARY STUDIES

ANNUAL VOLUMES

Volumes marked * are, at the time of publication, still available.

1971	James Hogg, *The Three Perils of Man*, ed. Douglas Gifford
1972	*The Poems of John Davidson*, vol. I, ed. Andrew Turnbull
1973	*The Poems of John Davidson*, vol. II, ed. Andrew Turnbull
1974	Allan Ramsay and Robert Fergusson, *Poems*, ed. Alexander M. Kinghorn and Alexander Law
1975	John Galt, *The Member*, ed. Ian A. Gordon
1976	William Drummond of Hawthornden, *Poems and Prose*, ed. Robert H. MacDonald
1977	John G. Lockhart, *Peter's Letters to his Kinsfolk*, ed. William Ruddick
1978	John Galt, *Selected Short Stories*, ed. Ian A. Gordon
1979	Andrew Fletcher of Saltoun, *Selected Political Writings and Speeches*, ed. David Daiches
1980	*Scott on Himself*, ed. David Hewitt
1981	*The Party-Coloured Mind*, ed. David Reid
1982	James Hogg, *Selected Stories and Sketches*, ed. Douglas S. Mack
1983	Sir Thomas Urquhart of Cromarty, *The Jewel*, ed. R.D.S. Jack and R.J. Lyall
1984	John Galt, *Ringan Gilhaize*, ed. Patricia J. Wilson
1985	Margaret Oliphant, *Selected Short Stories of the Supernatural*, ed. Margaret K. Gray
1986	James Hogg, *Selected Poems and Songs*, ed. David Groves
1987	Hugh MacDiarmid, *A Drunk Man Looks at the Thistle*, ed. Kenneth Buthlay
1988	*The Book of Sandy Stewart*, ed. Roger Leitch
1989*	*The Comic Poems of William Tennant*, ed. Maurice Lindsay and Alexander Scott
1990*	Thomas Hamilton, *The Youth and Manhood of Cyril Thornton*, ed. Maurice Lindsay
1991	*The Complete Poems of Edwin Muir*, ed. Peter Butter
1992*	*The Tavern Sages: Selections from the 'Noctes Ambrosianae'*, ed. J.H. Alexander
1993	*Gaelic Poetry in the Eighteenth Century*, ed. Derick S. Thomson
1994*	Violet Jacob, *Flemington*, ed. Carol Anderson
1995	*'Scotland's Ruine': Lockhart of Carnwath's Memoirs of the Union*, ed. Daniel Szechi, with a foreword by Paul Scott
1996*	*The Christis Kirk Tradition: Scots Poems of Folk Festivity*, ed. Allan H. MacLaine
1997–8*	*The Poems of William Dunbar* (two vols.), ed. Priscilla Bawcutt
1999*	*The Scotswoman at Home and Abroad*, ed. Dorothy McMillan
2000*	Sir David Lyndsay, *Selected Poems*, ed. Janet Hadley Williams
2001	Sorley MacLean, *Dàin do Eimhir*, ed. Christopher Whyte
2002	Christian Isobel Johnstone, *Clan-Albin*, ed. Andrew Monnickendam
2003*	*Modernism and Nationalism: Literature and Society in Scotland 1918–1939*, ed. Margery Palmer McCulloch
2004*	*Serving Twa Maisters: five classic plays in Scots translation*, ed. John Corbett and Bill Findlay
2005*	*The Devil to Stage: five plays by James Bridie*, ed. Gerard Carruthers
2006*	*Voices From Their Ain Countrie: the poems of Marion Angus and Violet Jacob*, ed. Katherine Gordon
2007*	*Scottish People's Theatre: Plays by Glasgow Unity Writers*, ed. Bill Findlay
2008*	Elizabeth Hamilton, *The Cottagers of Glenburnie*, ed. Pam Perkins